THE RED APPLE

JONATHAN LEVITAN

Çitlembik Publications 138

*For my wife, Stacy, and
childen, Jacob and Maya*

Acknowledgements

A certain amount of pretension goes with writing a book. But no book is truly the work of one person.

No acknowledgement would do that did not start with thanking my wife, Stacy. She is the foundation for all that I do and my compass for all directions. Her contributions to the editing of *The Red Apple* were invaluable.

My son, Jacob, consumes a seemingly countless array of novels with speed and discernment. I held my breath to see how he would rate *The Red Apple*. His thumbs-up declaration was welcomed with a heavy sigh of relief.

My young daughter, Maya, brings sunshine wherever she goes and fills my heart with joy. She is my muse.

My father's enthusiasm for learning lies deep within me. That trait made doing the research for this project a pleasure. My mother was the editor of my earliest writings. No run-on sentence stood a chance. Thanks for winning the battle.

My brother, Dan, was a passionate editor. His enthusiastic desire to see the project succeed was a constant confidence builder.

I owe a special thanks to my cousin, Rachel Levitan, and her husband, Yigal Schleifer. Their wonderful journey to Istanbul led me to Çitlembik.

Finally, I want to thank Nancy Öztürk and Vanessa Larson at Çitlembik for the interest and professionalism they brought to the project.

Table of Contents

The Gathering • 1430 11

On to the Straight Path. 29

Justinian's Globe 46

The Sky Began to Turn • 1437 71

The *Orta* 84

The Race to Jajce 99

Dervish Tales 116

Marching to Varna • 1443 to 1444 135

The Last Crusade 153

The Hexamilion • 1446 170

The Frontier • 1448 187

The Courtship 207

"Let Those Who Love Me Follow Me" • 1451 222

Urban's Canon • 1453 238

The Red Apple • May 23, 1453 256

Seventy Thousand Sons of Isaac 276

"The City is Ours" 291

Vanquished 309

The Gathering • 1430

The harsh whine of the cold wind whistled in the boy's ears and stung his eyes. Manuel had endured the Thracian winter with his usual indifference, but he now cursed the volatile spring weather. Manuel again counted his flock of sheep. They were huddled together in a dense single mass, collectively bleating a muffled drone.

"Seventeen," Manuel angrily shouted into a gust of wind that was gaining momentum as it swept over the hill. The wind seemed to pull the words from his mouth before he could finish. Shaking his head in frustration, Manuel turned his back against the assault. He watched the short, sparse blades of grass yield to the wind and point towards a distant, wooded hill.

The surrounding rolling hills looked pale and uninviting under the gray, late afternoon sky. Manuel wondered why a single sheep would wander away from the protection of the flock on such an inhospitable day. Stumped by his own question, he counted his charges for the fifth time.

Manuel dreaded his mother's fury. Except for the vegetable garden outside of their cottage, they depended solely on the flock to sustain them. Excuses would not replace the money that the sheep's coat brought them each year.

If she were merely angry, he could expect a lengthy harangue in which his mother called upon the spirit of his dead father to descend from heaven and beat some sense into their undisciplined boy. But if she wished to reach his soul, she would quietly remind him that no sheep had been lost while Thunderbolt, their old sheep dog, was alive.

Thunderbolt's death only months earlier had deprived him of his only friend and ally in keeping the flock together. Manuel mourned Thunderbolt's death daily, feeling the fresh wound of his absence every day he brought the sheep out to pasture.

No matter the approach she took, Manuel would hang his head in shame waiting for the storm to pass. There was no reason to ignite her rage with some shallow excuse. In the end, she was sure to burst into tears and hug him so tightly that he would have to plead for his release in order to breathe.

Manuel's guilt was made still worse because he had been lost in reverie. From the time he was five years old, his mother had sent him into the hills with the flock. These last five years of solitude in the same few hills had left him pining for adventure. Except for his mother and the rare visit to the nearby town, his only outside contact came from the hospice of Mevlevi dervishes settled in the next valley.

The Mevlevis benefited from the Sultan's interest in their mystical teachings. They received generous awards of funds to build their hospices and *tekke*s throughout the Ottoman Empire. In the last few years, they had established a hospice for the constant stream of travelers who crossed the countryside. The dervishes won over many of their grateful visitors, causing the hospice to grow so quickly that it rivaled the nearby, centuries-old Christian village.

On most days, the dervishes' seductive music could be heard wafting up into the hills. During their frequent visits with Manuel, they gently encouraged him to join the faithful. Although he enjoyed the visits, Manuel did not dare show any eagerness for the dervishes' teachings. He assumed that the dervishes, like his brethren in the village, would forget about him if he entered their fold. Manuel preferred to appear aloof or tease them with faint hints of interest while extracting information about the outside world.

Affecting an aloof air came naturally to him. Years of solitude and no formal education had made him feel insecure around others. Although unable to envision a life separate from his mother, Manuel innately believed that he was more than just a poor shepherd boy. Oftentimes he imagined that his father was descended from a noble but exhausted family that had become destitute. As the family's last scion, Manuel dreamed that he would reclaim its glory. A tremendous need to protect his personal dignity and prove his worth to others pervaded his thoughts in every encounter.

Whenever a stranger passed and waved his hand in greeting, Manuel responded with a curt, disinterested nod. If nothing else, these were his hills and he wished all who passed to accept him as their sovereign. Having spent countless hours in self-satisfied introspection and dreaming that he might live a hero's life, he continuously fostered a belief in his superiority. Only his mother was allowed to penetrate his insulating exterior and know his fears.

Heaving a frustrated sigh, Manuel concluded that the lost sheep had been driven off by the wind. Taking a chance that the rest of the flock would remain huddled together while he searched, he followed the blades of grass.

Manuel quickly reached the foot of the hill. The wind briefly subsided and he thought he heard a low, guttural growl. A dull ache filled his stomach as he nervously made his way up to a clump of thick bushes knitted together halfway up the hill. As Manuel crept closer, the growling grew louder and seemed to overlap on itself. Carefully pushing a small portion of the bushes apart, he peered outward and gasped.

Less than twenty feet away, a pack of wild dogs were snapping at each other as they picked over the remains of Pan. Their short, wide muzzles were soaked in the sheep's blood. Although little remained, the dogs lingered over the carcass, not content until the sheep was utterly consumed.

Manuel was drawn to the pack leader, a gray-backed mongrel whose greasy coat was pocked with ancient battle scars. Standing a half head higher than the other dogs, the pack leader periodically circled back to maul the carcass, clearing a path with ferocious snaps of his razor-sharp teeth. Hunger gave way to survival instinct as the rest of the pack cautiously avoided offering up parts of their bodies as fresh morsels.

Manuel seethed with anger and his eyes filled with tears. Pan had been his favorite since he was old enough to hug her back on rides around the cottage. Always a gentle soul, Pan had never strayed far from the flock until now. It was nearly certain doom to leave the protection of the flock. Manuel believed that his sheep instinctively understood this peril. But as he stared deeply into her lifeless gaze, Manuel thought he detected a look of contentment.

Eyes locked on the leader, Manuel blindly fumbled for a weapon. Coming upon a large jagged rock, he muttered, "You will not enjoy your prize."

Just as he was about to throw the rock, a strong gust of wind roared up the hill, nearly knocking him through the bushes. The dogs instinctively pushed themselves low to the ground and then popped up again when the wind subsided. Their demeanor had changed. Clearly agitated, they began to snarl and look side to side. The pack leader seemed to be peering through the bushes directly at him. For a moment, Manuel thought he could feel the dog's warm, sour breath lapping his face.

Manuel was transfixed by the pack leader's fierce, proprietary gaze. The rest of the world seemed to disappear into the dog's rapacious eyes. Although well sated by Pan, the dog hungered for its next feast. He looked at the other dogs, whom he now counted. All eight of them wore the same frightening gaze.

Manuel slowly released his grip on the rock. His face became flushed as he realized that the few rocks strewn about his feet were his only means of defense. Manuel wondered whether the gust of wind had alerted the dogs to his scent. All thoughts of avenging Pan disappeared as he now plotted his escape. Manuel pressed his body to the side of the hill and gradually slid back to its base. Heart pounding painfully, he kept his eyes on the bushes. At any moment, he expected the dogs to burst through this thin layer of protection.

On reaching the base, Manuel turned on his heel and raced back to the flock, not daring to peer over his shoulder to see whether the dogs would make him pay for his folly. Upon reaching the flock, however, Manuel's thoughts returned to Pan. He felt a sense of betrayal. Safely away from the dogs, he was ashamed of his cowardice and wondered whether the dogs would have scattered had he attacked them.

Bitter tears now streamed down his cheeks. "Never again. I swear I will not run," he told his flock.

A scarlet sunset painted the horizon as Manuel led the flock back to the paddock behind the small, tired cottage. The gate clicked shut. Sighing heavily, he turned to face his mother. As he made his way to the front of the cottage, a man's voice said, "I'm merely a messenger. Plead your case to the Turks."

Father Isaac was standing next to his mother. Her arms were folded tightly together across her chest, lips turned down in a frown. Undaunted by his authority, her chin was aggressively thrust upward at the much taller, young man, whose slender build swayed awkwardly away from her.

Manuel had seen the priest only once before, when his mother had taken him to Mass on Easter. The priest had done little to impress him, stumbling through the service without any of the practiced elegance of his predecessor.

Father Isaac had been sent from Constantinople to replace Father Ignatius, who had died the previous year. Most people found Father Isaac overbearing and mourned the loss of the saintly old priest. Remembering Father Ignatius when he first arrived, the village elders assured their children that Father Isaac already showed far more common sense and kindness than Father Ignatius had during his first years. "It's hard to break learned men from their ignorance of the world. They must first test everything for themselves before listening to the common man," the elders advised, glad for this rare opportunity to share their wisdom.

"You are more than a messenger," Manuel's mother snarled through the wind, taking liberties with his easy acceptance of her impertinence. "It is your duty to protect my son against this outrage."

"My power is limited to the spiritual world," Father Isaac demurred in a calm voice that masked his true discomfort. "The Ottoman authorities have ruled this land for decades. If you deny their demand to produce your son in the village tomorrow, it is their authority to which you will have to answer."

Manuel's mother bit her lip and scowled at the priest. "An easy excuse for someone who doesn't wish to help. You say the Turks want to select boys between the ages of eight and twelve to serve in the Sultan's armies?"

Father Isaac nodded.

"Now why do the Turks want to bother with boys for their army? Surely you've made a mistake."

Father Isaac did not like being told he was wrong, but he calmly replied, "I'm told that they are increasing the ranks of their elite Janissary infantry corps. I can only assume that their traditional method of recruiting Christian captives to their corps has not kept pace with demand. How children will help makes no sense to me either. Let us pray that they've embarked on the road to ruin— even if we must suffer their inhumanity. But you shouldn't fear so much for your son. They don't intend to take every boy."

"How can I survive without my son? Who will watch my sheep? Who will protect me? Who will care for me in my old age? It won't be you. You priests are more concerned about the Pope than protecting the everyday needs of your people."

Father Isaac's eyes opened wide in surprise.

"Oh yes, I've heard," Manuel's mother said slyly, emboldened by the young man's surprise. "I was in the market just last week. A merchant from Ancona was telling stories about how the Emperor was going to force the Patriarch to give up his Orthodoxy and follow the ways of the Latin Church so that Constantinople can be rescued from the Sultan."

"Constantinople should run red with the blood of the Emperor and his family before such a deal is made," Father Isaac blurted out, face suddenly flushed with anger. "If the city is destined to fall to the Turks, then let God's will be done. Adopting the Latin heresy in exchange for a few dirty coins is not worth the price of eternal suffering."

"If the Turks capture Constantinople, they won't stop with the Emperor and his family," Manuel's mother snorted. "My husband died on the walls of Constantinople eight years ago when the Sultan besieged it. He was in the city selling our woolens when the Sultan's army arrived. My husband was Emperor Manuel's loyal subject. That is why we paid the Turks' poll tax instead of converting to Islam and freeing ourselves from that levy. So my husband fought and died for his Emperor. Now you and the Turks say that more of my family's blood is demanded." She shook her index finger at the priest and snapped, "My debts are paid in full. Tell your Turkish overlords that my cottage is not part of the town and that my son's name should be taken off their horrid list."

"The list cannot be changed," Father Isaac said in obvious discomfort. He regretted his uncharacteristic outburst and struggled to regain his composure. "I was ordered weeks ago to produce all of the boys whose names appeared on the baptismal rolls between eight and twelve years ago. Manuel's name is on the list. I dare not imagine what they'll do if even one of the boys isn't present. Now is not the time to try playing tricks on the Turks. Their power grows by the day. With it grows their intolerance of those who try to deny them. I've only just learned that they took Salonica from the Venetians."

Manuel's mother stepped back, stunned.

"Yes, it's true. I hardly believed it myself. The flag of St. Mark no longer flies over that great city. No doubt the Turks are swollen with pride. When the power of Venice is impotent against them, what hope can there be for a lowly priest to save your boy?"

Horrifying reports about the demise of Salonica had been filtering north for a week. The city had suffered the fate of all cities the Turks took by storm: three days of sanitizing pillage. Salonica echoed with the screams of violated women and children, their husbands and fathers massacred. Churches and palaces were ransacked. The great Church of Panagia Acheiropoietos, which had served as a beacon to Christians for nearly one thousand years, was converted into a mosque. The Venetian governors were the only ones to escape unscathed.

Unsated, the Ottomans were already sweeping westward to Epirus in search of further conquest. The rolling menace of Ottoman expansion left little time to rest for their enemies, who were too often divided to rebuff them through a unified front.

"I fear that any protest I might make to spare your son would only incite them to take him. Place your faith in God. If your boy is destined to be taken by the Turks, then it is God's will. You will have to accept it."

"Then convince them that Manuel is weak in mind and body. Tell them he's a Gypsy."

"And what of the rest of the boys? Am I to plead only for your son?"

Tears streamed down his mother's chapped cheeks. "I cannot concern myself with them. Manuel is a gentle soul. He knows nothing but the simple life we live together," she moaned. Sobbing softly, she fell to her knees and hugged the priest's legs.

"The Lord will provide for you, my child," he said artificially. He reached down and pulled her up, keeping her at a healthy arm's distance.

"We will come tomorrow," she said, voice hollowed with defeat. "Will you at least pray for us?"

"I always do."

She shook her head in frustration and then noticed Manuel, his mouth agape, standing by the side of the cottage. She ran to embrace him.

"But you said they don't intend to take every boy," Manuel plaintively reminded her again. He kept thinking of Pan and the dogs as he shared his mother's sense of dread. He found it easier to discuss tomorrow than to be alone with his thoughts.

His mother held him tightly and stroked his thick, wavy hair. Instead of trying to push away at the first chance of freedom as he usually did, Manuel accepted her embrace and rested his head on her shoulder. He wondered what would become of her. She had lavished all of her strength on him, sparing herself nothing. Manuel could not imagine his mother surviving without him.

"You will play the fool tomorrow," she finally said, voice trembling. "The Turks are looking for the best. Don't look them in the eye. Don't respond immediately to any question. Do anything you can to look undesirable. That is our only chance."

"I know, Mother. You've told me already."

She smiled at him as only a mother can smile at her son. "You're a good boy. You're my boy."

"If I'm taken, will you be all right, Mother?"

Releasing him, she rubbed the tears from her eyes with her fists. "No matter what happens, you must not worry about me. All young men must live their own lives at some point. If your day begins tomorrow, then you will do so knowing that you grew up with love and a mother who will cherish the thought of you until her last day.

"I have one final duty for you. When your dear father left us for Constantinople, you were but two years old. Of course, you don't remember those days. Those memories belong only to me. But I will tell you that you and your father loved each other dearly. The best moments of his day were spent with you. I pray that you have a child so that you can know that love. Your father was a cautious man and knew all too well that we lived in dangerous times. He wanted to make sure that you knew the same advice passed down by generations of his family. So he told me in case he wouldn't be able to tell you himself."

She took a deep breath and held him by the shoulders. Looking deeply into his soft, brown eyes, she said, "Discover what you covet most and pursue it endlessly. Never settle for less than what you truly desire, no matter how much another prize glitters before you. Only then will you have lived a life worthy of God's gift."

"Did my father live by those words?"

His mother smiled knowingly and said, "Take your time discovering your true desire."

"Father loved you very much, didn't he?"

"Each day you are more and more like your father. He too had a way of asking a question that wasn't a question at all."

Having heard his mother describe his father so many times, Manuel sometimes thought he could remember him. He often fantasized about his father and himself fighting back the Turks from high atop Constantinople's ancient walls, the Emperor having promised the restoration of their family's former estates in exchange for their heroism.

"I thought I wouldn't survive his loss, but here I am. You needn't worry about me. If God wills that we be separated, then we will accept his judgment in peace."

"If I'm chosen, I swear I'll escape. I'll be back tending the flock within the week." He thought about Pan and decided that his mother would not want to hear about her loss now.

"Promises should be made with care," she reproached him, unable to resist playing the role of the teacher.

She gently kissed his forehead. "Now rest. We'll have plenty of time to talk more in the morning," she said unconvincingly.

"Mother," he nearly sobbed, sounding like a small child. "I don't want to leave you." He wanted to stay awake all night talking to her even if it meant rehashing the same tired conversations over and over again.

A single tear clouded her eye and then escaped, quickly disappearing beneath her quivering jaw. No longer able to contain himself, Manuel rushed into her waiting arms and clutched at her with all of his strength, tears pouring down his cheeks. Her little body felt frail under his crushing embrace, but she did not flinch. Rocking back and forth and stroking his back like she had done when he was a newborn, she gently sang songs that had been locked in the deep recesses of his memory. As her voice drifted out of the cottage to be carried off by the wind on the crisp night air, he wondered what songs would reach his soul in the years to come.

The next day, Manuel stood alone in the church courtyard watching fourteen other boys mill about in small groups. He wanted to appear brave, but could not stop stealing glances at his mother.

She stood apart from the fathers of the other children. Her lips were tightly pursed shut and her cheeks sucked in, contorting her normally pert features into a brooding mask. Unconsciously imitating her movements, Manuel arched his shoulders towards the ground and rocked on his heels with his arms wrapped around his waist and hands balled into tight fists.

The villagers were as much perplexed as outraged by this blood tax. The Ottoman arrival in the Balkans more than seventy years earlier had been a boon to the Christian peasants. The Ottomans had expelled the hereditary landowning class that had oppressed the peasantry. As the new overlords, the Ottomans granted the peasants much greater freedom. Taxation was limited and forced, unpaid labor was abolished.

The other boys talked softly to each other. They had played together during the more carefree days of their youth and still spent Sunday afternoons playing games after Mass.

The village and its children were strangers to Manuel. Resentment built up in him as he envied the comfort the boys found in each other and the curious looks they occasionally cast his way.

The midday sun flickered through the gray sky, casting intermittent rays of light on the decaying wooden church. The powerful gusts of wind from the day before had drifted off, replaced by a light, energizing breeze. Manuel looked up into the sky and prayed that God would have mercy on him.

As Manuel finished his prayer, the two large doors of the church were thrown open. Three men wearing Turkish robes and turbans over their shaved heads emerged, followed by Father Isaac. Ninety boys from other villages were left inside.

The leader was dressed in a fine woolen robe interwoven with silk and velvet, contrasting sharply with the weathered appearances of the hulking drover and rail-thin clerk standing obediently behind him. Each disdainfully surveyed the boys and their parents. The Ottomans were clearly undaunted by the mass of villagers, who could have easily overwhelmed them.

After several minutes, the drover broke the uncomfortable silence. "Colonel, shall I have the boys drawn up in order?"

The colonel nodded.

"Get in line. Get in line," the drover snarled.

The boys immediately scrambled to obey. No one wanted to draw attention to himself by being disobedient.

The drover looked at the boys and shook his head in disgust. "Worse than the last lot," he said, swallowing his words as he struggled to stifle a stale belch. The drover then walked the line and straightened each boy by the shoulders. Placed in the middle of the line, Manuel flinched as the drover's fierce fingers dug into him.

"I count only fifteen," the colonel quietly said to Father Isaac. "I was told that this village contained seventeen boys of suitable age."

Feeling the understated menace in the colonel's tone, Father Isaac's face turned crimson. "An understandable mistake," he stumbled. "Two boys whose names are listed on the parish register were sent to Constantinople for advanced religious training a few weeks ago."

A discontented murmur arose from the parents. The two boys were the sons of a wealthy merchant.

A wide smile crossed the colonel's face. "Should I suppose that they won't be returning for some time to come?"

Steering his back towards the parents, Father Isaac looked at his feet and said, "It appears unlikely that they will be home for quite some time."

"Your church could use some maintenance," the colonel opined, not bothering to glance at the building. "It's a pity when a place of worship ceases to be a source of pride to those who worship in it. You and I will have to discuss what funds have been set aside to maintain it. I'm rather skilled at organizing the finances for building projects."

"Thank you for your kind offer," Father Isaac meekly replied.

The colonel turned his attention to the drover. "Let's get started. I'm tired of scouring the district looking for perfection. Find ten boys who will be able to hold a scimitar without cutting off their own hands. I want to be in Edirne by tomorrow evening."

The drover respectfully nodded his head to the colonel. He then turned to the boys and gladly rubbed his meaty hands together. "Take off your robes," the drover ordered in a harsh tone that demanded instant obedience.

Like the rest of the boys, Manuel shuddered. Shaking uncontrollably, he wondered what the drover was seeking and what it would take for him to be passed over. Unknowingly catching the attention of the colonel, Manuel leaned forward to observe the drover as he stood before the first boy in line, who was trembling violently.

"Let's see whether you've been earning your supper," the drover cackled in broken Greek, absorbing the frightened soul in his bloodshot eyes. With surprising speed for such a giant man, he buried his powerful fingers into the boy's shoulders and squeezed, all the while staring deep into his eyes. The drover methodically worked his way down to the boy's feet. He then clamped his hands on the sides of the boy's head and roughly snapped it to and fro before prying open his mouth to inspect his teeth. With none of his earlier violence, the drover then ran his hands through the boy's hair, only stopping briefly to probe the bulges on the boy's head. When he was done, the drover smiled almost kindly at the boy and slapped his hand on his shoulder.

"Stout lad," the drover called back to the colonel in Turkish. "I expect he'll grow another six inches—fill out nicely in the process. Needs to watch his calves, though. Don't quite match up with the rest of his legs. Left eye wanders a little bit and there's some rot in the mouth. Nothing that would stop him from splitting open the head of a Hungarian farm boy, mind you."

"But can he think?" the colonel interrupted, anxious to quicken the process.

"I've felt worse skull bumps," the drover replied, annoyed that his analysis had been interrupted. "Of course, I don't think he'll be fortunate enough to rise to your rank, Sir."

The colonel's eyes arched in surprise as he wondered whether the drover was being impertinent. "Well, get on with it then," he snapped.

The drover repeated the process with the next eight boys before reaching Manuel. Unlike with the rest of the boys, he took a long look at Manuel, whose eyes were locked on his feet. "Look at me, boy," the drover growled.

Remembering his mother's counsel, Manuel slowly raised his chin and stared blankly ahead, affecting a dull expression.

The drover squinted his eyes. "Bit of a challenge here, Colonel," he shouted over his shoulder.

Manuel was taller than most of the other boys, but frightfully thin and awkward. His square shoulders and pointy elbows shot out at sharp angles and his knees bulged over his spindly calves. Even his chest seemed to sink sharply inwards.

"Haven't been eating much, have you, boy?" the drover asked sympathetically while narrowing his gaze on Manuel's large hands and big hips.

Manuel was surprised by the drover's sudden warmth. He could not decide whether an answer was expected. An uncomfortable silence followed before Manuel finally stammered, "I, I, I ate just last night."

"You look like you're used to feeling the sting of hunger," the drover said, inspecting Manuel's flat stomach. He then slapped Manuel on the back. The drover's thick fingers tried to push into the muscles above Manuel's shoulders but made little impression. Next, he made his way down to Manuel's feet. Rather than yielding to the assault, Manuel could not resist tightening his muscles. Although outwardly frail, Manuel's wiry frame was taut and his joints firm.

The drover shook his head appreciatively as if to tell the colonel that the boy was no longer a mystery. Before probing Manuel's head and inspecting his teeth, the drover took another long look at Manuel, who was no longer averting his gaze. The physical assault had awakened Manuel's overriding sense of personal dignity. Under his thick mop of tangled, curly, black hair, which hung down to his shoulders, his long, narrow nose, full lips and round, slightly protruding chin were drawn up into a sullen countenance.

Satisfied that Manuel was no longer trying to deceive him, the drover's friendliness melted into his more natural malevolent smile. He then ran his hands over Manuel's head. Several times the drover stopped to examine small protrusions, always editorializing with a different sigh or shake of his head.

"Don't let his physique fool you, Colonel," the drover reported in Turkish. "He's a healthy lad. He's got the good, swarthy skin to prove it. Work him hard for several years and he'll be crushing pomegranates in his fists and swilling flagons of wine in a single gulp. I can't say that he has much of a mind or that it will develop like his body, though. Some of the bumps on his head tell me he's a slow one."

Manuel had learned a fair amount of Turkish from the dervishes. His face relaxed into a wide smile as the drover finished the report.

"I don't suppose that he'd even be able to learn Turkish then, would he?" the colonel asked coyly.

The drover laughed. "Oh no, Sir. Out of the question."

"Suppose then you tell me why the boy is smiling. It appears that he knows our language."

For an instant, Manuel's face returned to stone. He cursed his foolishness. As the drover studied him, Manuel smiled again, hoping to make the Turks believe that he was an imbecile who unwittingly smiled in the face of danger.

The drover was embarrassed by the colonel's challenge. "With all due respect, Colonel, this boy would probably smile if you told him to burn his cottage."

"Smart enough to smile, not dumb enough to do as you suggest," the colonel replied. "You may continue your inspection."

The drover frowned and moved on, finishing rapidly. He then reported back to the colonel, who motioned for the clerk and Father Isaac to join him. After consulting for several minutes, the clerk began to write madly and then handed a piece of paper to the colonel.

The drover walked back over to the boys and patted some of them on the shoulder. As the drover approached, Manuel thought his chest would explode. His heart was pounding so wildly that he did not feel the drover's heavy hand fall on him. The world seemed to slow to a crawl as the boys who had not been chosen ran into the waiting arms of their teary-eyed fathers. They quickly rushed off to the safety of their homes.

Manuel looked at his mother. She was shaking uncontrollably. Her hands were pressed against her mouth as if to mute a scream that was struggling to escape.

"It is an honor to be chosen," a voice dully echoed in his ears. It was the colonel. He was standing alone in front of the new recruits, but his words were also directed to the parents. "A grand destiny awaits you." The boys and their parents slowly turned to face him. "Your lives will be dedicated to the Sultan and the advancement of his empire. In the years to come, you will face great hardships, but the rewards will be even greater. All will know that the engine of the empire is powered by your valor. Now say your farewells and cry your tears. But don't take too long. Your Sultan awaits."

Manuel rushed into his mother's arms. As they shared their pain, the momentum behind their sobbing built until a convulsive, unified wail thundered impotently from their lips.

Father Isaac had watched the entire process with growing frustration. The only risk he had been willing to take was to save the two sons of the village's most wealthy merchant. But now the colonel seemed intent upon taking the merchant's donation to the church as well. Father Isaac looked forlornly at his dilapidated church and wondered whether any of his flock would return. At least the colonel had promised not to take any more children for another seven years, he thought, eyes falling on Manuel and his mother.

"Colonel," he said, trying to sound authoritative. "Might I have a word with you?"

"Only if you're brief," the colonel answered, not bothering to face the priest. He was carefully watching the children say their goodbyes, judging when he could cut the cord.

"Do you see the young man with his mother?"

"I'm not blind," the colonel snapped.

"Certainly not," Father Isaac said apologetically, his courage draining. "I wonder whether it might be better to let the boy stay behind. You see—"

"You must be mad," the colonel interrupted. "I have my one hundred boys. It's time to return to Edirne and apologize for taking so long to find them. The boy must go."

"It's just that he is the woman's only child and she is a widow."

The colonel now turned and snarled at Father Isaac. "Why didn't you tell me earlier?"

Father Isaac did not have an answer. He wondered whether his silence stemmed from being intimidated by the colonel or whether he was striking back for being upbraided by Manuel's mother.

"No answer, eh?" the colonel scoffed. He looked up at the sun. "The day is being lost. I must reach Edirne by tomorrow. I will not be the last company to return to the capital. I need the boy. This burden falls on you, priest. I will not suffer for your meekness."

The colonel's contempt had grown beyond what Father Isaac could bear. "Is it not enough of an outrage that you take our children to be slaves in the Sultan's army where they will be called upon to fight their Christian brothers? Can you not find some mercy?"

"You judge me?" the colonel glowered at him. "Byzantium's emperors harvested soldiers from this land for centuries."

"But they were not forced to serve."

The colonel looked at Father Isaac with genuine puzzlement. Centuries earlier, the Turks had been enslaved by the Abbasid Caliphate in Baghdad. Rather than being dulled with resentment, they eventually rose to high positions and formed the backbone of the state.

"The other boys are assembled," the drover interrupted. He pointed to the ninety boys who had already been harvested. They were drawn up in two long lines in front of the church.

"Then it's time to leave," the colonel said. "Call the new recruits to order with the rest of the boys. I will be with you shortly. Father Isaac and I need to discuss his church's finances first."

"It's time to leave," the drover bellowed.

Manuel looked over his shoulder at the drover and jerked his head back into his mother's breast. "I will not leave you, Mother."

His mother wiped the tears from her eyes. Pasting a wan smile on her face, she firmly held him by the shoulders at arm's length. "It is time, Manuel," she said gently. "We must accept God's will."

Manuel looked over his shoulder again. The rest of the boys had said farewell and were slowly walking towards the waiting troop. "I will escape. We will be together soon," he sobbed.

She leaned forward and kissed him on the forehead. "Go. Go with God's love in your heart."

Manuel bit his lip and slowly backed away. As he fell into the rear of the troop, he saw the colonel emerge from the church, playfully tossing a pouch of coins in the air. Smiling brightly, he said, "On to Edirne."

"You heard the colonel," the drover snarled. "Move."

The troop began to trudge towards the end of the village. Manuel kept his head turned back as he marched. His mother was standing alone by the church, a stricken expression frozen in place. Afraid that she might be gone if he turned his head for an instant, Manuel continued to look back until she disappeared behind a small rise on the road leading away from the village.

On to the Straight Path

"I'll send you back to your mothers in thin strips if you don't pick up the pace," the drover thundered, relentlessly pushing the boys down the narrow, dusty road.

Only one short rest break was allowed every five hours. The colonel was not content to waste a single moment making his way to Edirne. He meant to march the boys at the same lightning-quick speed that the Janissaries were fabled to travel.

Manuel was too numb to do much more than watch one foot fall in front of the other. He felt like a heavy rock had been smashed against his forehead. His cheeks had no feeling and his mouth hung open, slowly and deeply inhaling with each anesthetized step he took.

The sounds of choked-back tears periodically caught his attention. These strangers shared his vulnerability and sorrow. Part of Manuel wanted to reach out to them, but he instinctively found it easier to remain remote. Manuel refused to yield a tear or sob that the others might notice.

They had passed through three towns during the first two hours of their journey. Manuel had not noticed which way the drover wove them through the towns or the nearly identical broken roads they tramped over. When the troop made camp at nightfall, each boy was hopelessly lost.

The drover and the clerk passed bread and canteens of water to the boys. Although a meager meal to most of the troop, it was a feast for Manuel. With his belly full, the numbness began to ease.

Having already lost hope that he could find his way back to the village, he concentrated on remembering the image of his mother. Manuel was seized with fear that he might forget her face. He wanted to make sure that he would recognize her even if years passed before they crossed paths again.

They were on the road again at sunrise. "We will reach Edirne by sunset or you will sleep at the bottom of the Meriç River," the drover growled for effect every time the colonel passed on his horse. The boys were now moving quickly on their own. They, too, had little interest in spending another cold night on the road, much less provoking the drover. The drover smiled to himself, pleased that the terror he had sown in their hearts was bearing fruit.

Manuel looked towards the front of the line and noticed that the boys who had been gathered previously were talking softly to each other. Soon the boys from his village followed suit. Satisfied with their progress, the drover did not silence them.

Manuel could not bring himself to speak to the boy marching at his side. He was not used to speaking to other boys and was afraid of appearing foolish. Perhaps sensing Manuel's discomfort, the boy ignored him. Both found it easier to march in silence.

Manuel knew that he should not have moved during the drover's inspection. But how could I not react when I understand their every word, he pleaded with himself. He cursed the dervishes two times over. Not only had he learned Turkish from them, but he had rejected their proselytizing efforts. If they had not stolen my hills from me, he sadly conceded, I might have converted to Islam. Then they would have never taken me.

Before long, morning slipped into day. The boys noticed the satisfied expression on the face of the colonel and concluded that Edirne must be close. The widening roadbed improved and was now heavily traveled with merchants and farmers. As the pale blue sky finally glowed red with the setting sun, Edirne stood in front of them. Sitting astride the Meriç River, the city's daunting fortifications were an awesome sight.

Once little more than a garrison town named for the Roman Emperor Hadrian, the Ottomans had taken Adrianople seventy years earlier and renamed it Edirne. Forever looking to expand their domains into Europe, the Ottomans embarked upon building the city into a great capital and base of operations.

The drover brought them through one of the city's fortified gates and immediately steered them into a nearby building, which opened onto a large, grassy courtyard. They were led into a long room with a high ceiling where a series of straw mats littered the stone floor. For a few moments, the boys stood silently, not sure what to do next.

A wiry, old man entered the room holding a basket overflowing with loaves of freshly baked bread. Before he could motion for them to come forward, the boys hungrily fell on the basket, devouring its contents almost instantly. Their bellies sank back into contentment, leaving only their hearts to flutter with anticipation.

With an amused expression, the drover said, "You've done well, lads. Bit of advice I have for you. Get as much sleep as you can tonight. You'll need all of your strength tomorrow. So grab a mattress."

He watched the boys scramble for the mats. For several minutes, the drover stood silently above them, watching his charges swiftly succumb to exhaustion. No one dared say a word. He then nodded his head several times and walked away.

"Allah is great. Allah is great. Allah is great. Allah is great," rang out in the chilly dawn air. Dozens of *müezzins* commanded the balconies of Edirne's slender minarets, joyously reminding the faithful that prayer is better than sleep.

As the first rays of light were fighting their way into the sky, drawing the sunrise behind them, the boys were startled from their slumber. They rubbed their eyes and then glanced over to the open windows with identical quizzical expressions. All country boys, none had visited a Muslim city and few understood Turkish or Arabic, the language of the call to prayer. Many wondered whether the city was on fire or under attack. Afraid to move, they sat on their mattresses waiting for the drover to return.

"....Come to prayer. Come to prayer.... There is no god but Allah."

Manuel listened with fascination to the *müezzins'* lyrical exhortations. He was drawn to the simplicity and fervor behind the message. The entire city is surely engaged in prayer, he fantasized.

Several minutes after the call to prayer ended, a warm murmur arose. The old man had returned with another large basket filled with bread. The boys eagerly swarmed around the man, who was undisturbed by the onrush. The sting of hunger once again removed, the hall was soon buzzing with trembling voices trying to talk over one another.

"Silence," a slender, middle-aged man ordered in Greek. Although he was outwardly unimpressive, his voice belied his size as it reverberated through the hall.

Obedience was immediate. The boys froze in place and stared intently at the small man, who was dressed in a black robe and wore a pristine white turban.

"Form four lines of twenty-five in the courtyard," the man said simply, now barely raising his voice.

The boys jumped to attention and were perfectly assembled before the man emerged from the hall. The sun was now rising and casting its warmth upon them. A hawk flew above them, stretching its wings upwards into the still-dim sky. Raised to see the world through superstitious eyes, the boys saw the hawk as a signal that their fortunes were about to soar.

"Disrobe," the small man said. He was now joined by the agha of the Janissaries. He was a distinguished-looking older man, who walked with his shoulders pinned back as he cast a judgmental gaze over the boys.

The courage they had found over the last day instantly vanished as they stood naked in the courtyard. Fresh tears appeared on their faces and sobs were choked back.

"You have been honored," the small man said earnestly. "The Captain General of your future corps will inspect you himself."

The agha walked over to each boy and performed a much more cursory inspection than the drover had inflicted. When he was done, the agha flashed a quick smile at the small man, who looked relieved.

"Congratulations," the small man said. "You have been well chosen. It is time to receive your first reward. You will begin a new life dedicated to walking the straight path. Now dress."

Ten armed men now appeared. The small man nodded towards the first boy in line. Two of the men grabbed his arms and led him out of the courtyard. As he left, the boy looked at his comrades from over his shoulder, a panicked expression etched on his ghostly face. Several minutes later, the process was repeated with the next boy in line.

After two hours, it was Manuel's turn. Seeing no point in resisting, Manuel took a step towards the armed men, hoping to receive better treatment by appearing cooperative. The men did not seem to notice. They roughly grabbed his arms, nearly lifting him off the ground, and directed him down a long hallway that led into another courtyard. As they entered the courtyard, a high-pitched scream, followed by convulsive sobbing, echoed from the opposite arcade.

One of the boys was brought from a small room by two men. His face was bright red and his chest was drawn to his knees. In between gasping for breath, he was moaning for his mother. As he watched the boy surrender to his agony, Manuel resolved that he would suffer with dignity whatever trial lay ahead.

"Your name has been Manuel," a heavyset man said to him as he was deposited into a well-lit room with a long table in the middle. "My name is Yusuf," he said with a warm smile. Two other men stood quietly by his side looking benignly at Manuel.

"It is my joyful duty to introduce you to the straight path. Please sit down." Yusuf pointed to the table.

"I don't think I can sit," Manuel croaked meekly, mouth dry and head aching.

Yusuf smiled at his colleagues. "The young man knows his mind." He turned to Manuel and said, "From this day forward, you will be known as İbrahim. Now we must prepare you for your initiation into the faith."

Yusuf examined İbrahim's head with a disapproving glare. He produced a pair of sharp scissors and said, "You wear your hair like a Mongol. Those who worship the true faith wear their hair close to the scalp and cover their heads. And so shall you."

Before İbrahim could protest, Yusuf had already cut off several large patches of hair in just a few snips of the blades. İbrahim watched his hair fall to the floor in a daze. He tried to convince himself that the pain he had seen in the other boy was somehow connected to the haircut.

After the last lock of hair had been shorn, one of Yusuf's comrades placed a bowl of water in front of İbrahim. "Take off your robe and wash your body," the man said.

İbrahim shrank back.

"You'll be fine," Yusuf laughed.

İbrahim took a deep breath and plunged his hands into the bowl of water. He quickly spread the water over his body while avoiding his groin.

"No," Yusuf said firmly. "You must cleanse all of your body."

İbrahim sighed deeply and obeyed. Not waiting for permission, he threw his robe back on as soon as he was done.

"Now you must profess the *shahadah*," Yusuf instructed. "Repeat after me: There is no god but Allah and Mohammed is His messenger."

İbrahim obeyed.

Yusuf said, "You are now a Muslim and an adherent of Islam. In the years to come, you will become a practicing Muslim through the strength of beliefs and virtuous acts."

İbrahim sighed. "Then it is over?" he said hopefully.

"No, my son," Yusuf replied solemnly. "You must submit to one last ritual symbolizing your acceptance of the faith. Please disrobe again and mount the table."

İbrahim slowly slipped off his robe and sat on the edge of the table. He thought of the boy who had preceded him and shuddered.

"Lie down, İbrahim," Yusuf said soothingly, gently applying pressure to İbrahim's shoulder.

Body shaking, İbrahim lay back. The two other men then tied his wrists and ankles down so tightly that he began to lose sensation. İbrahim tried to relax, but his body was already bathed in sweat and a pungent odor rose from him.

"All Muslim men must be circumcised," Yusuf said. "You will feel pain, but you must control your movements or risk grave injury. Do you understand?"

İbrahim did not understand what it meant to be circumcised, but was afraid to say so. Yusuf looked into the boy's eyes and understood. Gently stroking İbrahim's head, Yusuf said, "I will be quick."

Yusuf's two colleagues applied their weight to İbrahim's chest and legs. With his groin exposed and now unable to do little more than wiggle his toes and fingers, İbrahim was gripped with terror. He was on the verge of urinating when he saw Yusuf lean forward.

"Please, no," İbrahim pleaded, still not knowing exactly what was about to happen. "I swear that I accept Islam. I will follow your faith as if I were the Sultan."

"The Sultan is also circumcised," Yusuf said.

İbrahim was seized with pain as the foreskin of his penis was stretched away from him. Hands balled into white-knuckled fists and taking quick, gasping breaths, he desperately tried to raise his body. Suddenly, his penis felt like it was on fire. İbrahim vaguely sensed the warm trickle of blood that followed as the pain continued to build until he was sure he would soon die. İbrahim thought he heard the faint echoes of his own distorted voice begging to go home.

For a few more minutes, the two men continued to hold him still. As he lay on the table, the wound was treated with salve and wrapped in bandages. Almost imperceptibly at first, the pain slowly diminished. Another minute passed before he opened his fists. Small rivulets of blood appeared from where his nails had dug into his palms. Finally, the men released him. Although coated in his own perspiration, a chill descended on him.

"You were very brave," Yusuf said. "Courage is a quality that will stand you in good stead."

İbrahim forced a faint smile.

"May you enjoy your grand destiny," Yusuf said with pride.

Three days passed before the boys were called to order. No one had recovered yet. Except for two boys who were suffering from bad infections, the entire troop managed to form four lines in the same courtyard where they had previously assembled. Fear of never again seeing their families had been long since replaced by fear of what terrors might still await them. The boys stood motionless and silent, numb to all except the persistent pain in their groins.

The same small man who had introduced them to the agha now appeared. A troop of soldiers stood dutifully behind him. He cleared his throat and said, "Ten of you have been selected to study in the Sultan's palace here in Edirne. You have been so honored because of your superior intelligence."

The appeal of being chosen caused the boys to stir from their torpor. No one could imagine that more favorable options were in store for them. Although remembering the drover's judgment that the hills and valleys on his skull were unacceptable, İbrahim expected to be chosen.

When the drover finished calling the names of the chosen, İbrahim was left standing in line. The insult to his dignity surpassed the hurt to his body for a brief, unhappy moment.

"The rest of you will leave now for Gallipoli. There you will be hired out for the next several years to work the farms of great men. They will teach you Turkish and strengthen your bodies. You will learn to live as a Muslim. When you return to Edirne, you will be registered as cadets. And then," he beamed, "you will become Janissaries."

"Remember, boys, you are slaves to the Sultan and the Sultan is the state. Your fate will be intertwined with the destiny of the empire. So use your time well. The foundation you lay will decide the fate of nations for centuries to come."

The small man whispered something to the captain of the soldiers. The captain snapped to attention and vigorously nodded.

The captain waited for the small man to disappear before speaking. "Boys," he barked, "Gallipoli is one hundred miles from here. We will make the trip in four days."

A collective gasp filled the courtyard.

"I know you're in pain," the captain continued, "but that will not excuse you. If you fall behind, there will be punishment," he said ominously. "You must learn to move quickly no matter the adversity you suffer."

Like the other boys, İbrahim's mind could only absorb his pain as he trudged down the dusty road, blind to all else that lay in his path. İbrahim's sole focus was measuring his slow recovery from the wound. When Gallipoli finally came into view, the boys could not even muster a cheer.

Seventy-five years earlier, Gallipoli had been rocked by a horrible earthquake. The ruined city was temporarily abandoned. Taking advantage of this opportunity, the Ottomans had rebuilt the city and populated it exclusively with Turks.

The blow to Byzantium could not be measured. Now the Ottomans held the primary crossing point from Thrace to Anatolia. The Emperor impotently demanded Gallipoli's return, but the Ottomans replied that the city had fallen to them through God's will. And so it was from Gallipoli that the Ottomans first laid claim to dominion in Europe.

The boys were housed that night in an old soldiers' barracks near the docks. Sleep came easily to them. It was their only solace. The next morning they awoke to the now familiar calls of the *müezzins*. They were fed breakfast, instructed to clean themselves, and then led down to the docks.

A large group of men was waiting for them. As soon as the boys were assembled, the men advanced, subjecting them to another examination. By this time, however, the indignity of being poked and prodded was little more than a petty annoyance.

İbrahim barely noticed the men. Instead, he closed his eyes and sighed contentedly. İbrahim had never smelled the sweet aroma of sea air. He filled his lungs and wondered whether the seemingly gentle waters below him were as soothing to the soul. His reverie was soon disturbed, though, by a firm hand that gripped his left shoulder.

"You will come with me, İbrahim," the man said plainly.

A tall, elderly man stood before him. Under the man's turban was an impressive face, lined with deep crevices in his cheeks and a faded scar that started at the top of his forehead and ran diagonally down to his right eye, splitting his crooked, bushy eyebrow in half. His dark, brown eyes bore into İbrahim, exuding an unexpected warmth and projecting a keen intelligence. The bridge of his long, thin nose leaned to the right, then briefly straightened before turning back to the left and hooking towards his mouth. The man's features finally drained into his broad, square chin, which pushed upwards to keep his face from collapsing.

A lifetime of trials stared serenely back at İbrahim. Rather than focusing on a single, battered feature, İbrahim was fascinated by the man's overall regal bearing and countenance, which, cast alongside his spare, ramrod-straight posture, indicated a strength of personality and spirit alien to İbrahim's experience. Although the man was as old as any of the elders in his village, İbrahim was sure that he was a match for any of the soldiers who had escorted the boys to Gallipoli.

"My name is Mahmut," the man said, impressed by how İbrahim's eyes had rolled over him.

"İbrahim." İbrahim flinched each time he heard his new name.

"I will be your master for the next several years."

İbrahim nodded respectfully.

"We must hurry. The ferry will be leaving shortly."

Mahmut firmly took İbrahim's arm and led him to an old ferry, which was already tightly packed with passengers. As İbrahim and Mahmut made their way on board, the ancient ship groaned. İbrahim made eye contact with one of the boys from his village. The boy smiled—a kind face amid a sea of strangers. For the first time since he had left his mother's arms, İbrahim's spirit lifted. He tried forcing a smile but wondered whether he had even managed to turn his lips up. The ferry pitched away from the dock. The passengers stumbled into each other and struggled to keep their balance. When İbrahim looked up, the boy was gone.

The ferry slowly pushed its way east into the Dardanelles. İbrahim had never been on a ship. Not long into the voyage, his intoxication with the fresh sea air gave way to illness as the ferry sluggishly rolled from side to side.

"Open your eyes," Mahmut gently counseled.

İbrahim swallowed hard and obeyed.

With a commanding expression fixed to his already formidable features, Mahmut stared ahead, undisturbed by the voyage. "Now pick a point far in the distance and don't waver from it."

İbrahim looked out into the sea. The coastlines of Europe and Asia were equally distant. Then he gasped. A convoy of Venetian merchant galleys loaded with silks and furs was bearing down on them. Fueled by the powerful north wind behind them and showing no signs of veering from their course, the galleys looked like they would slice the struggling ferry in half.

İbrahim tugged on Mahmut's sleeve and pointed at the nearing convoy, which was cutting a wide, foamy swath in the sea. "They will ram us," he cried, speaking his first words to his master.

Mahmut sniffed loudly and said, "And dare placing their cargo at risk? I hardly think so."

Moments later, the convoy swept by the ferry, which had just narrowly crossed its path. The Venetians rained down a hail of invective, but the passengers did little more than turn their heads away. Rather than harming the ferry, the wake from the convoy lifted it up and propelled it towards Anatolia. The ferry captain turned to look triumphantly at the passengers, a wide, toothless grin beaming contentedly from his leathery face.

"They'd sell their souls to the devil if it meant filling their pockets with a few more ducats," Mahmut sneered. "Never underestimate them as an enemy, but remember that the dominion we seek will always outstrip their commercial obsession. Our resolve cannot be sated or dulled by material fulfillment."

After the fall of Salonica, the Venetians had quickly negotiated a new treaty with the Sultan, which allowed their subjects to move and trade freely throughout the Ottoman Empire. Back to business as usual, the Venetians were already transferring the base of their Aegean operations to Negropont on the eastern shore of the Greek mainland.

They pulled into port an hour later. İbrahim stood at the edge of the ferry nervously trying to decide when he could safely jump onto the dock from the heaving ship. Anxious to be on their way, the passengers pushed past İbrahim, who stumbled onto the dock and spun around just in time to see Mahmut nimbly disembark.

Struggling to adjust to being on land again, İbrahim slowly regained his balance. He marveled at Mahmut, who immediately walked in a steady, straight line.

"We will eat first and then pray," Mahmut said. He gripped İbrahim's shoulder to balance him and smiled.

"I don't know if I can eat." İbrahim swallowed hard as the thought of food revived his nausea.

"When was the last time you ate mutton?" Mahmut asked, surprised that any boy İbrahim's age might not be hungry.

İbrahim blushed. He and his mother had mostly eaten breads and vegetables.

"That long, eh? Well, I'll have you used to the taste of meat in no time," he said warmly.

They went to a nearby tavern, which was crowded with merchants and travelers making their way between the two continents. Mahmut ordered bread and mutton over the deafening din and then sat back to watch İbrahim, whose eyes were open wide. Strangers effortlessly mingled together, undaunted by the unfamiliarity of their surroundings.

"That's enough," Mahmut ordered as İbrahim reached for a second piece of meat. "We have a long trip before us. I don't want you becoming sick. Trust me. You will enjoy meals like this one for years to come."

İbrahim sighed and pulled back his hand. Eating the mutton was the first moment of real joy he had felt since his enslavement.

Mahmut stood and said, "It will be time for prayer soon."

İbrahim jumped to his feet and followed Mahmut. As Mahmut emerged into the bright midday sun, the *müezzin*s recited the call to prayer. Not waiting for İbrahim to catch up, Mahmut moved quickly down the crowded street, only looking back when he reached a nondescript ablutions fountain in the courtyard of a small mosque.

"We must cleanse ourselves," Mahmut said, nodding to the fountain, as İbrahim finally met up with him, still unable to walk without pain.

Mimicking his master's movements, İbrahim washed his face, hands and forearms. He then took his right hand and ran it over his head and finished by washing his feet.

Mahmut watched İbrahim with a satisfied expression. "Now we are prepared to worship."

"I don't know how," İbrahim said nervously, embarrassed by his ignorance.

A small smile cracked Mahmut's lips. "You will learn by doing as I do—exactly. Do not deviate in the least from any word or gesture I make."

"Of course," İbrahim said obediently, wanting to impress Mahmut with his ability to follow directions. Having expected the worst, İbrahim was baffled by the paternal manner in which Mahmut treated him. He was also fascinated by the constant dignity and deliberateness with which his master so effortlessly moved from one point to the next.

The mosque was packed with worshippers whose decorum was impeccable despite being crammed into such a small space. Mahmut removed his shoes and joined his brethren, who were pointed towards a large, ornately decorated niche in the wall facing south to Mecca.

Following the imam, the worshipers repeated the call to prayer. Then, raising the open palms of their hands level to their shoulders, the worshipers declared, "Allah is great."

Standing with his left hand tucked firmly in his right, İbrahim watched Mahmut pray.

In the name of Allah, most gracious, most merciful.
Praise be to Allah, the cherisher and sustainer of the worlds;
Most gracious, most merciful;
Master of the Day of Judgment.
Thee do we worship, and Thine aid we seek.
Show us the straight way,
The way of those on whom Thou hast bestowed Thy grace,
Those whose portion is not wrath, and who go not astray.

He is Allah, the one and only;
Allah, the eternal, absolute;
He begetteth not, nor is He begotten;
And there is none like unto Him.

İbrahim studiously copied his master, who now inclined the upper part of his body and rested his palms on his knees, saying, "I extol the perfection of my Lord." Mahmut then stood and said, "Allah is great." He then prostrated himself and continued to pray, before kneeling and touching the ground with his brow. Mahmut sat on the base of his heels before once more prostrating himself. Sitting back on his heels again, he said, "There is no god but Allah and Mohammed is His messenger. May Allah cause His prayers to descend on our lord Mohammed." Finally, Mahmut turned his head over his right shoulder and then over his left, each time saying, "May peace be upon you and the mercy of Allah."

The imam concluded the service by delivering a sermon and invoking the blessings of Allah on the community. Mahmut was completely absorbed in the ritual. His face glowed with deep satisfaction and a humble tranquility.

Religion had never played an important part in İbrahim's life. The dervishes had done more to provoke his disdain than spark his interest. But seeing the fulfillment on the faces of the worshipers wounded him. İbrahim felt that he had been denied their communal strength.

Mahmut patted İbrahim on the back. "Five times a day: before sunrise, midday, midafternoon, after sunset, and at night. That is when you must pray."

Unlike the dervishes, Mahmut had no intention of allowing İbrahim to exercise his own will. İbrahim accepted the order, perplexed by his own willingness to yield so easily.

Mahmut was eager to be on his way. Deftly maneuvering through the sea of worshipers, Mahmut swiftly covered ground with his long legs, again leaving İbrahim struggling to keep pace.

As they exited the courtyard and entered the bustling street, İbrahim's head swiveled side to side. From the towering minarets to the smallest shop, he wanted to absorb the city into his memory. After a while, İbrahim's jaw began to ache from the broad smile that was stretched across his face. His head was swimming with questions, but Mahmut was already out of earshot.

"Ah! You clumsy fool," an old man scolded him as the two collided. "Keep your head out of the clouds and on where you're going."

İbrahim looked down at the man and gasped.

The barefoot old man was wearing a dark, tattered robe that was far too long for his diminutive stature. His deeply pocked skin was tightly drawn over his sunken, oily face, which was smeared with filth. Dark, bloodshot eyes danced madly about, never focusing for more than a moment, but it was his rancid odor that set İbrahim back. He deliberately coughed several times, trying not to share the same air with the man.

"Won't even say you're sorry, eh?" The old man poked his bony forefinger into İbrahim's chest. "Looks like I'll have to give you a beating then."

"A beating?" İbrahim asked, the absurdity of the man's declaration finally awakening him from his stupor.

"You heard me right. You'll stand there and take it too. I can't be chasing after you after all."

"You expect me to let you hit me?" İbrahim's revulsion for the derelict now turned to contempt. "Out of my way, old man, or it is I who will give you the beating."

Searching for approval, İbrahim looked to see if anybody was witnessing the spectacle. To his surprise, even the people who maneuvered around him passed without a glance. It was as if he had been thrust into a separate world.

A confused expression descended on the old man. "Then why won't you give me my money back so I can a buy a stewpot?" he asked, suddenly sounding like he was about to break down.

İbrahim ignored the nonsensical question and pushed past his tormentor. He craned his head upwards in search of Mahmut. A sea of indistinguishable turbans bobbed ahead. A tremor ran through him as he froze in place.

"The pot must be deep, you understand," the old man muttered, twitching his head with irritation while positioning himself squarely in front of İbrahim.

"You must go," İbrahim ordered unconvincingly, eyes frantically searching for his master.

"No. No. I must have it." In a speedy, jerking motion, the man dug his fingers into İbrahim's robe and pulled himself close. "I want my spoon, too," he screamed. "How am I supposed to eat?"

İbrahim turned his head sharply to the side, failing to fend off the old man's putrid breath. "Let go of me," İbrahim weakly ordered, all pretense of his earlier bluster gone.

"It would be an honor to share my purse with you, Sir."

İbrahim spun his head around to see Mahmut, who had circled back to find him, standing over his shoulder. İbrahim could hear his own deep sigh above the commotion of the street.

"A true believer is what you are," the old man said, smiling gratefully. He released İbrahim and held out his hands like a cup.

Mahmut placed several coins into the man's hands.

"May peace be upon you and the mercy of Allah," the old man said before disappearing into the bustling street.

"Why did you give that man money?"

"It's our duty to give to the poor and needy."

"But do we have to give to any man?"

"You would have preferred if I gave the money to a more suitable person?"

"There must be others in this city who could have used that money too. That man was terrible," he concluded with a healthy dose of disdain.

"Your youth is no excuse for making such a harsh judgment," Mahmut said sternly. "It is not for you to decide who is worthy of Allah's bounty." Softening his tone, Mahmut said, "It is written, 'For those who give in charity, men and women, and loan to Allah a beautiful loan, it shall be increased manifold to their credit, and they shall have besides a liberal reward.'"

İbrahim was immune to the scripture. He was stung by the unexpected reprimand. Turning his chin upwards, he responded with a deliberately obvious petulant expression.

"You will have plenty of time to learn all you need to know," Mahmut counseled, deftly ignoring İbrahim's frustration. "It's now time for us to go home."

"My home is in Thrace," İbrahim bristled, wishing for his mother. He was disappointed that Mahmut had not risen to the bait.

"We will talk about your home another time," Mahmut said calmly. "In the meantime, we are on to Bursa."

"How long will it take to get there?" İbrahim asked, a hint of excitement returning to his voice. He had heard the dervishes talk with reverence about the great city.

"It depends on which road we decide to travel."

Justinian's Globe

Nothing escaped İbrahim's wide-eyed wonderment as he and Mahmut traveled down the ancient road leading east towards Bursa. Although the pain of being torn from his mother was constantly in his thoughts, he felt strangely liberated. A mesmerizing array of merchants, dervishes and soldiers shared his path. The travelers treated each other to friendly greetings and respectful acknowledgments. He tried to smile back.

The warm rays of the sun shimmered off the budding wildflowers and vegetation on the verdant plain, revealing an abundance that İbrahim had never imagined. He had been content in the rugged hills that his flock routinely ravaged. Now, he was ashamed of his humble beginnings as he absorbed the radiance of this new land and its purposeful people.

Mahmut rarely spoke during the journey. İbrahim assumed that the silence reflected Mahmut's disapproval over his behavior towards the street beggar. İbrahim found himself craving Mahmut's approval, if not his forgiveness. But it was curiosity that truly drove his interest. There was a long story written on Mahmut's battered face and İbrahim wanted to know it all.

Resting on the lower slopes of Uludağ, Bursa rose up before them on the fifth day of their journey—a glittering jewel sparking İbrahim's wonderment. A hundred years earlier, the starving population of the ancient city had been abandoned by the impotent Emperor in Constantinople. After a ten-year siege, they finally yielded to the inevitable and opened their gates to the besieging army of the dying Sultan Osman. His son, Orhan, promptly made Bursa the imperial capital. For the next thirty-five years it served as Orhan's base for organizing the foundling Ottoman emirate into the chief Turkish power in Anatolia.

Although no longer the capital, Bursa remained the holy city of the empire. Renowned for its silk trade and commercial power, it was also the home of the Islamic religious establishment. Schools of theology and Islamic law, mosques, and *tekke*s dotted the streets along with the tombs of Osman and his successors, making Bursa a site of Islamic pilgrimage.

Mahmut stopped when they reached a fork in the road leading to Bursa. He had seen the city more often than he could remember, but his heart still stirred with pride. "May he be as good as Osman," Mahmut whispered.

İbrahim wondered whether his master was speaking about him.

After several minutes passed, Mahmut smiled pleasantly and said, "If you work hard and immerse yourself in Islam, I will take you to the city one day." He then turned onto the fork in the road that led away from the city.

İbrahim's heart sank. He thought of a dozen different protests, but his lips were frozen shut.

They walked for another hour until they passed through a gate and onto the grounds of a centuries-old Byzantine villa. Although the color of the stone was worn gray, the rest of the villa was in remarkably fine condition. Behind the estate house lay a large barn, which commanded rich wheat fields and groves of peach and mulberry trees on either side.

"My home," Mahmut said with a hint of pride that surprised İbrahim. "The Sultan granted my family hereditary rights to this land. A rare honor," he explained, noticing İbrahim's reaction.

"I would be pleased to meet your family," İbrahim said, unsure of what to say.

A dark mask momentarily passed over Mahmut's normally warm demeanor. "You and I have much to talk about before there can be such familiarity," Mahmut dryly replied.

"I didn't mean to offend," İbrahim said defensively.

Mahmut's gnarled features relaxed. "Of course you didn't. Now follow me to your quarters."

Expecting to be led into the villa, İbrahim's face fell as he followed Mahmut to the barn. Am I to be nothing more than livestock, he wondered as his feelings of conciliation soured into raw indignation. A pungent odor struck him as they entered the barn, which was fully stocked with well-fed livestock.

"You will sleep here," Mahmut said. He was standing in front of a stall containing a thick straw mat.

Wearing a sullen expression, İbrahim mumbled, "Is this how a Janissary sleeps?"

"Even the elite are sometimes fortunate enough to have a thick roof over their heads and a soft mattress to sleep on," Mahmut answered wryly. "It will be sunset shortly. You will join me and my farmhands outside the villa for prayer."

Mahmut left the barn, pausing briefly on his way to pet affectionately the muzzle of a horse that leaned out of its stall. İbrahim looked around his new home, shaking his head in frustration. "This is my grand destiny?" he demanded of a cow that was dully chewing its cud.

Mahmut's farmhands silently studied İbrahim, clearly unimpressed. Although prematurely aged by the rigors of their work, they possessed an air of confidence that distinguished them from the men İbrahim had seen at home.

"I have a gift for you," Mahmut said, almost smiling. He handed İbrahim a prayer rug. "May you never pray on defiled ground."

The rug's bright red and blue colors meshed together to form an elaborate, graceful pattern. It was the most beautiful object İbrahim had ever possessed. "I will cherish it always," he gushed, clasping it to his chest.

"Let its use give you fulfillment," Mahmut preached. "But remember, it's merely an object."

"Of course," İbrahim happily agreed.

The farmhands smiled at each other before beginning their prayers. Already, İbrahim had nearly perfected the ritual. Affecting the zealousness of a true believer, he stole glances at Mahmut, who, as always, was absorbed in prayer. When they were finished, the men carefully rolled up their rugs and began to chat amiably among themselves.

Two servants brought out a large stewpot from the villa and placed it in front of the group.

"Will you be joining us tonight?" one of the men asked Mahmut.

"He will not," said an old woman, who had come out of the villa unobserved.

İbrahim fixed his eyes on her. Although she was nearly as old as Mahmut, her refined features retained much of their youthful beauty. Like Mahmut, her small, delicate body bore a stately aspect, but she was not blessed with any of the outward signs of serenity that marked her husband. İbrahim could not decide whether the deepening wrinkles in her brow and the sharp lines arching down from her thin mouth reflected sorrow or anger.

Mahmut smiled at the men as if to warn them against judging her too harshly. "I will be enjoying the company of my wife tonight. Come, İbrahim. Please greet my wife, Safiye."

"It's an honor," İbrahim said, respectfully bowing his head.

"Humph," Safiye snorted. "How do you expect to get any work out of this one? A good breeze will break him in half."

Mahmut ignored his wife's criticism and said, "İbrahim, I will join you before sunrise tomorrow. Now eat well." He took a step towards the villa and then leaned back. "Remember, İbrahim must eat more than any of you," Mahmut instructed the farmhands.

İbrahim and the farmhands watched Mahmut and Safiye disappear into the villa. One of the men handed İbrahim a bowl and spoon. "Your master is right. You need to get some meat on your bones. My name is Sait."

"Thank you," İbrahim said uneasily, wondering whether he had been insulted.

Sitting in a tight circle around the pot, the men silently devoured their stew. Before pouring themselves another bowl, they waited for İbrahim to catch up. As they finished their second bowl, the men seemed to relax.

Sait turned to İbrahim and asked, "So where were you captured—Salonica?"

"I don't think I was captured," İbrahim answered, unsure of whether he had understood the question. "They told me I was levied just like the rest of the boys." İbrahim went on to tell his story.

"The world is changing faster every day," Sait mused. "All of the other boys the master trained were captured. The last one was a Genoese boy kidnapped by pirates who were sailing off the coast of Chios. I suppose the Sultan has decided that the only way to increase the size of the Janissary corps is to have a steady stream of recruits."

"I hope the master will find me worthy," İbrahim said nervously, obviously worried about Safiye's criticism.

Sait had heard other boys express the same concern. "Don't worry about the master's wife. You won't be seeing much of her."

"You think she doesn't like me?"

"Don't take it personally, boy," Sait counseled. "It's not as if she likes anybody. I've worked this farm for what must be over twenty years now. I haven't seen her smile once in the last eight years that I can remember."

"It's because of her boys," a man named Ragıp explained. "She lost them eight years ago when the Sultan besieged Constantinople."

"Lost them?" İbrahim asked.

"They were killed," Ragıp said.

İbrahim's face turned red, embarrassed by his lack of comprehension. He thought of his father dying on the very walls that Mahmut's sons had attempted to breach and wondered whether Mahmut might somehow blame him for his own sons' deaths.

"Sait is right," Ragıp said with a defensive hand gesture, ignoring İbrahim's discomfort. "She spends almost all of her time locked inside the villa. She doesn't live in this world anymore. She might as well—"

"Watch yourself," a farmhand named Ömer snapped, his words more command than objection.

Ragıp cut himself short and dropped his head submissively. Ömer was the oldest of the group. Despite his earlier silence, he was clearly the leader.

Ömer cleared his throat and somberly warned, "It's not our place to judge the master's wife. I've worked this land longer than any of you. Her love for her boys is no different than that of any other mother. I'll tell you now, and don't make me remind you again, it doesn't matter whether your son is a *gazi* warrior fighting to expand the dominions of Islam or a sickly child who drains your body and soul; it is impossible not to lose the best part of your soul if your child dies."

İbrahim's heart sunk under Ömer's words as he considered his mother's anguish.

"Ragıp didn't mean to offend," Sait spoke in his friend's defense. "He was only trying to make the young man feel more comfortable."

"If you want young İbrahim to feel more comfortable," Ömer answered, "you should tell him that Allah has blessed him with the most noble master. Young man," Ömer said, tilting his head towards İbrahim, "the master has been training young boys for over twenty years. You're the fourth boy I've known. None of the boys ever loved their fathers more than they loved the master when they left. Tears in their eyes, every last one of them."

Eyes wide open and lips pursed shut, İbrahim respectfully nodded his head, absorbing Ömer's every word. Already upset about his earlier gaffe, he did not dare make another mistake.

"A *sipahi* cavalryman to the end," Ömer continued. "I'm told that his great-grandfather was so fierce in battle during the siege of Bursa that he won the gratitude of Sultan Osman himself. That's why his family was given the honor of hereditary title to this land. Of course, the master is no less a hero. He rode cavalry against the Serbs at Kosovo over forty years ago and helped destroy the Crusaders at Nicopolis."

"Perhaps that's what he intends to talk to me about tomorrow," İbrahim said hopefully.

The men smiled.

"You're better off getting a good night's sleep than thinking about it," Sait said. "It's the master's job to work you hard—and he takes his duties very seriously."

"He won't give us much more consideration," Ragıp yawned as he inspected the bottom of his bowl.

The men said their goodbyes and headed home to their families. İbrahim watched them disappear into the rapidly cooling night air. Feeling the dull ache of loneliness, he was already thinking about sunrise as he made his way back to the barn.

"It's time," Mahmut said.

İbrahim rubbed the sleep from his eyes and pulled himself to his feet. He picked up his prayer rug and followed Mahmut out of the barn. They began their prayers as the first rays of sunlight filtered into the sky.

They then ate their breakfast in silence. As they shared their morning bread, İbrahim studied Mahmut. He could not fathom how a man who mourned the loss of his children could exhibit such contentment. The ache in his own heart over being separated from his mother had left him desolate. He could not imagine ever achieving Mahmut's tranquility.

"We are clearing a new field. I assume you've never done that before."

"I was a shepherd."

"We clear fields a little differently from your sheep."

İbrahim followed his master to the edge of a cornfield. Mahmut's farmhands were busily chopping down cypress and plane trees. The men collectively called out, "May peace be upon you." Mahmut nodded his head appreciatively and returned the salutation. İbrahim quickly followed suit.

"İbrahim, you will take orders from Ömer," Mahmut said.

"Work hard and do exactly as he says."

"I will do my best," İbrahim dutifully answered.

"You must," Mahmut agreed, and turned to leave.

İbrahim was stunned as he watched Mahmut head back towards the villa. İbrahim looked at Ömer and wondered how the lessons that needed to be learned could come from such an ordinary person. The camaraderie he had felt with the men the night before was replaced by a sense of superiority.

"Have you cleared a field before, boy?" Ömer repeated Mahmut's inquiry. He was already bathed in perspiration despite the cool breeze steadily blowing across the field.

"I was a shepherd," İbrahim answered haughtily.

The men erupted into laughter.

"Where about, boy?" Ragıp managed to ask.

"Two days' travel from Edirne," İbrahim answered proudly.

"Good hunting in those hills," Sait joined the conversation. "I've heard it said that the capital was moved from Bursa just so the Sultans could be near the game in those hills. Didn't know hunting sheep was such good sport."

The men continued to laugh until İbrahim, his face becoming a dark shade of scarlet, demanded, "Exactly what is so funny?"

"We're not laughing at you, son," Ömer apologized. "Well, at least not as much as you might think. It just strikes us as funny that the Sultan now prefers to grant shepherds entry into the Janissary corps instead of the stout lads he used to collect from conquered lands."

"What's wrong with being a shepherd?" İbrahim fumed.

"Come now, İbrahim," said another farmhand, named Ali. "Your sheep do all of the work. Besides, we're not nomads wandering from one watering hole to the next. We control the land," he said proudly.

İbrahim could see that arguing was pointless. Changing his tactics to affecting indifference to their criticisms, he coolly asked, "Where can I find an axe?"

"You won't be needing one," Ömer answered cheerily. "I can't have you hurting yourself. You're pulling the rocks out of the ground and putting them into that wagon. We'll take care of the trees." Ömer tossed a shovel at İbrahim's feet. "I want that wagon filled before the master returns."

"When will that be?" İbrahim asked anxiously.

Looking slyly at him, Ömer said, "You're better off worrying about filling that wagon than trying to figure out how much time you have to get the job done."

Although humor and good feeling rang in the men's voices, İbrahim resented their laughter. He grabbed the shovel and began to search for his first rock.

"Leave them be if the rocks are smaller than your foot," Ömer called over to him.

İbrahim soon found a boulder jutting out of the ground. He set to work, first digging around its edges and then straight down. After an hour of digging, the full size of the boulder began to be revealed. It was buried three feet deep in the ground and showed no signs of yielding when he tried to pry it loose. Sweat pouring into his eyes and muscles burning from exertion, he fought a losing battle, all the while growing more upset at the thought of the empty wagon. İbrahim was still struggling to work the boulder free when Mahmut returned just as the sun was reaching its zenith. The boulder had consumed time as quickly as it had his energy.

Rather than inspecting İbrahim's efforts, Mahmut walked over to Ömer. "How did the boy do?"

İbrahim's head snapped towards Ömer. He had not noticed Ömer sparing him a glance. The empty wagon was sure to be Ömer's only guide, İbrahim despaired.

To his surprise, Ömer answered, "Worked hard. Doesn't have any idea about what he needs to do, though."

"No one told me what to do," İbrahim loudly interjected.

Mahmut silenced him with a cross expression. "You will speak when I ask you a question."

Embarrassed, İbrahim bit his lip and looked to see if the others were listening. All eyes were on him.

To his relief, Mahmut took out his prayer rug. Following prayer, lunch was quickly eaten in silence. İbrahim then went back to work. He excavated an inclined trench and the earth on all sides of the boulder. Pleased with his preparations, he took turns pushing with his back and then his hands and chest, but the boulder did not acquiesce. İbrahim urged himself on, smarting from Ömer's criticism. The battle between flesh and rock continued on for the rest of the afternoon.

Ömer finally released İbrahim from the struggle. "You've worked hard. Now it's time to fill your belly."

"But I've done nothing," İbrahim confessed with a resentful glare at the boulder. The sun was dipping below the horizon. Again, he was astonished by how quickly the time had passed.

With a bemused expression, Ömer said, "You can worry about filling the wagon tomorrow."

İbrahim followed the men back to the villa. Mahmut was waiting for them, prayer rug already laid out. İbrahim was again disappointed when Mahmut left them to their evening meal. Starving for the bottom of the stewpot, the men demanded that İbrahim fill his bowl until he could hardly breathe.

İbrahim listened in silence to the farmhands, who spoke to each other with the relaxed familiarity reserved for close family. He studied his comrades, whose bodies abounded with scars and knots. The marks of battle, İbrahim decided.

İbrahim returned to the barn, alone. As he lay on his mattress, his thoughts alternated between the mystery that was his master and the question of how he would defeat the boulder. He had little time to solve these riddles. Sleep soon overcame him.

Mahmut's call to prayer the next morning was far less easily received than his call from the previous day. The throbbing tightness in İbrahim's overworked muscles had left him weak. He steeled himself for the struggle against the boulder.

On arriving at the field, İbrahim briskly waved to his comrades and sought out his newfound nemesis. He renewed his assault with fury, driving the wedge of an iron shovel underneath the boulder. İbrahim threw himself against the handle until his feet were dangling in the air. As he bounced on the wooden shaft of the shovel, it groaned and then splintered. Like a bird struck by an arrow, İbrahim toppled awkwardly to the ground. He tried to jump up but his aching legs betrayed him. Sprawled helplessly on the ground, he felt his ears ring with laughter.

"It looks like that wagon is going to stay empty for a long time," Ömer howled along with the other farmhands.

Slowly straightening himself, İbrahim leaned against the boulder. "I need a hammer and a spike," he snapped.

Still shaking with laughter, Ömer pointed to a pile of tools. "Don't break anything else," Ömer managed to say, eyes twinkling with delight, as İbrahim stormed passed him. "Remember, it's our job to build the estate, not tear it apart."

"I'll break the boulder into a thousand pieces," İbrahim announced brashly.

"It's your rock," Ömer giggled like a child.

"Rocks," İbrahim corrected the older man. He marched up to the boulder and began to chip at it. Deciding to cut it in half, he started at the top of the boulder and carved a shallow line down to its base.

İbrahim sustained the assault for the next five days, unwilling to admit defeat and swallow his pride. His efforts had only produced a shallow, unimpressive trench in the boulder. Ömer had left İbrahim to his own devices. If he were still amused by the young boy's folly, Ömer no longer said anything.

The boulder was gone when İbrahim arrived at the field on the seventh day. Eyes racing frantically across the field, he finally located it in the wagon, completely intact. He marched up to Ömer and demanded, "Which one of you moved my boulder?"

"Which one of us?" Ömer laughed. "Don't be absurd. How could one man possibly move such a boulder?"

"So how did it end up in the wagon, then?" İbrahim stamped his foot angrily.

"We tied a rope to it and then had a horse drag it down your trench and onto the wagon. Great idea, your trench," Ömer said appreciatively. "It made things much easier."

"So none of you was able to best the rock either?" İbrahim asked triumphantly.

"It's in the wagon, is it not?" Ömer answered.

"But it took all of you to do it."

"How else could it have been done?"

"If that is so, why didn't you say so earlier?"

"You said it was your rock," Ömer answered simply. "It was up to you to decide how you would get it in the wagon. If you wanted our assistance, you only needed to ask."

"What should I do now?" İbrahim asked humbly, shoulders slumped forward.

It was a familiar scene, Ömer thought, fascinated by the uncertainty on the boy's unblemished face. "Your job hasn't changed. Clear the field."

İbrahim wistfully watched the men return home to their wives and children after finishing dinner. The wound in his heart opened anew and he yearned for his mother.

"It's a fine evening."

İbrahim spun around, heart racing, to find Mahmut standing behind him. The last faint rays of the sun seemed to be absorbed into Mahmut's ancient face, which glowed with satisfaction.

"Ömer tells me that you have learned a lesson in humility."

İbrahim's face contorted with pain and anger over what he felt was Ömer's betrayal.

"You must miss your home. Tell me about it."

İbrahim brightened and began describing his flock and the hills he had tried to rule. But after a few minutes, he drew silent, surprised by how little he had to say.

"Do you not have family besides your sheep?"

"Of course I do," İbrahim said, embarrassed. Trying to make up for his gaffe, he launched into a detailed description of his mother.

Mahmut smiled. "She sounds lovely. And your father?"

"Mother and I were alone." He hung his head and tried to fight back tears.

A worried expression crossed Mahmut's brow. "Your father is dead?"

A chill ran through İbrahim as he pondered whether he should reveal where his father had died. After hesitating for several seconds, he finally nodded his head.

"So your mother is alone now?"

İbrahim could no longer control himself. The tears cut streaks through the dirt on his face as he croaked, "I will never see her again, will I?"

"This should not be," Mahmut said, looking stunned. "I was told that an only child would not be taken from his widowed mother. Did they know that your mother would be alone?"

"I want her," İbrahim pitifully squeaked.

Mahmut looked up to the sky and heaved a heavy sigh. This boy should not be here, he realized. Mahmut thought of the corps İbrahim was destined to join. The Janissaries' strength was based on their indomitable esprit de corps. Their success was dependent upon the willingness of each man to sacrifice at any time for the good of his comrades and Sultan. Already, İbrahim's immature social skills were a source of concern. Mahmut had hoped that İbrahim's obsessive desire to move the boulder without assistance was merely childish pride. Now, he worried that İbrahim's behavior reflected a deeper character flaw that would make him forever incompatible with his future.

Mahmut's heart ached for İbrahim. He had never felt pity for the boys he trained. Although slaves, theirs was a happy bondage in which they were to become the elite. Each boy had quickly adapted to his new surroundings and eventually welcomed the long journey back to Edirne. But İbrahim was different. If it were possible, Mahmut would have gladly sent İbrahim home.

"It is too late to reunite you with your mother. You are no longer the young man you were a month ago." Mahmut surveyed the anguish in İbrahim's face and thought of his own boys when they were young. "I know it must be painful, but you must accept what you are now," he said, echoing the advice he had given himself every day for the last eight years.

"What am I?" İbrahim asked.

Spirit lifting, Mahmut patted İbrahim on the back and said,

"You are many things. First among them is that you are a Muslim. It is time that you began to study the Koran." He reached into his robe and produced a worn volume. "It is the word of God," he said reverently, "given to the world by His prophet, Mohammed."

The idea of receiving any gift thrilled İbrahim. As he examined the holy book, his sagging spirits began to lift. "I can't read," İbrahim finally admitted, embarrassed by his ignorance.

"I didn't expect you could. Besides, it's written in Arabic."

"Then how will I ever be able to understand it?"

"You and I will study together every night."

Perhaps he will tell me his stories, İbrahim thought.

"Of course, you will have to work hard in the field."

"Of course," İbrahim agreed. Cradling the Koran like a baby, he skipped back towards the barn.

Mahmut watched his charge disappear into the night and whispered, "May the mercy of Allah shine on the boy." He was too humble to pray for anything else.

As he clasped the Koran tightly to his chest, İbrahim's heart raced with excitement at the chance to learn more about his mysterious master. The scar—I must learn how Mahmut was wounded. And his boys—somehow I must learn what happened to them. He fought back sleep while spending the next several hours creating a list of questions.

İbrahim was waiting for Mahmut the next morning. With a cheerfulness that Mahmut had never seen from his young charge, İbrahim called out, "May peace be upon you, Master."

"And upon you, İbrahim," Mahmut replied, his scar contorting as his brow furrowed in partial amusement and bewilderment. "Shall we begin?"

İbrahim nodded and launched into the morning prayers, all the while anticipating Mahmut's answers to the questions he would ask during their walk to the field. It was not to be. When they completed their prayers, Mahmut wished him a good day and returned to the villa. Baffled, but still excited, İbrahim felt the day pass quickly. He hardly noticed his fellow farmhands as he filled five more wagons without assistance. By evening, however, his soul sank. Mahmut was nowhere to be seen. Feeling cheated, İbrahim returned to the barn with his chin hung down over the taut muscles of his rapidly maturing chest.

"Just how am I to become this great warrior, a man of destiny," he scoffed, "if I'm to be treated no differently than you?" İbrahim shouted at a cow, who contentedly looked past him.

"You would do better to ask how you might learn to be a responsible member of the community," Mahmut answered, standing by the door in the last shadows of twilight.

İbrahim spun around with a broad smile on his face. "I was hoping you would come. I have so many questions."

Mahmut gestured for İbrahim to be silent. "First you will listen. When it is time, I will let you ask your questions. If they are worthy of being answered, I will do my best to satisfy your curiosity. Now sit. We must discuss your future."

İbrahim raced over to Mahmut and seated himself reverently at his master's feet.

"It is my charge to send you back to Edirne well-mannered, faithful, sincere—and sociable. These qualities are essential if you are to be a true believer. Otherwise, you will undoubtedly stray from the straight path. I've seen too many men who truly believe themselves to be Muslims engage in low behavior. Self-deceit can be the worst kind of foolishness and the most offensive vanity. I cannot abide it. You will be a true believer."

İbrahim vigorously nodded his head in agreement. "I can be what you ask."

"You must. Words are not enough. It hasn't escaped my notice that you prefer to work alone and mix uneasily with the others. I'm sure you have your reasons. You may even be conscious of some of them. Still, it cannot be."

"But surely my work has pleased you," İbrahim said, stunned by Mahmut's critique.

"You did well for a man working alone, but the field would be cleared of those rocks by now if you had sought Ömer's help.

That is why you have not yet proven yourself to be an asset to this farm and why you'll never be an asset to your future corps unless you change who you are. Virtue and reward come from devotion to the community, not to one's self." Mahmut could see İbrahim's face turning red with resentment. "Criticism is not an evil, either," he said flatly.

Conscious of the blood rushing to his cheeks, İbrahim begged for his master's forgiveness. "I don't know your ways, but I will try to learn."

Mere words, Mahmut thought to himself as he struggled to find a way to reach İbrahim. "Two hundred years ago, my fore-fathers roamed the steppes; they were barbarians. No one thought that nomads could emerge from those dry grasslands and create a state. But it happened. Do you know how? It's because they became warriors for the faith. And for that, we were promised worldly dominion.

"Yes, it is true. The great Sultan Osman's father, Ertuğrul, led a mere four hundred horsemen into Anatolia. One day he chanced upon a battle between the Mongols and the Seljuk Sultan Alaeddin of Konya. Ertuğrul threw his lot in with the Sultan and together they won a great victory. The Sultan awarded Ertuğrul a small fief in northwestern Anatolia, near the lands of the Byzantines.

"*Gazi* warriors and adventurers seeking booty flocked to Ertuğrul's lands and began the fight to expand Islam into Byzantine territory. With each success, more warriors came. Families settled the land and a mighty state took form.

"But what set our tiny emirate apart from all of the others that dotted Anatolia? It was more than our good fortune to be bordering a decrepit, rudderless state. Allah smiled upon us through Osman, who became enraptured by the eternal word of Allah in the Koran.

"One night Osman stayed the night in the home of a judge whose daughter's hand he had sought for two years. As he slept by the side of the judge, Osman dreamed that a lush tree rose out of his loins. The tree grew quickly and cast its shadow over the world. Soon Osman was perched atop the tree gazing down at the Balkan, Taurus, Atlas and Caucasian mountain ranges together with the Tigris, Euphrates, Nile and Danube Rivers. The lands were rich and the cities, enriched by Islam, radiated power and refinement unmatched in history. The leaves of the tree then turned into the blades of shimmering scimitars, all pointing toward Constantinople. The great city sparkled like a pristine jewel under the hot glare of the summer sun. It then became a brilliant ring. As Osman reached out to put the ring on his finger, the dream was broken. When Osman told the judge about his dream, the judge knew that the young suitor was blessed with Allah's revelation. He gave his daughter in marriage to Osman."

Mahmut paused and stared deeply into İbrahim's eyes. Satisfied that he held the boy's full interest, he continued, "Osman's dream of placing the ring on his finger did not end that night. In Constantinople, a massive statue of the great Byzantine Emperor, Justinian, sits in front of Hagia Sophia, Christendom's greatest church. In the right hand of the statue rests a globe. We call it the Red Apple. It is the symbol of worldly dominion and our greatest desire. One day you and your comrades will burst through Constantinople's formidable walls and claim the Red Apple for Islam and your Sultan. 'On to the Red Apple.' It must be the cry that burns in your heart above all others."

As much as İbrahim wanted to embrace the future Mahmut had laid before him, he hesitated. He thought of his father's counsel that he pursue that which he coveted most. Was the conquest of Constantinople truly to be his Red Apple, he wondered skeptically. How could so many share the same goal?

"Your lust for the Red Apple needn't start now," Mahmut added judiciously, sensing İbrahim's reluctance to fully release himself. "Unless desire comes from the earnest belief that what you seek is bound in virtue, it can only lead to sin. In time, you will experience sacrifice and loss for your faith and the Sultan. One day, a day that starts like any other, the frightening realization of your mortality will unexpectedly but forever attach itself to your soul. Then your heart will stir and you will yearn to make an in-delible mark on this world. That is when you will claim Justinian's globe from his giant hand."

There was no sense denying Mahmut's counsel, İbrahim de-cided. Not only did he not want to arouse the disapproval of his master, but he wanted to make sure that Mahmut continued to shower him with stories. Although self-reliance was deep-ly imbedded within him, a life of loneliness had no appeal. If he could embrace the Red Apple, İbrahim decided, perhaps he could find the fulfilling attachment to community that Mahmut preached.

"It is time for you to rest," Mahmut said. "Tomorrow evening we will begin our studies."

The next evening İbrahim gulped down only one bowl of stew before rushing back to the barn. Ömer peered into the pot, which was still brimming with stew. His stomach growled angrily as he watched the boy disappear into the shadows.

"The young man forgets that he has other bellies to feed," Ömer informed Mahmut as he emerged from the villa.

Looking disappointed but not surprised, Mahmut inspected the stewpot. "It is true. He has much to learn."

"Perhaps while you're teaching him you might allow us to eat more bowls than the boy," Sait requested. "Certainly, the food should not go to waste."

Ömer froze Sait with a lethal gaze. "It's a good thing you're not responsible for İbrahim's training," Ömer scolded his friend. "He'd learn all the wrong lessons. İbrahim must bend to the rules. The rules cannot bend to İbrahim. In the meantime, our bellies will have to adjust."

Mahmut smiled at his old friend. "Ömer, you are a blessing to this land. I trust you will make sure that the stew is brought to the village and distributed to the poor." As Mahmut walked past Sait, he patted him on the shoulder.

As he came upon the barn, Mahmut saw İbrahim completing his last prayers of the day. A quick study, Mahmut mused.

"Well done," Mahmut greeted İbrahim when he was done. "The study of the Koran and the Tradition will occupy us now. Come."

For the next seven years, Mahmut had come every night and instructed İbrahim about God's decrees. İbrahim had ravenously consumed Mahmut's every lesson. He stayed awake late into the night repeating Mahmut's injunctions and mouthing them under his breath as he worked in the field.

As his mind grew, so did his fluency in Arabic and Turkish. İbrahim reveled in his newfound education. No bit of knowledge was too small to be absorbed into the lockbox that was his mind. He thirsted to know more and wash away the blight of his ignorance. Knowledge was to be a finely cut tool through which he would overwhelm friend and foe with his arching intellect. He systematically committed to memory more and more verses of the Koran until he could out-quote his teacher.

İbrahim's fascination with Islam far outstripped that of any of Mahmut's previous charges. Unlike the others, though, İbrahim rarely asked questions about how the underlying bases for the injunctions were to be bound to his own life. A collector of facts, not ethics, Mahmut feared. Mahmut wondered whether İbrahim had any more belief now than when they had first met on the docks of Gallipoli.

Mahmut had committed far more time to him than to any of the other boys. He felt the frustration of a devoted father. A crushing sense of failure pervaded his thoughts as he imagined İbrahim living an empty life with nothing to assuage the inevitable suffering of a warrior.

Death was the only topic that elicited deep personal reflection from İbrahim. Mahmut taught İbrahim that his life was in God's hands and that he should not fear his end. The true believer, Mahmut explained, would enjoy eternal life if his death came in battle for the advancement of God's will.

Dissatisfied with this lesson, İbrahim would endlessly rephrase questions about whether true belief was necessary to receive eternal life. It was during İbrahim's frustrating pursuit of a more palatable answer that he finally overcame his hesitancy and asked, "How did it feel to stand in battle?"

As he often did, Mahmut paused to consider the question. Several minutes passed during which the striking features of Mahmut's battered face eventually relaxed, unveiling his advanced age. Mahmut's eyes lost their focus as he drifted into another time and place. Finally, he said, "You cannot anticipate your own fears by knowing mine. Measuring your resolve on the battlefield against my faded memories will not help you."

"Then tell me your stories so that I may know the glory that awaits me."

"You're certainly no longer the timid pup I collected on the docks of Gallipoli," Mahmut laughed.

In the past, İbrahim would have blushed and apologized endlessly while wondering whether he had just suffered a subtle rebuke. Although those thoughts lingered, they were banished to the farther reaches of his mind, especially where Mahmut was concerned. The old man was now more father than teacher.

"My first battle was fought nearly fifty years ago against the Serbs at Kosovo," Mahmut relented.

İbrahim's face sprang to life. He leaned forward, already fearing that he might miss something.

Mahmut's severe mien was momentarily replaced by amusement at İbrahim's youthful fascination. "It was a great and terrible day for our empire," he said, mindful of the historic magnitude of the story he was about to tell. "Fortunately, our neighbors were no more united than they are now—always at war with each other. The Serbs had already done us the favor of destroying the Bulgarians a half century earlier. And of course the Byzantines were hardly better off than they are today. Survival was the extent of their ambitions. And so the Serbs were our only true opposition, but even they had seen better days. Still, they are a hardy people, fierce in battle. You must not forget that when it's your turn to take the field," he added with paternal gravity. "The Serbs had gained a great victory over us the year before at the Battle of Plochnik. National pride blossomed. Like fickle but excited children, the Slavs flocked to the Serbian Tsar Lazar's banner.

"Sultan Murad used the full wisdom of his seventy years as he studied the threat. He knew their unity was thinly greased by brashly spoken, grand words. The Sultan held us back in Asia, letting time eat away the Slavs' enthusiasm. When their internal squabbles grew loud enough, we crossed into Europe."

"Were you excited?" The question nearly burst from İbrahim's racing imagination.

Mahmut smiled wryly. "I was inexperienced. My heart fluttered like the wings of a young bird learning to fly. I wanted to strike the deathblow to Tsar Lazar myself. I thought nothing of how badly outnumbered we were as the Sultan marched us onto the Plain of Blackbirds.

"My excitement did not survive the first hour on that field," Mahmut shuddered. "It was a desolate place and I was sure that the cold wind blowing from the enemy camp would strip the skin from my bones. Still, my comrades and I stood our ground, certain that victory would be ours.

"Looking back, I've wondered why I felt that way. Why do birds know when to head south for the winter?" He mused. "Perhaps we are guided by the same natural instinct.

"The Sultan drew us into our customary battle order: In the center stood the Sultan with his Janissaries and cavalrymen; Bayezid, the Sultan's eldest son, commanded the European troops on the right flank; and Yakub, the Sultan's younger son, commanded the Anatolian troops on the left flank. It was with Yakub that my comrades and I stood that day.

"At first, the Serbs were strong. Sometimes I think I can still hear their war cries when the wind howls. Their shrieks fell on us like the whine of the earth splitting open during an earthquake. Men cannot make the sounds they made. The devil had made his home in their tongues. They bored into our left flank, raking us with their swords as though they were clearing a wheat field. I can't remember falling from my horse. All I recall is being swept backwards like a piece of debris being carried out in the foaming sea. We should've been doomed, but the treachery of Vuk Brankovic, Tsar Lazar's son-in-law, saved us."

"The Tsar's son-in-law betrayed him?" İbrahim's eyes had ceased to blink. "Who could be so corrupt?"

"Know your friends, my boy," Mahmut implored his young charge. "Move quickly once you suspect their betrayal. When betrayal comes, it comes at the worst times. That was so for the Tsar. Vuk Brankovic withdrew twelve thousand soldiers from the battle just as victory was within his father-in-law's grasp. I can't tell you the reward the Sultan promised the young man for betraying his blood, but it couldn't possibly have been worth the Serbs losing the field and their independence soon thereafter.

"But all was not well. Treachery is a dangerous cancer that stalks friend and foe alike. During the battle, Milosh Obilic, another of Tsar Lazar's sons-in-law, also gave himself over to the Sultan on the pretense of changing his allegiance. But Obilic's heart remained true to his nation. Upon being presented to the Sultan, Obilic plunged a hidden dagger into Sultan Murad's chest. Of course Obilic was immediately killed. Tsar Lazar was also executed.

"No great man should be murdered so basely," Mahmut mourned. "Sultan Murad was a just man who did more than build a state. He showed us the righteous way of reaping our rewards. Even the Patriarch in Constantinople, always an implacable foe, had once proclaimed that Sultan Murad had left his Church in peace.

"The throne passed to Prince Bayezid. It was now his duty to preserve the empire. He started his reign by soaking his scimitar in the blood of the Serbian nobility. He then strangled his brother, Yakub, to ensure that his succession to the throne would not be challenged. Next, Bayezid turned his rage on Hungary. When his raids on Hungarian territory finally provoked King Sigismund to attack, we were ready.

"King Sigismund and a Crusader army of French, English, Scots, Germans, Wallachians, Poles, Italians, Spanish, and Knights Hospitallers took the field against us. We met them along the Danube before the fortress of Nicopolis.

"It is said that King Sigismund declared, 'If the sky fell on our army we should have enough lances to uphold it.' I would've believed it as well. Unfortunately for King Sigismund, the sky was not his enemy. That distinction belonged to Sultan Bayezid and King Sigismund's allies, whose foolish pursuit of personal glory doomed the Crusade. Instead of attacking in tandem with King Sigismund's Hungarian infantry, his Crusader knight allies charged at us—alone.

"It was a brilliant spectacle. The knights' armor glittered like rays from heaven over the field. I had battled the Christians long enough to know that their strength came from their valor, not their professionalism. They would wreak havoc with a glorious attack, hoping to overpower our discipline and mobility. I'm quite sure they didn't even bother to scout us before starting their charge.

"The knights charged uphill, easily dispatching our outposts and scattering our cavalry. I was lucky to escape with but a few wounds. After their initial charge, they dismounted and pushed their way up the hill with their armor and swords drenched in blood. Imagine their surprise," Mahmut allowed himself a crisp laugh, "when they saw sixty thousand fresh men set to fall on them. The poor fools had exhausted themselves mostly on shock troops. Unhorsed, they couldn't even flee.

"Sultan Bayezid enjoyed his victory well. He ordered a general massacre of the many thousands of prisoners. Only a few captured French counts were left alive to tell the tale. But first they were forced to watch their comrades beheaded and left for carrion."

"And what of King Sigismund? Was he killed as well?"

"He held his forces back. Sigismund is the Holy Roman Emperor today. The cautious man often reaps rewards that others might have gained," Mahmut soberly counseled.

İbrahim was enthralled, but he was also disturbed by Sultan Bayezid's bloody excesses. Remembering Mahmut's lessons, İbrahim asked, "Is it not so, 'Whoso is slain wrongfully, We have given power unto his heir'?"

Mahmut smiled wanly. "Many things occur in war that call

into question our morality. Who is to say, but perhaps Sultan Bayezid suffered for slaughtering his prisoners.

"I stood by my Sultan several years later outside of Ankara when the great Mongol warrior, Tamerlane, incited by Sultan Bayezid's insults, took the field against my master. Tamerlane was nearly seventy years old—and lame as well. No matter. It didn't take long before most of our soldiers were running for their lives. Only the Janissaries and a few loyalists like myself stood by the Sultan until the end. After fighting until I could barely lift my sword, I was knocked from my horse and trampled. I bear those wounds on my face now." He gently ran his fingers down the craggy chasm and mournfully shook his head. "Unlike the Sultan, though, I was lucky to escape. It is said that Sultan Bayezid was taken alive and paraded through Anatolia in a cage while Tamerlane enjoyed the Sultan's harem. In shame, Sultan Bayezid crushed his skull on the bars of his cage."

İbrahim studied Mahmut's jagged scar and thought he could feel the skin over his own forehead constrict. "And then you retired?"

"I only wish I could have laid down my scimitar," Mahmut said forlornly. "Although only in my early thirties, my body ached from years in the field and I suffer to this day from having failed my Sultan. But the empire disintegrated into a terrible civil war. Duty called. It took ten more years before Sultan Mehmed, a truly decent and faithful man, defeated his enemies and reunited our people. Once, I expected to take Constantinople. Instead, I spent the last years of my career trying to preserve one hundred years of hard-won gains."

For a moment Mahmut appeared overcome by emotion. Then he clasped İbrahim's shoulders with both hands in a vice grip. "It will fall upon you to claim the Red Apple, İbrahim."

İbrahim strained against the pressure applied by Mahmut's arthritic hands. The old man's unflappable serenity had momentarily given way to the desperation and pain he held deep in reserve.

Grateful for Mahmut's trust, İbrahim's eyes clouded with tears. "Why am I happy?"

A sense of relief spread over Mahmut. A connection had finally been made after seven years, he thought. For the last six months Mahmut had held a note from the agha of the Janissaries ordering İbrahim's return to Edirne as soon as possible. The tone of the note suggested an urgency that made Mahmut wonder whether a major operation was being planned. Although always mindful that his first duty was to the state, Mahmut had not been able to release İbrahim. Biting his lip, he wondered whether the boy might surprise him after all.

The Sky Began to Turn • 1437

Mahmut could not help but be impressed by İbrahim. Hard work had layered his nearly six-foot frame with thick muscles. Each evening İbrahim indulged his youthful fascination with his strength by playfully hoisting Ömer onto his broad shoulders and parading him back to the villa for the evening meal.

A fine weapon, Mahmut mused, contemplating İbrahim's energy being molded to the purposes of the Sultan. Where is the sullen young man who first came to this land, Mahmut wondered as İbrahim grinned brightly at him. The boy's features sparkled in the light of the early morning sky. Although deeply tanned, his skin still exuded a youthful delicateness that belied the assertive boulder of a chin that petulantly projected upward from under his long, angular nose and broad, furrowed brow. Yet for all of İbrahim's outward signs of strength and familiarity with his comrades, Mahmut still saw İbrahim flinch and quickly turn away when confronted or caught stealing a glimpse at another.

İbrahim cursed his shyness. When will it lift, he asked himself every day. During his first years on the farm, he assumed that the passage of time would wash away his discomfort. Instead, the shyness continued to grow, even as he became more focused on the weakness. He was troubled still further knowing that he did not have much time before he would be sent away. The thought of being separated from Mahmut and his friends on the estate left him with a perpetual ache in his belly.

"I have good news," Mahmut announced flatly.

Watching the stony expression pasted on Mahmut's face, a shudder ran through İbrahim. He intuitively realized that the moment he had dreaded for so long had arrived. His comrades seemed to realize it too. They somberly stood with their hands fidgeting by their sides.

Mahmut cleared his throat and continued, "Edirne beckons, my boy. I have been commanded to bring you to the capital, where you will be entered into the ranks of the cadets. There you will complete your training and become a Janissary."

"When do we leave?" İbrahim asked, trying to sound brave.

"Tomorrow morning."

A gasp escaped from İbrahim. He turned to look at his comrades. They had experienced this moment before and spared their young friend further pain by avoiding his gaze.

"A Janissary doesn't have time for long farewells. The rest of the day is yours to do with as you please."

"Then this is goodbye," İbrahim said, looking at Ömer.

With genuine fondness, Ömer smiled and said, "You were an asset to this estate, İbrahim. We will miss you. I pray that you live a long life that brings glory to the empire and a happy retirement on a fair estate."

Over the years, İbrahim had developed a sense of brotherhood with these men. He grew to covet every moment of their fraternity. Yet he constantly questioned the permanency of this happy condition and whether his feelings were reciprocated.

"I will carry my memories of you for the rest of my days," İbrahim assured them, his voice cracking as he succumbed to the moment. Searching their faces for affirmation, he said, "I hope you will remember me with equal fondness."

"Of course we will," Ragıp said merrily, "at least until the next young man is brought to us."

It was a tired joke that Ragıp had shared with all of the previous boys. Still, his companions broke into laughter. Unlike during his first days on the farm, İbrahim enjoyed the joke. With their laughter ringing in his ears, he left the orchard.

Feeling the same dull numbness that he had experienced during his first trip to Edirne, İbrahim trudged back to his barn. The animals welcomed him with the familiar cacophony of braying that he had happily grown accustomed to over the years. As he surveyed his friends for the last time, he laughed at the absurdity of his attachment to this place. It was never meant to be home, İbrahim decided. Why else would Mahmut have quartered me here? It is my destiny to move on.

Carrying his treasured Koran and prayer rug, İbrahim stepped through the gate of the estate for the first time in seven years without so much as a glance over his shoulder. He remembered only too well the pain of looking back once before. When they reached the intersection with the main road, Mahmut pivoted and said, "Do you remember the promise I once made to you?"

İbrahim's heart skipped a beat. "You promised to bring me to Bursa if I learned my lessons well," he answered, surprised that Mahmut had remembered.

"And have you?"

"I know each chapter of the Koran by heart." İbrahim knew Mahmut suspected that his intellectual curiosity had not matured into deep belief. Not wanting to lose his chance at the prize, he truthfully said, "I pray for the day when the light of Islam brings me peace."

"As always," Mahmut chuckled, "a well-considered answer, worthy of a jurist. By any account, I'd say you've earned the right to visit the city."

İbrahim's heart raced with excitement as they passed through the southern gates of the city's ancient citadel. The pounding buzz of activity from the crowded, narrow streets immediately thrust itself upon him as they began to wind their way past the ancient houses, whose overhanging balconies afforded welcome shade against the late summer heat. Pushing past the throngs of people, they enjoyed the parks and gardens that dotted the city. İbrahim eventually found himself in the covered market, where peaches, candied chestnuts, silks, towels and cottons were being sold amid a frenzy of competing buyers who hovered over the well-provisioned stalls. The enticing aroma of grilled meat and melted butter permeated the air. As Mahmut had suspected it would, the seductive allure of this prosperous city had dulled any lingering regrets İbrahim had about bidding farewell to the pastoral life.

"What a wondrous place," İbrahim shouted to Mahmut above the din of the market.

Mahmut nodded his head in agreement and said, "Only to be surpassed by the city's marvelous tombs and mosques."

After walking east for several more minutes, they finally came upon the Green Mosque. "Green Bursa," Mahmut murmured, gazing proudly at the emerald green tiles atop the mosque and its minarets.

The mosque had been built during the reign of Sultan Mehmed I. Following custom, construction had stopped when the Sultan died. Still, its beauty knew few rivals in the Islamic world. Eyes wide with wonderment, İbrahim found himself standing before the northern portal. The words "Here is a building such as no nation has been presented with since the sky began to turn" were inscribed above him.

"May we enter?" İbrahim asked hopefully.

"Of course. That is what pilgrims do."

They spent the next few hours visiting the tombs of Sultans Osman and Orhan. A world of ever widening wonders opened up to him as İbrahim effortlessly meshed with the other pilgrims.

Standing reverently next to Sultan Osman's tomb, Mahmut said softly, "I dream of going on the hajj to the sacred monuments in Mecca before I lose my strength. As my time in this world grows shorter, my nightly dreams are filled with visions of myself, the light of Allah upon my face, praying before the Kaaba and seeing the Black Stone. Each night the urgency grows for me to fulfill that sacred duty. Sometimes when I awaken, I start packing my belongings."

"What makes you stay?" İbrahim asked, honored by the unexpected intimacy of Mahmut's confession.

"One duty at a time." Mahmut fixed on İbrahim the same fatherly expression that had touched him from the first moment they met. "But enough talk about an old man's dreams. You will be pleased to know that Bursa is known for more than its tombs and peaches. Its baths have soothed spirits and bodies for centuries."

Mahmut brought İbrahim to Kaplıca. A powerful sulphuric odor wafted towards them as they entered the bath. Grinning broadly, Mahmut sighed, "Come. It's time that you learned to measure hardship against pleasure."

For nearly an hour, they lounged lazily in the soothing, hot waters of the spa, steam clouding the air around them. İbrahim stared intently at Mahmut, whose body seemed to relax more and more with each passing moment. Of all the many stories that Mahmut had shared with him, Mahmut had never spoken about the fate of his boys. It was the story that İbrahim longed to hear most. Nights had passed slowly as İbrahim jealously wondered whether they had had the same affection as he for Mahmut or whether Mahmut showered him with the same fatherly love. Feelings of betrayal never ceased to creep into these ruminations, as İbrahim struggled to reconcile his affection for Mahmut with his idealized love for his natural father.

Time is again my enemy, İbrahim groused to himself. His time with Mahmut was quickly disappearing like the last sands descending in an hourglass. "We cannot part company before I tell you about my father."

"What more could you tell me than what you told me years ago? Did not your father die when you were a very small child?"

"Yes, Mother told me that he died fighting the Sultan's armies during the siege of Constantinople fifteen years ago." As he quickly finished his confession, İbrahim carefully watched Mahmut's face for a reaction.

"Did you fear telling me about your father?"

"I still do."

"I would never hurt you," Mahmut said with a pained expression.

"Oh, I've known for years that you would never raise your hand against me. That is not what I fear now."

"You can no more blame the enemy for defending himself than

you can expect him to relieve you of your pain." Mahmut sighed heavily. "We cannot concern themselves with who may have killed whom in war."

Always the teacher, İbrahim reflected, feeling relieved of the burden he had worn like a millstone around his neck for the last seven years. Minutes evaporated like seconds as the steam seeped deeper into İbrahim's now relaxed body. Yielding completely to the steam, he turned to Mahmut and said, "For some time now, I've thought of you as my father. Does that mean I've betrayed my true father?"

Mahmut understood the young man's pain only too well. He had often looked back with regret over the times he told his own father, in reverent tones, stories about how his commanders possessed unmatched qualities. "We spend our lives making new attachments and disentangling ourselves from others. But never forsake your bond to the Sultan. That is for a lifetime."

Even among his enemies, Sultan Murad II's reputation was that of an upright, religious man, albeit with strong mystical leanings. He was more disposed towards peace with Christendom than war. Nevertheless, he was a mighty warrior whose gift for commanding men made him beloved. Stories abounded of how he would take meals with the men and speak as a commoner while his aloof advisers shook their heads in exasperation. There was no challenge the army was unwilling to take for their Sultan.

"I'm afraid that I might not be able to serve him as I served you, Master. I know nothing of fighting."

"It's better that way. The men who train you will prefer working with a blank slate. If it's courage you think you're lacking, though, I can only tell you that the trainers will give you nothing more than discipline. Whatever strength you bring to the battlefield has lain deep in your breast since birth. No experience can rival the feeling of discovering that power. In those times when you doubt yourself the most, remember that the Red Apple beckons to you. Let its power fill your heart."

Edirne's minarets glistened brightly before them in the midday sun. İbrahim looked south and mourned for his mother. Despite his best efforts, her memory had dimmed over the years, a victim of time and his fresher bond with Mahmut. As his last moments with Mahmut were coming to an end, the wound of his separation from his mother bled anew. Wondering whether Mahmut's sense of loss would match his mother's, he turned to Mahmut and shakily asked, "Will you be taking on a new boy?"

Mahmut detected a mixture of jealousy and anguish in İbrahim's voice. "You were quite enough, İbrahim." He playfully slapped İbrahim on the back. "Even an old warhorse like myself is entitled to a few days of rest. I thank Allah that I'll be able to live out the rest of my days knowing that you will bring honor to my name."

Although basking in Mahmut's approval, İbrahim noticed that his master's face was drawn tight and that he was dragging his left leg behind him.

Winding their way through the streets, they finally came upon a large, gray stone building. Battered by the weather, it had obviously stood for centuries. Two young men nodded respectfully at Mahmut as they passed through the gates of the building into a large courtyard. Hundreds of older men and their young charges were milling about.

As İbrahim surveyed the scene, he saw a heavyset man with a narrow, gray beard that drew a thin line between his swollen cheeks and the billowing folds of his neck. The man's eyes lit with recognition and he rushed forward. "Mahmut, old friend, I was beginning to wonder whether you would ever deliver this boy."

"It's good to see you again, Mustafa," Mahmut replied warmly. "The strong young man at my side is İbrahim."

İbrahim respectfully nodded his head.

"İbrahim, this man commands the cadets. Do as he says."

"That's the best introduction you can make?" Mustafa laughed.

"Is more needed?"

"Mahmut, you might tell İbrahim that you are my oldest

friend." Mustafa faced İbrahim and said, "You needn't worry about disappointing me, young man. I doubt very much you will see me at all during your training. But on to more important matters. You might be interested to know that your master saved my life and many others at Ankara against Tamerlane."

İbrahim's eyes opened wide in surprise.

"Just as I thought," Mustafa chuckled, "another one who doesn't know that he's been tutored by a hero."

"Memories and folklore will not bring us the Red Apple. Only the strength of our commitment to Islam and ethics will bring us Allah's bounty." As he spoke, Mahmut's face suddenly turned ashen and his breath became labored.

İbrahim had noticed the deterioration in Mahmut's condition but was afraid to say anything out of fear that he might embarrass his master. Mustafa also saw Mahmut's distress.

"You must rest," Mustafa said gently. "It's been a long journey. Here, take my hand."

"It's nothing," Mahmut weakly protested. "It's just an ache in my left arm. I've had it for the last several days. No need to worry. It always passes," he grimaced. "I must say, though, this pain is far worse than the last time."

"Perhaps I should send for a doctor," Mustafa said.

"So he can waste all of our time by telling me that my arm is arthritic like the rest of my body? You needn't bother." He grimaced more severely.

"Stubborn as those old mules you used to ride into battle," Mustafa tried to joke, unsuccessfully masking his concern. Mahmut was clutching his arm now and his face was growing increasingly ashen.

"İbrahim," Mahmut groaned.

With a sharp pain stabbing at his gut, İbrahim watched Mahmut drop to his knees.

"Call for a doctor, boy," Mustafa ordered.

"No," Mahmut croaked. "The boy stays."

"I want to stay," İbrahim confirmed, tears pouring down his face as he leaned over Mahmut.

"İbrahim, my son," Mahmut said panting, "I must bless you now before it is too late."

The word "son" hung in the air, increasing İbrahim's misery. "It's not too late." İbrahim knelt down and stared at Mahmut in disbelief.

"You are every bit as much a son to me as my own boys," Mahmut admitted, voice becoming eerily weak. "Just as the great Sheikh Hacı Bektaş blessed the first Janissary over a century ago, I foresee that your visage shall be bright and shining, your arm strong, your sword keen, your arrow sharp-pointed. You shall be victorious and ever return in triumph."

The shadows cast from curious onlookers now shaded Mahmut's stricken body from the bright sunlight. The faces of İbrahim's fellow cadets peered down on him, calm and dispassionate.

"I suppose I won't be seeing the Kaaba after all," Mahmut wheezed, clutching his chest.

As his face turned a darker shade of gray, his breath quickened into an irregular pattern of staccato-like pants. Mahmut turned his head upwards and with his remaining strength declared, "There is no god but Allah and Mohammed is His messenger." A long, soft breath escaped from him as the last words trickled out.

"He is gone," Mustafa said solemnly after a long, reverent pause. "A man for the ages." Pushing his massive bulk erect, Mustafa lurched past the crowd of boys and called for assistance.

İbrahim cradled Mahmut's head in his lap. Suddenly, a wrenching sob erupted from deep within him, followed by a torrent of sobs that were beyond his control. His body jerked upward as his chest continued to fill with air. Salty tears drained into his mouth and a clammy chill took hold of him.

The cadets crowded closer to İbrahim. A heavyset boy with a small forehead and bulbous nose snorted, "I only wish it was my overseer who was lying there now. I've got scars on my back just because I'd forget my evening prayers sometimes."

"No mistake there," another boy chimed in. "I would've liked to have given my master a taste of the lash a few times."

"I'll be thinking of my overseer the first time I take the head off of some Wallachian peasant," a third boy spit.

A chorus of criticism aimed at their overseers drowned out İbrahim's sobs.

The heavyset boy clapped his hand on İbrahim's shoulder and with a knowing wink said, "Mustafa is well out of earshot. You needn't make a show for us." He nodded towards Mahmut's lifeless body. "I imagine he was every bit as bad as the rotten bastard who beat me."

The boys echoed their approval with a chorus of laughter.

Stung by their harshness, İbrahim looked up at the boys with disbelief. "He was a good man," İbrahim said, struggling to think of what he could say that would convince them.

"You must have gotten your beatings on the head," one of the boys called out.

The mocking jeers grew even louder, but now the jeers were aimed at İbrahim.

İbrahim's pain and confusion began to jell into rage. He wanted to wrestle each one of the boys to the ground and drag them around the courtyard behind an oxcart until their bodies were scoured with wounds. İbrahim had hoped that their shared experiences over the last several years would bind them like brothers. Seeing that he was sorely mistaken opened up old wounds and fears of rejection that had never truly healed.

Rising nobly to his feet while affecting utter disdain for the boys, İbrahim sneered, "Your ignorance will condemn all of you to putrid lives of wasted service."

To his surprise, he was greeted with howls of laughter. Though he was only feet away from the nearest boy, a deepening chasm separated them. Smarting from their ridicule and unable to silence them, İbrahim felt his world collapse.

"Silence," Mustafa thundered over the commotion as he approached with a small troop of soldiers. "Report at once to your captain."

Within seconds, İbrahim was alone with Mustafa and the soldiers. "May I stay with him?" İbrahim asked solemnly.

Mustafa smiled kindly and said, "Say your farewells quickly and then you must join your comrades."

Conscious that Mustafa was observing him, İbrahim felt pressure to prove his fidelity to Mahmut. As he knelt down, a myriad of memories flitted through his mind, but he could not give them expression. He slammed his fists into his legs and looked up at Mustafa with sorrow and frustration etched on his face.

"It's all right, boy. Your master knew you well."

"I will prove myself worthy," he said bravely. İbrahim stole a final glance at Mahmut and bolted past the soldiers.

İbrahim ran over to join the cadets, who were already in formation at the far end of the courtyard. Unable to resist, he looked over his shoulder to see Mahmut one last time, but his master was already gone.

"Thank you for joining us," a stentorian voice wisecracked.

İbrahim's head snapped to attention. A slightly built man with an oversized head and a stern, hawkish expression fixed on his florid face was facing the boys. "I'm sorry, Sir," İbrahim stuttered. "I was saying goodbye—"

"I'm not interested in your excuses," the man glowered.

The boys choked back their laughter as İbrahim's face turned a bright shade of crimson.

"I'm not in the habit of repeating myself," the man said, "but it will serve both of us well if I make this one exception. I am your captain. That is more than my rank. It is the sole name by which you will know me. You will obey me at all times—absolutely. Failure to do so will result in the harshest discipline you can imagine.

"These are exciting times. Each day there is new word out of Hungary that King Sigismund is on his deathbed. Better still, I've been told that no strong successor is waiting to succeed him. If all of this news is true, then the Sultan will surely march. The spoils of a weakened nation beckon to us.

"So what does this mean to you, worthless dogs that you are? If our armies march, you and other cadets will be charged with manning this city's walls and policing its inhabitants." With a wolfish scowl, he stared down the boys and said, "Don't believe for one moment that I think you'll prove yourselves worthy of this charge. You're still boys who are more likely to terrorize those you've sworn to protect than do honor to the corps. I will be watching carefully. Rest assured, I have eyes that will surround you wherever you venture. When I discover your misdeeds, there will be punishment."

The boys collectively averted their gaze from the captain. The certainty of punishment at the hands of such a fierce man made them long for their former masters.

"Of course," the captain continued, "your principal duty will be to learn your trade as infantrymen. You will be drilled until your instincts for war are as natural as that of your lungs filling with air." An unexpected glow came over him. "The Empire has prospered because of the valor of the Janissary corps. For years *sipahi* cavalrymen, like your former overseers, have greedily claimed credit for the expansion of our lands. Nothing but self-delusional dandies, I tell you. It is infantry that holds ground and breaks the resolve of our enemies with an irresistible advance. The success of the empire falls to you.

"Remember, you are slaves of the state and the Sultan. Serve the Sultan with a glad heart, for he is the Shadow of God on Earth, and know that Sultan Murad does more than bestow offices. He will lead you from the stirrups as well."

Adopting a more officious tone, he then said, "You'll find your barrack assignments posted on the wall behind me. Get a good night's rest. The rigors of your last years will pale in comparison to the trials that lie ahead of you."

İbrahim surveyed the barracks. His eyes slowly climbed the sturdy, thick walls. The stones were knitted closely together and conveyed a sense of permanence and power that seemed to validate the captain's boasts. Fifteen feet from the floor was another tier, which, like the base below it, contained firm straw mattresses, enough for eighty cadets between them. Broad, wooden rafters crisscrossed below the heavily thatched ceiling, which towered over the hexagonally wedged stone flooring.

New faces mixed with the boys who had stood next to him in the courtyard. The room was filled with eager, confident young men who were anxious to get to know their comrades. Amiable conversations surrounded him even as he surrendered to the solitude that inexorably pulled him inward.

"He's the one I was telling you about," one boy laughed as he pointed out İbrahim to a group of cadets standing on the far side of the barracks.

İbrahim glowered at the group. Anxious to build relationships, they mimicked the boy's disdain.

Ömer had needled İbrahim for years. More than just catering to his own playful desires, Ömer had tried to break İbrahim from his obsessive need to be constantly treated with dignity. As the years wore on, İbrahim came to accept Ömer's jokes with the proper spirit. İbrahim had left his master's estate confident that laughter would never wound him again.

But this group's laughter was much different from Ömer's fatherly quips. A cruel edge pervaded their heckling. If he had grown up among other boys, İbrahim would have answered with an even sharper, leveling remark, or laughed off the joke with the same brash, youthful confidence with which it had been said to him. Instead, İbrahim assumed that the boy and his newfound compatriots were motivated by deep malice.

Reinventing the same aloof air that he had worn during his early days in Thrace, İbrahim proudly turned his head away from the group. He pulled his Koran from the small sack in which he had carried his meager belongings from Mahmut's estate. Delicately cradling it like a newborn child, he let the book fall open and began reading a chapter. As his eyes absorbed the familiar words, he was certain that his knowledge of Islam was surely greater than that of any of the shallow boys he would meet.

The *Orta*

Hungary's crown passed to Sigismund's son-in-law, Albert of Austria, who immediately was at odds with the Hungarian nobility. Europe's primary bulwark against Ottoman expansion was now in turmoil. Hungary's troubled rulers in its capital of Buda wondered where the inevitable Turkish strike would occur.

Behind the Hungarians was a sea of self-interested, grasping competitors who were more focused on making their own claims than joining forces against the Ottomans. Even in Rome, the Pontiff's primary concern was returning Constantinople's Patriarch to the Western fold rather than defending Constantinople's dwindling population. Desperate for the Pope's support, the Byzantine Emperor John VIII Palaeologus and a large delegation of Orthodox clergy were holed up in Florence's cathedral making ecclesiastical concessions that were sure to demoralize further their beaten subjects.

Sultan Murad II was driven to exploit this unique opportunity. A steady stream of Anatolian regulars was brought across the straits. Edirne was aglow night and day with activity as the offensive came closer to being launched.

Although its legend and effectiveness in battle made foreign armies exaggerate its numbers, the Janissary corps numbered little more than several thousand men. New men were desperately needed. Mustafa demanded that the cadets be hurried through their training.

In the dead of winter, İbrahim and his comrades were subjected to a relentless hail of instructions and drills. Each morning, the cadets were marched outside of the city's walls to a parade ground. They were taught how to use halberds, scimitars, bows, crossbows, mortars, and, always open to innovation, the rarely reliable flintlocks. Handling these weapons with equal familiarity, they marched endlessly to a foreboding cacophony of music produced by the mixture of enormous kettledrums, cymbals, trumpets and treble pipes.

"Janissaries take ground," the captain growled at them when they were finally given a brief rest from their drills. "You are not Swiss pikemen protecting the beds of their virgin daughters. You will take the offensive and march without flinching into the teeth of every blow our enemies can render until they surrender or are slaughtered to the last. If you run, you'll be traitors to the Sultan. Your name will be stricken from the corps. You will be executed, cast aside to rot with the vermin. More importantly, you'll be traitors to your comrades who are relying on you to be part of the same impenetrable phalanx. Pillars of the empire you may be, but only if you have unswerving loyalty to the corps first."

The cadets were afforded little time to recover from their daily ordeal. Their Janissary brethren had already vacated the city, leaving many tasks to be done. When night fell, groups of cadets were sent out to man the walls. Upon being relieved, they were often too exhausted to return to the barracks. Instead, they chose to sleep in the watchtowers. Others were set to work policing the streets, guarding the royal buildings, and performing maintenance on the walls.

By autumn, the first news from the front filtered back to the capital. Reports of large Ottoman raiding parties crossing the Danube and pillaging the Transylvanian countryside electrified the city. With their fields ablaze behind them, tens of thousands of Transylvanians were marched off to the slave markets. The Sultan then turned southward into Serbia, capturing every castle and monastery in his path.

As spring passed into summer, the first companies of soldiers were cycled back to Edirne for rest. The city was abuzz with excitement as the soldiers regaled the eager populace with inflated stories of their bravery. "Serbia will soon be ours," they boasted, "and then it will be on to Buda."

The exhausted cadets desperately wished to be freed from the daily rigors of their training. To their delight, word passed that they were about to be assigned to their *ortas*.

The *orta* was built on more than the fierce spirit of its men. A finely defined command structure was its backbone. Each *orta* was commanded by a colonel, who was assisted by six staff officers, a clerk, an imam, and a battery of sergeants. One of the colonel's lieutenants commanded the barracks hall and was supported by fellow officers and the cook.

With his razor-sharp knives, the cook played a dual role in the corps. Unlike other armies, whose daily rations were principally made up of stale, crusty biscuits, the Janissaries enjoyed freshly baked bread along with their ration of mutton, rice and butter. More than a baker and butcher, the cook was also responsible for discipline. His unmatched skill with a knife made him the company's executioner.

Along with several other recently graduated cadets, İbrahim walked, mouth agape, into the barracks hall. Able to accommodate over one hundred men, the majestic hall contained brilliant turquoise tiles which were illuminated in the glow of the lamps that hung from the gilded ceilings. The marble-floored hall opened onto a spacious courtyard where a steady stream of crystal clear water poured from the mouth of an equine fountain. Storerooms, privies, and small chambers for the officers rounded out the surroundings, which were duly dominated by a giant flag emblazoned with a camel, the emblem of the First Orta.

The other graduates quickly assimilated into their surroundings by striking up conversations with battle-scarred veterans. Much to İbrahim's surprise, the veterans pulled the newcomers into their own close-knit circles. Soon the hall was echoing with riotous laughter as veterans and newcomers traded stories about their training.

"I thought my overseer was rotten too," a former cadet named Ali sneered as he stood well at ease next to a young veteran, "but Ibrahim here thinks that his overseer was a great man."

Although shorter than most of his peers, the veteran's barrel chest and thickly muscled arms and legs matched his wide brow and bulging chin to convey a sense of unshakable confidence and spirit.

Enjoying Ali's humor, the veteran broke into hard laughter. "I've never heard of such a thing. The man must have coddled him. We'll have to keep an eye on this one," he shouted over his shoulder.

"But don't get too close," Ali chimed in. "He might accidentally cut you with his scimitar if he decides to imitate his old overseer."

"A war hero, was he?" the veteran laughed contemptuously.

The rest of the world seemed to cease as Ibrahim concentrated a malevolent glare on his tormentors, his rage bubbling outward uncontrollably. Ibrahim lunged forward and slammed their heads together. Both men stumbled away in opposite directions. Ibrahim leaped on Ali, knocking him unconscious with a quick succession of blows to the head. He then turned on the veteran, who was rapidly blinking his eyes, struggling to regain his senses.

The rage continued to build until Ibrahim's heart pulsed madly and his eyes throbbed. He threw himself headlong into the veteran, lifting him off his wobbly feet. Ibrahim landed with his shoulder buried in the man's sternum. A reptilian hiss burst from the veteran's lungs. Desperately trying to regain his breath, the man hardly raised his hands to defend himself against the torrent of blows raining down on him.

Several veterans rushed over to rescue their comrade. Ibrahim was sobbing uncontrollably as he was hauled off the battered man.

"You must be mad," the veteran shouted. Two gaping cuts were oozing over his swollen right eye. "You're about to learn your place, boy." He raised his fist in the air and brought it down towards Ibrahim's face.

His arms held tightly behind his back by the other veterans, İbrahim could only close his eyes and brace himself.

The blow never landed. Instead, he heard the veteran yell, "Let go of my arm, Ahmet. This is not your concern."

"But it is, Şemsi. Everything that happens in this *orta* is my concern. I'm particularly interested when a young lion isn't afraid to bear his fangs. Sometimes even the youngest members of the pride know when their senior is a liability."

İbrahim opened his eyes to find a wiry, fair-skinned man with crystal blue eyes restraining Şemsi. Although he strained to hold off Şemsi, a broad, rakish smile was pasted across the fine features of Ahmet's long, narrow, handsome face.

"Someone peel this fool off my arm," Şemsi howled. His wounds began to bleed more heavily as his face blazed with fury. "I'm in no mood to suffer your foolishness today."

"A man who aspires to such great heights shouldn't moan like a small child," Ahmet slyly chided him. Inciting him further, Ahmet pinched his fingers deeper into Şemsi's arm.

"Let him go, Ahmet," an enormous man with a pendulous belly hanging over his waist ordered. Rivulets of sweat raced down his swollen, florid cheeks before disappearing into the dense brush of his snowy beard. Crusty, old, brown bloodstains covered his frayed, white apron.

Şemsi smiled triumphantly and indignantly pulled his arm free. "Thank you, Rüstem. This young man could use your special disciplinary skills." Şemsi strolled towards İbrahim and patted his cheek paternalistically. He then violently jerked his knee into İbrahim's groin.

Almost instantly, a wave of pain surged through him, which continued to grow until İbrahim thought he would lose consciousness. He was allowed to slump to the hard, cold floor, where he balled himself up into a protective shell.

Amid the roar of laughter, Ahmet knelt over İbrahim and said, "Take a deep breath. You needn't worry too much about my friend Şemsi. You still have more manhood than he. I dare say that you're the first man he's dropped in a year."

A previously silent group of men joined in the joke while others stared at Ahmet in stony silence. The newcomers noticed the tension and averted their eyes from the developing conflict.

"I warned you not to try my patience," Şemsi screeched madly, his voice hitting a piercing pitch. He drew his leg back to kick Ahmet. But before he could bring his leg forward, Ahmet reached up with lightning quickness and grabbed Şemsi's groin. With his eyes popping wide, Şemsi fell on the back of his head, legs sprawled akimbo, unconscious.

"I was right," Ahmet said, looking at the hand that had gripped Şemsi's groin with mock surprise. "This boy does have more manhood."

Gazing at the spectacle of Şemsi on the floor, everyone laughed this time.

"Enough," Rüstem growled menacingly, "or you'll all join Ahmet and his foolish young friend in my kitchen." Calm was instantly restored.

"Scullion duty?" Ahmet said resignedly.

"Scullion duty," Rüstem answered, flashing a crooked smile sparsely riddled with jagged, orange teeth.

"I didn't hear you mention my sleeping friend," Ahmet said, turning serious.

"Şemsi didn't start the trouble," Rüstem said flatly.

Ahmet considered Rüstem's words for a moment and then said, "What's your name, boy? We have some hard work ahead of us."

"You've made yourself quite a formidable enemy," Ahmet chuckled, "and within only minutes of entering the *orta*."

They were sitting next to each other on a long table in Rüstem's kitchen, trying to catch their breath. For the last several hours, they had been disposing of a shipment of rotten lamb. With the greasy remnants of the lamb caught under their fingernails and smeared across their arms and faces, the debilitating stench clung to them.

"When we're relieved of these duties," Ahmet continued, "the men will take a deep breath and perhaps even tremble for a moment before tattooing the *orta*'s insignia on your shoulder and leg. A wild one is what they're thinking. Of course, they'll expect you to display that same rage in battle."

İbrahim had noticed a small tattoo of a camel near Ahmet's ankle. "Was it such a grave mistake? You certainly belittled Şemsi as if he were nothing but a fool."

"Şemsi?" Ahmet said. "Hardly. He's actually quite lethal with the scimitar, not to mention one of the *orta*'s finest marksmen with a crossbow. He's my leading rival for becoming the *orta*'s next sergeant."

"Şemsi doesn't seem to share the same lighthearted view of your rivalry," İbrahim observed, warming to the conversation. "It's obvious to even a newcomer like me that you're more than his match when it comes to making him look foolish."

"A weakness I enjoy exploiting," Ahmet admitted. "Perhaps you're a thinker as well as a warrior. I'll make a deal with you. Why don't you scrub the grease off of the floor while I sit here. If Rüstem approves of your work, I may be able to find a place for you in my circle of friends."

"That's quite all right."

"You don't think you need my help?"

"Not unless I'm looking to find a quick way back to scullion duty after I leave here."

"A wit! Perhaps you can help me advance into that sergeant's position. Too many of my friends are content to simply follow my lead. One needs true helpers who state their mind when the hard times come."

"How long has this sergeant's position been open?" İbrahim had not realized how much he missed the pleasure of having such a simple conversation. A sense of gratitude towards Ahmet warmed his neglected heart.

"It's not open. But in war, positions have a way of opening up rather quickly. One must be ready to seize the opportunity."

"It sounds like you're fighting a war inside and outside of the *orta*. I was led to believe during training that all who served in my *orta* would be true brothers. You make it sound like I'll have to watch my back on the battlefield."

"You should fear no such thing. What your captain told you is so. We all believe in the *orta*. Not one of us would hesitate to lay down his life for another in battle."

"You would do so for Şemsi?"

"Of course. I want the First Orta to be known as the most gallant company in the corps. God willing, our company will be the first men to snatch Justinian's globe from his hand. That means the *orta* must succeed. You see, my competition with Şemsi can only help my Sultan and me."

İbrahim stared deep into Ahmet's unflinching eyes. Though they seemed outwardly warm, İbrahim detected a harsh edge shimmering off the deepest point of Ahmet's pupils. He wondered why a man with such confidence would show so much interest in a raw recruit. İbrahim guessed that Ahmet's overture was a ruse aimed at manipulating him. Still, İbrahim was willing to take that risk. The chance to share his thoughts had excited him. Besides, he reasoned, I will surely be able to unearth any manipulation Ahmet may try before I come to harm.

Ahmet returned from his reverie and smiled appreciatively at İbrahim. "It was my intention to learn more about you, but here we are speaking about me. Tell me why you attacked Şemsi and his young friend."

İbrahim sat back, digesting the question. After a long pause, he said, "I don't know."

"Come now. How can you not know?"

"I know why I was angry," İbrahim answered defensively, "but I've never lost control of myself like that before."

"Well, I suppose that's a relief. Don't ease the minds of your new friends, though. You might avoid the hazing your fellow newcomers are experiencing while you're stuck on scullion duty if the veterans think you might snap at any time."

İbrahim shook his head in amusement. "That's not the type of reputation I want."

"As you like. Now tell me your story."

"He'll tell you another time," Rüstem barked, returning from the bakery. "I want this floor sparkling brighter than the sun at noon, you worthless Ragusan pirate," he ordered almost fondly.

"I was never a pirate," Ahmet laughed.

"All Ragusans are pirates," Rüstem snickered. "How could you not be? After all, you were spawned by the Venetians."

Ahmet turned to İbrahim, a broad smile pasted on his perpetually animated face. "Rüstem has a bad habit of mixing the facts. I was kidnapped by Turkish pirates while sailing on my uncle's merchant galley. Daring group of brigands they were, too. We were only thirty miles away from home when they attacked. Along with the cargo, I was the only sailor spared by the pirates. That was my beginning."

"I didn't mix a thing," Rüstem protested. "I've never met a Ragusan merchant who is anything but a pirate. Ask any Venetian or Genoese."

"You're confusing piracy with driving a hard bargain. Speaking of bargains, though, what will it take to convince you to send me and my young friend back to the barracks?"

Rüstem's eyes twinkled mischievously under his bushy eyebrows. "Ahmet, you can return right now, but your friend will have to stay twice the time in order to do your work."

Ahmet shook his head in mock exasperation. "You're a rotten soul, Rüstem. At least do me the favor of treating Şemsi with the same consideration when he runs afoul of you."

"It's about time Rüstem released you, my friend," İshak shouted. "It's been five days since you abused Şemsi."

"Six days," Ahmet corrected him. He leaned towards İbrahim and whispered, "You would not have made that mistake."

Three other young veterans rapidly made their way across the crowded barracks to greet Ahmet.

Ahmet surveyed his four closest supporters and said, "İshak, Cem, Sinan, Hüsrev, meet your new friend, İbrahim."

The four men shrank back, mouths aghast. "You don't mean to say that we are going to allow that madman into our ranks, do you?" Hüsrev nearly pleaded.

"Don't you trust my judgment anymore, Hüsrev?" Ahmet asked, undisturbed by the challenge.

"Well, we were beginning to wonder why you had yourself placed on scullion duty for a brand-new recruit," Sinan probed.

"Sometimes limits need to be tested," Ahmet answered cryptically.

Ignoring Ahmet's attempt to be subtle, İshak excitedly blurted out, "We've gotten word that we'll be marching back into Serbia in little more than a week. Isn't that grand? More chances for spoils."

"And glory," Hüsrev added.

"Of course, but give me the spoils first," İshak beamed. "I just want to know how we're going to prepare ourselves for this grand event."

"Well, if you haven't spent your last coins yet," Ahmet said slyly, "perhaps we might chance upon a tavern where we can spend some time and enjoy some very personal entertainment."

"I was praying you would suggest that very thing," Cem howled with delight, finally joining the conversation. The other men enthusiastically nodded their heads in approval.

In his travels with Mahmut, İbrahim had spent many nights in taverns. Although he had always enjoyed these visits, İbrahim could not fathom why Ahmet's friends were so excited.

"Come, İbrahim," Ahmet amiably ordered. "A new experience awaits you—one of the true pleasures that a Janissary has to look forward to in this world."

Dusk was descending as the men made their way through the city's labyrinth of streets. Dressed in their rich robes and sturdy boots, they cut an impressive swath through the meek mass of residents scurrying home. In contrast to the uneasy, stealthy glances İbrahim had experienced as a cadet, he was met with a wide array of respectful gestures and muted greetings. His companions appeared unmoved by the humble solicitations, but İbrahim's self-esteem soared as he absorbed the dignity bound in his position.

As Ahmet led them deeper into the city, the streets narrowed until passersby had to turn their shoulders to squeeze by one another. The perpetual buzz of the crowded streets was lost in these suffocating alleys, replaced by the eerie echoes of their purposeful footsteps and the occasional whispered greeting. Without warning, Ahmet stopped abruptly in front of an old, unmarked wooden door that had not been painted in years. The rest of the building was equally nondescript, merging seamlessly into the adjacent buildings.

"My friends," Ahmet said warmly. "Remember, tonight belongs to you, but tomorrow belongs to the corps. Just try not to embarrass me."

Ahmet threw the door open and nearly tripped headlong into the tavern. Three jagged steps, soaked with wine, led down to the bowed wooden floor below.

İbrahim was immediately at Ahmet's side, afraid to break the connection. "What was that you were saying about us embarrassing you?" he laughed gently.

"You've grown quite bold in the short time we've known each other," Ahmet snorted, unable to muster an effective retort. Trying harder, he warned, "I don't need friends who laugh at me in public. My rivals will fill that role quite nicely."

"I'm sorry, Ahmet."

İbrahim was surprised by how easy it was to apologize to Ahmet. Even Mahmut had not earned anything more than a few grudging concessions of wrongdoing. With each passing day on scullion duty, İbrahim had volunteered more information about himself. Ahmet had never cut him short. Instead, Ahmet listened with the same intensity with which İbrahim memorized chapters from the Koran. Most of the time they spoke as equals, but Ahmet always managed to subtly convey that he was in control. He did not let even the most mundane conversation conclude without having said the last word.

Recovering quickly from his misstep, Ahmet smoothly maneuvered through the crowded, dimly lit tavern, which appeared to stretch nebulously into the distant shadows. As İbrahim eagerly took in his surroundings, he noticed that the tavern was a cavernous collection of several buildings joined together by roughly created holes in the walls. The bare walls and creaky floors, littered with food and wine, were merely a pale depository for the life infused into them by the spirited patrons. The tavern was a home of the Janissaries.

Often interrupting their conversations mid-sentence, senior Janissaries warmly greeted Ahmet and regaled him with their heroic adventures. Trailing quietly behind their leader, Ahmet's companions patiently waited for the respectful acknowledgment that was ultimately reserved for them as well. Like a true master, Ahmet never failed to introduce İbrahim, who was instantly accorded the same greeting.

Flagons of wine were being eagerly consumed by the Janissaries, who were either locked in animated conversations or making their way from one source of entertainment to the next. At the far end of the tavern, a puppet show depicting the conquest of a Serbian village was being performed to raucous acclaim. A beautiful young woman was dancing on the opposite side of the tavern, flirtatiously waving her veils at the huddled mass of men hovering over the stage.

"What do you think?" Ahmet asked, noticing İbrahim's fascination with the dancer.

"She's beautiful," he blushed.

"Beautiful, yes, but not all that she seems," Ahmet said coyly.

İbrahim stepped closer to the stage and squinted hard. After a few seconds, he turned back to Ahmet, who was wearing a broad smile. "I don't know what you mean," İbrahim confessed, unable to decipher the riddle.

"Of course not. You would have to get a lot closer to him than you are now."

"Him?"

"A very talented young man, from what I can see," Ahmet confirmed dispassionately. "He has quite a following. Since it appears that he has caught your attention, you may wish to ask yourself whether it's women or merely their image that interests you. You can find both here." Ahmet gestured for İbrahim to join him at a table where his friends were busily drinking.

"Drink," Ahmet said, raising a glass of wine. "It's time to make our first toast."

"Here, here," Cem said, his face already aglow.

"Is this permitted?" İbrahim asked.

"Wine," Ahmet laughed. "It's the water of life. No good Janissary could live without it. Exercises the senses." He pushed a glass of wine into İbrahim's hand and declared, "May you ever be victorious in your march to the Red Apple."

"To the Red Apple!" the men cheered, clanking their glasses together and then rapidly emptying them. İbrahim followed suit. His face turned a bright shade of red as the wine burned the back of his throat and soaked his belly.

The men laughed wildly.

"Look at him. I told you this wine has been in the barrel no more than a day," Sinan crowed at İshak.

"It could burn the hair off a wild boar's ass," Hüsrev agreed.

To show that he was up to the challenge, İbrahim poured himself another glass and drank it whole. As the raw taste of the wine washed over his palate, he could feel his face growing warm. The tension in his body eased and he smiled genuinely at his new companions, who nodded their heads approvingly.

"What a handsome young man," a woman's voice said from behind.

Startled by the closeness of the voice, İbrahim spun his head around to find a middle-aged woman pushing her way past the back of his chair and onto Ahmet's lap. She had wild, tangled black hair, laced with silver, curling down to the small of her back. Her dark eyebrows framed coal black eyes that were steadily taking in İbrahim's body. Although her skin was slowly surrendering to the vagaries of age and a hard life, her face retained the beautiful essence of her youth.

Wrapping her arms possessively around Ahmet's shoulders, she said, "Hasn't seen a day of battle yet, has he?"

"In neither of our arenas, I imagine," Ahmet laughed lewdly.

A bright gleam filled her face. "My name is Irene. I work here." She leaned forward and smiled.

İbrahim's eyes were irresistibly drawn to her breasts, which heaved outwards until they nearly escaped from the top of her low-cut chemise.

"I was hoping we might find him someone closer to his age."

"Age has nothing to do with what this boy needs," Irene chastised Ahmet as she transferred onto İbrahim's lap. Her hair brushed gently against İbrahim's face, further intoxicating him. "I know things about making a man happy that this boy will never forget."

"No one doubts your skill, Irene. I'm just afraid you might hurt him."

Ahmet's friends obediently burst into laughter.

"Your friend doesn't seem to have any objections," Irene smiled. She writhed slowly on İbrahim's accepting lap and pressed her breasts firmly against his side. As the blood rushed downward, İbrahim found himself instinctively matching her rhythmic gyrations with awkward thrusts of his own. "In fact, he's growing to like me from where I sit," she cackled.

"She'll be the only woman you truly remember, İbrahim," Ahmet warned, observing his friend's growing interest. "Of course, you could do worse than an experienced Greek whore."

İbrahim closed his eyes and tightly wrapped his arms around Irene's waist. Sighing contentedly, she slid her worn hands on top of his own and guided them between her thighs.

Sinan smiled and said, "Our friend is lost."

"Congratulations, Irene," Cem cracked, "I'm sure you never thought you'd bed down such a young man again."

"Go on and make your jokes," Irene said, unfazed. She turned her head and filled İbrahim's mouth with a long kiss.

"It pains me to mention such a small detail, Irene," Ahmet said, "but perhaps you might like to tell me how you'll be paid for your delicious services."

Irene spun towards Ahmet, eyes wide with panic. "Don't tell me they haven't paid the poor boy yet."

"Not a single asper," Ahmet smiled.

"Ahmet," she pleaded, the glow from her face vanishing.

Ahmet waited a moment and looked at İbrahim, who was trying to mask his disappointment. Finally, he snorted, "Who am I to stand in the way of love?" He reached into his robe and tossed a small bag of coins at İbrahim. "To a true Janissary, the contents of that bag are far more valuable than anything Irene can offer. Remember that when she confesses her love for you while reaching into your pocket."

The Race to Jajce

The air hung heavily over İbrahim's head as the late summer heat drew moisture from the nearby Danube. Along with the rest of the massive Ottoman force securing the siege camp, he was overcome with torpor while waiting for the Serbs to end their bitter resistance.

Led by the Sultan himself, the Ottoman army had been encamped around the walls of Smederevo for almost three months. Brankovic's eldest son heroically led the exhausted garrison, which stood stalwartly behind the city's vast fortifications. Knowing that Serbia would lie open to him once Smederevo was taken, the Sultan ordered that nothing so large as a rat should find its way free from the teetering city.

The camp exemplified the superiority of Ottoman organization and arms. The Sultan's silk tent, embroidered with vegetation in hues of red and green, stood at the center of his geometrically ordered army. The tent resembled a walled castle with an imposing two-tiered gate. A towering pole with nine horsetails hanging below a golden ball, which contained a horned moon for a crest and a small Koran in a silver case, was planted in front of the tent to signify his exalted rank. War councils met in an even larger tent located close by.

The rest of the camp symmetrically converged around the Sultan. A series of roads radiated outward, dividing the camp into districts, at the center of each which was the company commander's tent. Around him were the precisely aligned tents of his men.

Unlike the filthy camps of their adversaries, the Ottomans took special care to construct latrine pits and ablution tents to preserve sanitary conditions. Leaving nothing for granted, each district had its own food shops and assorted craftsmen.

The Janissaries were encamped close to the Sultan in their conical cloth tents. Except for manning the mortars and firing the cannons at the fortifications, they had passed the time slowly, all the while craving open conflict.

İbrahim watched his comrades sink into depression and wondered what special joy they could possibly derive from butchering their enemies. Still, he was not prepared to reject their passion. If he were to survive, he knew that their zeal would prove invaluable.

"I hear that the city has been without water for a week," Ahmet announced. "If that's so, we'll be on our way to new conquests in the south any day."

Noticing that none of his friends cared to probe further, İbrahim asked, "How did you come by that information?"

With obvious delight, Ahmet answered, "The colonel told me. It seems that a poor rug merchant was captured last night trying to escape from the city."

"So you've become good friends with the colonel," İshak said, becoming interested. "It won't do us any good unless there's fighting. You could lick the colonel's boots, but if no sergeants die, you're going to be stuck where you are."

"I agree," Ahmet said, wiping a thick layer of sticky perspiration from his brow. "I swear that breathing this wet air can only lead to illness of the mind and body. That's why I volunteered all of us to head south immediately before Smederevo throws open its gates."

"Immediately?" they all gasped, except for İbrahim.

"That's right," Ahmet said, feigning surprise at the strength of their response.

İshak protested, "We've sat still for nearly three months waiting to enjoy this prize. Even worse, we haven't been paid in weeks. My purse has run dry. Let us take our reward and then move on. Surely we've earned the right."

"Of course we've all earned that right. It takes a special kind of patience for men like us to wait out the poor fools trapped behind those walls. But let's examine how our rights can be best served. Dare we miss out on the chance to be the first to take Novo Brdo?"

"That town sits on top of silver mines, does it not?" Sinan asked, suddenly interested.

"Indeed it does, my friend," Ahmet smiled wolfishly. "It would be a horrible misfortune if we missed out on the opportunity to pocket real wealth simply because we're feeling the pinch in our wallets right now. What do you think, İbrahim?"

"Don't waste your time asking him any questions," Cem said. "He can't hear you. Our poor friend has been firing cannon shot at the walls for the last several hours. Besides, İbrahim is still dreaming about that old whore every waking moment. We'd all have a few more aspers right now if we hadn't loaned so much money to our desperate friend."

"Another fine reason to abandon this place. It seems that we need to find our young friend a new, worthier passion," Ahmet said. "What can he possibly learn about our world if he merely spends his days firing mortars and cannons at the walls of a doomed city? It's time for him to whet the greatest appetite."

"I don't suppose there's any point in trying to dissuade you?" İshak asked rhetorically.

"It's on to glory," Ahmet beamed.

Along with a sizeable contingent of lightly armed Janissaries, Ahmet's band left the siege of Smederevo in its eleventh hour and headed south to Serbia's Novo Brdo region. The unprepared populace fled in disarray as the Janissaries covered territory with their legendary speed. But as night fell on the seventh day of their journey, a Serbian army, high atop a hill, stood its ground before them.

"Several thousand men on higher ground," Ahmet told his friends, obviously not concerned. "Looks like the usual mixture of poorly trained soldiers and scared farmers."

"But we are only half of their number," İbrahim said, mouth turning dry. "Aren't we going to wait for reinforcements?"

Ahmet gazed past İbrahim's head to where the red and yellow flag of the Janissary corps was rippling in the steady breeze sweeping through the rugged hills. Emblazoned in its middle, the cleft sword of Ali fluttered ominously towards the Serbian host. "We are more than a match for this army. Remember your training and you will be fine," Ahmet confidently assured him.

Early the next morning, İbrahim was awakened by the sounds of drums pounding. For a moment, he thought he was back on the parade grounds. He rubbed the sleep from his eyes and reached for his prayer rug.

A powerful hand gripped his shoulder and yanked him upwards. "We can pray later," Ahmet said. "The fools are giving up the high ground and moving on our camp."

İbrahim hurried towards his comrades, who were already facing the enemy in well-formed, unflinching order behind a series of makeshift earthworks. As he steeled himself for his first taste of battle, he squeezed his scimitar until the blood ran dry in his frozen knuckles.

"Take this," a familiar voice ordered. İbrahim spun around. Şemsi pushed a crossbow and quiver of arrows at him. To İbrahim's surprise, no hint of enmity showed on Şemsi's brutish face. "Make your shots count. We need to even the odds a bit before leaving our redoubts."

The roar behind him continued to grow as the drummers furiously pounded their great drums. Intermittently, the sounds of trumpets blaring and cymbals crashing together penetrated the din. As the pain in his ears grew, İbrahim was certain that his head would explode.

Face glowing with delight, Ahmet hollered into İbrahim's ear, "It's grand, isn't it?"

The furor of the band drowned out the hellish war cries from the Serbs, who were now madly charging down the hill. When their chaotic advance came within one hundred yards, the Janissaries coolly unleashed a deadly hail of arrows. Taking careful aim, İbrahim methodically fired his bow, dropping every man who chanced into his line of fire. Although the enemy was closer, it struck him that he was engaged in no less sterile an exercise than when he had fired cannon shots into Smederevo's walls.

The Serbs were now stumbling towards the waiting Janissaries, who laid down their crossbows and drew their scimitars. Raising their voices above the drums, the Janissaries unleashed a hellish war cry of their own that sent a shudder down İbrahim's spine. As their voices joined as one, İbrahim felt electrified. Without even realizing that he had opened his mouth, he found his throat aching and growing hoarse as he lent his voice to the noise of war.

Now they were moving, rushing towards the Serbs, who appeared dazed. The collision seemed to happen all at once. Certain that victory belonged to them, the Janissaries hacked at the Serbs with merciless vigor. As the Serbs stumbled backwards over their fallen comrades, the enveloping pressure was too great for them to take flight. Instead, they held up their swords and pikes, hoping to somehow weather the assault.

Infused with the bravery of his comrades, İbrahim sprinted forward and struck his first blow at a teenage boy, whose face quivered with fear. İbrahim's scimitar easily slashed past the parrying blow. Not realizing that he had severed the boy's neck, he raised his scimitar to strike again and then stumbled forward as he swung into empty air. İbrahim looked down to see the boy's terrified brown eyes staring up at him as the life poured from his body.

Before he could contemplate his first kill, İbrahim's momentum brought him up against a burly Serb who was madly swinging his pike in a wide circle. İbrahim paused for a moment to study his foe. Again, he was drawn to his enemy's eyes, which were partially obscured by his rapidly fluttering eyelids. Like the boy, the man was more concerned about warding off harm than striking a blow. With a confidence that surprised him, İbrahim timed the Serb's swing and buried his scimitar in the man's chest.

Awash with success and seduced by the frenzy around him, İbrahim felt the bravery he had borrowed from his comrades replaced now by his own martial spirit. Sparks of madness flitted through his mind as a guttural roar anticipated each blow that sprang so lethally from his scimitar. Like a threshing machine, he plowed blindly onwards, his mind racing with excitement. Only his training, embedded deep within him, allowed the hostility he unleashed to be channeled. When the order to withdraw was given, İbrahim reluctantly lowered his scimitar, his passion unsated.

"You look like you've bathed with the devil himself," Ahmet called over to him as the scattered remnants of the Serbs limped back to the safety of the forest. "I hope none of that blood is your own."

İbrahim patted himself down to make sure that he was unharmed and then broke into a cold sweat. Unable to answer his friend, İbrahim sank to the ground and thanked God for his mercy.

Ahmet made his way through the fallen and sat down next to İbrahim. "A nice little victory. You should be proud. I saw you hacking your way deep into the Serbian lines. A few times I thought they would swallow you up, but sorry was the man who crossed your path. You'd do well, though, to remember to stay with us. You can't always expect to be so fortunate."

I find ways to isolate myself even in battle, İbrahim laughed to himself. He was fascinated by the heartless animal that had emerged so easily from within him but now seemed so well under control. No wonder my fellow Janissaries strut through the streets with such pride, he decided.

"Now is the time that we pray to Allah," Ahmet said, rubbing a handful of dirt across his bloody brow. "And then, we will attend to the needs of our brethren."

Sitting around their stewpots, richly filled with lamb, the Janissaries recounted their heroics later that evening. Estimates about the size of the Serbian host continued to multiply until many were sure that they had defeated a force ten times their number. They feasted on the broad tales. Only a few casualties marred their celebration, but their fallen comrades were celebrated with raucous toasts rather than mourned.

The wide circle included more than just Ahmet's close comrades. Everyone in the *orta* who valued Ahmet's esteem was present. İbrahim searched for an opening. He wanted his fellow Janissaries to know that his bravery had exceeded the most fanciful
tale. As he thought of ways to proclaim his valor, İbrahim found
himself demeaning the accomplishments of others. He ultimately
decided it was better to keep quiet.

Noticing his friend's reticence, Ahmet said, "None of your stories can compare to the bravery of my good friend." He pointed
to İbrahim, whose face became flushed. "I've never seen a new
man take so well to battle. It's as if he were born with a scimitar
in his hand."

"And what would you know of judging a man in battle?" Şemsi
interjected, pushing his way into the circle. "Or perhaps you know
a great deal," he pretended to correct himself. "I imagine one has
plenty of time to watch others during a battle when safely tucked
away behind the lines."

"You're better off not using your imagination, Şemsi," Ahmet
replied smoothly, disguising his surprise at Şemsi's unexpected
arrival, "unless, of course, you've been dreaming of reporting to
me."

The men around the pot made sure to let Şemsi know how
much they enjoyed the joke.

Knowing that he was in hostile territory, Şemsi did not get
angry. Instead, he affected his most dignified expression and said,
"It is you, Ahmet, who will have to do the dreaming. It would
seem that a sergeant's position became available this morning and
it has been promised to me."

For an almost imperceptible moment, Ahmet's face fell. Then
he said, "That's wonderful news, Şemsi. If indeed you are destined to be a sergeant, then I'm sure your men will gladly stand
behind you while you lead them into the enemy."

"I thought you would be pleased. Perhaps I'll find some time
one of these days to teach you how to advance in the corps." With
his face aglow with satisfaction, Şemsi took his leave.

"Do you think it's true?" İbrahim whispered to Ahmet.

"Of course it's true," Ahmet replied. "Şemsi doesn't make an announcement unless he's checked and rechecked his information several times over." Ahmet stood up and smiled at his companions, who did not know how to respond. "Brothers," Ahmet declared grandly, "enjoy the feast."

Ahmet motioned for İbrahim to join him as he walked into the night. "So why do you think Şemsi was promoted ahead of me?"

İbrahim shook his head.

"İbrahim," Ahmet gently scolded, "if I wanted silence, I wouldn't have invited you. Now tell me your thoughts."

İbrahim confronted the riddle. "Surely Şemsi's valor in battle has not outshone your own," he cautiously decided.

"But for exceptional feats of heroism, it is quite difficult to set oneself apart in battle," Ahmet agreed. "Then what would've attracted the colonel's attention?"

İbrahim remembered his friends' lust for gold. It had occurred to him that the acquisition of riches was the unifying focus of every conversation. "Are you suggesting that Şemsi has bought his position?"

"I would never suggest that the colonel's favor was for sale, but a well-timed gift can be just the trick to catch your commander's attention. I didn't see Şemsi's prized emerald ring on his finger when he came by our fire tonight.

"It might interest you to know that Şemsi did quite well for himself during our raid into Transylvania. That ring was just one of the many trinkets he recovered. It seems that he stumbled onto a local noble's cache of family heirlooms while raiding a castle. Since Şemsi isn't one to share the wealth with his friends, I imagine he brought home a tidy little fortune, certainly more than enough to interest even the well-fed tastes of our colonel."

"You don't sound like you disapprove of Şemsi's methods."

"My lone regret is that I wasn't the first man into that noble's home."

"And that is why we're marching on Novo Brdo," İbrahim exclaimed.

"Now you've got it!" Ahmet cheered. "Yes, I'm in too much of

a hurry to hope that riches will find me. That's why we're marching to a place where gold and silver pour from the ground faster
than rain falls from the sky."

Screwing his courage together, İbrahim asked, "Doesn't it
bother you that Şemsi was promoted before you?"

"Şemsi is only a competitor. He's not the measure of my success. I can't waste my time worrying about Şemsi's career."

"Are you sure that's wise?"

Ahmet saw the fierce insecurity in İbrahim's eyes, but İbra-
him's skepticism struck a nerve. "I leave it to you to keep an eye
on Şemsi. You will let me know if he deserves my attention." Ahmet then spun around and headed back to his friends around the
stewpot.

Alone in the dark, İbrahim watched his friend gracefully slide
back into the circle. İbrahim welcomed the comforting cloak of
darkness that wrapped around him. Except when he was with Ahmet, İbrahim felt uncomfortable, always suspecting that he was being judged. Even his best efforts to repress this emotion could not
change the suffocation he felt from the unrelenting closeness of the
orta. The brief respite drove him inward, back to the battle.

It all seemed like a dream. Only his exhaustion convinced him
that he was truly the weapon Mahmut and his captain had predicted he would become. İbrahim had believed his was a peaceful
spirit. Now, he wondered whether a hidden terror resided deep
within him which, when released, ruled him.

The memory of his first victim's eyes distressed him. Who was
he? İbrahim wondered. His eyes closed tight. The world around
him disappeared. The young man was a farmer, the fourth of
nine children. He was in love with a girl he had spied from a distance several times on market days. Her silky, smooth golden hair
floated in the wind, bewitching him like a siren's sweet song. She
would be his wife some day and they would have nine children of
their own before dying happily in each other's arms.

So much of the world had been hidden from him that he assumed this simple, pristine vision was the life shared by most people. But as much as this illusion allured him, İbrahim was more

enthralled by the seductive thrill of battle. Denying the dreams of others in battle was strangely satisfying. Guilt ate at him, but he found it easier to cast it aside and relive in his mind the awesome power he had experienced. His appetite well whetted, he lusted for more.

"On your feet," the sergeant barked, waking İbrahim from his deep slumber. "The colonel has ordered a raid."

A collective groan rose up from the camp as the men stood to find that the sun had yet to peak above the horizon. They had counted on a day of rest to recover from the rigors of battle and their nightlong celebration.

"Yunus," Ahmet called out testily to the sergeant, "when is this raid to begin?"

"As soon as you finish your prayers and empty your bladders," Yunus said flatly. "A village lies a short march to the south of our camp. When you're done with the village, you can satisfy whatever appetite you wish. Now let's move."

As the Janissaries quickly made their preparations, İbrahim coyly asked Ahmet, "Is the colonel afraid this village might disappear unless we attack it now?"

"It's not the village he's worried about," Ahmet responded seriously. "I suspect the colonel believes that the village supplied many of the men we fought yesterday. No doubt that's where the survivors are licking their wounds. Why risk fighting a man more than once when you can finish him off for good? Besides, a particularly nasty early-morning punitive raid has a way of paralyzing the remaining countryside with fear."

The sun was just beginning to fight its way through the mist trapped in the craggy hills when the village came into view an hour later. Except for the occasional barks of a few dogs and the clucking of roosters searching for their morning meal, the village remained asleep.

"The colonel wants it bloody," Yunus quietly ordered as he walked down the line of men, who were positioned behind the trees ringing the village. "But make sure you leave a few survivors to tell the tale. We wouldn't want to see your work go unappreciated," he snorted. "Now move. I want to be eating my breakfast within the hour."

First moving forward with catlike stealth, torches in their hands, the Janissaries soon broke into a chorus of war cries as they descended upon their hapless prey. In minutes, towers of smoke were rising from the thatched roofs of the cottages. Anguished screams followed. As the villagers poured out of their homes, they were greeted by scimitars, flames reflecting brightly off their still unspoiled steel.

İbrahim's back stiffened and his legs rooted themselves to the ground as he watched the villagers being butchered. A mother calling after her daughter was cut down several feet away from him. An unanswerable accusation was frozen in her lifeless eyes. A dark puddle of blood slowly ebbed towards him. Nausea crept up his throat and he puzzled over how the blood from the day before could have meant so little to him. A dull ache wrenched his belly as he remembered his mother's eyes during their last moments together. Never before had her pain seemed so real.

"İbrahim," Ahmet called to his friend, blood dripping from his scimitar. "What's wrong?"

İbrahim answered him with a disbelieving expression. "This is madness. How can we be doing this? How can you?"

"War does not require excuses," Ahmet reproached him.

"War is the name you use for what's happening here?"

"Can you think of a better word?"

İbrahim gazed at the dead and dying. "Yesterday, I thought I could follow my *orta* down any path. Now I don't know if I could ever participate in this kind of slaughter."

Always appreciating the voice of the outsider, Ahmet resisted the urge to be judgmental and said, "Do as your conscience tells you to do. You'll be sparing yourself—and me—a great deal of trouble, though, if you don't draw attention to your rebellion." He winked at İbrahim and ran off to join the rest of his comrades.

"I can hardly see my feet," İbrahim shouted to Ahmet. "The column should be stopped before we all fall to our deaths."

They had been marching in a torrential downpour. Thick, oozing flows of mud slid over their boots as they trudged up the narrow trail hugging the mountainside. Above their heads, the murky sky flickered with lightning and rolled with thunder. In the two weeks following his first battle, this was the first time İbrahim had felt vulnerable.

Under the withering assault of the blinding rain, the Janissaries' murderous march into the heart of Serbia was now a distant blur. But only the day before, when the sun lit his path, İbrahim's spirit had danced. Suffering no more than a few minor wounds, he and his comrades had easily swept aside all opposition. In the wake of the retreating Serbian forces, towns were abandoned and the land yielded its bounty. Churches and nobles' homes were looted and set ablaze. Having access to the livestock left behind, they marched on contented stomachs.

İbrahim had felt indestructible as he waded through the sea of death and putrefaction. He viewed his survival as proof of his natural superiority and favor with God. The guilt that had first dogged him had retreated deep into his consciousness. The eyes of his victims were now no more than lifeless stones.

Ahmet pretended not to hear İbrahim's warning. It had been his good fortune to be placed in the vanguard of the advancing Janissaries. Taking over one hundred of his closest followers, Ahmet pushed well ahead of his colonel and Şemsi, determined to be the first Janissary to reach Novo Brdo.

İbrahim tugged on Ahmet's shoulder and said, "You'll spend the rest of your life on scullion duty if you lead the rest of us off the side of this mountain."

"Where's that crazed courage of yours?" Ahmet called back to him. "How can such a scourge on the battlefield be pestered by the weather?"

İbrahim was used to Ahmet's humor, but the challenge to his bravery struck a deep chord. "It's not our safety that concerns me. We may get lost in the storm."

"Over one hundred Janissaries never get lost."

"Perhaps you're right. We will not get lost, but we risk the main body losing track of us. If we're engaged by a large force, we may regret the speed of today's advance."

As always, Ahmet listened carefully to his young adviser. He hesitated for a moment and then turned to stare İbrahim directly in the eye. Neither man flinched. Finally, Ahmet laughed and said, "You win, my friend. We'll stop as soon as we get off of this accursed mountain."

The word was passed back. Bodies straightened and faces glistened with cheer. Within the hour, they had made it to the bottom of the mountain and were preparing to make camp.

Their reprieve was short-lived. A train of three covered wagons, guarded by fifty heavily armed Serbs, was spotted a short distance away in a small, muddy clearing. Ahmet's scouts reported that the wagons were stranded in the mud, weighted down with a heavy cargo.

"I'll wager a month's salary that those wagons are filled with gold and silver," Ahmet said hungrily.

İbrahim looked at Ahmet with fascination. The lure of riches was still one appetite that was alien to him. But to the rest of the corps, filling their lungs with air and pursuing money were equally necessary tasks. As slaves and new men to the empire, each of the Janissaries knew that he could never rise to the elite status of the noblemen. Only the leveling force of money could lift a Janissary's status beyond his accomplishments in battle.

Ahmet quickly rallied his exhausted men and restored them with dreams of riches. Convincing them to abandon the dryness of their tents was easy. In minutes, they had stealthily positioned themselves around the entrenched wagons.

Viewing the torrent of rain as a sufficient guarantee against an attack, the Serbs had laid down their weapons and were putting their shoulders into the sinking wagons. The battle did not last long. The rain masked the Janissaries' attack until it was too late for the Serbs to recover their weapons. Their doomed cries for help barely escaped their mouths.

Ahmet's men dutifully waited for him to climb aboard the nearest wagon. He did not try their patience. Leaping onto the wagon, scimitar drawn as a precaution, Ahmet ducked inside. Five metal trunks, tinged with rust, awaited him. He thrust his scimitar back into his scabbard and threw open one of the trunks. His eyes opened wide and from outside the wagon his men heard him cry, *"Allahu akbar!"* He exited the wagon holding two fistfuls of gold coins.

"It seems that we will have our payday after all," Ahmet proclaimed triumphantly. "Look." He held up a single coin. "It's the face of the Despot Brankovic, no doubt fashioned by a Ragusan mint master. In becoming rich, we'll probably create a mutiny in the Serbian army when they miss their pay."

The men howled their approval and then boarded the wagons to see for themselves. Confident that he would have his share of the spoils in due time, İbrahim watched from a distance as his comrades fumbled madly over each other to get their hands on the treasure.

"Quite a find," Ahmet said, standing at İbrahim's side and watching his men rejoice. The sky was beginning to clear and the raindrops now only flicked lightly at their faces.

"Will the colonel let you keep it?"

With a wolfish glint in his eyes, Ahmet answered, "I imagine that the colonel would let me sleep with his favorite mistress after I honor him with half of our gains."

"And a sergeant's position as well," İbrahim added, appreciating Ahmet's willingness to part with the money to secure his higher goals.

"Let's just say I expect to be first in the colonel's thoughts when the next position becomes available."

"Why wait?" İbrahim counseled. "Cannot the colonel create a position for you? After all, haven't you been leading our party as if you were already a sergeant?"

"The rules aren't good enough for you, are they, İbrahim?"

İbrahim blushed for a moment and then said, "What's the use of following a rule that fails to serve the guiding principle upon which all of our rules stand?"

"And what might that be?" Ahmet said, listening closely.

"The betterment of the state, of course. Shouldn't you remind the colonel that great deeds can only be accomplished by men who are willing to go beyond the call of duty? Such men must be rewarded. How else can they be expected to continue serving the state with such ardor?"

"Keep quoting principle, İbrahim," Ahmet beamed.

"Ahmet," Cem interrupted, a courier at his side. "This man has a message for you."

"I have an urgent message from the colonel," the man said. "You are to halt your advance on Novo Brdo and wait for the main body to arrive."

"That's absurd," Ahmet snapped. "The Serbs are reeling and we're so close."

"Those are the orders," the courier apologized. "The colonel says that the Sultan now intends to absorb the Novo Brdo region at his leisure. In the meantime, he wants the army to move into Bosnia. It seems that the roads there are wide open."

"I've never heard of that land yielding any great treasure," Ahmet sighed. "It appears that someone else will get our fortune, İbrahim."

"But you've already won a great fortune," İbrahim said. "Isn't this enough for now?"

"There are only so many fortunes that are waiting to be won," Ahmet explained. "One does not turn away from a place like Novo Brdo easily satisfied. Still, I suppose it speaks well for my prospects that I may be the one to have benefited most from this campaign so far. I can't imagine anyone else impressing the colonel more than I will."

As a sergeant, Ahmet led his men northwest into the nearly un-defended Bosnian countryside. Moving with the rest of the Janissary *ortas*, they covered twenty miles a day. Soon they reached Sarajevo and then penetrated all the way to the outskirts of Jajce, the Bosnian capital.

Word of their advance spread like wildfire through the hills.

Most of the villages were abandoned well before the Ottomans' arrival. Still, an unfortunate few did not escape the wrath of the conquerors. İbrahim quietly patrolled the perimeter of the villages while his comrades sowed hatred into the hearts of the survivors.

By October, the Sultan's forces were pressuring Hungary from the east and south. Only the formidable fortress of Belgrade protected the Hungarians against Murad's offensive. The prospect of another siege burdened Ahmet and his followers, particularly since they knew that the fight for Belgrade would be a life-or-death struggle for the Hungarians.

Walking about the camp on the outskirts of Jajce, İbrahim looked back over the last several months. He had yet to receive anything more than a scrape. Each new success had heightened his desire for more conflict. Is it really so easy, he wondered.

"So where have you been lurking all day?" he asked Ahmet upon seeing his friend emerge from behind a row of tents.

"Ali and I were speaking," Ahmet winked.

"So you're on a first-name basis with the colonel now?"

"He's promised to make me an officer once the spring campaign season begins." Ahmet leaned close and whispered, "The colonel told me an interesting story about the state of affairs in Hungary. It appears that the political landscape has become even murkier than usual. While making his way to Vienna, King Albert, much to the delight of his own nobles, fell ill with dysentery and died. Already, the question of succession is creating turmoil. It seems that Brankovic's son and the Lithuanian Jagellon dynasty are squaring off for the prize. Let's hope they throw the country into civil war. Who knows, perhaps then we can just walk into Belgrade."

"Since when have you been interested in politics?" İbrahim asked, bemused.

"The colonel made it very clear to me that rising in the corps requires knowing more than just the politics of the *orta*."

Becoming interested, İbrahim asked, "And this information is reliable?"

Ahmet nodded his head. "We captured one of Cardinal Cesarini's couriers on his way back to Rome with a report to the Pope. It didn't take much to make him talk. I'm told that a dying man's words are quite reliable."

"You make it sound like it's more dangerous behind the lines."

"I'm beginning to think that may be so," Ahmet reflected.

"But you're intent upon entering that world?" İbrahim asked, voice dripping with disapproval.

"Don't worry, my friend. I don't intend to enter that world tomorrow. You and I will have plenty of time to find our way."

Dervish Tales

"It is nothing but betrayal," the old priest berated the merchant. "This is not the first emperor who has tried to force the Roman way down our throats in exchange for a few gold coins. I don't care if the Pope restores the imperial treasury so that it matches the days of Justinian or compels the return of all the relics stolen by his Latin brethren. No payment is enough."

The merchant protectively wrapped his arms around his thick waist. "You've found the wrong man to bear your anger. I'm just a poor merchant from Venice trying to survive the winter away from home. It's true that my people hold close to our Church, but we've also had more than our share of disputes with the Papacy over the years."

"Ha!" the priest snapped. "You think that I'm some kind of fool? You can't hide behind the disputes of yesteryear when this Pope is one of your Venetian brothers."

A nervous twitch began to distort the merchant's left eye. "Please leave me in peace before the authorities throw us both out of the market."

"Are your precious silks and furs all that matter to you?" the priest thundered as he picked at the merchandise neatly laid out on the counter of the stall.

Steam rose from the merchant's forehead as beads of perspiration mixed with the icy, winter air. Cursing the priest under his breath, he pretended to focus his attention towards the back of the stall. No sooner had he turned away than he was met with the sound of the counter being overturned. "Why are you doing this?" the merchant pleaded, frantically gathering up the silk brocades and furs scattered on the muddy ground.

Dozens of curious onlookers flocked to the unfolding drama. His face purple with passion, the priest demanded, "Who has heard about the abomination born out of Florence? Do you know that the Emperor and his handpicked clergy—godless stooges— have tried to sell our Church to the Pope? They wish to foul our churches and deny us our heavenly reward."

The priest was met with blank stares.

"I will tell you the heresy that the Emperor has agreed to foist on us. We are now to believe," he sneered contemptuously, "that the Holy Ghost proceeds not just from the Father, but the Son as well!" He thrust his hands toward heaven and lamented, "Does damnation have a price in this world?"

İbrahim and Ahmet watched the priest rage from the far corner of the marketplace. They had been patrolling Edirne's Christian quarter all morning. It had been a tiresome exercise and they now welcomed the diversion.

"Surely Belgrade will be ours once spring arrives," Ahmet said, bracing himself against an unexpected blast of cold air. "Our enemies are hopeless."

İbrahim nodded. "So much anger and distrust." He was engrossed by the priest's venom, which grew with each new onlooker who joined the throng. Playing on their fears, the priest focused on the loss of paradise that surely awaited anyone foolish enough to adopt the Latin theology.

Ever since returning to the capital several weeks earlier, İbrahim had reflected on the campaign. Removed from the excitement of the battlefield, his role in the death of others and the risks to his own mortality nagged at him. A desire to fasten himself to God dominated his thoughts. Each day İbrahim looked to his treasured copy of the Koran for answers, but his frustration continued to grow.

"What of this life?" İbrahim mumbled.

"What did you say?" Ahmet asked.

"This priest speaks with passion about the afterlife and the people listen with rapt attention. Shouldn't there be fulfillment in this world as well?"

Ahmet leaned forward, interested. "You surprise me. I didn't know you were interested in the spiritual well-being of our Christian neighbors."

"I'm not," İbrahim answered flatly.

"Then these are questions you've asked yourself," Ahmet concluded.

"Don't you ask yourself the same questions, Ahmet? How can you spend a life on the battlefield and not ponder your role in this world? My master told me that fulfillment would come from serving my Sultan. One day I would realize that my greatest accomplishment and satisfaction would come from taking the Red Apple. What if he was wrong?"

Ahmet thoughtfully absorbed İbrahim's plea. "There are people who can help. I will introduce you to them."

Back in the barracks, İbrahim paced like a caged tiger. "You don't expect answers all at once, do you?" Ahmet teased. Motioning for İbrahim to follow him, Ahmet walked out of the barracks into the twilight.

They stood side by side as they made their way through the streets. Just short of affecting a swagger, İbrahim walked with his powerful shoulders pinned back and his chin thrust outwards. He cast a proprietary gaze over all that chanced his way. Finally, Ahmet nodded at a building attached to the side of a modest mosque located on the far edge of the city. Several Janissaries, their heads directed downwards, were carefully stepping over the threshold.

"Have you ever been inside a *tekke*?"

İbrahim shook his head.

"This *tekke* belongs to the Bektaşi order of dervishes. Most of us belong to this order. In time, you will call this place and others like it a second home."

İbrahim followed Ahmet into the *tekke*, mimicking his friend's avoidance of the threshold. A dimly lit prayer hall filled with worshipers who had just completed their evening prayers greeted him. Janissaries and devout ascetics, humbly dressed in threadbare robes, mixed contentedly together.

To İbrahim's right was the meeting hall, followed by the kitchen, bakery, and monastic cells. Designed for utility, the *tekke* was a well-organized home and haven. Chips of plaster hung from the discolored white walls, which were sparsely dotted with framed pictures of masterfully crafted calligraphy. A stale odor, heavy with moisture, persuaded İbrahim to breathe through his mouth. Still, an enticing air of mystery permeated the otherwise dreary room, irresistibly drawing İbrahim forward.

"So this is where I'll find answers?" İbrahim asked, with more suspicion than hope.

Ahmet frowned. "Arrogance and skepticism will not always stand you in good stead. If you wish to find fulfillment, you need to open your heart to more than the Koran and *hadith*."

İbrahim stared at his friend with surprise and said, "You wish me to become a heretic?"

"Our detractors often accuse us of being heretics," Ahmet admitted. "The Bektaşis have merged many of the beliefs from Islam, the steppes and Christianity. It's better that we don't flaunt our doctrines. Secrecy is the best policy in all that happens here, even if only for the sake of secrecy itself. Why take unnecessary risks?"

"Does this mean you are a dervish?"

Ahmet chuckled and said, "No, but I have sworn allegiance to Sheikh Bektaş. For that, I've been invested as an associate."

"So when are you going to introduce me to these beliefs?"

Ahmet laughed. "I'm afraid I'll never be anything more than a student, and even then my training lies more with learning how to participate in rituals than true scholarship." He respectfully waved at an old dervish to join them.

The dervish, dressed in a frayed robe, slowly made his way across the room. Each labored step was taken with care. His bent frame looked as though it might topple over if he took his eyes off the floor for a single instant.

"Shouldn't we go over to him?" İbrahim suggested.

"And insult him? Of course not," Ahmet answered, looking ready to dash across the room to catch the old man.

The dervish's thin, brittle skin was tightly drawn over his face. His mouth was sunken inward, hiding darkened teeth, which clung precariously from their roots. He must never eat, İbrahim decided, revolted by the man's ghostly mask.

"You've brought a new boy to see me, Ahmet," the old man said upon finally reaching them. His faraway, watery eyes studied İbrahim with a combination of passion and placidity. "He doesn't care for what his eyes see," the dervish finally concluded with a judgmental sigh.

"He spares no one," Ahmet explained, "not even himself. That's why I wanted him to meet you."

"Is he willing to learn? I'm too old to waste my time."

"He will accept your guidance."

"Then you may introduce him to me."

Ahmet cleared his throat and said, "İbrahim, it is my honor to introduce you to Binali Baba. He is a great *baba*."

"Have you studied the Koran?"

"Every day," İbrahim answered proudly.

"And has it brought you closer to Allah? Do you feel Allah's presence within you?"

"I don't know," İbrahim answered, puzzled by the question.

"Isn't that what you want?"

İbrahim thought for a moment and said, "I suppose I would be a fool to say that I didn't want such a thing."

Binali Baba grinned and said, "But you've never believed that it was possible." He grabbed hold of İbrahim's hand, digging his gray, bony fingers into İbrahim's pink skin, and pulled İbrahim towards a pair of sheepskins covering a large, ornately woven rug in the corner of the room. A four-step set of stairs was flush against the wall. It held several long candlesticks along with an incense holder and rosewater sprinkler.

Music was now wafting towards them. İbrahim detected a surge of energy shoot through the room.

"Sit with me," Binali Baba urged. "If I stand too long, I'm sure to fall. At my age, falling on the ground can be just as deadly as falling on a razor-sharp scimitar."

Settling on the sheepskin, Binali Baba gently whispered, "You partake of Allah's essence every moment of your life. You must unite with Allah while in this world. Find immortality while possessing your consciousness. If you can unite yourself with the presence of Allah that lies within you, you will find what you need."

"How am I to find this unity? Must I study the Koran more?"

Binali Baba smiled. "I don't believe that knowledge of the law is enough to find answers. Open yourself up to song, dance and wine. Release your reserve. Give in to your senses."

He pitied İbrahim. The boy had an undefinable emptiness in him, Binali Baba thought, concluding that it was unlikely İbrahim would succeed in his quest. Still, he wanted to help him.

"I will tell you the story of the blind ones and the elephant." Binali Baba settled deeper into the sheepskin and said, "There was a city whose inhabitants were all blind. One day, the city was visited by a king and his army, whose centerpiece was a great elephant. The people were thrilled by the thought of this beast. Some ran out to inspect it. They surrounded the elephant and groped it until each man was certain that he understood its nature. Upon returning to the city, the man who had felt the ear said that the elephant was a large, rough animal. The man who had felt the trunk dismissed this report and said that the elephant was shaped like a long, hollow pipe possessing tremendous power. With equal certainty, the man who had felt the legs said the elephant was like a mighty pillar. Of course, they were all wrong. Knowledge does not reside with the blind."

"Must you speak in riddles?" İbrahim complained.

"Don't put too much stock in my words. Only the effort to understand will change your life. Now leave me. I'm tired and you have much to think about."

Although frustrated by the old dervish, İbrahim was strangely drawn to him. Even Mahmut had not possessed this man's quiet, unyielding authority. İbrahim felt like a unique opportunity was slipping past him.

"You mustn't monopolize Binali Baba's time," Ahmet said, coming over to collect his friend. "It's time we returned to the barracks."

"But we've only just arrived," İbrahim protested.

"Just arrived," Ahmet laughed gently at the stunned expression on İbrahim's face. "We've been here for hours."

They slowly made their way back to the barracks. The crisp night air washed over them, sharpening their senses. With a broad grin, Ahmet broke the silence and asked, "Did he tell you the tale of the elephant?"

"He told you that tale too?"

"On occasion Binali Baba will share that story," Ahmet said. "You have been honored by his interest."

"Why do you think he chose that tale?"

"You're wasting your time looking for answers to his stories from anyone else but yourself."

"I must know what Binali Baba knows."

"You can't follow his path, İbrahim. Swear allegiance to the order, but remember that you're a Janissary above all else, not a dervish."

"Then why did you take me to the *tekke*?"

"You would prefer to live in ignorance?"

İbrahim struggled with the question. It offended him to accept that he would not be able to match someone else's knowledge. To accept what Binali Baba had to offer without ever having the hope of matching him meant making a painful admission.

After a few minutes of silence passed, Ahmet asked, "Is it really that hard a question to answer?"

"Of course not," İbrahim answered, head hung low.

İbrahim spent a restless night digesting Binali Baba's parable. The simplicity of the tale and its seemingly obvious lesson troubled him. It was too obvious. What mystery eludes me, he wondered, wanting to race back to the *tekke* and demand the answer.

The world had seemed so clear on the battlefield. There was life and death. Conquest and survival walked hand in hand, a comfortable guide. İbrahim felt like one of his hapless victims, vulnerable and pleading for help with no chance of escape.

When the cries of the *müezzin*s finally filtered into the barracks, İbrahim leaped from his mattress and began his morning prayers. His frustration continued to build as he knelt down on the prayer rug. No relief presented itself.

İbrahim found Ahmet shivering in bed with beads of sweat rolling off his forehead. "You'll have to find someone else to patrol with you today," Ahmet croaked.

"But you were fine last night," İbrahim said.

Ahmet smiled weakly. "It's this easy living. It will turn the sturdiest man soft."

"İshak and Hüsrev are paired together, as are Cem and Sinan. Maybe I'll patrol on my own until you're well."

"Don't be ridiculous," Şemsi said cheerfully. "We can't have you on your own. You might get hurt."

İbrahim spun around, eyes open wide with surprise. Despite his girth and plodding gait, Şemsi had an uncanny way of disguising his approach.

"What do you suggest?" İbrahim asked suspiciously.

"No suggestion," Şemsi said. "You and I will patrol together today."

"I thought you and Tarik were assigned to the waterworks," Ahmet wheezed, struggling to push himself up on his elbow and protect his friend.

"My rank carries with it certain privileges, does it not?" Şemsi snarled, obviously pleased by Ahmet's discomfort. "İbrahim, meet me at the fountain in ten minutes."

They watched Şemsi strut through the barracks, barking out orders as if he had been born to the sergeant's rank. "What do you think he wants?" İbrahim asked nervously.

"Say only what you must. Don't forget a word he says. I want to know all."

"I thought you weren't worried about Şemsi?" İbrahim taunted his friend.

"I'm not," Ahmet answered defensively, "at least not yet."

İbrahim was leaning over the fountain in front of the barracks, still struggling with Binali Baba's parable, when Şemsi hammered his back with the palm of his hand. "Time to work."

İbrahim cast a lethal gaze at Şemsi, whom he expected to shrink back in fear. Instead, Şemsi smiled placidly. If he had any lingering concern that İbrahim might snap at him, it was well hidden in his broad, flat face.

"Don't look so sore." Şemsi let out a lighthearted laugh. "I was just getting your attention."

"What do you want?"

"First, I want you to remember that I'm a sergeant," Şemsi barked, abruptly changing his tone of voice. "Ahmet isn't here to undermine my authority. So remember, I ask the questions. You will keep silent unless I give you permission to speak."

It was soon clear that they would not be patrolling the city. Şemsi led him through Edirne's main gate. Outside the walls, the buzz of the city faded, replaced by the cold gusts of wind swirling around them.

"We'll inspect the walls," Şemsi explained, almost as an afterthought. He looked over his shoulder several times to see if anyone was nearby. "I hear you acquitted yourself with great valor during the campaign."

İbrahim nodded, surprised to hear Şemsi speaking to him in such a respectful manner.

"You're still new to the *orta*, but haven't you wondered why you weren't recognized for your valor?" Şemsi slyly prodded. "A real love for battle is what I'm told. Men have been decorated for less. Of course, I had to make that judgment without help from your so-called friends.

"You need true allies if you are to rise in the corps. I speak to the colonel as much as your dear friend Ahmet, but I never heard the colonel say one word about you. You can imagine my surprise, particularly since the colonel is well versed in the feats of Ahmet's other friends.

"Naturally, I expect you believe that I'm lying to you. But put aside your emotions for a moment and think. If you were Ahmet, would you want to risk your standing with the colonel by publicizing your link to a man who's at war with members of his own *orta*?"

"I'm at war with no one in my *orta*," İbrahim protested.

"Silence," Şemsi snapped. "If you interrupt me again, you will spend the rest of your life cleaning up for Rüstem." Şemsi paused to regain his composure and said, "The colonel has many cares and he is slow to take notice of some things. But he is neither a fool nor a blind man. The colonel will notice that Ahmet has distanced himself from you. He will ask Ahmet to explain himself. Political expediency is Ahmet's credo. If I know my friend, he will abandon you."

Şemsi paused and look at İbrahim. "So why am I sharing this information with you?" Şemsi devilishly cackled. "I won't deceive you. I have no love for you. As things now stand, your value as a soldier makes you tolerable. You're fortunate that I'm a practical man with goals. I believe we can overcome our differences and help each other. I propose a simple deal: I will become your advocate in exchange for you supplying me with certain information."

"What makes you think I want an advocate?" İbrahim asked contemptuously, daring to break his silence. "You've misjudged me if you think I aspire to the same heights as you."

Ignoring İbrahim's insolence, Şemsi smiled slyly and said, "You wear your ambition too openly for me to believe such nonsense. I know the look of a man who craves recognition. My contest with Ahmet will have its high and low points; no well-fought battle doesn't. But rest assured, I will prevail. Those who stand with me will enjoy the benefits of my success. Those who don't—" Şemsi shrugged. "Well, you're a bright lad."

"So you think I can be bought with fanciful promises of riches laced with threats of retribution?"

"Don't expect me to waste too much time trying to sway you. The facts are in front of you. Convince yourself. Already you've seen Ahmet serve scullion duty while I sat comfortably in the barracks. You've seen him scramble to match my promotion, and only do so because he blindly stumbled on that accursed wagon. Haven't you noticed that the circle around Ahmet's stewpot isn't as large as mine?"

"His followers love him," İbrahim defended his friend.

"A fickle emotion. Now, the men in my circle like me well enough, but more importantly, they wouldn't dare disappoint me. Which response do you think is more likely to ensure the success of the *orta*?"

Unsure of whether he was truly interested in Şemsi's offer or simply carrying out his mission for Ahmet, İbrahim asked, "And what is it that you expect me to do?"

Şemsi beamed triumphantly. "Ahmet spends a great deal of time with you. Why?"

The question was an invitation to his first betrayal. "I couldn't even guess."

Şemsi's face turned bright red, but in an evenly modulated voice he pressed on. "You needn't tell me the reasons for his interest in you. Why don't you tell me what you discuss instead?"

"But we discuss so many things. They all seem to merge together," İbrahim said, trying to persuade Şemsi that there was no point in pursuing the matter further.

"Do you discuss Ahmet's dealings with the colonel?"

An overpowering urge to answer the question descended on İbrahim. He could not decide whether he was reacting to Şemsi's authority or an inner desire to impress Şemsi with the depth of his information. Finally breaking free from the compulsion to answer the question, İbrahim demanded, "What do you want?"

"Nothing that will harm you. I simply want you to tell me about Ahmet's activities."

"I won't argue with your idea of harm, but neither will I be your spy. You'll have to best Ahmet in a fair fight."

"I'm not interested in fairness, just winning," Şemsi growled.

"You'd do well to remember that. When you've changed your mind, let me know. Until then, think long and hard before getting in my way." He snapped his large jaw shut like a crocodile and spun around. İbrahim watched Şemsi depart with newfound respect as he pondered his dark warning.

İbrahim stood over Ahmet's bed, watching his friend slip in and out of consciousness, consumed with delirium. Ahmet's clammy skin had a ghostly pallor and his beard was soaked with perspiration. Şemsi could not have picked a better time to attack. The contrast between Şemsi's abusive swagger and Ahmet's weakened body seemed to validate Şemsi's arguments.

"Is that you, İbrahim?" Ahmet asked. He shook his head to free himself from the cloud hanging over his head, but the desultory gaze that had sunken into his eyes refused to yield.

İbrahim patted Ahmet on the shoulder. "Sleep. We'll talk later."

"We'll talk now," Ahmet insisted. "All day, only questions have occupied my mind. I need answers before I'm driven mad. Tell me what Şemsi said."

İbrahim hesitated. Was it possible that even some of what Şemsi had said was true? If so, was it wise to share this information with Ahmet? Imagining Şemsi's habitual sneer, İbrahim understood that he had fallen victim to the very suspicion that Şemsi had worked so cunningly to create. Still, he could not free himself from his concern.

"You really must rest," İbrahim said, hoping to buy more time to consider Şemsi's overture.

"I won't be tortured for another moment," Ahmet exploded.

İbrahim sighed and quickly rattled off, "He wants me to betray you. I rejected his offer. He threatened me. Now sleep."

"I didn't ask for a summary. Tell all."

İbrahim relinquished an assenting nod. After providing his friend with an unedited account, İbrahim expected an impassioned defense. Instead, Ahmet stared stolidly at İbrahim as if he were watching the clouds roll past. When İbrahim finished, an impish twinkle sparkled in Ahmet's eyes.

"Stand away from him," Hüsrev shouted from across the hall.

İbrahim spun around to see Hüsrev racing towards him, gesturing madly. "Half the city is sick with influenza," he coughed. "Get away from Ahmet before you catch it too. He needs to be isolated from the rest of us."

İbrahim obediently retreated. He had heard of whole cities being decimated by such epidemics. "Before I go," İbrahim said to Ahmet, "do you want me to do something?" His dissatisfaction with Ahmet's reaction had increased his inner turmoil.

Ahmet smiled contentedly and lay back down. "You and I have much to talk about—later. For now, simply keep listening and don't become anyone's enemy."

"It may be too late for that."

"Perhaps I may have taken your advice too lightly where Şemsi is concerned, but you needn't worry about him. At least for now, he's content to play games."

"Enough," Hüsrev said, tugging on İbrahim's sleeve.

As they walked down the long corridor of the barracks, Hüsrev casually said, "So, tell me about Şemsi."

İbrahim wondered whether Şemsi had also approached Hüsrev and the others.

"Hüsrev, forgive me, but I cannot."

Hüsrev snorted lightly, just loud enough for those passing by to know that he was angry. "Don't make the mistake of thinking that you've risen above our friendship with Ahmet simply because you own a secret. We've been with him from the start."

"Don't be absurd, Hüsrev. We're all friends."

"But some friends stand above others, don't they?" Hüsrev groused, stifling a cough.

"I don't understand," İbrahim answered with mock innocence.

Hüsrev turned bright red and thundered, "You dare to trifle with me, boy? I'm not some ignorant sheepherder."

"Of course not," İbrahim contritely agreed, pricked by Hüsrev's well-chosen insult and alarmed by his hostility. It had been quite some time since İbrahim had questioned the tenuous nature of their relationship. Now, İbrahim wondered where he might stand with Ahmet's followers if Ahmet were to be claimed by the epidemic. Şemsi was right. Friends were a necessity.

Hüsrev felt a pang of compassion as he observed·the conflict etched on İbrahim's face, but he did not restrain himself. "Don't think that we haven't noticed how your pride has swelled. I don't know what value Ahmet finds in you, but you might want to remember that Ahmet isn't the only member of the *orta*."

İbrahim smiled wryly. "I know."

Within days, Edirne was reeling from the epidemic. The mournful wails of the survivors grieving their losses weighed heavily on İbrahim. The aura of invincibility that he had nurtured on the battlefield was lost. Terrified of catching the influenza, he limited his interaction with people as much as possible. Each day he prayed for the city to be delivered even as he wondered how God could show the Sultan so much favor in war but devastate his capital only months later.

New questions, spawning additional unanswerable questions of their own, filled his mind each day. Contentment became a distant illusion. He set out to see Binali Baba, prepared to demand answers. More importantly, he needed to assuage the guilt that dogged him over his inability to dismiss Şemsi's solicitation.

An eerie silence met him on the streets. Although it was only midafternoon, the people had abandoned all commerce and fled to the illusory safety of their homes. It was as if they believed that the contagion lurked only in the deserted pathways. A restored sense of invulnerability grew within him as the echo of his boots pounded the streets. Except for the rare soul who nodded respectfully towards him, he felt as though he was the only life left within the city.

It was only when İbrahim cautiously crossed the threshold of the *tekke* that his conceit faded. Even inside its normally lively walls, silence reigned. Only a few dervishes and lay adherents milled about. To his relief, however, İbrahim spotted Binali Baba sitting on a sheepskin. He was gently resting his paper-thin hands on his crossed legs. The ancient *baba*'s eyes were sealed shut, enclosing him within the serenity of his meditation. His entire body, slumped forward, seemed ready to lose its structure as Binali Baba slid deeper and deeper into a state of spiritual ecstasy.

İbrahim cursed his bad luck. He knew that he could not interrupt the old dervish, especially if he expected to receive his aid. Nevertheless, İbrahim was content to observe Binali Baba. Disease lurked on the streets and in the barracks. Waiting for Binali Baba to complete his meditation held far greater appeal than leaving the *tekke*. Perhaps Binali Baba's wisdom will flow out from him and into me while I wait, İbrahim thought.

He settled himself on top of several nearby cushions and closed his eyes.

"I didn't expect to see you again so soon," Binali Baba said, awakening İbrahim from his slumber.

İbrahim's startled eyes searched for a window. It was dark. Hours had passed.

"So tell me what makes you brave Allah's wrath?"

"I need answers," İbrahim said simply.

"I thought I'd already given you instruction. It's too soon to return to me. You could not have struggled enough."

"I'm willing to keep struggling with the spiritual world," İbrahim conceded, "but I need your help in this world."

Binali Baba waved his hand in protest. "Don't believe that my spiritual powers reflect temporal knowledge. Know also that I have no wish to become involved in such common matters. Too often they lead away from the true path."

"But I risked much to see you," İbrahim said, crestfallen.

Again Binali Baba sensed the inner demons tearing at İbrahim and was moved. "Very well, I will listen."

İbrahim's face lifted. "Oh, thank you, *baba*. I will try not to overwhelm you."

İbrahim spent the next hour explaining the predicament Şemsi had created. Binali Baba's eyes flickered shut several times, followed by heavy breathing. Finally, İbrahim concluded by telling

Binali Baba about Ahmet's apparent disinterest in Şemsi's accusations.

"Let us not dally," Binali Baba said, once it was clear that İbrahim had finished his tale. "Are you asking me whether you should shift allegiances?"

İbrahim now understood why Binali Baba had not been interested in the details of the story. To him, the issue merely revolved around the underlying morality of the choice at hand.

"I'm not even sure where my allegiances should lie right now," İbrahim countered, trying to make Binali Baba understand the depth of his confusion.

"The answer will present itself to you. You simply must continue to look for it."

"Time is a luxury I don't posses."

Binali Baba smiled at İbrahim's youthful insistence on immediate gratification. "What use can an answer be to you if you can't solve the riddle on your own?

"This order's venerable patron saint, the Hacı Bektaş Veli, may Allah the most high bless his mystery, once said, 'If you wish to be always under the protection of Allah, keep in your heart the following counsel: Act with loyalty toward Allah, with justice toward His creatures, with desire to oblige toward the great, with compassion toward subordinates, with forbearance toward enemies, with fidelity toward friends, with discipline toward yourself, with liberality toward dervishes, with humility toward the learned, and with silence toward the ignorant.'"

A satisfied smile warmed the *baba*'s face as he nodded his head towards İbrahim. "Now you may return to the just path."

İbrahim spent the rest of the evening digesting Binali Baba's counsel. Although Binali Baba had purported to stand away from the conflict, there could be no mistaking his message. İbrahim wondered whether the protection of God would be enough to shield him from Şemsi.

Following his morning prayers, İbrahim visited Ahmet in a separate barracks hall that had been set aside for care of the sick.

As he entered the hall, he was assaulted by a malodorous stench. "How can anyone survive in such a place?" he muttered under his breath as he searched for his friend.

"You're better off pondering that question in the safety of your own barracks," a doctor said, rushing over to him. "That is, of course, if you value your health."

"I felt safer on the battlefield," İbrahim said.

"That may have been so," the doctor agreed. "Disease has killed more men than you and your friends ever will. Still, you shouldn't think too well of your battlefields. I have little doubt that the disease afflicting this city was brought here by our armies. Too many men together, surrounded by filth and death. Quite an irony, isn't it? If the Sultan keeps the peace, the empire doesn't grow; it will wither and die. If he fights the infidel, his capital is wracked with disease."

"Enough, doctor," Ahmet called out. İbrahim looked up to see his wan but cheerful friend gingerly walking towards him with his old smile. "My poor friend is more likely to grow ill from listening to you than from being in this wretched place."

The doctor smiled. As always, Ahmet had managed to make an important friend.

"I'm being released today, İbrahim."

"Wait one moment," the doctor protested. "I said that we would wait to see whether your chest was clear."

"Then let's get it over with." Ahmet bared his chest in the middle of the hall.

The doctor shook his head with mock disgust. "Go. Leave this place before you drive me mad," he laughed.

Back on the streets, Ahmet breathed deep and said, "I was beginning to think I might never escape from there." He turned to İbrahim and said, "You know that you were foolish to come."

"I thought it was more important that I see you."

"You want answers to Şemsi's accusations."

İbrahim nodded.

"I've often marveled at the destructive power of an accusation. It's worse than a curse. Of course, the hateful man absolutely believes the accusation. The rational man is far more frightening, though. He believes that he'll reserve judgment while waiting for the proofs to appear. He's certain that if the proofs don't support the accusation, he can cast it aside as if the words were never uttered. Of course, he's wrong to place so much faith in the power of his intellect. The lingering doubt that clings to even the most absurd slander is far too powerful. It's this mixture of self-deception and futility that slowly turns friends into enemies."

"So what hope is there? You believe that those are the only responses to an accusation?"

"The only hope is that the friends will overcome the accusation with acts of good faith," Ahmet explained.

"I never said I believed Şemsi's accusations."

"But you want me to respond just the same."

A painful silence fell between the two friends.

"I won't muddle your thinking with explanations that may sound like excuses. But, I'll help you in your task." Ahmet smiled devilishly and said, "I want you to betray me to Şemsi."

"An act of good faith?" İbrahim asked, puzzled.

"Can you think of a better one?"

"You want me to gain Şemsi's confidence."

"Obviously. If I truly must watch my rival, who better to do it for me than the man whom Şemsi believes is my closest confidant, now turned traitor? Of course, it would only be a ruse where you and I are concerned."

"I may be the perfect man to keep an eye on Şemsi, but then you're playing his game," İbrahim warned. "Are you certain you're up to it? He seemed rather comfortable making his offer."

"Why wouldn't I be up to it?" Ahmet could not imagine Şemsi besting him. "The man may have grand schemes, but he's a plodder."

İbrahim thought for a moment. It truly was an act of good faith. Ahmet was willing to risk İbrahim turning to Şemsi. As much as he wanted to profess his loyalty by rejecting the suggestion, İbrahim could not help but think that such an arrangement could secure his position with whomever ultimately won the contest. "So when would you like me to offer my services to Şemsi?"

"It's too soon since you rebuffed him. You'll have to wait. Otherwise, he'll be suspicious. I imagine that we'll know the right time when it occurs. Until then, let's pray that this winter passes quickly so we can return to the safety of our battlefields."

Marching to Varna • 1443 to 1444

The dull thud of axes chopping into ancient beech trees echoed through the narrow mountain pass. Muffling this assault was a veil of snowflakes, which were slowly descending from the gray sky, mixing with the unsoiled blanket of powdery snow rising up to the men's knees. Only the constant strain of their labor kept them from succumbing to the frigid blasts of air that periodically buffeted them. They had been working since before dawn.

İbrahim took a deep breath and exhaled loudly. He winced as the cold air circulated in his lungs. He lifted up his axe, which seemed to weigh more with each passing moment, and drove it deep into a tree trunk. A telltale crack answered him. The tree pitched forward and began its crashing descent into the gorge below. Pulling loose rocks in its wake, the beech joined a collection of trees and rocks blocking the pass.

"I almost hope that Yanko brings his Hungarians into this pass," İbrahim called over to Ahmet, who was busily working on his own tree. "I'd hate to think that we wasted our labor."

"Yanko is no fool," Ahmet huffed. "He'll scout this pass like all of the others. Let's just make sure that he won't be able to make his way through our pass."

"What's to stop him?" İbrahim asked. "If a tree can be chopped down, it can be cut through as well."

"But not nearly so easily if the tree and the rest of the land around it are frozen," Ahmet shot back.

İbrahim laughed. "You're still trying to get that stream diverted into the gorge?"

"Then you haven't heard the news. Cem tells me that the trough is ready. All we have to do is break the dam holding the stream back and the trees lying at the bottom of this pass will be frozen solid."

İbrahim was astonished. After so much disappointment and failure in the last two years, he had come to doubt whether he and his comrades were still capable of great deeds. They had been confronted by a revitalized foe who had stolen their initiative. The Ottomans' first setback had come when the Sultan tried to take Belgrade. Realizing that he was unable to hold this key to Ottoman expansion, Brankovic delivered the fortress to the Hungarians, who soon repulsed the Ottomans.

Although thwarted, the Ottomans had maintained their advance on both sides of the Danube. To the north, Turkish expeditions wreaked havoc in Transylvania and Hungary. To the south, the consumption of Brankovic's Serbia continued. Ultimately, Novo Brdo had surrendered. Dispossessed, Serbia's old despot had submitted himself to Hungary's new king. Now that the Ottomans controlled so much of the Balkans, even the fiercely independent Ragusan seafarers reluctantly agreed to pay a tribute of one thousand ducats' worth of silver plate a year to maintain their trading rights.

Brankovic's submission was soon transferred to King Ladislas III of Poland, who had successfully asserted his claim to the Hungarian crown after King Albert's death. Although only fifteen years old, the king had the foresight to appoint John Hunyadi, the Prince of Transylvania, to lead his armies. It was to this brilliant general that the Hungarians owed their salvation.

Hunyadi was known as the "White Knight" to Christendom and as "Yanko" to the Ottomans. He was rumored to have been fathered by King Sigismund himself on the king's way home from the debacle at Nicopolis. The royal blood flowing through Hunyadi's bastard veins had spawned an unsurpassed ambition. An adventurer and shrewd businessman, his true vocation was that of a Crusader who dreamed of driving the Ottomans from Europe.

Beginning with defensive raids, Hunyadi enjoyed startling victories that left the Ottomans reeling. Captured Ottoman banners and insignia were proudly displayed in churches throughout Hungary. Excited by Hunyadi's success, Pope Eugenius IV called for a Holy War. Unfortunately for the Hungarians, the Pope was mostly ignored, except for by the Poles and Wallachians.

Adding to the Sultan's problems was his hostile brother-in-law, İbrahim Bey, ruler of the Ottomans' Karamanid neighbors in Anatolia. Acting in concert with the Hungarians, İbrahim Bey attacked. The Sultan found himself surrounded by his enemies.

Then King Ladislas struck. Accompanied by the papal legate, Cardinal Cesarini, and the Serbian Despot, Brankovic, he set out from Buda with twelve thousand horsemen led by Hunyadi.

Hunyadi's Crusaders swept aside the Ottoman forces standing against them. Penetrating deep into Bulgaria, the Hungarians sacked Sofia. Within three months of their setting out from Buda, Edirne lay within a week's march. Faced with disaster, Ottoman resistance stiffened. Every road and pass were heavily guarded and blocked with debris.

As İbrahim considered the peril facing the empire, he heard the first rumblings of Ahmet's water swamping the fallen trees and rocks.

"Is ice our only weapon now?"

"If our lot is this harsh," Ahmet said, rubbing his frozen hands together for warmth, "then the Hungarians' suffering must be doubly bad. This cold could freeze the will of the Sultan himself. But at least we're on our homeland."

"You think they'll turn back?"

"Yanko hasn't fought past the traditional campaign season for no reason. He expects to win. He surely won't turn back if he thinks there's still a chance that he can warm his feet in the Sultan's palace. We'll have to do more than block Yanko's path with frozen debris. The colonel says that we're to head toward the town of Panagyurishte. That's where we'll make our stand."

İbrahim sighed and said, "Then it's another march through a thick forest."

"Hopefully, it will be a march worth taking. If we don't succeed, we're finished in Rumelia."

"When do we leave?"

Ahmet gazed at the frozen road of water that now coated the pass. It was all he could do to restrain the rage that welled up inside him. Hunyadi's successes had eliminated the opportunity for advancement. Promotions were not born from lost struggles. Ahmet's battle with Şemsi was little more than a memory. Internal strife within the *orta*, no matter how minimal, was a distraction that neither man was prepared to tolerate.

İbrahim understood his friend's frustration. He too had been plagued by Hunyadi's successes. It was much harder to march on one's heels. Dogged by death and misery, he wondered whether his eyes shimmered with the same fear that he had seen in the faces of his victims.

They trudged through the snowdrifts in silence. Although trained to resist the fear of battle, each man in the *orta* trembled at the thought of another loss. On the fourth day of their journey, the massed Ottoman forces appeared before them. A sense of desperation greeted them.

The colonel called his men to order before allowing them to enter the camp. In a year full of surprises, the colonel's decision to address them was no less remarkable. If not detached, he was certainly a reserved man who sheltered himself from his men.

With his shoulders pinned back and eyes gazing scornfully through the frigid gale, the colonel was the picture of pride as he stood before them. In contrast to his men's tattered clothes, his pristine, neatly pressed silk and velvet uniform looked as though he was ready for an evening's entertainment at the palace.

"Your pockets are empty," the colonel reminded them without sympathy. "You must decide whether you will someday enjoy the Sultan's purse or suffer his wrath. I love my master. But I wonder whether you do. How can an army that only recently held Serbia firmly in its grasp be on the verge of collapse? Will you allow some low adventurer and his collection of rabble to undo over one hundred years of glory? I am ashamed to be standing here today when I should be lounging comfortably in Belgrade, if not Buda. What will you do to reclaim your pride? What will you do to prove yourselves worthy?"

The colonel watched the glum expressions fixed to their faces. He despised their weakness. "As always, this army will take its lead from your ranks. You must show them the way. Don't expect an Anatolian *yaya* to save you. Oh, he'll fight hard, but he'll still have a home waiting for him if Yanko succeeds. It is you who will be homeless. You will lose all.

"And those of you who wish to be more than you are now, I will not allow a single one of you to rise while my career languishes because of your failures. So fight for Allah because that is the path of the righteous. Fight for your Sultan because to him you are bound. Fight for yourselves because you are men of valor and pride. And don't forget to fight for me because I will condemn you to a short, terrible life in the salt mines if you fail." With a contemptuous glare, the colonel whirled around and headed back to his tent.

"I suppose we're meant to be inspired?" İbrahim asked Ahmet sarcastically. "Do you believe he's serious about this threat?"

"He wants you not to know."

"So what are we to do that we haven't been doing for the last year?"

"Not give an inch," Ahmet said, thinking of the colonel's promise to freeze promotions.

The sun had not risen high enough to dull the cold winds when Hunyadi attacked early the next morning. İbrahim jealously watched the enemy's confident advance. Although wasted away by their meager rations and their arduous journey, the Hungarians were convinced that they were on the doorstep of the great victory that would save Christendom.

Yanko's men cut into the Ottoman army in loosely organized waves. Resistance by the demoralized *yaya*s quickly melted away. The wings of the army began to collapse inward. The makings of another disastrous defeat were well under way. As the army fell into disarray, İbrahim and his brothers marched forward.

"Who is ready to die for their Sultan?" Ahmet yelled, his voice carrying over the heart-thumping beat of the Janissary band.

He was greeted by a chorus of "Long live the Sultan!" followed by a wild roar that İbrahim had not heard for so long that it seemed to come from another world.

Sprinting side by side with Cem and İshak, İbrahim crashed into the Hungarians. The clash of steel and anguished cries surrounded him as he hacked madly at his enemies. Invigorated by this pivotal struggle, İbrahim was determined to reclaim the excitement of battle.

The battle had been raging for an hour when İshak, his voice barely penetrating the howling wind, called out, "İbrahim, fall back. We need you."

İbrahim glanced over his shoulder to find İshak and Cem struggling with five Hungarians. A thick line of dark blood was pouring over Cem's eye. Blinded by his zeal, İbrahim had advanced ahead of the line. Rather than confronting such a fearsome juggernaut, the Crusaders had deftly allowed İbrahim to slip into their ranks, assuming they would consume him later once he was sufficiently separated from the main body.

The peril to İshak and Cem was immediate. Despite their skill, they would not be able to last long against such numbers. İbrahim cursed his lack of discipline. He picked up an abandoned pike and, with a petrifying yell, launched it into the back of one of the Hungarians fighting Cem. The man fell forward, an explosion of blood spurting from his mouth. İbrahim then drove his scimitar through the head of Cem's other attacker.

İbrahim smiled at Cem and waited for words of gratitude. Instead, Cem's unobstructed eye squinted tightly and peered past İbrahim. "Behind you," he yelled with no small hint of exasperation.

İbrahim knew better than to look first. He lowered his shoulder and drove his body into a tight corkscrew. Pivoting underneath the swords of two Crusaders, he hacked at their midsections, slicing their entrails. When he regained his balance, İbrahim noticed that Cem had already joined İshak, who was stumbling backwards in the face of three men.

Two Janissaries against three Hungarians is more then a match, İbrahim tried to convince himself. He then looked at Cem's face and realized that Cem could only see from one eye. İshak was fighting defensively, trying to protect his friend. İbrahim hurled himself at their attackers. He made sure his first blow counted, driving his scimitar through one man's midsection.

Seeing their comrade fall, the two other Hungarians spun around. Cem took advantage of the confusion and struck one of the men in the back. The man fell towards İbrahim with his sword outstretched, which forced İbrahim to dance awkwardly backwards within the eager reach of the remaining Crusader. As he stumbled backwards, İbrahim sensed he was easy prey. In desperation, he swung his elbow up at a sharp angle, expecting his arm to be hacked. To his surprise, İbrahim felt his elbow snap the man's head backwards. The Hungarian reeled out of control towards İshak, who was racing forward to help. Before İshak could get out of the way, the man's sword was buried in his chest. Both men gasped as their eyes locked on each other, only inches away. Fearing for his life, the Hungarian abandoned his sword and fled back towards the safety of his own lines.

İshak fell to his knees. An astonished expression was fixed on his face. Gurgling blood, he fell sideways into Cem's waiting arms, a futile appeal set in his eyes.

"This cannot be," İbrahim said, shocked by the strange twist of events.

"It should not be," Cem seethed. "Why don't you return to your battle now? Fight Yanko hand to hand. That's what you must want. You obviously don't need us."

"I didn't mean to advance so far," İbrahim tried to explain. Dissolving into a blur of sound and color, the rest of the battle disappeared, replaced by a numbing sense of shame. He felt as though he had murdered İshak himself.

"Save your excuses. I have no use for them. Your wild runs

into the enemy have always been nothing but selfish conceit. Now see the consequences of holding yourself apart from us."

Both men looked down at İshak. Their friend's eyes no longer stared back at them.

The battle ended in a draw. The lack of supplies and the awful cold could no longer be ignored. Aching with regret, Hunyadi ordered his men to turn back. The Ottomans tried to gain the upper hand by renewing their attacks on the now retreating Crusader army. Not far from Sofia on Christmas Eve, Hunyadi's starved army snapped back and throttled the Ottomans.

Hunyadi's six-month campaign had been marked by stunning victories, but it would be a cruel illusion to believe that a new order had arrived. The Ottomans had suffered a sobering setback, not a shift in power. Much of Hunyadi's army had been lost to starvation, cold and Ottoman arms. Still, Hunyadi had unmasked the image of Ottoman invincibility. When he marched his army through Buda's gates in February, he was treated to a hero's welcome.

Rebellions broke out in Albania, southern Greece, and Serbia, and the forever hostile Karamanids in Anatolia were once again threatening war. A quick, generous peace was the only way for the Sultan to make sure that his enemies did not march against him in unison.

By early summer, the Sultan had secured his Rumelian possessions by agreeing to a ten-year truce with Hungary. Serbia and Wallachia were freed from their vows of allegiance to his empire. In return, the Hungarians promised not to cross the Danube or pursue their claims in Bulgaria. With due solemnity, the Sultan swore an oath on the Koran to observe the treaty and King Ladislas did the same on the Bible.

The Sultan was now free to turn his attention to the Karamanids. Although willing to live with the peace he had made, the Sultan was less confident that his western foes would forego further conflict after their recent successes. Contingents of Janissaries were left behind to guard Edirne and strengthen its walls.

İbrahim hoped that Edirne's distractions would dull the animosity he felt from his friends. Their anger seemed to grow every day since İshak's death. Only Ahmet continued to greet him with sincere cheer.

"I've heard it said that our young Prince and the Grand Vizier do not enjoy a good relationship," Ahmet shared with İbrahim as they inspected the city's fortifications. "It seems that Prince Mehmed doesn't care for those of noble origins."

"And whom did you hear that from?" İbrahim marveled at Ahmet's ability to discover the most confidential information.

Ahmet smiled mysteriously. "I'll tell you in a moment. First, you can congratulate me on my promotion. As of this morning, I'm an officer."

"Congratulations," İbrahim said, proudly slapping his friend on the shoulder. "I thought no one was receiving a promotion. Şemsi will be mad with jealousy when he hears about your news."

"Perhaps you should tell him."

İbrahim frowned. "Why does an officer have to compete with a mere sergeant?"

"You were the one who warned me about Şemsi."

İbrahim smiled appreciatively. "Tell me about Prince Mehmed."

"He's not like his departed older brothers, may they be enjoying the fruits of heaven. They were of a noble union. Mehmed's mother is a slave. Even worse," Ahmet whispered, "some say his mother is a Jewess."

"Why would someone think that?"

"She was born in Italy and her name was Estella."

"I don't understand."

"Of course you don't. You didn't have the benefit of trading with the Italians as I did. The Italian Jews are known for naming their daughters Estella."

"Not exactly hard evidence, but what if that's so? He's the Sultan's son. Why would it matter if his mother is a Jewess?"

"Merely an interesting piece of information. But it might explain why the young man is so hostile to the nobility. He is only half of their stock. I'm told that blood ties breed a special kind of loyalty."

"As long as the Prince is like his father, I'll have no complaints," İbrahim said hopefully.

"I'm afraid you'll have quite a few complaints then. The boy fancies himself to be the next Alexander the Great. I've already heard it said that he intends to seize Constantinople at the first opportunity. Mehmed is at war with everyone. He yields to no one. Did you know that the Sultan gave the Prince's tutor permission to use the rod? And so he has, many times."

"Who but the Grand Vizier would know that?"

"A new friend," Ahmet said proudly.

İbrahim gasped. "What would Halil Pasha want with you?"

Ahmet shrugged. "I think he's looking to draw as many of us into his ranks as possible. He's searching for leaders."

"But it sounds like the Prince is more likely than the Grand Vizier to favor new men such as us. Shouldn't we support Mehmed?"

"When are you going to realize that you are the establishment?" Ahmet reprimanded him.

"Watch yourself, Ahmet. I suspect the Grand Vizier's loyalty is fickle."

"You worry too much, İbrahim."

"You may be right. I have too much time to think about my sins."

"What sins are those?"

İbrahim shook his head dejectedly. "Don't forget about me when Halil Pasha makes you agha of the Janissaries. If you do, I won't have any friends to keep me company."

"I was wondering when you would talk about İshak."

"You're the only one who hasn't said anything to me about İshak's death."

"What is there to say?"

İbrahim laughed cynically. "I could spend the next hour repeating Cem's comments alone. Don't you know İshak would be alive today if it weren't for me?"

"Is that so? I didn't know there was such certainty in war."

"Tell your friends that," İbrahim replied.

"They're your friends too."

"Only because you demand it of them."

"Don't blame the men because they haven't embraced you. You must want to be close to them."

İbrahim opened his mouth to protest.

"Come now, İbrahim," Ahmet silenced him. "What can you tell me about Cem? Does his mouth curve up or down when he's had too much to drink? Which leg does Hüsrev drag when it's cold? Where was Sinan born?"

İbrahim hung his head.

"They could answer dozens of similar questions about you."

İbrahim scrutinized his friend. "Why are you able to forgive me so easily, but they cannot?"

"They expect you to act like they do. I have the benefit of knowing your nature."

"What does that mean?" İbrahim snapped.

"There are some things that a man can't change. His nature is one of them. İbrahim, you can't resist the urge to set yourself apart. It is both a weakness and a strength. I know that you genuinely regret İshak's death. That's why I won't waste a moment blaming you."

Ahmet's judgment stung him. Still, İbrahim could not muster an argument in his defense. "Honest intentions don't seem to carry as much weight as they should," was the best answer he could produce.

Ahmet smiled wryly and said, "You needn't explain yourself to me. It'll do you little good. As I've told you before, I don't hold the answers to your questions."

İbrahim fought to overcome the feeling that he was being abused. He screwed his resolve in place and suggested, "Then I suppose there's nothing left for us to talk about."

"I quite agree. This subject is closed—at least as far as I'm concerned. It's time we discussed my old friend, Şemsi. While I have the upper hand, it's the perfect time for you to offer yourself to him."

"You may be better off explaining your trust in Halil Pasha than playing with Şemsi," İbrahim warned.

"More warnings," Ahmet laughed.

"Good advice."

"I'll think about it if it makes you feel better. Of course, you'd probably be the first to admit that some advice is hard to accept."

"Ahmet," the colonel warmly called out as he approached them mounted on a brilliant roan.

They bowed respectfully at their commander, who nodded at Ahmet while ignoring İbrahim.

"You and I have an invitation to the palace."

Ahmet smiled broadly at İbrahim and then followed after the colonel. Not bothering to bid İbrahim farewell, Ahmet rushed back into the city, brushing the dust off his uniform as he eagerly hurried along.

The sun was still high in the sky. İbrahim decided to stroll the streets. Allowing his broad shoulders to drop, he melted into the masses. Soon he was swept along with the ebb and flow of street traffic.

A sea of colors and sounds greeted him as the world of the common man rubbed against him, breaking down the reflective polish of his hardened exterior. Soon bits of conversations from the people passing by tantalized him.

"The price of bread rises," an old man wearily complained.

"But you must admit, the Prince is handsome," a middle-aged woman insisted.

"Then he will be burned as a heretic," a young artisan replied with shocked innocence.

Simple and earnest conversations eventually materialized as his hearing became more sensitive. Gestures were restrained. No one spoke in the boasting, exaggerated manner of his comrades, who were constantly trying to out-duel each other.

With a baffling mixture of longing and scorn, İbrahim wondered what it must be like to live their lives.

İbrahim reached the city's central bazaar and leaned against a wall. No one seemed to notice him. Undisturbed, he watched an endless stream of people fight their way through the tumult. The jolting collisions between these faceless souls struggling to reach the stalls reminded him of battle. No one seemed to mind.

After watching for an hour, he pushed himself away from the wall. Before taking a full step, he collided with a girl rushing past him. Her shoulder caught his chest, causing her to spin into the back of a large man, who dropped a basket of apples.

The man spun around and growled, "You've ruined my fruit."

Squinting in pain, the girl rubbed her shoulder and stuttered, "It was an accident. I didn't mean—"

With a sour expression fixed on his face, the man waved his hand for her to stop speaking. "You will pay me."

İbrahim thrust his shoulders back and took a menacing step towards the man, who immediately snapped to attention.

"Look what this awkward girl did."

İbrahim gazed deeply into her. She can be no older than fourteen, he decided as his eyes worked their way down her short, slight body. Rich, dark brown eyes sparkled against her ivory white complexion. Her full, rich lips quivered uncontrollably as she tried to contain her fear. With white-knuckled fists, the girl nervously clutched balls of her long, silky black hair under her chin. With her hair tightly drawn to both sides of her face, she looked like she was in mourning.

Touched by her discomfort and feeling guilty over his role in her plight, İbrahim was moved to pity her. There was no room for pity on the battlefield. It disturbed him to realize how such a basic emotion had been so thoroughly purged from his consciousness.

"It was an accident," she timidly pleaded, now on the verge of breaking down.

"What does it matter how it happened?" the man sneered. "I'm not interested in excuses."

İbrahim silenced him with a withering glance. "You will let her speak."

The girl flashed a smile. İbrahim was thunderstruck. For that brief moment, a dazzling glow radiated from her. Her features came alive, foreshadowing the beautiful woman she would soon become. Mixed with her beauty was the essence of her sweet and compassionate nature.

She is filled with innocence and goodness, İbrahim marveled. I must know her. For a long, ethereal moment they gazed into each other's eyes, joyfully separated from the rest of the world.

"She says nothing," the man finally said in exasperation. "What do you intend to do?"

"Mihrimah," a slightly built middle-aged man called out in obvious relief. "I was afraid I might never find you."

The girl burst into tears and threw herself into her father's waiting arms. "Oh, Father," she cried. "I'm so sorry."

"What happened?"

"She destroyed my basket of fruit," the large man barked, deliberately hovering over the girl's father.

Mihrimah's sobbing increased as she buried her head in her father's chest. Ignoring the developing confrontation, İbrahim tried to catch another glance at the girl by maneuvering to her father's side.

"Your daughter has no manners," the large man spit. "You'd do well to mind yours and pay me three aspers for my trouble."

"Three aspers," Mihrimah's father gasped. "Your fruit couldn't possibly have cost so much."

"I said for my trouble," the large man scornfully replied while arching his body down towards the smaller man.

"Aspers won't remedy your troubles if you try to extort a single coin from these people," İbrahim interjected. He put his thickly calloused hand on the large man's chest and effortlessly pushed him several feet backwards. "Go in peace," İbrahim gently said to Mihrimah's father.

"But I must owe this man something?"

"You and your daughter have more than paid him back by enduring his insults."

Mihrimah turned to look at İbrahim. Her face was flushed with gratitude. Once again she melted him with her smile. A sweet, yearning throb wrenched his heart as their eyes met. He could feel the blood rushing into his face. Inhaling deeply, İbrahim reflexively dropped his chin and averted her gaze. A light, warm laugh, filled with delight, escaped from Mihrimah, who quickly muted it by shyly clamping her delicate hands over her mouth. İbrahim responded with a smile that grew until his cheeks ached.

Mihrimah's father noticed the exchange and pulled at her arm. "It's time to go, Mihrimah," he ordered, a hint of alarm in his voice. "Thank you, Sir," he added before disappearing with his daughter into the swarming bazaar.

İbrahim pushed himself up on his toes trying to steal one final glance at her, but they were already lost in the tide.

"And what am I supposed to do?"

İbrahim exhaled loudly and reached into his uniform. "For your trouble," he sneered while smashing several coins into the man's chest before turning to walk away.

"Thank you," the large man said, joyfully clutching the coins with both hands. "You are most kind. May Allah be with you and your most brave brothers," he called after İbrahim.

"Mihrimah, Mihrimah, Mihrimah," İbrahim whispered to himself. It was the most perfect name he had ever heard. Not even his happiest dreams had given him as much pleasure as the thrill of looking into Mihrimah's bewitching face. In a daze, he worked his way back to the barracks, periodically stopping to look over his shoulder. He wanted to race back to the bazaar and find her. Knowing that she was surely gone by now, he vowed to return to the bazaar every day until they met again.

İbrahim did not know what he would tell her once they met. Introductions will hardly be necessary, he decided as he nurtured the memory of her smile. Our bond is already strong. We need only remake our acquaintance. He imagined Mihrimah leaping into his arms at the first sight of him. Her rich hair would caress his cheek as he breathed her sweet breath through his eager lips. His hands would wrap around the small of her back and...

"How many times must I call to you?" The sharp tone of a

familiar voice faintly penetrated his reverie. "Are you ill?"

İbrahim rejoined his world with a sorrowful jolt. "I'm fine," he answered sourly. To his surprise, the barracks hall loomed in front of him.

"You look like you've been lost in meditation," Ahmet laughed.

İbrahim suppressed his annoyance over being awakened from his fantasy. With a wide smile, he said, "I met the most extraordinary—woman." He was not certain whether it was appropriate to call her a woman just yet.

"So this is how you've responded to my advice," Ahmet howled. "You've turned your passion back to women. So whom have you found? Does she know new tricks?" he added with a knowing arch of his eyebrows. "Of course, you'll have to show her to me. Perhaps she can entertain both of us at once."

İbrahim looked at his friend with alarm. "She is not for sale."

Ahmet frowned. "It's best that you stay away from such a woman, then. Don't tease yourself with thoughts of living an ordinary life. You cannot marry."

İbrahim had not yet considered how his link to the corps might block his dreams.

Ahmet noticed his friend's discomfort and changed the subject. "You'll tell me about this woman later if you like. It's more important that you learn about events happening in the palace. The young Prince is truly a different man from his father. We have much work to do."

Always ready to assist his friend, İbrahim blocked out his own concerns and said, "I'm not so sure I want to get involved in a game of politics that involves the Prince. You'd do well to have the same reservations."

"You and the rest of the corps may not have a choice. Remember, although we are servants, we are also the state."

"Are you speaking for yourself or Halil Pasha?"

Ahmet frowned and said, "I don't need your insolence now. I need your loyalty. While the Sultan is off in Anatolia, Rumelia is being governed by a boy who shows no respect for the old ways. He means to make sure that 'new men' rule the empire. The course that has brought us so much success is under attack."

"Halil Pasha is not a 'new man,' is he?" İbrahim quipped. "It seems that he has much to lose if the Prince's preferences are as you say. Besides, why should we throw our lot in with the Grand Vizier? We are the very definition of 'new men.' Shouldn't we support the Prince and his agenda? Are you throwing your support behind the empire or the Grand Vizier?"

"I quite agree that in the end our loyalty must first be to the empire. Believe me when I tell you that support for Halil Pasha and the empire are one and the same. Have you heard about the Persian heretic who has been making his way through the streets?"

"Of course," İbrahim said. "I hear the Grand Mufti is ready to see the fanatic burned alive."

"This Persian is already developing a wide following. That includes the Prince, whose protection the man enjoys."

"So the Prince has an appreciation for freethinkers."

"Whether our beliefs are sufficiently orthodox to meet the Mufti's tastes will not affect the fate of our state. The same is not true of the Prince. He must swallow his personal preferences and support the establishment at its core."

"So how is this our business?"

"Because it weakens the state," Ahmet forcefully answered. "Worse still, it weakens the state at a time when it can least afford to be divided. Halil Pasha has shared with me ominous news from the West. The Hungarians have betrayed their oath and repudiated the peace treaty."

"How can that be? They swore on their Bible."

"Indeed they did," Ahmet said wryly.

"Are you certain?"

"Halil Pasha told me himself. I'll grant you, though, that it is hard to believe. What makes it even harder to believe is that King Ladislas was advised to repudiate his oath by Cardinal Cesarini, the papal legate."

"What possible justification could there be for violating his oath?" İbrahim skeptically pressed.

"Halil Pasha believes that Cardinal Cesarini convinced King Ladislas that an oath sworn to people who do not believe as they do is invalid."

"Has the rest of the West joined in this perjury?"

Ahmet smiled. "The Emperor in Constantinople won't support King Ladislas. He's too weak and afraid. More importantly, though, Brankovic is not lending his support. The Sultan is a clever man. He pried the Serbs apart from the Hungarians by signing a peace treaty that allowed Brankovic to recover most of Serbia. There is nothing left for the old despot to gain. He only stands to lose his lands again if he supports the Hungarians and things turn bad. As an added piece of good news, Brankovic also agreed to block the Albanians from joining Ladislas."

"And what of the Venetians?"

"They are supposed to provide naval support to King Ladislas," Ahmet sneered. "I'm more concerned about Yanko."

"So we'll be back in the field soon," İbrahim sighed.

"Let's hope that the Sultan quickly defeats the Karamanids. We can't let the Prince bring us into battle."

"Ahmet, what ideas has Halil Pasha been putting into your head? Do you truly believe that you can affect whether the Prince commands us?"

"I am more than an individual, İbrahim. I speak for many."

"That may be true, but you don't speak for enough Janissaries to make them raise their voices as one against the Prince."

"I wouldn't dare incite a single man to rebel against the Prince," Ahmet said, lightly feigning mortification. "That would be treason. But I might suggest that we receive a long-overdue pay increase."

İbrahim sighed heavily and said, "Do you expect the Sultan to outlive his son?"

Ahmet frowned for a moment before saying, "I suppose I'll have to place my faith in the Grand Vizier."

"Then let's hope that your important friend keeps his head."

The Last Crusade

"The bazaar is on fire!" a frightened woman screamed to no one in particular. "The devil has taken this place."

The warm summer night air echoed with panicked cries as people raced down the streets in a desperate bid to stay ahead of the flames that were quickly engulfing Edirne. An immense fortune in materiel had been sent to the city in order to prepare for hostilities with Hungary. Now it was burning along with the brittle wood houses dotting the capital.

Rumors were already spreading that the Janissaries had set the fire because they had not been paid their stipend. Instead of joining the bucket brigade bringing water from the river to fight the fire, most of the Janissaries were comfortably camped on the hill in front of the palace.

Sitting perched on the hill with the rest of his comrades, İbrahim silently watched the fire leap from one street to the next. Like rays of light shimmering off the choppy sea, the flames flickered in a constant, aimless path, steered by a mischievous breeze. The fire's appetite knew no bounds. The homes of the rich and poor were afforded the same mean consideration.

While thousands of his Janissary brethren watched the fire's progress with fascination, İbrahim's eyes were locked on the central bazaar. Only ashes remained of what hours earlier had been the heart of the capital. Dreams of renewing his acquaintance with Mihrimah now seemed as ethereal as the silhouettes of the people rushing for safety below him.

As he had with everything else that had excited his passion, İbrahim yearned for Mihrimah completely. Her absence made her more precious. Fearing that he would soon lose her memory, he desperately wanted to hold her.

"We want our money," a chorus of Janissaries from the Fourth Orta lustily yelled towards the palace.

Halil Pasha was set on protecting the privileges of the established families and teaching the Prince a lesson. Knowing that Mehmed's tutors had used the rod and failed, the Grand Vizier took pains to make sure the boy suffered an especially stiff lesson that would compel his allegiance to the old guard. Halil Pasha invoked the aid of the state's most conservative and reliable engines, the religious order and the military.

Halil Pasha had first turned to the Mufti. Feigning interest in the Persian heretic's views, the Grand Vizier invited the rabble-rouser to his home. Lulled into a false sense of security, the heretic liberally expounded on his views, not knowing that the Mufti was hiding behind thick curtains. When he could no longer bear to hear the heresy, the Mufti leaped forward and tried to wring the Persian's neck.

The Persian managed to escape to the palace. Close on his heels was the enraged Mufti, who demanded that Mehmed surrender the man. Grudgingly, the Prince offered up the Persian to his fate at the stake.

Halil Pasha then turned to the Janissaries. With the help of leaders such as Ahmet, he ordered a raid on the home of the Chief White Eunuch, Sabahattin Pasha, another favorite of the Prince. Even worse, he was a new man—a natural enemy.

Spurred on by these events, the Janissaries were ripe for insurrection. The Grand Vizier convinced them that the only way they would fill their purses again was to force the Prince to open the treasury. Little effort was necessary. Aside from their lust for wealth, the Janissaries did not like the Prince. Already, Mehmed's overbearing nature and arrogance were widely condemned throughout the ranks. Prayers for the Sultan's health and continued rule were on every Janissary's lips.

"Listen to them," Ahmet proudly said, sauntering over to İbrahim. "That is the sound of power."

"Ahmet," İbrahim said bitterly, "the city is in flames. Who knows how many have died?"

"Cities can be rebuilt," Ahmet said, unconcerned. "I'm more concerned about the number of lives that will be lost if the Prince is not reigned in."

"Halil Pasha would be proud of you. You speak his words like a trained parrot."

"You'd do well to remember who your friends are," Ahmet peevishly reprimanded İbrahim. "I need your support even if you don't agree with me."

İbrahim sighed. As he watched the smoldering ashes of the central bazaar drift away in the warm night air, he wanted to strike a blow against those whose ambitions had undermined his own. As much as he considered Ahmet to be his true friend, he could not help but include him among those who had harmed him. Grudgingly, he offered, "You always have my support."

Ahmet smiled and patted his friend on the back. "I haven't seen you lately. You were supposed to join us for the raid on Sabahattin Pasha's house. You missed out on a treasure trove of fine jewels."

"I was ill," İbrahim lied unconvincingly.

"Lovesick for that girl, eh?" Ahmet smiled, having already surmised the reason for his friend's absence.

Instead of answering, İbrahim sighed again and returned his attention to where the central bazaar had stood. It was Ahmet's turn to sigh. He had a talent for understanding his friend's thoughts. "You have a grievance with me." Ahmet's sharp tone demanded a forthright answer.

"How will I ever meet her again? Who would stay in this place now?"

"İbrahim," Ahmet said, reducing his tone of voice to a gentle whisper, "how often must I remind you what you are? You cannot have this girl or her life. Let her go. In time, your heart will be restored like the city below you." Rather than waiting for a reply, he rejoined the ranks of his aroused followers.

Even as the fire began to ebb, the demands for money echoed with increasing ardor. Not a single Janissary showed the slightest intention of returning to the barracks. If there was a time when their demands were nothing more than empty bravado, that time was long past.

"Your friend is quite a success," Şemsi said, sidling up to İbrahim. "My closest followers are standing by Ahmet's side demanding their money." He shook his head in disgust.

Looking at Şemsi's downtrodden face nearly released İbrahim from his melancholy. "Why are you sad, Şemsi? I would think you would be pleased."

"And why would I be pleased?" Şemsi snorted in disbelief.

"I always thought teachers were pleased when their pupils followed their path. Haven't you shown your men that the way to success is through a deep pocket?"

"I never taught them to mutiny," Şemsi indignantly replied.

"It is a sad state of affairs," İbrahim agreed.

"Then you do not support Ahmet?" Şemsi asked, the frown on his face beginning to lift.

"Let's just say I'm not pleased with what has occurred during the last several days."

"Perhaps I misjudged you, İbrahim. You may not be a fool after all."

"Look," a chorus of men shouted. "A messenger has been sent out from the palace."

"It's the Prince's tutor," another Janissary added.

All heads turned towards the main entrance of the palace. An elderly mullah dressed in a fine silken robe approached the mutineers without an escort. His face betrayed no concern even as he was showered with a hail of invective.

"I want my money, old man," a young Janissary growled.

The Prince's messenger smirked. "You needn't waste your time abusing me. I'm too old to worry about the coarse threats of spoiled children."

"Tell us why you're here then," another man shouted.

"The Prince wishes you to know that he holds you personally

responsible for the damage to his city. As far as your request for old and new monies," the mullah paused to savor the tension, "the Prince has found favor in your position even as he condemns your low conduct. You will be paid all monies owed to you tomorrow. You will also receive a ten percent increase in your wages. Spend it well and next time remember whom you serve." With a disdainful sniff, he returned to the palace.

Wild cheers rolled across the hill. "This will teach the young Prince a lesson he'll never forget," one man said to a friend as they walked past İbrahim and Şemsi.

"He's right," İbrahim said. "Mehmed surely will not forget this lesson."

Şemsi nodded. "Nor those who taught it to him."

"No doubt it's a long list," İbrahim said. "I wonder if it's reasonable to expect that the Prince would learn the names of all who provoked this mutiny."

"A truly difficult task. I suppose even a Prince needs help at times," Şemsi answered. "Just like a Grand Vizier, Princes can use friends as well."

The threat to Ahmet was clear, but İbrahim hid his concern. "Knowing when to make a friend can be a very difficult judgment. Bad timing can cause terrible problems."

"I like the way your mind works, İbrahim. Rest assured, I will not set myself against a man as powerful as Halil Pasha. Of course, a day may come when the Grand Vizier's power is not what it is today. After all, youth is on the side of the Prince. One day young Mehmed will rule his father's lands. Then those who had vision and patience will be served."

"I suspect you're right," İbrahim conceded. "Many years may pass, though, before that day comes. You never know when the next minute will be your last."

"I've always told my friends that those who can gain even a little insight into the future can survive the storm others cannot. Then they can live and prosper. They can also reward their friends," Şemsi said, extending himself to İbrahim. "I need to know if my name is spoken even by accident to Halil Pasha. Will you help me?"

"You speak of a tree that may one day yield rich fruit. It is barren today. I've grown concerned that some games may be too dangerous for me to play. That's why I'm very careful about where I shade myself. I need time to consider your request."

"Take your time, İbrahim," Şemsi smiled pleasantly. "Just remember, I will not always be licking my wounds. You will not always have this offer to consider." Without a hint of rancor, Şemsi walked away, head slightly tilted downwards.

İbrahim watched Ahmet's rival depart. This was Ahmet's day and Şemsi was a solitary character. His vulnerability could not be disguised. To his credit, Şemsi did not bother to try.

Şemsi's offer was the entree İbrahim needed to spy for Ahmet. Still, İbrahim wondered whether he should take the overture seriously. He knew Şemsi was right. No amount of power Halil Pasha amassed could change the fact that Mehmed would one day be the Sultan. If İbrahim indelibly linked himself to Ahmet, then he was sure to fall with him.

İbrahim slowly rose to his feet and surveyed the hill. Faces beaming contentedly, the Janissaries headed down to start fighting the fire, unperturbed that they were responsible for its start.

As the people of Edirne returned to their damaged homes, they had little to make them smile. With the prospect of the Hungarians storming the charred city, many questioned the wisdom of rebuilding until Hunyadi could be stopped.

Spurred on by the feverish zeal of Pope Eugenius IV, the Hungarians intended to strike a deathblow to the Sultan's empire in Europe. Despite fierce resistance from the Ottoman garrisons in Bulgaria, the Crusaders had managed to slug their way towards the Black Sea. Their goal was to join with the papal fleet, whose twofold mission was to meet its allies along the Black Sea coast and prevent the Sultan from bringing his army back into Rumelia from Anatolia.

Throughout his tenure, Murad had brilliantly guided his army while surviving the most well-conceived plans of his enemies. With his usual ease, the Sultan defeated his Karamanid brethren. Now put to the test as never before, he took up the daunting challenge of maneuvering forty thousand soldiers around the papal fleet. If his soldiers could not reach the European side of the straits, the undersized army he had left for his inexperienced son to command was sure to meet its doom.

Showing their indifference to the crusading zeal of their fellow Christians, the Genoese introduced themselves to the drama. For a rich endowment from the Sultan's purse, the Genoese gladly ferried the Ottoman army to Europe under the cover of darkness. The Pope responded with a bull excommunicating those who had aided the Ottomans, but the damage had been done.

The Janissaries were thrilled by their master's return. A sense of order fell over the corps. Their enthusiasm for the Sultan's return was only exceeded by that of the Grand Vizier's relief. Rumors had been circulating for weeks that Halil Pasha had all but summoned Murad back to the capital. As his relationship with the Prince continued to worsen, Halil Pasha's need to have Murad take up residence in Edirne became increasingly important.

In a series of northbound forced marches through the early November Bulgarian countryside, Murad's army covered territory with electrifying speed. On the seventh day of his advance, the army was ordered to halt. Positioned on the heights overlooking the Black Sea port city of Varna was the Crusader army. Nowhere to be seen was the papal fleet.

İbrahim and his comrades huddled close to one another around the stewpot. Few words were spoken as they nibbled on their fresh biscuits. They understood what a defeat would mean to the future of the empire. Past squabbles melted away as they tried to draw strength from each other.

"Why the dour faces?" Ahmet asked, trying to break the tension. "Our scouts say their army is a quarter of our size."

Ahmet's enthusiasm fell on deaf ears. His friends continued to concentrate on their biscuits.

Ahmet frowned before continuing on with greater zeal. "How dare they call themselves an army? Our master has assembled hunting parties larger than Yanko's ragged collection of Hungarians and Wallachians. We will end this madness once and for all tomorrow. Before sunset they'll be running home with their tails between their legs."

"Don't worry about us," Hüsrev offered. "We'll be ready."

"We'll fight like one," İbrahim added. He forced a smile in the direction of Hüsrev, who responded with a scornful sniff before looking away.

İbrahim surveyed his comrades. They had deftly edged their backs towards him as Ahmet walked off to join the colonel. Heaving a heavy sigh, İbrahim said, "Surely Yanko's army will not have the support of heaven tomorrow. A price must be paid for violating an oath sworn on their own scripture. Don't you agree?"

Except for Sinan, who grudgingly nodded his head, the others ignored him. Why must they make it so hard, he agonized.

After several more minutes passed, the men stood to leave. Hüsrev said, "It's best that we all sleep well. It will be a long day tomorrow."

"Wait," İbrahim blurted out, seeing his chance to make amends about to disappear. The men turned to look at İbrahim, lacing him with exasperated sighs. "Tomorrow is too important a day that we not say a prayer for our fallen comrades before resting for the night," he stammered nervously.

"Who are you—" Cem began to say before being silenced by a wave of Hüsrev's hand.

İbrahim ignored Cem's accusation. "I too mourn their loss. I cannot purge those faces, nor would I. Battles demand loss even from the victors. I've wondered whether we would be here today if their lives had been spared. Would we have taken their places if they had lived? Is the price we pay for own survival the loss of our friends? If that is so, then we are here now because of their sacrifice. So let us pledge together that we will do honor to their memories. Tomorrow, let our faces be bright, our arms strong, our swords keen, our arrows sharp-pointed, and may we return to Edirne flush with victory."

His comrades stared blankly at him for a moment. Then Hüsrev grinned broadly and said, "I miss them, too, İbrahim. We will avenge their deaths tomorrow—together." Hesitant smiles from Sinan and Cem followed.

As he watched his comrades depart, İbrahim's thoughts drifted back to the central bazaar. The sweet smile on Mihrimah's face beckoned to him. In his heart, İbrahim was certain that he would see her again if he survived. The stakes tomorrow will truly be high, he thought, his heart fluttering.

The midmorning sky darkened over the heads of the two motionless armies. A lacerating west wind swept over them, bringing with it increasingly loud claps of thunder. "Someone's bad omen," men on both sides of the field whispered to each other as they tried to mask their fear.

Only twenty thousand strong, the Crusaders were indeed an undersized force, particularly compared to the nearly eighty thousand men the Sultan had drawn to the battle. King Ladislas had been unable to rally other Christian states to the cause. Even the young king's friends and allies had been appalled by his sacrilegious repudiation of the oath he had taken on the Gospel.

Although the constantly opportunistic Serbian despot, George Brankovic, had deftly avoided King Ladislas's call to arms, the Prince of Wallachia was not so fortunate. Bound by his oath to defend and propagate Catholic causes, Vlad Dracul had reluctantly sent several thousand of his Wallachian cavalrymen to join the battle. In so doing, the Wallachian Prince broke his own oath of allegiance to the Sultan and risked the lives of his two sons who were hostages in the Sultan's court.

The cloudburst struck the Crusaders with magnetized focus while the Ottomans were only speckled with a few raindrops. The wind wreaked havoc throughout the Christian lines. Banners were shredded and supply carts upset. The men leaned into the gusts and struggled to root their feet to the ground.

When the wind finally began to subside, news of the first encounter echoed through the lines on both sides of the field. An Ottoman party of irregular cavalry and infantry forces had initiated a skirmish. A more serious attack followed. Finding their courage, the Hungarians fiercely drove them back.

Yielding to the demands of Hunyadi, King Ladislas held the center of his army while Hunyadi fell upon the attacking *sipahis*. It was the king's task to hold the army together while his general garnered the glory.

The Crusaders' numbers were magnified by their ferocity. As the battle wore on, they gained strength, feeding off of the Ottoman failure to break their lines. The Hungarians began a steady and lethal advance. Rather than overwhelming the Crusaders with their sheer numbers, growing elements of the Sultan's army lost heart and began to break away from the field, eventually swelling into a mass desertion. Most were headed back to Gallipoli and the safety of Anatolia. An historic victory lay within King Ladislas's youthful grasp.

King Ladislas's Polish knights advised him that it was time to seek out glory. He gladly abandoned his critical position and led a charge of five hundred cavalrymen into the heart of the remaining Ottoman forces.

"The Sultan is leaving the field!" Ahmet screamed to İbrahim over the thunderous din of the battle, face etched with horror.

Several nearby members of the *orta* looked over their shoulders. Seated high on his horse, the Sultan's back was to the charging Crusaders. The fight began to drain from their hearts. Only their deep reserve of discipline kept them from breaking rank.

"We are doomed if the Sultan departs." Ahmet's eyes locked on İbrahim in a desperate appeal.

İbrahim tried to muster an answer as he pushed back a thickly armored horse with his pike. Without thinking about what he was saying, İbrahim blurted out, "Then we will stop him."

Ahmet's eyes sparkled. "That is exactly what we will do. Follow me!" he called out to İbrahim, Sinan, Cem and Hüsrev.

They obediently followed Ahmet towards the Sultan, who was looking over his shoulder with an agonized expression. Amid the frightened screams of the wounded and dying, Ahmet and his followers made their way back from the front line. Even in the darkest days, İbrahim had never seen so many casualties among his corps. Still, they fought on, refusing to yield under the Crusaders' hell-bent assault.

Ahmet pushed his way up to the Sultan's horse and grabbed hold of its bridle. The horse came to an abrupt stop, jolting Murad forward in his saddle. Two guards moved towards Ahmet but were roughly pushed aside by Cem and Sinan, who froze the Sultan's protectors with malevolent glares.

Unperturbed by the disturbance around him, Murad calmly fixed a quizzical look at Ahmet. Standing by Ahmet's side, İbrahim stared deep into his master's eyes. Except from a distance, he had never seen the Sultan.

With his long, thin nose and neatly groomed, graying beard, the Sultan was the picture of refinement. His regal features, however, were a thin mask for the rigorous resolve that radiated within him. Murad's warm brown eyes glowed with a reassuring combination of intensity and restraint. İbrahim jealously craved the inner comfort and spiritual satisfaction possessed by the Sultan. He had never seen someone who projected such serenity. My master is truly the Shadow of God on Earth, İbrahim decided in awe. I will lay down my life for this man if I must.

"Who is it that takes my mount from me?" the Sultan demanded in a clear, understated voice.

"Your most loyal and humble servant," Ahmet answered resolutely.

"I will not question your loyalty for now," Murad said, "but you have certainly shown a lack of humility."

"Then please forgive my boldness. The urgency of the battle has shorn my manners from me. May I speak?" Ahmet asked respectfully, fist still tightly wrapped around the bridle.

The Sultan nodded.

With his chin thrust doggedly forward, Ahmet said, "The battle is not lost. Don't abandon the battle because those pampered *sipahi*s failed and the Anatolian *yaya*s are more interested in running to their homes than defending your Rumelian possessions. Your Janissaries can hold this field. Stand firm and let us bring you victory."

For a long moment, Murad's eyes poured into Ahmet. Then he graced Ahmet with the earnest countenance that had endeared him to the Janissaries and his people. "I will savor the memory of watching you break this accursed army. Let the world know the price for sacrilege."

Ahmet nodded respectfully at the Sultan. "Come!" he triumphantly ordered his comrades.

As İbrahim quickly picked his way past the fallen bodies, the thunderous clap of galloping horses roared towards him and shook the earth. Hundreds of Polish cavalrymen were charging headlong at the line. With lethal precision, they pointed their lances at the Janissaries' phalanx. Leading the charge was King Ladislas himself. His silver armor sparkled brilliantly across the battlefield. All eyes were drawn to him as he wielded his lance.

"The King belongs to the Tenth Orta," a voice bellowed above the din.

İbrahim's eyes fell away from the king and swung to his right. The hawk on the Tenth Orta's flag rippled threateningly towards the Crusader king.

Every Janissary wanted to claim the king even as each was committed to holding his position. Each man kept one eye on King Ladislas while subconsciously pushing towards the Tenth Orta's position.

The collision between the Tenth Orta and King Ladislas and his knights rang out across the field. The wrenching cries of dying men and the awful braying of crippled horses followed the clash of steel, all harmoniously blending with the strident rhythm of the Janissary band playing behind the line. Every terrible note inflamed the Janissaries' appetite until each man's blood pulsed through his veins like a swollen mountain stream.

İbrahim stood back from the line and gazed over at King

Ladislas. Bedecked in the finest armor his Hungarian craftsmen could fashion, he hovered grandly above the fray. Each thrust of his sword struck down a new claimant for the prize. Still, masses of Janissaries continued to rush at him until he was nearly cut off from his knights. Unable to pull the king to the ground, they finally drove a pike through the breastplate of his mount. Rising up on his hindquarters, the king's horse vented a stricken cry and then collapsed under its master, who was catapulted to the ground.

The king pulled himself to his feet and surveyed the scene. A dozen Janissaries, scimitars dripping with blood, had surrounded him. The king's only chance of rescue lay with his knights, themselves consumed in a desperate fight. Limping noticeably from the fall, he swung his sword in a protective arc while waiting for the first attacker to present himself.

A large Janissary emerged from the pack and engaged Ladislas. Grunting loudly, he launched himself at the king, who stumbled backwards under the assault. Utterly exhausted, Ladislas labored under the weight of his sword, swinging it in ever wider, less effective arcs. The Janissary took advantage of an opening and rushed forward. He clutched the king by the throat and hurled him face-first to the ground with a mighty yell. Panting heavily, Ladislas balanced himself on all fours and stared at the mud oozing over his clenched fists. The gleam of a leveled scimitar caught his eye.

A triumphant cry rose from the Tenth Orta. All heads turned. Ibrahim thought he saw King Ladislas mounted high above the battlefield. Confirming his vision, a Janissary mourned, "The King is saved."

Ibrahim's brow knitted together as he studiously observed the king's head. Against the graying sky, the head bobbed up and down before falling forward at a dramatic angle. "No. He is dead," Ibrahim crowed. "Ladislas's head is mounted on a pike."

As others began to recognize the king's fate, the sound of clashing steel faded until a hush momentarily fell over the battlefield. The Crusaders were finished. Now only thoughts of escape filled their spirits. The Ottomans rejoiced, mixing thankful prayers to Allah with contemptuous jeers toward the retreating enemy.

Hunyadi despaired as he watched his army dissolve into a vulnerable pack of fleeing rabble. Wading through his retreating army, he led a charge of Wallachian cavalrymen against the Janissaries in the hope of recovering Ladislas's body. On this day, there was no reward for his courage. His charge was easily rebuffed. Escape was his only fortune.

As his comrades' cheers rang ever louder, İbrahim's joy turned to concern. He saw the camel-emblazoned flag of the First Orta and rushed back towards his comrades. The first familiar face he saw belonged to Cem. In a moment borne from pure reflex, İbrahim embraced Cem, hoisted him off his feet, and declared, *"Allahu akbar!"*

For a moment Cem looked at İbrahim with suspicion. Pure exaltation beamed up at him. "İbrahim," Cem relented with a broad smile, "I will pray with you now."

"We will all pray with you," said Hüsrev, who along with Sinan was now standing by them.

"And what of Ahmet?" İbrahim asked, concerned.

"Oh, don't worry about our friend," Hüsrev chuckled. "He's already off with the colonel to see the Sultan."

"I hope to plead for the Sultan's mercy," Sinan said. "Our protest seemed so natural at the time. Now, I can't believe how we spoke to our master."

"Ahmet did the talking then," Hüsrev counseled, "and that's why he is there now. Don't concern yourself. After so many of the Sultan's captains and generals ran today, Ahmet's courage will surely lead him to higher rank."

The debilitating putrefaction permeated İbrahim's senses as he toured the battlefield. The celebration that had immediately followed the battle was already a distant memory. Rumors abounded that the Crusaders had not run for their lives after all. Instead, they were said to be lurking in the nearby hills, waiting for an opportune moment to attack. For the next three days, the Sultan's victorious army held its position.

Never before had İbrahim seen such carnage. Tens of thousands of Ottoman soldiers, including Janissaries, were dead. Seeing the fallen Crusaders next to his brethren was little solace to İbrahim. Shaken with guilt, he could not fathom how he could have experienced such elation after the battle.

As he numbly surveyed the field, a seemingly distant voice said, "Is it not amazing that the Christians are all young men? Not a single graybeard is among them."

İbrahim turned to find the Sultan. He was accompanied by a large retinue of advisers. Far in the back was Ahmet, whose face wore the broadest grin İbrahim had ever seen. "If they had graybeards among them, perhaps they would not have sought us out," İbrahim heard himself say.

The Sultan nodded his head in agreement. He too was clearly moved by the sight of the carnage. İbrahim sensed that the Sultan was also affected by rage.

"What do you think should happen to men who allow their brothers to be slaughtered?" the Sultan asked.

"It is not for me to say," İbrahim humbly answered.

"It is if I ask you the question," the Sultan corrected him.

"All of the army must know that some failures will never be tolerated," İbrahim blurted out. His face turned a bright shade of red as he nervously awaited the Sultan's reply.

"Should the judgment be more harsh for those of higher rank?"

"If they were the cause of their men taking flight, then yes," İbrahim answered more steadily.

Murad gestured at the distinguished-looking man riding by his side and said, "You see, Halil Pasha, those generals must suffer for their cowardice. I will spare their lives, but they will be dressed as women and marched through the camp. Let them understand true humiliation."

Halil Pasha was the picture of restraint as he calmly replied to the Sultan's uncharacteristic display of rage. "Prince of Princes, might I suggest again that we let more time pass before carrying out such a judgment. Our resources are short enough already. We may still need these men before leaving this field."

The Sultan sighed heavily and smiled warmly at İbrahim. Suddenly, Murad's face sparkled with a look of recognition. "You were one of the men who held me to this field."

İbrahim nodded.

The Sultan got down from his mount and clapped both hands on İbrahim's shoulders. "You have my everlasting gratitude, young man. May Allah be with you always in your struggles."

"Ahmet," the Sultan called out. "Do you know this man?"

Ahmet dismounted and hurried over to the Sultan. "His name is İbrahim," Ahmet said, his face bursting with pride. "He is a close comrade of mine from the First Orta."

"The First Orta produces men of good stock," Murad said, patting İbrahim on the back before leaping back on his horse. "Now you must return to your comrades. The time to tarry on this field is long past. I need every strong hand I can muster to chase down my enemies."

İbrahim stared after his master. He could see why Ahmet was obsessed with advancement. If the reward was serving at the Sultan's side, then the risks were eminently worth taking.

"Good work," Ahmet said as he nudged his horse past İbrahim. He had deliberately let himself fall back from the Sultan's entourage. "I was proud to call you my friend." Before İbrahim could answer, Ahmet had already spurred his horse forward.

İbrahim arrived back at camp to find his comrades advancing across the battlefield towards the Crusaders' wagon train. The tight formation of wagons was only protected by a ring of shields. Its guards had left behind a fortune in spoils.

Word was sent back to the Sultan, who ordered the countryside cleansed of the retreating enemy. Within the hour, a lethal frenzy was unleashed that turned the hills red.

After several days, the Sultan set off for Edirne, from where he sent letters to his fellow Muslim rulers proudly declaring the victory. The head of King Ladislas was preserved in a cask of honey and then sent as a gift to the people of Bursa.

After being in Edirne for no more than a couple of months, the Sultan shocked his subjects and enemies. Only forty years old, the world-weary Sultan Murad II abdicated his throne in favor of his young son. Not even the relentless pleadings of Halil Pasha could make him change his mind. The Sultan had reassured himself that no new threat could come from the West for years to come. He assigned the Grand Vizier to guide the new Sultan, certain the path of his empire would remain constant.

With his customary lack of fanfare, Murad left the capital with a small entourage of his closest associates. He was off to Manisa in Anatolia to lead a life of quiet study. Before Murad's train was a day's march from the city, competing factions were busy securing support. The battle between the old guard and the "new men" was underway.

The Hexamilion • 1446

Several hundred of Mehmed's falconers and kennelmen scoured the Thracian countryside looking for game. At Halil Pasha's urging, the young Sultan indulged his passion for the hunt and left his capital. As a reward for his ceaseless efforts to draw the Janissaries away from the Grand Vizier's orbit, Şemsi was invited to serve in Mehmed's personal bodyguard. Exercising similar largesse, Şemsi invited İbrahim to serve as well. Together, they manned the entrance to the Sultan's tent.

Over the last two years, İbrahim had won Şemsi's confidence. Murad's retirement had heightened Şemsi's need for intelligence about Halil Pasha's plans. Even though Mehmed was now the Sultan, the reigns of power were still in the Grand Vizier's jealous grasp. But lately, members of the ruling class were wondering whether Halil Pasha's career had passed its peak.

İbrahim claimed he was not prepared to risk Mehmed's wrath by being too closely linked with Ahmet and, in turn, the Grand Vizier. In exchange for information about Halil Pasha's activities, İbrahim extracted Şemsi's promise that he would receive rich estates outside of Bursa when Halil Pasha retired.

Ahmet happily supplied İbrahim with information about Halil Pasha's plans. Although none of the information amounted to critical intelligence, it was sufficiently intimate to make Şemsi believe that he was linked to Halil Pasha's inner circle.

The words flowed easily from İbrahim, since he truly believed that Halil Pasha was destined to suffer a cruel fall from grace.

He also reveled in the attention and the realization that he was perfectly positioned to prosper no matter how the struggle concluded. If nothing else, Ahmet and Şemsi were sure to credit him with at least some measure of whatever success they achieved.

The hunt was a failure. Halil Pasha's assurance that the hills were laden with game was sheer fantasy. Except for yielding a few young stags, the forest had been eerily silent. The falconers and kennelmen cursed the Grand Vizier on behalf of the young Sultan.

A burly kennelman approached the Sultan's tent and curtly demanded, "I need to address the Sultan. Move."

Şemsi was a full head shorter than the kennelman, but he stood his ground and blocked the intruder's advance. "The Sultan's tent is not open to the likes of you today. It's you who will move along unless you prefer that I send you back to your dogs as a thinly sliced feast."

"Do you know who I am, fool?" Looking down at Şemsi, he bragged, "I am Hamza—"

Şemsi withdrew his scimitar and said, "Didn't you hear me? I said return to your dogs. Now!" he shouted.

For a brief moment, Hamza stared in amazement. Then he sneered contemptuously and raised his hand to brush Şemsi aside. Şemsi responded by driving the butt of his scimitar into Hamza's forehead. The kennelman hit the ground unconscious, blood pouring from a gaping wound.

"I cannot stomach these fools," Şemsi complained, looking at İbrahim for sympathy. "They lead idle lives but think that they have the ear and mind of the Sultan."

"Still, one shouldn't take them too lightly," İbrahim warned. "Their numbers are as great as our own."

"The only thing they share with us is that they too are slaves of the Sultan. Do not fear them. Unlike us, the state does not rest on their slack shoulders." Şemsi sighed. "I suppose every reward has its price. As much as I've enjoyed my entree into the Sultan's confidence, I find it almost impossible to be civil in the presence of these peacocks."

"I'd say you failed on this occasion," İbrahim quipped. "I've seen this man before," he said, pointing to the still-unconscious kennelman. "The Sultan likes him. This may be difficult to explain."

"If asked, you and I will say that Hamza tried to slash me with his knife." Şemsi leaned forward and pressed a knife into Hamza's limp hand. "It will be his word against the two of us. I'll take my chances."

İbrahim could not help but admire Şemsi. Long gone was the contempt with which he had once viewed his one-time antagonist. Şemsi had stayed true to his vision. It would have been so much easier for Şemsi to have attached himself to Halil Pasha. Instead, he let the whole world know that he had rejected the Grand Vizier. Mehmed appreciated Şemsi's commitment and often hinted that one day Şemsi would become agha of the Janissaries.

İbrahim was content to watch others ascend. He now found it satisfying to subtly manipulate the course of events from a safe vantage point. That was liberty, İbrahim decided while watching even the Sultan and the Grand Vizier victimized by the self-aggrandizing plans of others.

The Sultan's tent erupted behind them. Mehmed burst through its entrance, nearly falling over Hamza. His brow furrowed in disgust as he glanced down at the kennelman. Though the Sultan was not yet fourteen, his still-soft features had hardened into a terrible mask. "Is this news from Edirne true?" he spat at Şemsi.

Şemsi's face froze with fear. He stole a desperate glance at İbrahim, who shook his head. "I do not know of any news, oh Prince of Princes."

"Cabir," Mehmed bellowed.

A frightened messenger, covered with dust from his journey, emerged from the tent. "Yes, Master," he trembled.

"Tell Şemsi, my ever reliable eyes and ears, the news from my capital."

Cabir swallowed hard and said with a dry tongue, "The Sultan's father is on his way to the city."

Mehmed cast a lethal gaze at Cabir, who turned away.

Cabir croaked, "They say the Sultan's father is traveling with several thousand warriors. The Janissaries have taken to the streets in celebration."

Şemsi's face fell. He looked at İbrahim, who continued to look blankly at him.

"We are returning to Edirne immediately," Mehmed declared.

"What should I tell the men?" Şemsi meekly asked.

"Nothing," Mehmed answered, letting his displeasure with Şemsi show in each frustrated syllable he forced from his tongue. "I will meet with my father and accept his judgment." With a resolute look, Mehmed returned to his tent.

Şemsi collected his thoughts and then charged İbrahim, "How could you not know?" Flush with rage, he stomped on Hamza's head.

İbrahim hardly noticed the assault. Instead, he was busily repeating the same question to himself. Surely, Ahmet had known. Why would he not tell me, İbrahim wondered.

"Either you are no use to me or you've betrayed me," Şemsi said, intent upon punishing İbrahim with the same reproachful tone that Mehmed had inflicted on him. "Which is it?"

Perhaps Ahmet no longer trusts me with such sensitive information, İbrahim speculated, or he doesn't think I can hide what he tells me. İbrahim remembered the many times Ahmet had teased him about being unable to hide his emotions.

"I suppose I'm of no use to you," İbrahim simply answered after a long pause. He almost laughed as he considered the irony behind his admission.

İbrahim's earnest response muted Şemsi's anger. "Ahmet shared none of this news with you?" he asked, wanting to believe in İbrahim.

"Not a word." He was finding it satisfying to blunt Şemsi's thrusts with honesty. Perhaps I should thank Ahmet after all, he decided.

Şemsi continued to search İbrahim's face for a hint of deception. Finally, he ruefully shook his head and said, "I can't decide which one of us is the greater fool. If Mehmed has truly been deposed, then my future is bleak."

"It may not be as bleak as you believe," İbrahim consoled Şemsi. "Even if Murad has resumed the throne, Mehmed will most certainly reign again."

"Murad is only forty-two," Şemsi mumbled.

"And has already retired once."

"You may be right. But even if you're wrong, I've already attached my fate to Murad's son. I have no choice but to follow him. What of you?"

"I will stay with the *orta* in Edirne until the next campaign." His thoughts drifted back to Mihrimah. For the last two years, he had been searching for her among the swarming throngs that flocked to the rebuilt central bazaar. Each fruitless day added a new layer of frustration to his anguished soul. Still, he was prepared to search for her until the end of his days.

"It may become a quiet place for awhile," Şemsi predicted.

"If I'm lucky," İbrahim answered soberly.

It had been over two years since İbrahim had set foot in a tavern. He had forsaken that life since the day Mihrimah's visage favored him, but his Janissary brethren were not to be denied. Seeing his uniform, they demanded that he join the celebration. It was pure foolishness to protest. After a brief sigh, he joined the parade through the streets, which rang with prayers for the long life of Sultan Murad II. As the sun fell, the festivities were brought inside the taverns.

Mehmed graciously submitted himself to his father without complaint. After a brief interview, it was Mehmed's turn to retire to Manisa. Unlike his father two years earlier, though, Mehmed did not desire a quiet life of spiritual devotion.

Şemsi knew that he could no longer survive without Mehmed's support. Returning to his *orta* would surely mean suffering one indignity after another. He knew that a man can only endure so much punishment before being reduced to a rudderless shell. Doing his best to conceal his depression, Şemsi volunteered to follow the young Prince into exile.

İbrahim stood in a darkened corner watching the multitude of familiar faces. Janissaries from several *ortas* seamlessly merged with the prostitutes, who were doing a brisk business. The tavern was packed with drunken celebrants. Each face beamed with equal delight.

Their cheer should have been infectious, but nothing stirred İbrahim, who felt like he was helplessly watching a poorly matched couple celebrate their wedding. The only question to be answered was how soon their dreams would be rawly exposed.

"So that's where you've been hiding," Ahmet shouted, fumbling his way through the crowd. "I was hoping to find you." When he got within a couple of feet, he lowered his voice and said, "Who better to mark this day with than you, my dear friend?" He raised his voice again and roared, "Now come join us at our table. Hüsrev, Sinan and Cem have been asking about you."

"They're probably wondering how I've betrayed them."

"And why would they do that? I thought you had reentered their good graces after Varna."

"I had, but Varna was two years ago. Since then, you've had me spend my time with Şemsi. No doubt they believe I'm involved in some kind of plot to undermine the Grand Vizier's power."

"I hope you realize that I cannot disabuse them of that perception," Ahmet soberly replied. "If I did, I'd have to worry about word leaking out. Few stories told to more than one man remain a secret for long."

"Sadly, I must agree. You've taken on far too much risk. I told you from the start not to play this game."

Ahmet smiled and said, "You worry too much. We've won. By the time the boy regains his throne, he'll be a mature man who will not waste his time seeking vengeance over what occurred when he was an unworldly fourteen-year-old."

İbrahim followed Ahmet over to the table, where Hüsrev, Sinan and Cem were waiting. They manufactured brief smiles and politely pointed to an empty seat.

Ahmet cheered, "This is a day for celebration."

"I wonder," Hüsrev said, his voice dripping with insubordination, "is it a day of celebration for everyone?"

Ahmet glared at Hüsrev until he turned his head away. "We are all bound to the empire. As this is a great day for the empire, so it is a great day for all."

No longer feeling up to challenging Ahmet, Hüsrev changed the subject and asked, "So we will not be fulfilling Mehmed's dream of marching on Constantinople?"

"Not if Halil Pasha has his way." Ahmet flashed a knowing smile. "We need to deal with Constantine Palaeologus, the Emperor's younger brother in the Morea, before we can set our sights on that prize. Byzantium's Emperor is far less of a threat to us than his brother. Ever since Varna, Constantine Palaeologus has been crossing the Isthmus of Corinth and making inroads into Thessaly. He must be stopped before all of Greece is in turmoil."

"And what of Skanderbeg and his Albanian countrymen?" İbrahim added. "They've been wreaking havoc on our lands as well. Mustn't we put them down before moving on Byzantium?"

Ahmet nodded. "Palaeologus and Skanderbeg come first. We cannot commit the total resources needed to breach Constantinople's walls if we have such formidable enemies at our backs. Launching a campaign under such circumstances would be a disaster. I dare say that if Mehmed had shared this opinion, Halil Pasha would not have pleaded for the Sultan's return from Manisa. But all the boy could think about was Constantinople. What else could the Grand Vizier do?"

The cracks in Halil Pasha's grip over Mehmed had become too great to be ignored. The Grand Vizier had witnessed too many promising careers quickly fall apart once the smallest sign of decline appeared. He had no intention of being such a man. Mehmed's preoccupation with Constantinople had given Halil Pasha the excuse he needed to shock Murad out of retirement. In short order, Halil Pasha had reaffirmed his position while embittering Mehmed. If Mehmed was truly the empire's future, Ahmet now had to trust the Grand Vizier to make a difficult peace or suffer the consequences of choosing the wrong side.

"So now that you have your precious Sultan back, how do you plan to celebrate?" Irene asked, sidling up to Ahmet.

Ahmet was relieved to see her. "I've been asking myself that very question, Irene. What do you suggest?" He pulled her onto his lap and ran his hand around her waist.

Irene giggled and said, "I hate to admit it, Ahmet, but I really am too old now. I stopped working the floor last year. No one wants a middle-aged woman when new girls keep coming in from the country every day. Now I help manage this place." She looked around the table until her eyes fell on İbrahim. "I'll have to be content to savor the memories of past conquests, especially those who don't bother to stop by anymore," she playfully accused him.

Ahmet laughed and fondled her breasts. "You don't sound like you're pleased with your retirement."

Irene heaved a heavy sigh. She turned around on Ahmet's lap, straddled him and then pulled his face into her breasts. "A single asper would be enough to buy an hour of perfection," she said with a coquettish wink.

"I cost more than one asper, Irene," Ahmet teased. "I'll charge you three aspers to spend the next hour with me."

Irene's face fell. "You'll charge me? How dare you! Oh, you're an evil one, that's what you are." She jumped off him and started to leave.

Ahmet grabbed her hand and reeled her back into his lap. "What kind of manager allows a petty insult to interfere with business? Why don't you find us your five best girls?"

"Make it four," İbrahim corrected him.

"You're not interested, İbrahim?" Irene asked, shocked. "This is a day of miracles."

Ahmet laughed. "I'm afraid it's true. Our poor friend is lovesick for a girl he met in the central bazaar."

"That sounds romantic. Why tease him?"

"Because after meeting the girl for only a few minutes, he hasn't looked at another woman since. His search for her has been his lone passion for the last two years."

"That truly is romantic," she jealously concluded. "I didn't know Janissaries had passion for anything other than gold."

"My friend likes to be an exception," Ahmet explained. "It's an unfortunate character flaw that has disappointed more than one person."

Hüsrev, Sinan and Cem exchanged perturbed looks.

"İbrahim," Hüsrev smiled awkwardly, "why haven't you told us about this girl? We thought your new love was politics," he said, almost ready to forgive İbrahim for having spent so much time with Şemsi.

Ahmet peered into İbrahim's eyes, asking the same question. "Yes," Ahmet said, "why haven't you told your friends? They certainly seem interested."

İbrahim blushed, not knowing what to say.

Three girls arrived at the table and slid onto Hüsrev, Sinan and Cem's laps. Their tongues flickered in the men's ears, seductively promising new, creative thrills. Moments later, the three friends, hands pressed firmly against the women's wriggling hips, were on their way to the back rooms.

"Irene, I'd like a moment alone with Ahmet," İbrahim said stonily.

Ahmet slapped Irene's buttocks as she roughly pushed herself off his lap, in search of new prey. "Maybe I should come back later instead of giving you up to one of my girls."

İbrahim turned to Ahmet and asked, "Are we still friends?"

Ahmet laughed. "Are you making some kind of joke?"

"You know that joking is not one of my talents. Now answer my question. Are we still friends?"

Ahmet pushed a glass of wine in front of İbrahim. "Drink," he calmly ordered.

"First, answer my question."

"İbrahim, you've spent nearly eight years giving me advice. Now let me give you some advice of my own. There's truth in wine. So let's drink one glass to wine itself, another to the Sultan and another to the First Orta. Then I'll answer any question you ask."

They drank in silence for the next several minutes. Ahmet smiled contentedly and said, "You're my good friend, İbrahim."

"I didn't think good friends withheld information."

"A good friend makes sure his friends don't come to harm."

"That's why you didn't tell me that the Sultan was returning to Edirne? I can keep a secret better than you may realize."

"You may," Ahmet admitted. "But that wasn't my choice to make. Halil Pasha made it very clear to me that I was to tell no one."

"It sounds like Halil Pasha was worried about a fight."

"Why do you think the Sultan traveled with four thousand warriors? He also rewrote his will before leaving Manisa."

"So you're still my friend, but your position with Halil Pasha demands that there be limits on our friendship."

"Not anymore. Now that Mehmed is being packed off to Manisa, Halil Pasha will relax."

"So, what will be your reward? Will you be made a colonel of your own *orta*?"

Beaming with pride, Ahmet said, "After the next campaign."

"Next campaign?"

"Constantine Palaeologus needs to learn his place."

"So it will be the Morea."

"Yes," Ahmet beamed. "Now you own a secret."

The explosion from the cannon rang in İbrahim's ears. The stone walls of the Hexamilion were bursting apart like dry kindling wood thrown into a raging fire. Facing out onto the Gulf of Corinth, the Hexamilion was a six-mile-long string of bulwarks whose strength rivaled the formidable walls of Constantinople. It protected the narrowest stretch of the isthmus that separated Constantine Palaeologus's Morea from the Sultan's lands in Thessaly. Behind the walls lay a free Greek state, shaking with fear.

A cool breeze blew in from the isthmus, causing a shiver to run through İbrahim. "When will we be ordered to advance?" he shouted to Ahmet.

"Patience," Ahmet counseled. "The Sultan didn't march us

out of the barracks in the middle of November to start a long siege. We'll be on the move soon."

"Good," İbrahim shouted, his voice lost amid the sound of an overheated cannon bursting apart. "We should be back in Edirne. Whoever heard of beginning a campaign right before winter?"

Ahmet nodded. His normally confident expression faded. "Do you ever worry about being killed on campaign?"

"I haven't feared dying since my first battle," İbrahim answered, puzzling over why Ahmet would ask such a question.

"And why is that?"

"Because I believe I'll know when my time has come."

Ahmet laughed. "You never know when you're going to die."

"Well, perhaps then I have a sense of a life that still must be lived."

"And that gives you comfort?"

"It allows me to fight without fear."

"I wish I had your simple faith. After this battle, I will be a colonel with my own *orta* to command. My dreams are coming true. Why, then, am I certain that an arrow will find my heart? Ever since we marched out of our barracks on this campaign, I've been haunted by the same dream every night," he said, voice dropping to a mournful whisper. "I'm lying unconscious in a muddy ditch. My spirit rises out of my body and I see my blood slowly mixing with the filthy mire that is my tomb. My body fades and soon only my mouth remains, stretched wide in agony. My lips are peeled back and my teeth are jagged razors. I cannot tell whether my suffering comes from my death or because I must journey into an empty eternity."

İbrahim had never seen his friend unnerved. As Ahmet's power had grown, so had his composure. "Don't tell me you've lost heart now?" İbrahim teased, wanting to ease his friend's pain and boost his confidence. "You're still a long way off from being made our agha."

Ahmet smiled and said, "That's the problem. It's all so attainable. What can stop me except a stray arrow?"

"Which is why you shouldn't worry. What is the likelihood of that stray arrow striking you down? Now be the Janissary you're always telling me to be. If you're going to waste your time worrying about something, then worry about what you will do when we no longer march in the same *orta*."

"Keep your faith, İbrahim, and I will try to hold onto mine."

It was early December when the Sultan ordered the assault. The massive gaps in the Hexamilion's crumbling walls beckoned to the Ottomans, who dutifully threw themselves at the demoralized Greeks, who darkened the sky with a steady hail of arrows.

Driven forward by the menacing beat of the band behind them, the First Orta raced ahead, undaunted. The excitement of battle never ceased to send the blood pulsing through İbrahim's veins. With his scimitar raised high in one hand and his round shield in the other, he unleashed a rabid howl.

As they advanced, the steady stream of arrows took a heavy toll on his comrades. Falling with deadly force, the arrows sliced through their leather-bound wood and wattle shields. The wounded and dying overcame their pain long enough to demand that their brethren continue the charge.

An arrow blazed by İbrahim's shoulder, neatly slicing a thin tear in his uniform. For a brief, intense moment, his shoulder was aflame. He reflexively turned his head and watched the arrow plow deep into the shield of the charging Janissary behind him. Before the dull, heavy thud had resonated back at him, İbrahim was driven to the ground. He tried to raise his body but was met with an excruciating wave of pain that nearly made him vomit. "I've been hit," İbrahim finally moaned between increasingly rapid pants for breath, struck more with surprise than fright.

İbrahim propped himself up on his right knee. Gritting his teeth as he tried to resist the rising pain, he extended his left leg outward. The shaft of a long arrow stood bolt upright from the front of his thigh. Out from the back of his leg hung the arrowhead, a thin sliver of bright red flesh dangling on its rusty point. His eyes locked on the flesh, which seemed strangely alien to his body.

İbrahim snapped the arrowhead free from the shaft. He briefly inspected the torn tissue on the tip of the arrowhead before tossing it away in disgust. He gingerly wrapped his hand around the back of the arrow and took a deep breath. Just as he was ready to yank it free, his hand jumped away from the arrow. His entire body convulsed in pain. Another arrow had impaled itself inches from the first wound. A deep burning sensation rose from his hip. His leg and the ground around it were bathed in blood. Never before had the sweet, sickening smell of blood offended him. In seconds, it had become a pestilence.

Flat on his back, İbrahim tried to move, but felt pinned to the ground by an enormous weight. The pain was rapidly overwhelming him. He struggled to mute the scream poised on the edge of his lips, futilely looking for help while a swirling torrent of sensations dissolved his focus. The mud-caked boots of his comrades rushing past his head became a hazy, disorienting blur. As his grip on consciousness slipped away, İbrahim could not tell whether the empty roar rumbling in his ears was a distant cheer or the sound of his lost control.

"İbrahim," a familiar voice called out to him. "I thought you were finished."

İbrahim shook his head and tried to focus through a dense haze, but a debilitating lassitude held sway over him. The slightest turn of his head caused him to reel in pain and lapse into nausea. Finally, his eyes locked on Ahmet, who was staring down at him with a jittery expression. "What is this place?" İbrahim sputtered, his tongue cracking. His neck burned as he labored to pronounce each syllable.

"You're safe," Ahmet answered, obviously glad to hear his friend's voice. "You're in the infirmary."

İbrahim glanced up at the high, vaulted ceiling of the tent as he groped the thick sheepskin underneath him. The foul mix of pungent odors and the bitter moans of the wounded slowly invaded his senses. "How long have I been asleep?"

"Four days," Ahmet said.

"How can that be?"

"You're lucky to be alive. So much for your boast that you're invincible in battle," Ahmet said, forcing a laugh.

"My wounds couldn't have been that serious."

"Three arrows anywhere on a man is enough to spell the end."

"You mean two arrows," İbrahim corrected his friend.

"Three. You were hit in the leg, hip and neck."

"I remember only being hit in the leg and hip."

"Then you must've been hit in the neck while you were lying unconscious. I've seen many men spout a deadly plume of blood when struck just so in the neck. The wound cost you a lot of blood. You'll be weak for some time." His face turned grave. "The doctor says infection has set in. It's serious."

"Nonsense," İbrahim answered. "I'm not hot."

"That's because the fever just broke. You were raving like a madman only an hour ago."

"What was I saying?" İbrahim chuckled, amused by the disclosure.

"Mihrimah."

The humor drained from İbrahim's face.

It was Ahmet's turn to laugh. "You will count your blessings if you live to hear the jokes that will come your way."

"I wouldn't have thought you would be amused."

"You're fortunate I was here to speak for you. I told everyone that Mihrimah is a prostitute of wondrous talents with whom you've been fascinated." Ahmet saw the pained expression on his friend's face and quickly added, "Forgive me, but they seemed to accept what I told them."

İbrahim did not argue. He tried to move his left leg, but only his toes twitched. He gently ran his hand along the leg, which felt like it had been roasting over a fire. His face turned ashen. "Will I be able to walk again?"

"The infection is in the leg," Ahmet answered. "We'll have to wait and see. But don't worry, you won't have to recuperate in this wretched place. I've arranged to have you sent back to Edirne along with members of the Sultan's divan. You'll be treated by the best physicians."

"So tell me, were we victorious?"

A bright gleam radiated from Ahmet's face. "We smashed them. The Greeks ran for their lives, Constantine Palaeologus included. All of the Morea lies open to us. Hüsrev, Sinan and Cem are tracking down our enemies as we speak. The Greeks will be in complete vassalage soon enough. Halil Pasha says it's just a matter of time before Palaeologus sends an envoy formalizing the cessation of hostilities."

"And what of you? What *orta* do you now command, Colonel?"

"The First," Ahmet beamed.

"Our *orta*? How can that be?"

"The colonel was made a member of the Sultan's divan immediately after the battle. His first act was to reward me with his former position. So you see, it has all worked out for the best." Ahmet paused playfully for a moment and then said, "Congratulations on your promotion. You're an officer now, my second in command. Of course, your leg will have to heal before you can take your rightful place by my side."

İbrahim beamed with pride as he imagined being saluted by his fellow Janissaries. "If only Şemsi were here," he laughed.

"I can just see it," Ahmet howled, convulsing in such loud laugher that even the worst of the wounded turned their heads.

"Well, neither one of us will get to see Şemsi's reaction to your triumph. I imagine he'll remain safely tucked away in Manisa with the Prince for quite awhile."

"I hope so." Ahmet gained control of his laugher. "I want to be certain that my grip on the *orta* is firm before Mehmed regains the throne."

İbrahim was startled by Ahmet's confession. It was the first time he had heard his friend acknowledge the peril to which he had subjected himself. "You think that commanding our *orta* will be sufficient to protect you?"

"Halil Pasha thinks so," Ahmet said with more than a hint of uncertainty in his voice. "Of course, I hope to have risen higher by the time I'm faced with a new Sultan."

"So why this sudden change? You didn't use to worry so much about Mehmed. You came through the battle unscathed. Doesn't that convince you that your dreams of doom are mere fantasy?"

"I didn't tell you everything the other day," Ahmet said, eyebrows knitted with concern. He leaned forward to whisper in İbrahim's ear. "You were right to warn me as you have in the past. Halil Pasha's grip on power was slipping worse than I let on. I can't begin to tell you the tirades he had to endure from Mehmed. Every time he tried to focus Mehmed's attention on the more pressing threats to the empire, Mehmed accused him of being afraid to besiege Constantinople.

"The Prince is a powerful personality. But conquering Constantinople is hardly the extent of his dreams. When that city falls to him—and rest assured that even its fabled walls will be no match for Mehmed's will—a new Red Apple will dominate his quest for total dominion. Rome and Buda will shake with fear. He's driven to get what he wants and seems certain to punish those who stand or stood in his way."

"Then you'll have to make yourself an indispensable asset to the state," İbrahim advised.

"Agreed. I may also have to reach out to Şemsi while I still hold the upper hand. Once I begin to lose ground, I'm lost. Şemsi will punish me for his exile."

"Is it becoming warm?" His cheeks and ears were turning ruby red and a dull ache was beginning to pulse inside his head.

Ahmet smiled paternalistically at İbrahim. "Rest."

İbrahim nodded. "First bring me some food before the fever returns. After all, a Janissary travels best on a full stomach."

İbrahim was jolted awake as the supply cart carrying him and booty from the Greek despot's camp careened through a deep rut in the road. The lower left side of İbrahim's body ached horribly. He stifled each moan while never yielding to a deep sleep. Better to lose precious sleep, he decided, than for the world to see him suffer like any other man.

The physicians had attended to him as though he were the Sultan himself. Fresh bandages and treatments to his wounds were applied several times a day. The feverish spells were replaced by an acute awareness of the pain in his left leg. Besides the horrific damage to the muscle tissue, the arrow had scraped the bone. The physicians had confidently assured him he would live, but carefully avoided answering questions about whether he would regain the full use of his leg.

When he managed to ignore his damaged leg, İbrahim remembered Mahmut's assurances that he would devote himself to capturing the Red Apple once confronted with his own mortality. Instead, he yearned for Mihrimah as never before.

No longer was she simply a tantalizing vision of purity. She was an essential element of his being. "Mihrimah is the answer to my empty heart. My Red Apple," he whispered to himself. İbrahim remembered the advice his father had passed down to him through his mother. I will pursue her until she is mine, he swore to himself.

The Frontier • 1448

İbrahim dragged his leg behind him as he tried to push through the crowded bazaar. Each step caused a wrenching wave of pain to radiate up from his thigh and into his neck. Unable to generate any power, he could not cut through the masses with his customary bluster. İbrahim cursed his misfortune and finally gave in to his anger. "Move," he barked into the frigid air.

The crowd obediently stepped aside. İbrahim tilted himself up on the tip of his toes and surveyed the bazaar. "It is she," he rejoiced. İbrahim saw the back of the girl's head, silky black hair delicately bouncing, beckoning to him. Her baskets were full and she was rounding a corner. "I will lose her," he gasped, suddenly realizing that she was leaving the bazaar.

İbrahim took a deep breath to steel himself against the coming ache before launching himself forward. Muttering curses like a senile beggar, he pointed his head down and raced ahead like a tormented bull. "Out of my way, vermin! I'm here on the Sultan's business." When he got within several feet of the girl, he reached for her shoulder. His fingers clutched empty air. İbrahim's delicate balance was upset and he clumsily stumbled into the startled girl, nearly knocking her to ground.

"I didn't do anything," the girl cried.

İbrahim's heart sank. He had been sure that she was Mihrimah.

"Did she steal something, Sir?" A young Janissary saluted İbrahim. He was accompanied by a cadet, who locked his hand on the girl's thin shoulder, causing her to blanch. They eagerly waited for a sign of approval from their superior officer.

İbrahim considered answering yes. He wanted to punish her for not being Mihrimah. After a lengthy pause in which the girl's face melted under a torrent of tears, İbrahim finally said, "Let her go. I thought she was someone else."

The cadet released the girl. They watched her sprint into the blinding sunlight. In seconds, she was gone, another bitter memory.

İbrahim was growing increasingly desperate. While supposedly rehabilitating his leg by taking every available patrol, he had scoured the capital during the last year. Risking the suspicion of others, he gave an exacting description of Mihrimah to every patrolman, with orders that she be brought to him. He told them she had stolen a rare heirloom from a member of the Sultan's divan. So far, nine girls had been produced, fear being their lone similarity.

"Did you think she was the girl?" the young Janissary asked.

İbrahim looked closely at the man. He had never seen him before. "Do we know each other?"

"No, Sir."

"My reputation precedes me," İbrahim sighed.

The young Janissary's face turned a bright shade of red. "I didn't mean to offend you, Sir."

"Of course not," İbrahim agreed, putting his subordinate at ease. "It's not your fault. You're dismissed."

The pain in his leg was becoming hard to bear. He limped over to a fruit stall and leaned against its counter. Months of frustration had taught him that the pain would dog him for days. He was beginning to believe that he would never walk right again, much less return to the battlefield.

"May I help you, Sir?" the owner asked, tactfully trying to move İbrahim off his stand.

İbrahim spun his head around and glared at the portly man, who recoiled.

"Please accept a gift," the merchant said, hoping to make peace. He held out an apple.

İbrahim inspected the apple and took it without so much as a nod. He continued to stare at the apple with an increasingly bemused expression. Finally, he closed his eyes and took a large bite. He savored the rich juices released from its firm texture. He opened his mouth to take another bite, but then snapped his mouth shut, put the apple down on the counter, and lumbered away.

"I will never find her in Edirne," İbrahim complained to Ahmet as he rubbed his leg. It was a silent compulsion that now marked his behavior.

They were standing alone atop a watchtower that commanded the Thracian countryside. Winter had come early. Heavy autumn rains had given way to frigid temperatures. A light coating of frost covered the muddy roads leading up to the gates, making travel a stubborn hardship. İbrahim shared the travelers' misery.

"No, you won't," Ahmet agreed. "She and her father have surely moved on."

"But where?" İbrahim asked. "If I were to search every hovel in the empire, I still might not find her. She may have left our dominions altogether to live among the infidels."

"İbrahim," Ahmet said soberly, "have you considered that she may be dead? Many noncombatants have died over the last few years. Even if she lives, she may be married. The likely reality is that you will never see her again. Perhaps it's time for you to be thinking about moving on before you forfeit your life to a dream."

"Do you wish me to give up my quest because you're concerned about how I may affect your political aspirations?"

Ahmet paused to let the tension drain from the air. "I will not apologize for my professional interests. But don't deny my concern for you. You've been a brilliant adviser to me but you're a fool when it comes time to counsel yourself."

İbrahim's face softened. "I'm sorry, Ahmet. But how can I give her up when I know she's alive?"

"And just how do you know that?"

"Because I wake up with hope in my heart every day."

"Save some of that mystical vision for the real world. I'll share a secret with you: We'll be marching on Albania by summer. If we're successful in the lowlands, we'll engage Skanderbeg deep in the Albanian mountains. I'm told that his mountain fortress at Kruje is impregnable. It's going to be a bloody fight. To make matters worse, Skanderbeg has worked his people into a frenzy. They're ready to bite and scratch at us until the Sultan recognizes their sovereignty, even if every last man, woman and child dies in the process."

"I can't possibly join you," İbrahim said. "You know that. I can barely walk the streets of Edirne. Hüsrev will have to stand at your side in my place."

"Of course he will," Ahmet agreed, "but you will still serve a very important role by staying behind in Edirne. It looks like the Sultan is preparing to bring the Prince back to the capital. Halil Pasha tells me that the Prince is already in Thrace. It seems that a slave girl bore him a baby boy in Dimotika a few weeks ago, a new heir—Bayezid. I suppose the Sultan wants to try his own hand at molding his son. I need you to keep an eye on things for me. If Mehmed returns, renew your friendship with Şemsi. Find that common bond that will draw us together."

İbrahim frowned. "You suppose that Şemsi still considers me a friend? He wasn't very happy with me when we parted."

"Even angry men like Şemsi want friends, especially if they believe there's value to the relationship."

As İbrahim perfunctorily nodded at his friend, his face drew inwards until deep lines crossed his forehead and his lips were nearly sucked into his mouth. "I can't stay in Edirne," he finally blurted out.

"But you've already agreed that you can't come with the corps to Albania. Edirne is where you're needed. Where else is there for you?"

"Anywhere but Edirne," İbrahim flatly declared. "I can't stay here anymore knowing that my search must continue elsewhere."

"And where would you want to go?"

"The frontier. I've heard that some of the people who were driven away by the fire headed towards the Danube. Have Halil Pasha commission me to tour the frontier along the Bulgarian-Wallachian border. I'll inspect the state of our defenses and strengthen our outposts. And I'll look for Mihrimah."

"You're speaking madness. Think about what you're saying. You wish to travel hundreds of miles on a bad leg hoping to stumble across a girl you met for a few minutes in the bazaar years ago."

"It's what I want. You owe me. If nothing else, at least you won't have to worry about me making a fool of myself in the capital while you're gone."

In a low, soothing voice, Ahmet said, "You've never been to the frontier. I spent the first two years of my career serving in garrisons along the Wallachian border. It's a memory I despise. Unless armies are on the move, practically nothing happens. You'll be cursing me for obtaining that commission in less than a month."

İbrahim stared silently into Ahmet's eyes. Minutes passed. Ahmet eventually heaved a heavy sigh. "So be it, then. You will curse me."

The Wallachian peasant was pushed by three burly guards into the cramped room that served as İbrahim's office and living quarters. Faded gray paint peeled off the cracked, wood-planked walls and a musty odor clogged the air. The exterior wall was punctuated by a small window facing a nearby storage shack, which cast a dark shadow on the room for most of the day. Except for the few dim rays of sunlight casting a flickering spotlight on İbrahim's straw bed, the room's sole illumination came from a rusty oil lamp placed thoughtfully next to a pile of correspondence at the center of his desk.

The peasant's feet became entangled in a worn throw rug, causing him to crumple face-first onto the cold stone floor. The sergeant commanding the guards grinned maliciously. "We caught him trying to set the armory on fire, Sir."

İbrahim slowly rose from the chair behind his desk and stared into the eyes of the prisoner, whose bloodied face was growing swollen from the beating administered by the guards. A defiant, unflinching stare met him.

"What is his name, Sergeant?"

"He won't say anything, but we heard his comrades call him Nicu before we killed them."

A bright fire blazed in Nicu's unblinking, petulant eyes. Rarely had İbrahim seen such hardened resolve. He fought the urge to look away. İbrahim ignored what lay behind the eyes and asked, "What infested rathole spawned you?"

Nicu sneered and spat, "It doesn't exist anymore. Your men destroyed my village and my family last week."

The sergeant smashed his boot into the side of Nicu's head. "I can't stand unfinished work. It's time for you to join your family." He withdrew his scimitar and raised it over his head.

"Sergeant," İbrahim stopped him.

"Of course," the sergeant apologized. "No sense making a mess here. I'll remove the prisoner. I've been at this post too long. These Wallachians make my blood boil."

İbrahim pitied the man. Still, he knew that Nicu's fate was to die. The punitive expeditions across the Danube struck İbrahim as folly. The Wallachians were not so easily cowed. Unless we subjugate them to our sovereignty, he decided, we are inviting more trouble than we are solving.

The sergeant waited for İbrahim to order the execution of the prisoner. Shaking his head to convey the absurdity of the situation, İbrahim ordered, "Make it quick."

The sergeant noticed the subtle rebuke and smirked. He turned to leave and then said, "Oh, I almost forgot. A letter came for you from Edirne." The sergeant handed the letter to İbrahim and beat a hasty exit, eager to enjoy executing Nicu.

İbrahim inspected the letter. The parchment was bound together by the unbroken seal of the Grand Vizier. İbrahim smiled and gingerly broke the seal.

Greetings, İbrahim:

I pray that Allah is in your heart and that you are satisfied with your commission. Forgive me if I write with a heavy hand. In these times, even the seal of the Grand Vizier is not inviolate.

Our spies in Buda say that Yanko is planning to take the field again. Apparently, it is not enough for him to hold the regency over Hungary. He thirsts for Edirne and the chance to regain his prestige. If we can prevent Yanko from linking his forces with Skanderbeg's Albanians, we may be able to stomp out his ambitions for good. He certainly will not find help elsewhere. Pope Nicholas V has shown that he is not worthy of his predecessor's valor. Except for granting an indulgence to those who join the fight, this peace-loving Pope will not rally Christendom to Yanko's cause. Help is also not likely to come from Venice. They are enjoying a profitable peace with us. Brankovic will not fight either. He is afraid to aid Yanko for fear that the Sultan will convert Serbia back to vassalage. Of course, Yanko always finds a way.

As I told you before you left, we will march against Skanderbeg's Albania. The Prince will accompany us. Mehmed has returned to Edirne, a new father and a willing son. Few of our brothers are smiling, unless you count Şemsi. Our old friend is different somehow. I saw him on the street. He simply nodded as if to say that I had been seen and that was all. It seems the volcano is extinct and a mountain remains.

I need you, my friend. Now is the time to make the peace with Şemsi. Only you can make that happen. So train your mind on uncovering the tie that will bind Şemsi to me. Remember, finding what you seek will do you little good if you don't get the chance to enjoy your prize.

Your loyal friend, Ahmet

İbrahim felt the thick parchment underneath his gloves and pictured the invigorating bustle of Edirne. Ahmet had been right. The frontier was a dreary place. He had visited four fortresses, each the same configuration of tightly knit palisades encircling weather-beaten barracks and a trading post. Inside were hundreds of bored soldiers. With Yanko silent since Varna, the only excitement came from raiding the Wallachian settlements on the northern bank of the Danube.

Rubbing his leg as he walked, İbrahim limped into the gray, early afternoon sun and squinted to adjust his eyes. The relentless cold had made a home in his leg, reversing the limited recovery he had experienced in Edirne. He hoped that his leg would rebound once he returned to the baths, but he readied himself for the worst. The longer the pain persisted, the more İbrahim decided that he was likely to die a cripple.

İbrahim looked over at the main gate. The sergeant had not wasted any time. Nicu's freshly severed head was mounted on a pike high above the gate. Below the pike was a scimitar planted butt-first in the ground, its freshly bloodstained blade curving upward with deadly menace towards the Wallachian.

"We usually have several heads adorning our main gate," the captain apologized. "Unfortunately, last week we had a severe rainstorm, which blew the heads away."

The captain stood a half head shorter than İbrahim, but with his deceptively long, sinewy arms and knotty fingers, he seemed İbrahim's equal. As with most middle-aged veterans, the captain's face described his career. Years of exposure to withering cold had dotted the thickened skin of his face with patches of burst capillaries, which drew attention to the growing network of deepening crags running down his pointy cheekbones. His broad nose was pushed inward so that his nostrils flared perversely into oblong slits. The only signs of life lay in his dry, hazel eyes, which patiently absorbed his surroundings with wry condescension.

İbrahim was surprised by the captain's unexpected appearance but managed to suppress any reaction. "A poor use of the scimitar," İbrahim coolly observed.

The captain smiled proudly. "We make it our business to let all know that punishment is swift and sure for those who would raise a hand against us. I have a scimitar planted blade up at the foot of every severed head to let our enemies know that my scimitar is upon them even in death."

"You have no need to explain yourself to me, Captain," Ibrahim said, affecting disdain. "Your men appear to be quite diligent in their efforts."

The captain smiled, deferentially masking his discomfort.

Halil Pasha had granted Ibrahim temporary command of each garrison he visited. The suspicious overtures of the captains were Ibrahim's lone source of amusement. He knew their interest was not genuine and did not waste time trying to cultivate new allies. Instead, Ibrahim took childish delight in reminding the captains that they were no longer the lords of the lands commanded by their fortresses. They responded to Ibrahim's abuse with respectful obedience. If they had any chance of being reassigned away from their miserable commands, they knew it was necessary to insinuate themselves into the good graces of men such as Ibrahim.

"Have you found the border secure?" the captain asked nervously.

"Heads on pikes tell me nothing," Ibrahim sniffed, deflating the captain. "I will inspect the lands around your garrison to see if the people are obedient." He had used the same simple statement to justify his endless tours of the villages surrounding the fortresses.

Stung by Ibrahim's condescension, the captain took a deep breath and forced a hollow smile. "I will assign several men to ride with you."

Ibrahim offered a derisive nod. After three months away from Edirne's comforts, he had discovered that the captains were cut from the same mold. Boring but effective, he concluded, deciding that the empire needed such men if its borders were to remain secure. "What's the name of the largest village in the district?"

The captain could not resist laughing at Ibrahim's question. "None of the villages in this district have a name. The largest village has not much more than two hundred people. No one wants to live this close to the border when they can live far more safely in the Bulgarian heartland. We attract runaways, fools and Wallachian peasants who steal across the Danube. If you're a Wallachian, I suppose any place is better than living in a village that is sure to be put to the torch," he chuckled.

İbrahim welcomed the news. One of his greatest concerns had been that Mihrimah might have left Ottoman territory entirely. "Have they converted to Islam?"

"These people are an independent-minded lot. They're not so easily led. Still, some have converted to avoid taxes."

"Hardly a noble reason," İbrahim observed.

"I suppose it doesn't matter how you find your way into a man's heart as long as you succeed, eh, Sir?"

The captain was now warming to İbrahim and said, "Perhaps you would like to ride my horse? She has been magnificently trained. She'll give you the most gentle ride. Keep your leg from aching, that's what she'll do."

"Thank you, Captain." Where his leg was concerned, İbrahim had no compunction about accepting the generosity of others.

With a pleased expression pasted on his usually gloomy face, the captain rushed across the compound to take care of İbrahim's needs. İbrahim watched the men snap to attention as the captain barked out orders.

After several minutes passed, three soldiers approached İbrahim on horseback, drawing the captain's horse behind them. The leader of the group was the same sergeant who had beheaded Nicu. He held the reigns of the horse in his fist as if he were a mother shielding her child from harm. The sergeant saluted İbrahim and respectfully said, "We'd best be moving along, Sir. The sun sets early this time of year."

İbrahim took the reigns from the sergeant's band. "Thank you, Sergeant. You needn't worry about the captain's horse," he said, discerning the trepidation that appeared on the sergeant's rugged features. "I'm in no condition to take this horse for much more than a stroll. Now help me mount this beast."

The two other soldiers dismounted and helped İbrahim climb into the saddle. It was all İbrahim could do to mask his pain as his leg banged against the side of the horse. Each vibration dominated his senses.

The two helpers effortlessly leaped aboard their mounts. It was obvious they had grown quite skilled while patrolling the countryside. Trained to be a foot soldier, İbrahim had never been impressed by the abilities of the *sipahi* knights. Horses were a sign of rank but seldom substance, he had decided. Like any other Janissary, İbrahim proudly claimed that the Sultan's victories came from the dogged determination of the infantry. But as he watched the two men confidently maneuver their horses, he had to stifle his jealousy.

"We are to escort you to the nearest village, Sir?" the sergeant asked.

İbrahim grimaced, which the men interpreted as a sullen nod of agreement. They stealthily cast sideways glances at each other as if to say, "Here is another fool from the capital."

The four men dug their boots into the sides of their horses and started for the village. A steady, cold breeze beat against İbrahim's forehead, slowly numbing his face. Aside from the horses' loping gait, only the low whisper of the wind greeted his ears. Empty and desolate, the snow-covered lowland landscape was cast under an ashen sky that disguised the underlying beauty of the country. The somber surroundings drained his hope.

Now I know why Ahmet so easily agreed to let me come here, he thought. He assumes this search will drain my last bit of hope. Mihrimah will become the distant memory Ahmet thinks she should be. With each passing day, İbrahim became more convinced that his Red Apple would elude him.

After riding for an hour, İbrahim became inured to the pain in his leg, which assumed a dull, throbbing ache. Relief came in the form of the village. The rich aroma of burning wood wafted towards them. Seduced by the allure of warmth, İbrahim and his escorts subconsciously dug their heels deeper into their mounts.

The village was a collection of unimpressive wooden hovels linked together by a series of disjointed muddy paths. The people stared up at İbrahim and his entourage with a mixture of fear and curiosity. Heads turned down as İbrahim slowly made his way towards the center of the village. The women and children scurried back inside their homes.

"What happened to this place?" İbrahim asked the sergeant.

"I'm not sure I know what you mean."

"Most of these buildings look fairly new."

A look of recognition passed across the sergeant's face. "Yanko. His army torched the village on the way to Varna."

A dry, hacking cough announced the presence of a middle-aged man, who began to cross their path. As he sped up his pace to avoid them, he made eye contact with İbrahim. Their eyes locked for an instant. Then the man snapped his head down and ran the rest of the way across the street.

Was it a look of recognition that he had seen in the man's eyes, İbrahim asked himself. He thought he remembered the man, but was not sure whether he was simply responding to the man's aspect. İbrahim drew his horse to a stop and watched the man hurry down a small alley. Every several feet, the man looked back over his shoulder.

"Is everything all right, Sir?" the sergeant asked.

"I think that man knows me," İbrahim answered, nodding his head towards the alley.

"Would you like me to bring him back to you?"

İbrahim thought for a moment and said, "I'm sure there are many men who have seen me while I have campaigned across these lands. I doubt our meetings were pleasant. It's unlikely he wishes to remake my acquaintance. I think it's time that we returned to the fortress. It's growing dark." He turned his horse around and started back.

The sergeant gazed upward. "We have a couple more hours of sun left, Sir," he said, obviously perplexed. "Plenty of time to inspect the rest of the village."

İbrahim ignored him.

The sergeant looked over at his men and groused, "Edirne shouldn't be worrying about us. The Sultan's divan should be worrying about its own emissaries."

He then spurred his horse forward and caught up to İbrahim.

"Is there anything else my men and I can do for you?"

"Do your men ever tour this countryside alone?"

"It's safe enough, if that's what you mean."

İbrahim smiled. "You and your men can warm your feet in front of a nice warm fire tomorrow. I won't be needing you."

İbrahim set off for the village early the next day after giving strict orders that he not be followed. He wanted to look the villager in the eyes once more. An inner voice had advised him to do so in privacy.

Realizing that his safety was the captain's responsibility, İbrahim assumed the captain would have him followed. Menace was the only deterrent İbrahim knew. He warned the captain that he would periodically double back to make sure his orders were being followed. If he found they were not, İbrahim promised that punishmet would be unreasonably severe.

The captain and his men were glad to be rid of İbrahim for the day. They had been able to bear İbrahim's condescension, but his growing peculiarity made them uncomfortable. The most seasoned member of the garrison had never known a visitor to tour the countryside without a patrol to protect him.

As İbrahim disappeared into the distance, the captain and the sergeant watched him from the tower of the main gate. The captain said, "A strange man indeed. You must tell me again what happened at the village. I want to know about this man he saw."

The sergeant repeated the story in exacting detail for the third time. Each time he embellished his own role as the attentive escort.

"These Janissaries are an odd lot," the captain concluded. "They think they're better than the rest of us. They even look down their noses at the *sipahi*s. That's not to say I won't give them credit for their courage and loyalty to the Sultan. I've seen their charges—fearless, sometimes suicidal. Who would believe such dedicated warriors are slaves, stolen from their families as children. Maybe this İbrahim thinks he's seen his long-lost father or uncle."

"I can still have my men catch up with him," the sergeant offered. "The man's leg is in no condition to do much more than a steady trot."

"Another oddity," the captain added, knitting his brow together in deeper thought. "Why would the Grand Vizier appoint a man who is practically a cripple to tour the frontier? Certainly there were able-bodied men available to do the same job."

"Perhaps we're better off not knowing the answer to these questions. I wouldn't want to make an enemy of the Grand Vizier."

"Nor I, Sergeant, but learning more about this man and running afoul of the Grand Vizier are not necessarily the same thing. Besides, some of my old friends in Edirne have told me that appointments in the empire won't always be tied to holding favor with the Grand Vizier. You never know when a small piece of information today can have great benefits tomorrow. Have our friend followed."

The sergeant arched an eyebrow as he saluted.

"A word, Sergeant: caution. The men you choose must be your best. If our friend learns about your assignment, I'll have you sown up inside a rug and thrown into the Danube."

The sergeant saluted again and said, "You'll have your first report by nightfall."

İbrahim had taken his time. He knew that there would be little activity until the village markets hit their stride at midday. In the meantime, he was content to struggle with the mystery. İbrahim had never been anywhere near this part of the empire. If this villager knew him, he had traveled far. Yet the captain had made it clear that most of the immigrants were from Wallachia. Where had this man been and why had he chosen a desolate village along the war-torn frontier?

İbrahim's entrance into the village was met with the same reaction as the day before. Although there was no escaping the notice that his rich uniform compelled, İbrahim tried to infiltrate the masses. He paid a modest fee to put his horse in a stable and started traveling by foot. It did little good. İbrahim towered over most of the villagers. His felt cap heralded his advance. Not surprisingly, the villagers beat a path away from him, heads pointed down.

İbrahim positioned himself at the central marketplace and waited. As the hours passed, he merged into the surroundings and the villagers' discomfort gave way to cautious acceptance. By midafternoon, the normal buzz of the marketplace had returned.

It seemed to be a hollow accomplishment. İbrahim's prey was nowhere to be seen. But just as he was ready to retrieve his horse, the villager emerged at the far end of the marketplace. Smiling broadly through his now distinctive hacking cough, the man bought a loaf of bread. He exchanged pleasantries with the merchant for several minutes and then waved farewell.

As the villager turned to leave, he fell into İbrahim, who had stealthily maneuvered his way across the marketplace. The man's eyes opened wide in surprise, his feet rooted to the ground. As İbrahim steadily gazed down on the slightly built man, his heart began to flutter. For the first time in nearly four years, a magnificent surge enlivened his dormant senses. The omnipresent pain in his leg and heart disappeared as though they had never existed. İbrahim warmly clamped his giant hands on the frightened man and said, "Mihrimah."

The man's face turned ashen. He looked as though he would faint. Smiling from ear to ear, İbrahim had to hold him steady. "Breathe, breathe," İbrahim gently counseled.

The man shook himself loose and bent over to grip his knees. A series of dry, wrenching coughs rocked him. Just as the attack seemed ready to stop, a new wave of convulsions gripped him. İbrahim stood back, unsure of what to do next. In between coughs, the man looked up with a panicked expression. The man then began to wave his hands frantically in front of him.

It was Mihrimah. She was running across the marketplace to join her stricken father. İbrahim watched her, utterly thunderstruck. She was more beautiful than he remembered. The girlish fullness of her ivory-complexioned face had been replaced by striking high cheeks, a delicate mouth and a strong chin. But her eyes moved him most. They were still the same rich, compassionate eyes that had filled his dreams with joy over the last several years. Watching Mihrimah rush forward, her face awash with concern, İbrahim felt the sweetness of her soul.

"Father," her voice cracked as she knelt down beside him. "What happened?"

"Go away," he coughed. "Now."

"No, you don't understand. It's Mihrimah," she pleaded, afraid that he had lost his senses.

He tried to speak but could only produce a vile deposit of phlegm. She wrapped her arms around him and whispered, "It's going to be all right." Tears poured down her cheeks.

"May I help?" İbrahim said in the most compassionate tone he could muster.

Mihrimah looked over at İbrahim, who was leaning over her father. For a moment, she was startled by his uniform. Speaking from reflex, she sputtered, "Thank you, but that won't be—" before coming to an abrupt stop.

İbrahim opened his mouth but his thoughts found no expression. He had been waiting for this moment for years. Beautiful visions, each more fanciful than the last, had seduced him. Never had he considered what his first words might be. Rather than holding her tightly in his arms as he had assumed he would, İbrahim found his face melting with perspiration.

Mihrimah did not notice his embarrassment. She was torn between aiding her father and looking at İbrahim. "I know you," she said in a halting whisper.

"No, Mihrimah," her father coughed. The attack was beginning to pass. "You don't know this man. Now go. I'll follow you shortly."

İbrahim's heart sank. He wanted to silence her father but did not dare contradict him. Instead, he humbly said, "You need not fear me, Sir."

Mihrimah placed her hand on İbrahim's forearm and shook her head to silence him. Just as İbrahim was certain that his world was crashing down around him, her long, thin fingers softly squeezed his arm for the briefest moment. Her touch was the essence of the heavenly spirit that had sustained him.

Fighting through a tingling fog, İbrahim drew himself up to his full height and said, "I will leave you in peace."

Mihrimah stood as well. She pursed her lips to hold back a smile, but her eyes glowed with a feverish warmth that filled his heart with joy. Mihrimah then whispered, "The marketplace is best enjoyed at noon."

With a grand, sweeping gesture of his hand that he had seen foreign emissaries bestow upon the Grand Vizier, İbrahim said, "May Allah be with you and your daughter, Sir." İbrahim then walked away. A sweet ache took root inside him. Although he was dragging his leg, his pain was a faraway thought.

With a more demanding edge to his voice, İbrahim repeated his warning to the captain early the next morning. To his surprise, the captain blithely wished him a safe journey, showing no hint of the obsequious affect that had previously marked their interactions.

Taking no chances, İbrahim set out in the opposite direction from Mihrimah's village. He quickly visited two villages, all the while keeping a watchful eye on the sky. By the time the sun had reached its zenith, İbrahim sat comfortably in the marketplace.

Mihrimah did not disappoint him. She was already in the marketplace. Trying not to draw attention to himself, İbrahim subtly waved to her. Caution did not enter her mind. She raced across the marketplace to join him.

For a long moment, they stared at each other with expectant gazes. Finally, İbrahim haltingly said, "My name is İbrahim."

I sound apologetic, he thought, certain that he had committed an unpardonable gaffe. To his surprise, Mihrimah maintained the same affectionate gaze.

"My name is Mihrimah," she blushed while sharply pointing her head downwards and suppressing a nervous laugh.

"I know," İbrahim said proudly. He forced himself to look directly at her. A tremulous wave of euphoria swept over him as the first feelings of a new kind of courage surfaced. "We met several years ago in Edirne. I heard your father call your name." He took a deep breath and said, "Speaking your name has been my greatest joy since the day I first laid eyes on you." This time the words resonated from deep within him.

The bare honesty of what he had said surprised İbrahim. He expected Mihrimah to blush. Instead she eagerly scrutinized his face. "I remember you well. You saved me from that horrible man. I never got the chance to thank you."

"You could have scolded me and I would have been grateful. I've been searching for you ever since."

Mihrimah's face continued to glow. Her face then sank abruptly. "But what does a Janissary want with me?"

İbrahim laughed. "My friends ask me the same question."

"And what did you tell them?"

"I'm not even sure. How do you explain such things?"

Mihrimah smiled warmly. "I understand perfectly. I too have thought of you often since that day we met."

"Then why was I not able to find you? I searched Edirne night and day more times than I can remember."

"Father and I left immediately after the great fire."

"Many left the capital after the fire," İbrahim said, embarrassed over the role of his Janissary brothers in creating the disaster.

"Father never told me why he wanted to leave. He simply said we were through with the city. Then we made the long journey to this place. Father said that he had a brother who lived here, but I knew he was lying. The truth is that we simply headed north until we reached the Danube."

"So why did you leave?"

"Are you asking because you really don't know the answer or because you want me to flatter you?" she asked coquettishly.

İbrahim blushed. Then he took another sip from his internal well of courage and answered, "I want to be flattered."

"Then you'll be happy to learn that I could not stop talking about you. Like you, I can't explain why I felt as I did—do," she blushed. "I spent the first two days after we met telling Father over and over again that you were the bravest man I had ever seen and that I couldn't believe a great warrior was so compassionate. And, of course, I asked Father if he thought you were handsome. When he grudgingly said 'yes,' I asked him what he found handsome about you." She laughed sweetly and said, "Oh, I must have asked him a thousand more questions about you.

"I finally realized my mistake one night when Father tossed his bowl of soup from the dinner table. It was the first time I had ever seen Father lose his temper. He told me that a good woman had no place in the life of a Janissary. I insisted you were different. He said it didn't matter. He claimed you were not allowed to marry. Of course, I didn't believe him, but I said nothing about you after that night. He used the fire as an excuse to keep us apart. But fate has brought us together. How else could you have found me in this sad place?"

Her words rang sweetly in his ears like a siren's song. "Your father still doesn't want us to be together."

Mihrimah nodded. "He's already warned me to stay off the streets. But Father might change his mind if I could prove him wrong. You are allowed to marry, aren't you?"

İbrahim was speechless. The pain in his leg suddenly burned with renewed ferocity.

"Oh, no," she moaned. "Oh, no." Her eyes filled with tears.

"Your father is right," İbrahim finally said. "The prohibition against marriage is clear and absolute. But that doesn't mean we must be apart."

"You would be willing to leave your friends for me?"

"Yes, but my will is not enough. Behind my rich uniform and training, I am nothing more than a slave. You are more free than I. I can't simply decide to leave the corps. I'd lose my head and put you in harm's way at the same time."

"Could you be granted permission?"

"There are those who have been granted retirement." İbrahim sighed. "Unfortunately, their retirements were rewards for some fabulous deed or because they had served a lifetime and could no longer benefit their Sultan. I've never heard of a man being released from his bonds for a woman."

"What of your injury, then?" Mihrimah pressed, looking directly at his leg for the first time. "How can you fight?"

"I'm young," İbrahim answered wistfully, "and young men are expected to recover from their wounds."

"Then how can we be together?" Mihrimah blurted out.

"We don't have to marry," İbrahim said softly.

Mihrimah reddened. "I'm no man's plaything."

"No, no," İbrahim raised his hands in protest. "I didn't mean we could never be together as man and wife. I only meant that we could not be together as man and wife now."

"What will change?"

"We live in a turbulent time. Borders change every year. Sometimes rulers change with the same frequency. In the last four years, Sultan Murad has stepped down and reassumed the throne. King Ladislas and Pope Eugenius are only memories. Brankovic is an old man and the Byzantine Emperor is dying. Surely there will be an opportunity for us."

"And in the meantime?"

"We'll get to know each other."

The Courtship

"Tell me again," the captain said, rubbing his hands together in delight.

The sergeant smiled. It was the fourth time he had been asked to tell the story, but he derived as much joy in its retelling as the captain did from listening to it. "They are like adolescents in love for the first time, constantly hiding in the most easily discovered places," the sergeant laughed. "They may be the only ones who don't know that their secret is all the village talks about. Yesterday, they slipped into a fallow cornfield, absolutely certain that no one was watching. They talked the whole day. It's been two months, but the man does no more than steal occasional kisses— and harmless ones at that. I managed to work my way through the stalks to get close enough to hear their conversation. Apparently, her father does not approve of our friend. He's insisted on a meeting." The sergeant choked back his laughter long enough to blurt out, "And like a young boy afraid to tell his mother that he hasn't finished his chores, he's in a complete panic."

The captain convulsed in laughter. "For the first time, I almost don't mind this Janissary. Until he arrived, I didn't realize just how starved I was for entertainment."

The captain's face then turned dour. "I still don't like the man being here, even if my garrison is only a distraction from his real goal. He parades his disdain for me for the whole garrison to see. Yesterday, in front of a peasant brought in for questioning, he ordered me, as though I was a raw recruit, to make sure his horse was properly groomed. He was talking about my horse!" He unconsciously bit down on his lip until his top row of teeth were stained red. "I've never been one to overreact to petty slights, but they become intolerable when they're suffered day after day. Besides, I want my command back."

"What will you do?"

"Every day I consider reporting his activities, but this man has powerful friends. My head could end up impaled on the palisades," he said, gesturing to Nicu's picked-over skull. "Since I must be the victim of his whim for now, I'll have to take my revenge a bit more slowly."

"If he's so untouchable, then what could you do to him? Besides, when he finally leaves, he'll be hundreds of miles away with his friends, well beyond your reach."

"I've considered selling his woman into slavery when he departs," the captain smiled maliciously, "but even that would not be sufficient repayment for his insults. He must know I'm the one responsible for his pain."

"How will you do that?"

"I know one of the Prince's favorites, a kennelman named Hamza," the captain sniffed self-importantly. "Hamza was taken prisoner as a young boy in a village not so far from here. I was in the company that took him to the capital. Well, the boy cried endlessly. It was torture listening to him. The whole company was ready to leave him for the wolves. I spent hours trying to convince him that a life filled with wonderful adventures lay before him. If I had known he would become a kennelman, I might have even been envious. After all, who wouldn't savor a life devoted to the pleasures of the hunt? In any event, a bond was formed. Over the years, Hamza and I have stayed close."

"How did such a boy become an important man?"

"Hamza was blessed with splendid gifts. He stands half a head over the average man and his intelligence is only matched by his ravenous appetites. My boy can fire an arrow farther and more accurately than the Sultan's most skilled archers. As the Prince grows, so does Hamza. While the Prince stands in the shadow of the Grand Vizier, Hamza can do little for me. But I'm sure the day will come when he can help me exact my revenge."

"So we wait," the sergeant concluded.

"Yes, we wait," the captain confirmed, "and learn everything we can about this Janissary."

İbrahim had studiously avoided Mihrimah's father, resisting her efforts to bring them together. After weeks of futile pleadings, she finally told him that her father would not allow their courtship to continue unless İbrahim presented himself.

İbrahim's heart was racing as he approached Mihrimah's cottage. The panicked expression İbrahim had seen on her father's face haunted his dreams. Maintaining his relationship with Mihrimah meant overcoming her father's prejudice. It was a task he felt particularly ill equipped to handle.

Loud, convulsive coughing greeted İbrahim as he reached the door. His illness can only make my task more difficult, İbrahim concluded. İbrahim peered into the cottage. He waited for his eyes to adjust to the dim light. The cottage, clean and well maintained, was not much larger than the stall he had inhabited in Mahmut's barn. The two straw mattresses placed on opposite ends of the room were the only furniture.

"Come," Mihrimah's father coughed.

"Where's Mihrimah?" İbrahim squirmed.

"I sent my daughter to the market. She won't be back for quite awhile. I thought it better if we spoke alone."

"Very well," İbrahim bravely replied. He leaned against the hearth, which housed the dying embers of a fire.

"Oh, don't make yourself too comfortable," Mihrimah's father croaked, his words drying up in his throat. "This is no place to—" Before he could complete the sentence, a wave of heavy coughing, born from deep within his diaphragm, lacerated his lungs and stopped him from speaking.

İbrahim took a step forward to help, but Mihrimah's father shook his hand at him. "You needn't bother. My legs are still strong enough to keep me on my feet." He held his breath for a moment and then quickly blurted out, "Kasım," before coughing again. "My name is Kasım."

İbrahim bowed respectfully and said, "How may I be of service to you?"

"I wish you had asked me the same question a few months earlier. I no longer know how to answer your question." Kasım walked out of the cottage, where he was greeted by several scrawny goats and sheep, which had invaded a large, meticulously cultivated garden. He picked up a rock and hurled it at a goat, which was gnawing at a radish. "Get," he snapped. Unimpressed, the goat continued to chew lazily on its meal while beating a slow retreat. Kasım squinted into the sun. "This is no place to live," he lamented.

"Why don't you move back to Edirne?"

"My sweet daughter has truly muddled your senses if you truly believe I can travel. She cannot face my condition. She refuses to mention it. Sometimes I think she believes that one day she'll wake up and find my cough gone. For now, I'm content to let her confront my condition in her own way. But you," he wheezed, "recognize a dying man."

"Surely your condition is not so serious," said İbrahim, trying to sound hopeful.

Kasım smiled. "My father had the same cough before he died. His illness spread from his throat and lungs until his entire body was riddled with disease. Now it's my turn. Each morning I wake up and search my body for those same lumps that disfigured my father. I wonder whether each new ache I feel means that the illness has finally begun to spread. It's a terrible thing to count down the days of your life, especially when you have a wonderful daughter who will one day be alone."

"I'd like to put your mind at ease where Mihrimah's concerned," İbrahim said. "Her life will be happy."

"I find that hard to believe. You've doomed her to a life of sadness. What will become of her when you leave?"

İbrahim opened his mouth to answer.

"I don't desire your answer, young man." Kasım choked back a cough and hoarsely continued, "You and I know that you cannot stay. You think you'll bring us back to Edirne, but you're wrong. I won't allow my Mihrimah to be your concubine."

İbrahim's face turned red. "I've never touched—"

"So Mihrimah tells me," Kasım cut him off. "She says that you only want her as a bride. I believe my daughter. She doesn't have a trace of guile about her. But how long will this resolve last until both of you change your minds—several more months, a year perhaps? Since you can't marry her, what else can she become to you? You expect her to follow a dream and me to follow along as well like a whipped dog? You'll turn her into a kept woman, who one day will learn that her great protector has finally been lost to a better-aimed arrow," Kasım said as he stared at İbrahim's ruined leg. "She'll have no choice but to sell herself to the highest bidder until the day comes when age and disease have washed away her beauty. I will not allow it."

"I will find a way to make her my bride. I gave Mihrimah my word. Now I give it to you," İbrahim desperately assured Kasım.

"You're a resourceful man. How else could you have found us? But we live in a cruel world where there are more limits than possibilities. Your word is not enough."

"You would rather have your daughter live out here?"

"Until you came, yes. In time, I would've found a husband for her. But you've destroyed that, too. The whole village knows of your courtship. What man would risk making you his enemy? Worse still, once you leave, no one will smile pleasantly at my daughter. They'll call her a whore behind her back. We will be shunned, outcasts."

"Then come with me," İbrahim pleaded.

"No, we will find a new place—" A wave of convulsions riddled Kasım, who bent forward and wrapped his arms around his chest. Finally, he managed to say, "This accursed coughing either leaves me gasping for breath or my ribs aching. My throat and lungs are an inferno." Tears streaked down his cheeks. "Leave me now."

"But I thought we might pray together." İbrahim had planned on sealing his bond with Mihrimah's father by uniting in prayer.

Kasım opened his mouth to speak but then thought better of it. Looking as though the cares of the world had suddenly become too difficult to bear, he trudged back to the cottage.

İbrahim knew it was useless to continue the debate. Temporarily resigned, he despondently hung his shoulders and slowly walked towards his horse.

The journey back to the fortress seemed particularly long. Is it a sin to despair, he wondered. "That old man will not deny me, not after all I've overcome," İbrahim complained to a flock of birds soaring overhead.

Except for defending himself against Kasım's charges, İbrahim had not spent any time thinking about Kasım's pain. İbrahim closed his eyes until all he could sense were the warm rays of the sun beating down on him. He tried to imagine how he might feel if his lone daughter had been consigned to such an odd destiny. After several minutes, he violently shook his head to dissolve the vast upset swirling within him.

As İbrahim continued to make his way down the dusty road, the solitary figure of an ancient beggar cast a thin shadow towards him. As much as he had tried to master his contempt for beggars over the years, İbrahim could not mute the reflexive revulsion he felt. A disconcerting need to show off his superiority always seemed to bubble to the surface.

"Good Sir," the beggar flashed a stale, toothless smile. "A mere asper would earn my eternal gratitude."

A horrific stench wafted upwards, causing İbrahim's mount to back away while uttering several disapproving neighs. The beggar's discolored, cracked face was stained with several layers of grime caked onto it. Badly malnourished, his temples were sunken inwards. Only two squinty points pierced through the darkness of his cavernous eye sockets.

"I'd prefer that you bathe rather than that I accept your gratitude."

The beggar answered İbrahim with a confused expression.

İbrahim was about to strike the man with another nasty quip, but stopped. A wide, ingratiating smile spread across İbrahim's face. He lowered himself from his mount and said, "A thousand pardons for my rudeness, Sir. Please accept these few coins as my apology." İbrahim reached into his uniform and withdrew his change purse. A month's salary was inside. He spread apart the string holding the bag shut and started gathering coins while considering how many aspers would be a just payment.

"You needn't empty your purse on my account," the beggar said thankfully. "Even a few coins would be enough to keep me for awhile."

Continuing to force a smile, İbrahim looked at the man, who stared blankly at İbrahim's chest. His only companion is his shadow, İbrahim sadly decided. He felt the man's desolation. Am I so different than he, İbrahim shuddered. He snapped the purse shut and handed it to the beggar. "I only wish I had more to offer you."

The beggar felt the weight of the purse and gasped. İbrahim embraced the dumbfounded beggar. Finding his strength, the traveler gripped İbrahim and released a torrent of tears. "Thank you," the man sobbed. "Thank you."

Looking like they were long-lost brothers, the two men clung to each other. Finally, İbrahim asked, "Will you pray with me?"

Hoping to exit as quickly as he entered, the captain pushed his way past the half-open door leading to İbrahim's quarters without knocking. "A letter from the front," the captain gruffly announced.

İbrahim was dreamily reading the Koran. He gently laid the book on his lap and offered a genuine smile. "Thank you, Abaza Bey."

The captain was stunned by İbrahim's unexpected warmth and respect. He sensed that İbrahim's greeting was sincere. For a fleeting moment, he regretted his plan to gain revenge.

"Do you have friends on campaign with the Sultan in Albania?" İbrahim innocently asked.

This rotten cur is mocking me, the captain decided, rekindling his anger. He doubly cursed İbrahim for making him doubt himself. "I'm only a humble servant of the State with a humble command," the captain answered coldly, his lips curling into a bold sneer. "I'm not privileged to know men who march beside the Sultan." He contemptuously flipped the letter on top of the Koran and tramped out of the room.

İbrahim was taken aback by the captain's response. A shudder ran through him as he reevaluated his initial judgment about the captain's significance. The thought of Mihrimah trying to fend off the captain caused his jaw to painfully lock shut.

Wrenched from his peaceful contemplation, İbrahim was too stunned to plan how he might safeguard Mihrimah. Instead, he numbly tore open the seal to Ahmet's letter. The date on the letter was mid-July, three months earlier. İbrahim took a deep breath in preparation for deciphering Ahmet's cryptic prose.

Greetings, İbrahim:

Even the best news these days is laced with ominous tidings. Our victory in the Albanian lowlands is complete. Skanderbeg seems intent upon cajoling us to follow him into his mountains. If only we would! I'd like to put his fortress at Kruje to the torch. Unfortunately, our provisions are far too meager to support such a costly offensive. Already the Sultan has retired back to Edirne, leaving only a small garrison to protect his hard-won gains. Meanwhile, Skanderbeg grows strong again. If he were not entangled with the Venetians, who knows how powerful Skanderbeg might be by now.

We will need all the support of heaven if Skanderbeg and Yanko join their forces against us. Already, there are rumors that Yanko has somehow mustered together yet another army. Only Allah knows who is left to fight his wars. Hopefully, Brankovic will deny Yanko access through Serbia.

Yet, the news is worse still, my friend. Halil Pasha tells me that the Prince will have an important command in the next campaign. Am I lost already? You must return to the capital. Bring your jewel if you must, but don't delay.

Your loyal friend, Ahmet

İbrahim sighed and balled the letter up in his fist. Ahmet is finished if I stay and Mihrimah will fall prey to the good captain if I leave. If only I could convince Kasım Bey to return with me. But how? He's certain a long journey will kill him. A divine act is what I need, İbrahim despaired. He cursed his own foolishness in provoking the captain.

İbrahim spent a restless night tormented by nightmares of the captain committing one atrocity after another against Mihrimah. In each nightmare, İbrahim pictured himself helplessly watching the spectacle from a faraway hill where he was tending a flock of sheep. When he awoke the next morning, heart still racing, his muscles had contracted tighter than a python's grip on a stricken rabbit.

He threw on his finest uniform and made his way to the stables. As he propelled himself across the compound, eyes locked on the path in front of him, İbrahim did not see the captain rushing to intercept him. The captain grabbed hold of İbrahim's arm, bringing him to an abrupt stop. Feeling as though he had been caught swearing some vile oath against God, İbrahim stared back into the captain's eyes with a stricken expression.

The captain grinned with delight, clearly enjoying İbrahim's discomfort. "The courier who brought your letter also delivered some other news yesterday—new news. We have joyous tidings from Kosovo."

"What's in Kosovo?" İbrahim asked.

"A great victory and on the same battlefield where the Sultan's grandfather crushed the Serbs fifty years ago. Only this time, Yanko is our victim."

İbrahim was thunderstruck by how quickly events had transpired over the last three months. "Yanko is dead?"

The captain shook his head and said, "Brankovic took Yanko hostage as he fled home and killed much of his army. Although I would've preferred Yanko's slaughter as well, his capture by Brankovic is fitting. It seems that Yanko stirred up Brankovic's ire by marching to Kosovo across Serbian territory without the old tyrant's permission."

"And what of Skanderbeg?" İbrahim pressed. "Did he join the battle too?"

"He was busy concluding a peace treaty with the Venetians. Skanderbeg's army was still days away when the broken pieces of Yanko's army began drifting towards the Albanian vanguard. No fool, Skanderbeg marched right back to his mountains." Knowing the Janissaries' antipathy towards the Prince, the captain coyly said, "You ask about Yanko and Skanderbeg, but have you no thought for the Prince?"

"The Prince is dead?" İbrahim asked, poorly disguising the hint of hope in his voice.

Looking as though he had caught a Wallachian peasant stealing across the Danube, the captain said, "The Prince is a hero. He and his Anatolians wreaked havoc among the Hungarians."

"That's wonderful news," İbrahim lied. He thought of Ahmet and suddenly had no more desire to learn about the battle. "Thank you for the report, Captain," he said politely. "I am going to make a final tour of the countryside. I'll be leaving you shortly."

"Don't you want to know more about our victory?" the captain nearly laughed, not surprised to hear İbrahim announce his departure plans.

İbrahim stared into the captain's gloating eyes and groaned inside. He's found out about Mihrimah, İbrahim thought. Then İbrahim realized that the captain had known for months. Mustering as much strength as he could, İbrahim answered, "You will tell me more on my return."

İbrahim rolled off his mount and let his momentum propel him past the open door of Mihrimah's cottage. His own fear inspired terror in the hearts of Kasım and Mihrimah, who were stunned by İbrahim's dramatic entrance. "You no longer have a choice. You must do as I say."

"What has happened, İbrahim?" Mihrimah asked, trembling.

"It's the captain. He knows about us."

"Why should that matter?" Kasım asked, perplexed by İbrahim's anxiety. "Doesn't he report to you?"

"He does, but something has changed. He is a different man now. He looked at me yesterday with a strange expression. And today, he took particular glee in telling me that the Prince had been heroic in a freshly fought battle where we crushed the Hungarians."

"You're talking nonsense. What is wrong with the captain being proud of the Prince?"

"The Prince and the Janissaries are not on good terms. You might remember the fire," İbrahim smartly added, his voice now choked with exasperation.

Mihrimah protectively rested her hands on Kasım's shoulders. "İbrahim," she said evenly, "we don't understand."

İbrahim took a deep breath. "Why would the captain dare to confront me now after months of suffering in silence? And why does the success of the Prince have meaning to him? I can think of only one answer: He is linked to someone the Prince favors."

"Does that mean he can hurt you?" Kasım asked.

İbrahim sighed. "He may try."

"And you think this captain hates you enough to harm my daughter and risk your anger?"

İbrahim nodded and looked expectantly at Kasım.

Kasım fought back a cough and said, "Then it's settled. Mihrimah and I will leave for the next village tomorrow."

"If that's as far as you're willing to go, then you might as well serve yourself up to the captain now. I no longer have time to debate you. I must leave tomorrow. You and Mihrimah must follow me back to Edirne. Trust me," he pleaded.

Kasım responded with a stony, impenetrable stare.

İbrahim turned to Mihrimah. She tried to look at him but was unable to pull her eyes away from the floor. The frustration became too much to bear. İbrahim burst back across the threshold into the raw shelter of the steel gray sky.

"İbrahim," Mihrimah sobbed, her voice trailing after him. "Don't leave me." Before he could fully turn his shoulder, she was burrowing her face in his chest.

As İbrahim surrounded her with his arms, he divorced himself from the crisis. There could be no pain when graced by her sweet touch. He stroked her hair and confessed, "Your father's stubbornness only compounds the damage caused by my own arrogance. Make him understand that the danger is real. Convince him that he has no choice but to agree with me." İbrahim lifted Mihrimah's chin and said, "Do you believe me?"

Mihrimah's eyes answered before her voice. "Yes," she said effortlessly. "I always seem to think like you," she soothingly reassured him.

The tightly sprung muscles in İbrahim's face melted into a relaxed smile. "I cannot delay my return to Edirne, but I will ride day and night until I get there even if it means ruining my leg forever. I'll then have an escort of loyal men bring you and your father to a safe place. If your father insists, you don't have to stay in Edirne. I can find a quieter place that is close enough for me to visit you often."

Mihrimah nodded her head and said, "I will make Father listen. He will not go happily. I expect you will never earn his good will."

"I will not rest until he embraces me as if I were his son."

"My Mihrimah is the most remarkable woman," İbrahim told Ahmet as the steam from the bathhouse meandered through their lungs. The bathhouse rang with the voices of relaxing Janissaries.

"So you've told me a dozen times since you arrived yesterday," Ahmet laughed at İbrahim's excitement. "When are we going to discuss what I want to talk about? Now that you're back where you belong, you mustn't forget that the peace we earned at Kosovo has made our enemies in Edirne strong. You must arrange a meeting with Şemsi."

It was a prickly subject that İbrahim was anxious to avoid. "Are things really so dire?"

Ahmet sighed. "Şemsi was at the Prince's side throughout the battle. I'm sure Mehmed will be a great conqueror one day. He'll have to be if the empire is to survive once the Sultan leaves his throne. The empire's enemies, beaten though they may be, are not without teeth. Even after all the setbacks, Yanko and his army fought like lions. They were quite a sight in their dark blue armor. It was their firearms, though, that were truly terrifying. They bled us as though we were cattle being led to slaughter. Only our superior numbers and the Wallachians' decision to change sides during the battle brought us victory."

"Did the Wallachians benefit from their betrayal?" İbrahim said, becoming absorbed in Ahmet's tale.

"The Sultan was tired of their fickle fidelity. I suppose they broke their vows of allegiance too many times in the past to be trusted anymore. He had his Anatolians slaughter them all."

"A fitting end for traitors, wouldn't you say?" Şemsi wolfishly snapped, appearing from the hazy mist like an apparition. To Şemsi's delight, İbrahim's and Ahmet's mouths fell open. "I see you're both happy to see me."

İbrahim stood and tightly wrapped a towel around his waist. With a wide smile fixed on his face, he walked over to Şemsi and said, "I'm told your Prince has brought great honor to the House of Osman." The words rolled over his tongue as though he had not missed a single day in the capital.

"Like most of our brethren, you've forgotten he's your Prince too. Of course, you decided to place your faith in the House of Çandarlı," Şemsi concluded, in a caustic reference to the Grand Vizier's family.

"I don't recall being invited to join the Prince in his exile to Manisa," İbrahim quipped.

"Don't try to toy with me. You know better than I that you wouldn't have come."

"İbrahim," Ahmet reproachfully interrupted, "please allow Şemsi his afternoon entertainment. He came here to gloat at my expense, not to argue with you. I wish to hear his best."

For a moment, Şemsi appeared shaken by Ahmet's boastful manner. He then thrust his thick chest forward and blustered, "You'll see how foolish you were to side against the Prince when he resumes the throne. Just how do you plan to fill your days and line your pockets when that day comes? Of course, I imagine you're feeling the pinch already. The Prince has been waging his own private war with the Venetians. Their ships and islands in the Aegean suffer at his whim. Riches flow to his favorites. Quite a contrast to Murad's rule, which is nearly as lifeless as Byzantium."

"The Byzantine Emperor is dead?" İbrahim gasped.

"Too much time in the wastelands," Ahmet laughed.

Before he realized it, Şemsi unleashed a hearty roar as well. Both men locked eyes and then abruptly silenced themselves.

"You'll be pleased to learn who has won the royal diadem, worthless piece of paste though it might be," Şemsi smirked at İbrahim. "Constantine Palaeologus, the deceased Emperor's brother and the man responsible for your deformity, now rules the Greeks and their decrepit city."

İbrahim ran his hand over his leg and frowned. The leg had given him little trouble over the last few months. Since leaving Mihrimah, the familiar old ache had returned.

Ahmet stared at Şemsi with the same effortless confidence that had won him so many friends. "So you think your ties to the Prince have raised you above me," he said pointedly. "Did you know that İbrahim once believed he was invincible in battle? And why not? He had never suffered more than a scratch until we assaulted the Hexamilion. Look now. One arrow has revealed all the frailty that had been so well hidden. My dear Şemsi, you never know when or where the blow will come. That's why you should always surround yourself with allies with broad backs."

Şemsi leaned forward and asked, "Are you making an offer?"

"An invitation, not an offer," Ahmet clarified.

"You make it sound like I have something to gain by a parley with you."

"Oh, don't be coy, Şemsi. It doesn't suit you. I know a changed man when I see one. Your interests extend well beyond mere gloating now."

"I'm keen to change as well. You once showered me with an endless stream of insults, but I do believe you just praised me."

Ahmet got down to business. "There are many who believe that Halil Pasha's power is waning."

"Isn't it?" Şemsi beamed triumphantly.

"On the day Mehmed takes his place on Murad's throne, do you really think he'll have the luxury of discarding Halil Pasha? The Grand Vizier's power will remain great for years to come. Is your patience equally great?"

"It has its limits," Şemsi conceded.

"Being given a powerful command early in Mehmed's reign would certainly place you ahead of many competitors."

"And Halil Pasha doles out the commands," Şemsi smiled knowingly.

"You know the Grand Vizier often asks me who are the outstanding men in the corps."

"An interesting coincidence," Şemsi coolly calculated. "The Prince and I have had many discussions about who can lead the Janissaries into Constantinople."

"Then an understanding has been reached," Ahmet declared.

Şemsi turned to İbrahim. "Take good care of your friend."

İbrahim watched with fascination as Ahmet's erstwhile nemesis disappeared into the bathhouse mist. "I have been away too long," İbrahim said, shaking his head in confusion. "Who would have believed it? Şemsi finally gains power after those bitter years in exile and then foregoes his triumph. The only thing that seemed real about Şemsi's conversation with you was his gloating, but even that didn't last. I cannot imagine why Şemsi so willingly reached an accord with you. You didn't need me after all. I might just as well have stayed with Mihrimah."

"I'm surprised as well. What disturbs me most is that Şemsi sought me out. He must have powerful competitors."

"Does your deal with him mean that his enemies are now your enemies?"

"I must assume it does."

"Then you have quite a problem," İbrahim warned. "How will you learn the identities of these men, much less keep track of their activities when they are based in Manisa?"

"I will have to find friends in the Prince's court."

"Find them soon. I fear the Sultan's reign is deep into winter."

"Let Those Who Love Me Follow Me" • 1451

"He can barely speak my name. His throat is swollen shut so tightly that I can only hear the whistle of his breath," Mihrimah sobbed. She buried her head in İbrahim's chest. "I used to fight so hard not to hear his terrible cough. Now I miss it more than anything."

İbrahim wrapped his arms around Mihrimah's delicate shoulders and drew her trembling body towards him. Despite İbrahim's endless stream of well-intentioned gestures, Kasım had never stopped viewing him with suspicion. Their competition for Mihrimah's affection only worsened the divide. As İbrahim looked over Mihrimah's head into the cottage, no amount of guilt could stop him from feeling a sense of relief.

True to his word, İbrahim had sent several Janissaries from the First Orta to retrieve Mihrimah and Kasım. Constantly doubling back to see if the captain was having them followed, it took several weeks for them to arrive at their new home, a nondescript but neatly furnished cottage. The cottage was tucked away in a small village centered around a Bektaşi hospice, only a two-hour horseback ride from the barracks.

İbrahim had tried to steal every moment he could with Mihrimah, but the demands of the corps meant lengthy separations. The Sultan had besieged Skanderbeg's vaunted mountain fortress of Kruje for five months. When the barrage of mortar fire failed to dislodge the Albanians, the Ottomans had tried to bribe the defenders before finally offering peace terms. The Albanians stood firm. In the end, the Sultan had returned home in defeat, deciding to spare his army the rigors of fighting in the mountains during winter.

The winter drove the prematurely aged Sultan to rest in his country estates outside of Edirne. He yearned to revive his fortunes but rebuffed all pleas for him to launch a winter campaign against Skanderbeg. Fearing heavy losses, the Sultan declared that he would not give one soldier for fifty such fortresses. The absolute ruler of the Ottoman Empire was reconciled to licking his wounds until spring arrived.

Kasım was not so fortunate. The cancer in his throat had spread throughout his wasted body, wreaking pain and dysfunction. Horrible tumors bulged from under his sallow skin. Robbed of his energy, Kasım had now succumbed to pneumonia. Each short breath set his chest afire. It was all he could do to make his mind stray from embracing the day when the disease would claim him.

İbrahim looked with pride at the pristine cottage and large, freshly painted barn, which was richly stocked with a broad assortment of livestock. İbrahim had spared no expense in making sure that Mihrimah was comfortable. Unable to release himself from the corps, he wanted to convince Mihrimah that he was making an investment in his future home.

"Father keeps asking to see you," Mihrimah said.

The tortured screams of the wounded and dying had followed him through victory and defeat, rarely touching his soul. But confronting disease was different. It was an enemy that could not be defeated or controlled. His friends had long ago convinced him that it was better to die in battle than fall victim to this silent destroyer. İbrahim was stung by the realization that such an end likely awaited him if he were to escape to a normal life.

"I thought you said he cannot hold a conversation?" İbrahim lamely protested.

Mihrimah's soft features hardened with disapproval. A life sown with peril and sacrifice had created a mature, practical woman subtly disguised behind a girlish veneer. Knowing that she did not have the luxury of tactfully stating her needs, Mihrimah firmly commanded her father and İbrahim. At times, İbrahim thought his actions were guided more from a desire not to disappoint her than from the seductive warmth and mirth in her eyes.

İbrahim sighed. "I will visit him."

"Hold his hand," Mihrimah plaintively instructed.

İbrahim nodded and dutifully walked into the cottage. A stale, rancid odor immediately assaulted him. He instinctively held his breath and snapped his head back. İbrahim looked over at Kasım, who was quivering under a thick pile of wool blankets. A snake-like hiss glided over the sick man's lips between irregular gasps for breath.

İbrahim and Kasım were separated by a thick cloud of dust illuminated by a broad beam of sunlight coming through the lone window of the cottage. İbrahim wondered whether Kasım's illness lurked within the dust, waiting to leech onto a new host. He deftly walked around the sunbeam and approached Kasım.

İbrahim looked down at Kasım, who was mired in a fitful sleep. His face had buckled inward. A haphazard web of deep lines was carved through his chafed, ashen cheeks. "Kasım Bey," İbrahim gently whispered. "It's İbrahim."

The loose folds of skin over Kasım's eyes snapped open. His hand bolted out from under the covers and locked around İbrahim's wrist. Kasım swallowed hard, trying to gather as much air as possible. Then, with a frightful hiss, he croaked through his blue lips, "Tell me."

İbrahim wrinkled his brow as he tried to decipher the request. He did not want to force Kasım to repeat himself. But after a few moments, İbrahim quizzically asked, "What is it you wish me to tell you?"

Kasım shook his head up and down and mouthed, "You know."

"I do?"

Kasım nodded his head again. "She," he sputtered, "waits."

İbrahim took his free hand and fondly patted Kasım's arm. "You want to know that your daughter will be safe."

Kasım winced. "More," he croaked dryly.

İbrahim agreed that Mihrimah deserved more than a life filled with promises. He was still no closer to finding a way out of the corps. Now was not the time for vain predictions.

"I've worked out a plan to fake my death during our next Albanian campaign," İbrahim lied, trying to pacify the dying man. "Before the summer ends, I'll return to this village, never to leave again. Then I'll start raising children with your daughter." His words took on a more convincing ring as he dreamily imagined his infant son nursing at Mihrimah's breast.

Kasım's eyes glistened and a wan, eerie smile flitted across his lips. He gripped İbrahim's wrist and managed to say with unexpected clarity, "Bring me my baby."

İbrahim tenderly freed his hand from Kasım's clammy grip and left the cottage. To his surprise, Ahmet was waiting for him. Eyes locked on Ahmet's grim countenance, İbrahim hardly noticed Mihrimah rush past him into the cottage.

İbrahim inspected Ahmet's neatly pressed uniform and scowled, "I've told you never to come dressed in uniform."

İbrahim had religiously changed from his uniform into peasant garb whenever he entered the village. After his experience on the frontier, he knew he would have to suppress his identity to live in blissful anonymity. But as much as he yearned to live a simple life with Mihrimah, İbrahim always regretted having to exchange the velvet finery of his uniform for the coarse peasant's tunic.

"I have grave news from the capital," Ahmet said, ignoring his friend's reproach, all the while looking dazed. "The Sultan died shortly after you left two weeks ago."

İbrahim felt like a dagger had been plunged into his stomach. "A truly just and pious man; I shall grieve his loss as though he was my own flesh and blood."

"Too young to die," Ahmet opined.

"No," İbrahim disagreed. "He aged before his time. How did he die?"

"Except to say that the Sultan suffered a seizure, Halil Pasha was uncharacteristically silent. Of course, there are the usual rumors, which range from the Sultan dying from too much drink to being frightened to death by an old dervish's prediction of his doom. It doesn't matter. The only thing that matters now is that Mehmed is our new master.

"It may take years before our Janissary brethren embrace the new Sultan. But there are others who love him dearly. I'm told that when word of his father's death reached him in Manisa, Mehmed jumped to his feet and said, 'Let those who love me follow me.' And they did. A powerful contingent of his followers quickly escorted him into Thrace."

"Şemsi was close at hand?"

"Of course, but so were many others. My informants in Manisa had plenty to say about some of Mehmed's followers, particularly when it came to a despicable kennelman named Hamza, one of Mehmed's favorites. It seems he enjoys slowly torturing to death wounded game. He's urged Mehmed to purge the corps and replace its officers with loyal kennelmen and falconers like himself. No wonder Şemsi needed me."

"And what of your friend? Has Mehmed forgiven the Grand Vizier for his past indiscretions?"

"Halil Pasha was invited to kiss Mehmed's hand and take his customary place at the Sultan's side, as if they had never shared a cross word."

"Perhaps Halil Pasha's days shall continue," İbrahim smiled.

Ahmet shook his head. "I'm sure our new Sultan is merely biding his time. As we speak, he's entertaining delegations from our enemies, who are promising peace and lavishing him with gifts. Mehmed has been welcoming them with open arms. Even the Venetians, whose possessions Mehmed mercilessly raided for the last few years, are being embraced. The Christians think they're buying a cheap peace from a weak, overmatched boy. They would change their minds if they learned what has become of Murad's infant son.

"Following Mehmed's installment, his stepmother paid her respects to Mehmed in the throne room. He was nothing but gracious to her. You would have never guessed that at that very moment he was having her son, his own half brother, drowned. Jurists are already praising him for justly avoiding civil war. Murad would never have contemplated such a deed."

"Then why the easy peace with the Christians?"

"Mehmed still needs to shore up his support in the army. Besides, the Karamanids will surely cause trouble. They always do when they think we're vulnerable. Better to keep the peace with the Christians until Anatolia is secure."

"Will the Janissaries fight for this Sultan?" İbrahim asked.

"I'm sure Şemsi will ask me that very question."

"And what will you will tell him?"

"The answer must be 'yes' or we risk Mehmed's retribution. Şemsi will expect me to guarantee their loyalty."

"Guarantee?" İbrahim gasped. "What if our brethren revolt despite your best efforts?"

"I will pray to Allah that no reckless decisions are made," Ahmet glumly answered. "We must leave for Edirne at once."

İbrahim looked back at the cottage. "Mihrimah needs me."

"I no longer have the luxury of allowing you to live this double life." Face suddenly flushed with rage, Ahmet shook İbrahim's shoulders, jolting his head backwards. "Because you're my friend, you've already enjoyed more freedom than any Janissary dreams about. But now our enemies surround us. Time is one of them. Thoughtful decisions will have to be made quickly. If you wish to keep Mihrimah, bring her to the capital."

İbrahim swallowed hard. He was sure Mihrimah would never exchange the pastoral bliss of the cottage for the harsh bustle of the city. Even if she might grudgingly consent to such a move, İbrahim did not want to expose her to the dangers of a capital in turmoil.

A shrill, rising wail resounded in İbrahim's ears. "Mihrimah," he gasped. The world is collapsing around me, İbrahim despaired, feeling as though he was trapped in an inescapable labyrinth.

Ahmet's face softened. "Go to her," he sighed.

İbrahim sprang into the cottage. The awful hiss was gone, replaced by Mihrimah's wrenching sobs. Mihrimah's arms were cradling her father's head as if she was cajoling Kasım back to life. It was a scene he had witnessed too often in countless villages plundered by the corps. He had always turned away, fearing that the survivor's mixture of grief and futility would weaken him. Now İbrahim's eyes measured every ounce of Mihrimah's emotion. Her soul was laid bare and he was driven to absorb her essence into his own consciousness. Each sob drained him until he collapsed at her side and buried his weepy face in her shoulder.

"Father, Father," she moaned, drawing Kasım's head to her bosom.

İbrahim silently cursed his obligation to Ahmet. I cannot abandon her, İbrahim decided. He was prepared to risk the executioner's knife to remain by her side. "Nothing will separate us," he whispered into her ear.

A dark feeling came over him. İbrahim snapped his head up and saw Ahmet peering into the cottage from the doorway. The sun was at his back, leaving his face in shadow. "A moment, İbrahim," he politely requested.

İbrahim broke free from Mihrimah and followed his friend outside. When they were out of earshot of the cottage, Ahmet swung around to speak. Before Ahmet could say a word, İbrahim blurted out, "I will not join you."

For a long moment, Ahmet said nothing. Then, his crystal blue eyes sparkled as in the days before he bore the sergeant's rank. "Allah will decide our lives," he said philosophically. "Do what you must. You will come when fate demands."

"I'm not coming back," İbrahim resolutely replied.

"If you're to disappear without suspicion, you will have to return first," Ahmet warned. "The inevitable campaign against the Karamanids will be the perfect cover."

"Then you will help me," İbrahim exclaimed in disbelief.

"You're my friend, İbrahim."

"It's simply not done," Ahmet upbraided Hüsrev.

Locked safely behind the closed door of Ahmet's modest office in the barracks, Hüsrev aggressively asked, "Is it really that different from when you helped engineer the rebellion against Mehmed in Edirne years ago?"

"I only organized a protest," Ahmet explained. "We are setting a dangerous precedent if we demand that this Sultan make a gift to us for mounting the throne."

"I'm more worried that Mehmed will devalue the currency after agreeing to our demands," Hüsrev blithely responded. "Besides, the Sultan is to blame for keeping us in reserve while he chased the Karamanids into the mountains."

As Ahmet had predicted, the Karamanids had challenged the young Sultan. With wolfish delight, Mehmed sprang at the opportunity to sharpen his blade, rapidly bringing his army across the Straits to deliver a crushing blow to the empire's historic enemy.

"At the same time we were emptying our purses in Bursa, Mehmed was claiming a quick victory. So now we have no chance to replenish our losses with plunder. Surely he must realize that we were denied our just reward. Are we really being so unreasonable?" Hüsrev's brow suddenly wrinkled. "Shouldn't these be your words, not mine?"

Ahmet's face turned crimson.

Hüsrev snickered. "You've made a deal, haven't you? What is it," he demanded, "or is İbrahim the only one entitled to such sensitive information?" He looked at İbrahim, who was sitting absentmindedly in a chair, staring into space.

"Are you challenging me, Hüsrev?" Ahmet snapped.

"Somebody must. Your second in command sits among us, but he's of no use. İbrahim's addled mind is fixed on his woman. The corps wants this gift from the Sultan. Don't you see that you'll lose the loyalty of your followers if you don't serve them now? Ask Sinan and Cem. They'll tell you the same thing."

"It's suicide," Ahmet tried to explain. "Mehmed is not a simpleminded boy and he has grown much since his first days in Edirne. Worse still, his cruelty matches his father's kindness. Those who try to humble him will live shortened lives."

Hüsrev shook his head in disgust. "May I leave now?" Before

Ahmet could answer, Hüsrev threw open the door, nearly ripping it from its hinges, and stalked away.

Ahmet sighed. "It wasn't so long ago that Hüsrev accepted my judgments with modesty and respect. Now he spits in my face as though I were some common thief."

"You were right. Hüsrev is making a grave mistake."

"How would you know?" Ahmet asked, turning his anger against İbrahim. "You never said a word in my defense."

"You shouldn't waste your anger on me. I told you years ago to make Hüsrev your second in command. Perhaps then you'd find him more manageable."

"He has nothing to complain about. I spend most of my time with Halil Pasha. In my absence, Hüsrev has run the First Orta as if he were its colonel. I can't remember the last time I counter-manded one of his orders."

"Which means you've only dug the knife deeper into the wound. Hüsrev yearns for recognition. By not elevating him to his deserved rank, you abused his dignity."

"Hüsrev's Red Apple," Ahmet sighed as though he had been ordered to march yet another mile on rubbery legs.

İbrahim nodded.

"Unfortunately, I do not have the luxury of viewing the Red Apple as anything but Constantinople. It is our young Sultan's great quest."

"Then he's in quite a predicament. How can he conquer the world if the Janissaries don't love him?"

"Mehmed understands. I'm sure he would prefer to gain our loyalty through grand deeds and thoughtful gestures, but he will not empty the treasury to do so. Hüsrev's plan will only incite Mehmed. If we will not give ourselves willingly, I'm afraid the Sultan will find an especially unpleasant way of making us bend to his authority."

"How? By bringing the regular army against us?" İbrahim skeptically speculated. "The empire would be devastated."

"The Sultan will flood our ranks with his accursed kennelmen and falconers," Şemsi thundered, his voice tinged with a mixture of rage and agony. His disquieting talent for sneaking up on people was sharper than ever. "They will be promoted to every position where the current officer's loyalty is questioned. He's been working on a long list for months now."

İbrahim and Ahmet snapped their heads toward the doorway. "How long have you been here?" Ahmet nervously laughed, still uneasy about his alliance with Şemsi.

"Long enough to know I have an ally who understands the danger before us." The strain from competing for Mehmed's favor had taken its toll on Şemsi. His once rigidly straight, iron-hard shoulders now lazily drooped to his sides. The rest of his body followed suit. Şemsi's posture had collapsed underneath him, forcing his belly to push downwards like the swollen udders of a cow. "You must stop Hüsrev. He is giving Mehmed the excuse he desires to put his foot on our necks."

"Mehmed would dare to debase our ranks with that filth?"

"He'll do it with pleasure. This Sultan sees the flames rising high over Edirne as though it were yesterday. I doubt he'll ever trust the corps. His kennelmen and falconers are another story. He believes their loyalty is absolute. He's probably right. Since their numbers are greater than ours, Mehmed's plan to overwhelm our ranks will surely succeed. In the end, the Janissary corps will swear true allegiance to him. The faces will just be different."

"If diluting our ranks is his best option," Ahmet said, voice rising with excitement, "then perhaps rebellion is the best answer after all."

"You achieved your rank too quickly, Ahmet," Şemsi said judgmentally. "If you had suffered in exile as I, you wouldn't propose such rash action. Convincing the corps to love Mehmed may yet persuade him not to undermine our ranks. You must begin this campaign today."

"And what will you do?"

"I will plant the seed in Mehmed's head that tampering with the Janissary corps will undermine its effectiveness for years. If he expects to establish his capital in Constantinople, he'll need the Janissaries to be strong and united.

"Of course, the Byzantines may end up inciting Mehmed more than Hüsrev and his friends. Constantine Palaeologus sent a delegation to meet with Mehmed. It appears they misjudged the true nature of our master. The Greeks must think he's still the same weak boy. Apparently, they are demanding—yes, demanding—that Mehmed double the allowance he pays to maintain Prince Orhan in Constantinople. As you know, it's been rumored that Prince Orhan is the great-grandson of Sultan Bayezid. Some say he has a legitimate claim to the throne. The Byzantines made it very clear that they would help the Prince make his claim if the Sultan did not satisfy their demands." Şemsi sniffed derisively. "Even as their empire disintegrates, the Byzantines' ability to scheme is boundless. Obviously they think they can intimidate Mehmed with the threat of civil war."

Proud of his master's quickly developing political skills, Şemsi beamed, "Mehmed was outraged but allowed the emissaries to leave with his goodwill. The Sultan will continue to lull the Byzantines to sleep until he's ready to shear them."

Ahmet's mouth hung open. "How did you learn about this insult?"

Şemsi smiled devilishly. "The delegation first met with Halil Pasha, who later passed on the information to the Sultan."

"Why was I not told?"

"A question that concerns me as well. Are things well between you and the Grand Vizier?"

"I hope so," Ahmet answered nervously.

"I hope so too," Şemsi agreed. "Our partnership has no value to me if I must tell you what Halil Pasha won't." Şemsi paused for a moment to let his words sink in. He then left the room without so much as a nod.

With a bemused expression lighting up his face, İbrahim leaned over to watch Şemsi leave. "At least some things never change."

"A little bit more of the world seems to slip beyond my grasp each day. Şemsi is right. I must stop Hüsrev and unite the corps with Mehmed."

"Then let's start," İbrahim said, disturbed by his friend's distress.

"They are no longer mine." Ahmet's voice dripped with defeat. "After speaking to Hüsrev, I realize that now. For the first time in years, I can't see my next step."

"You're fighting to survive," İbrahim observed. "No prize beckons to you. What then is left?"

Ahmet helplessly shook his head.

"Nothing," İbrahim answered his own question. "Bursa will be awash in chaos when the Janissaries demand their gold from the Sultan. Now is the time for us to go."

Ahmet looked at İbrahim as if he were mad. "Go? Where would I go?" he asked incredulously.

"You could come with me," İbrahim said, voice rising with excitement. "Mihrimah would welcome you as my brother."

"I've indulged your fantasy for years, but now you're speaking madness," Ahmet rebuked him. "I'm staying with my command. You should do the same."

"For what purpose?" İbrahim asked. "I'm useless to you. No one can help you with the Sultan and I certainly cannot survive another battle."

"That's absurd, İbrahim. You're the fiercest soldier I've ever seen."

"My leg will not allow me to charge the enemy or climb some Albanian mountainside. I might as well throw myself into the Bosphorus. The result would be just the same."

"But you didn't limp or grimace once during the march to Bursa," Ahmet protested.

"An effort I cannot repeat. It was all I could do to control my pain in front of the men to spare you embarrassment. But my self-control doesn't give my leg back its strength. It's time for me to go where I'm truly needed."

"You would risk being hunted down and executed like a common criminal for her?"

"I'd risk the wrath of Allah for her," İbrahim answered with soulful conviction.

"Then you must go," Ahmet nobly whispered, his face contorted in misery.

İbrahim was surprised by Ahmet's ready submission to the inevitable. "I haven't abandoned you. My home and counsel will always be open to you."

Ahmet shook his head appreciatively. "You've been a true friend. If you say that you cannot survive the next battle, I must believe you. How then can I ask you to stay?"

İbrahim swallowed hard. Measuring his words carefully, he offered his greatest thanks. "You have spared me from my loneliness."

As the words passed from İbrahim's lips, it occurred to him that Ahmet's vast network of contacts was quickly dissolving. Before long, Ahmet might experience the same desolation that had plagued İbrahim for so many years.

"You know you'll never wear the uniform again," Ahmet said.

"I'm satisfied to merely keep my uniform and scimitar as trophies. I will never raise my hand in battle again."

The uprising came with alarming swiftness. Within hours, Hüsrev had easily seduced his comrades' greedy spirits. With calls for a large donation, the barracks emptied. Starting mischief as though they were young cadets, the Janissaries upset market stalls and roughly pushed their way through the panicked citizenry. A series of small fires appeared, an ominous portent of the fate awaiting the city if the Janissaries were not satisfied.

İbrahim took advantage of the upheaval. Under the cloak of darkness, he slipped out of the city in peasant dress. İbrahim's white Janissary cap was replaced by an anonymous gray turban. As İbrahim made his way down the main road towards Gallipoli, the Janissaries' churlish demands were born away by a stiff seaborne wind.

İbrahim raced ahead until he came to the fork in the road leading to Mahmut's old estate. He stopped and wistfully gazed southwards. Tears welled up inside him. The lessons of his youth and Mahmut's affection stirred within him. As he rushed to his new life under the veil of the crescent moon, İbrahim resolved that he would redouble his efforts to live a pure, moral life.

İbrahim spent the next few weeks making his way back to Mihrimah. He had marched the same roads for years side by side with his Janissary brethren. A sense of invincibility was rooted in each step he had taken. Now, separated from the corps for the first time in over fourteen years, he was unnerved by the vulnerability of the solitary, anonymous traveler. İbrahim began to understand Kasım's fears for Mihrimah's safety.

İbrahim was tormented in his sleep. At times, he dreamed of Mihrimah being brutally murdered or raped. But the dream that tortured him the most was hauntingly simple: He returned to an empty cottage. The dream absorbed İbrahim's waking thoughts as well until he was riddled with doubt.

İbrahim arrived outside the cottage at dusk on the twentieth day of his journey. Mihrimah was working in the garden. Her slender back faced him. With her body swaying up and down as she vigorously dug a trowel into the soft earth, Mihrimah appeared deep in prayer.

İbrahim began to laugh. As he considered his earlier, morbid fixation, İbrahim's laughter grew more frantic until he thought his heart would burst.

Mihrimah turned her head. Her startled face instantly brightened with excitement. She threw the trowel to the ground and madly rushed to him. İbrahim tried to brace himself as Mihrimah burst into his arms. His body precariously swayed backwards before abruptly collapsing.

Face aglow with shock and amusement, Mihrimah giggled like a young girl. She smothered his face with a rapid succession of kisses and said, "I knew you would come back to me today."

İbrahim inhaled her sweet breath and sighed, "Now how could you have known I'd arrive today?"

Mihrimah playfully ran her fingers through his beard. "Because yours was the first face I imagined before opening my eyes this morning. But then," she admitted with a coquettish smile, "I've thought of little else since you left."

İbrahim slid his hands around the small of her back. He then slowly drew his hands upwards, finally caressing her shoulders with his strong fingers. He interrupted her contented sigh with a long, hard kiss, which was answered with Mihrimah's velvety rich lips. Every nerve in his body sprang to life, tingling with euphoria, as he voraciously consumed her passion. Finally, beaming at his beloved, he cryptically announced, "I have come home."

Mihrimah stared silently at him for a long moment. Then her eyes sprang wide open. "You've left the corps?"

İbrahim smiled and nodded his head.

"But how is that possible?"

İbrahim shrugged as he dourly reflected back on his last day in Bursa. "The Janissaries are about to be reborn and I do not belong to the new order. My mysterious departure is more likely to be welcomed than challenged."

"Ahmet didn't try to stop you?"

"I always thought he would. But when the time came, he surrendered easily enough. I think Ahmet believes he has become like a ship without a sail, cast adrift to flounder on the rocks. As I look back, Ahmet must have thought releasing me was the last thing he controlled. He demanded my company on his voyage for so many years. I think he wanted to make sure I landed unharmed even if he did not."

"You will see him again, won't you?" Mihrimah soothingly asked, wanting to ease İbrahim's upset.

"I'm sure that is his will. I'm less certain he'll have the opportunity. Enemies surround him. But enough of Ahmet," İbrahim beamed, his mood suddenly brightening. "You and I have waited years for this moment."

İbrahim pulled Mihrimah's waist against his own. She moaned lightly and rhythmically thrust her hips against him. "I want you to be my wife," İbrahim said with the shyness and purity of an innocent.

Eyes glistening with desire, Mihrimah stood up and looked down at İbrahim, who was still loosely sprawled on the ground. She walked to the cottage, not turning back to see if he was following. As she disappeared into the cottage, İbrahim sprang to his feet. An anxious shudder rocked him as he contemplated what awaited him inside.

When he entered the cottage, Mihrimah was standing naked before the bed, batting her eyes nervously. İbrahim had never seen her unclothed. Her long hair cascaded over her bare shoulders, drawing his eyes to her full, upturned breasts. Untouched by the sun, her cream-colored skin was invitingly soft. Taking in her full measure, İbrahim's eyes continued to drift hungrily downwards. As if a dark rain cloud was suddenly pushed out to sea by a soothing blast of warm, sweet-scented air, his inhibitions were released. He crossed the room to embrace her.

Urban's Canon • 1453

"Rüstem would fear for his job if he knew he had such a rival," Ahmet rakishly said to Mihrimah as he took another large bite of lamb. "I hope you'll invite me to your next feast."

Mihrimah was used to Ahmet's exaggerated praise but still blushed in gratitude. "You never need an invitation to our home," she playfully slapped his shoulder. Mihrimah deftly maneuvered her way around the table where Ahmet and İbrahim were ravenously devouring their afternoon meal. She walked over to the great fire and inspected the lamb slowly roasting on a spit. Its rich aroma soaked the thick walls of the fastidiously maintained cottage, awakening a sense of contentment among the three friends. She brought a leg of lamb over to İbrahim and reflexively ran her hands over his shoulders. İbrahim's shoulders instantly softened at her light touch.

With each new visit, Ahmet surveyed the humble surroundings with growing appreciation. "Seldom a day passes when I don't think back to our last day together in Bursa. I thought I was being invited to your exile, not a home. But look at you and your beautiful wife, an ideal."

"Do you still have a home?" İbrahim asked.

"Even if the Sultan guaranteed me a permanent position in his divan, the barracks will always be my home," Ahmet forlornly answered. "My ambitions have always been rooted within those halls. Unfortunately," Ahmet sneered, "those halls are now filled with wretched kennelmen and falconers who tell all who will listen that they are the Sultan's true Janissaries. By the way these new-comers talk, you would think they were the ones who brought the empire all those victories. I walk through the bloated ranks of the First Orta and see one unblemished face after another. No battle scars to tell the glory of our *orta*. A new history will be written by these men. Our stories will die with us."

İbrahim was not disturbed by Ahmet's prediction. "I have a very narrow audience these days," he beamed at Mihrimah, "and she is not impressed by tales of war. I find greater pleasure in bringing food to this table. You know I never felt comfortable sitting around the stewpots sharing stories."

Ahmet's face relaxed in quiet contemplation. "Meals are also not the same anymore, not since poor Rüstem was ordered to execute Hüsrev. I can't remember the last time Rüstem teased me about being a pirate," Ahmet nostalgically mused.

"I can't remember the last time I saw true joy on your face either," İbrahim observed. "Can't you and Şemsi find some way to overcome your adversaries?"

"Şemsi and I are like two doomed survivors of a shipwreck being tossed helter-skelter on a waterlogged raft. None of our plans produced the results we expected. At every turn, the newcomers are awarded the favors that rightly belong to us. Sometimes I wonder whether I should've joined Hüsrev in his folly. At least he died with his convictions firmly intact.

"Did I tell you that I was allowed into the Sultan's inner circle for an evening last week?" Ahmet held up his hand. "Don't rush to congratulate me. I've pillaged villages without a moment's remorse, but I've had a nightmare every night since my evening with the Sultan. It seems that Mehmed has taken to walking the streets of Edirne at night. He's trying to discover whether the populace has a taste for his planned push on Constantinople. Of course, Mehmed desires anonymity. We were walking down a quiet alley when an old man recognized the Sultan and said, 'Long live...' Before he could finish the salutation, Mehmed buried a dagger in the man's chest with no more emotion than a bird plucking a worm from the earth. I know I'm a fool, but I couldn't stop from kneeling down to look at the man. He seemed so familiar."

"Who was he?" İbrahim croaked, his mouth suddenly dry.

"I knew his face," Ahmet said. "He was a retired *sipahi* colonel. Until that moment, I never thought I could have any sympathy for those pompous peacocks. He stared into my eyes, lips quivering with his final prayer. My chest almost burst. Every feeling of betrayal in the man's soul flowed into me."

"Can't Halil Pasha help?"

Ahmet laughed contemptuously. "Oh, how the Grand Vizier's star has lost its luster along with his nerve. Only recently, Mehmed summoned Halil Pasha to the palace in the middle of the night. Fearing for his life, my old friend brought a bowl of gold. The Sultan sneered at this customary gift. He told Halil Pasha to keep his gold. He demanded that Constantinople be delivered to him and then sent Halil Pasha home again like a well-reprimanded schoolchild."

"That was the only reason for the summons?"

Ahmet nodded.

"He treats Halil Pasha so because of past slights?"

"That's what most people think, but I disagree. Mehmed is pushing him to exhaust his last ounce of strength in pursuit of the grand quest. The Sultan is forever working late into the night pouring over plans to capture Constantinople. He sketches the city's walls and draws up battle lines and positions for his siege engines. He consults endlessly with foreign military experts. He demands the same from Halil Pasha. Although nothing would've saved them, the Greeks were foolish to insult Mehmed by threatening to support Prince Orhan's claims. Now they will pay doubly when their city falls."

Shortly after defeating the Karamanids, Mehmed had wasted little time revealing his true nature and ambitions. The first step to strangle Constantinople was put in motion. The Sultan ordered the construction of a powerful fortress on the western shore of the Bosphorus. Mehmed selected a site directly across from Sultan Bayezid's fortress of Anadolu Hisarı and ordered the demolition of the churches and monasteries occupying the land. The site, which was actually Byzantine territory, commanded the narrowest part of the strait. Mehmed planned to strangle commerce from this strategic lookout and use the fortress as a base for the siege of Constantinople.

The Greeks were stricken with terror. The full measure of their opponent was becoming apparent. Byzantium's old threat to support Prince Orhan was rudely exposed as impotent bluster. The Emperor now resorted to a gentler form of diplomacy. Envoys were sent to Mehmed, reminding him that Bayezid had first asked for the Emperor's permission before building Anadolu Hisarı fifty years earlier. The envoys then sought assurances that the Sultan did not intend to make war on Byzantium. Mehmed refused to receive them. Two more delegations were sent from Constantinople. The last group finally drew Mehmed's attention. Their heads were severed.

Only four and half months after the project was begun, the five thousand masons brought from throughout the empire put down their tools. Boğaz Kesen, "cutter of the strait," cast its massive shadow over the Bosphorus. Called Rumeli Hisarı, the castle of Romeland, by the Greeks, it incited the demoralized populace of Constantinople to predict their own doom. "These are the days of the Antichrist" mournfully echoed through the ancient streets of the Greek capital.

Mehmed confirmed their worst fears. Once the fortress was completed, he marched his army to Constantinople and inspected the city's walls for three days. He left a five-hundred-man garrison at Rumeli Hisarı with orders to demand a tax from every passing vessel. Refusal was to be answered with six-hundred-pound stone cannonballs.

The Venetians were the first to test the strength of the fortress. Three grain-bearing vessels did not stop at the fortress. Two merchantmen were promptly sunk. Their crews swam to shore, where the Sultan ordered them beheaded and their captain impaled.

The cannons used to sink the Venetian merchantmen were

constructed by a Transylvanian cannon founder named Urban. Urban had first offered his services to the Emperor, who could not meet his steep price. Urban then turned to Edirne, promising Mehmed that he could produce cannons powerful enough to smash Constantinople's walls. The Sultan showered Urban with gifts and money. Seeing the results of Urban's cannons at Rumeli Hisarı, the Sultan ordered the cannon founder to produce a cannon that was twice as powerful.

"What will happen to the people of Constantinople?" Mihrimah asked. Gone was the innocent affect that usually marked her voice.

Ahmet shrugged. "I imagine their fate will depend on the will of their Emperor. If he cedes the city without a fight, Mehmed will likely follow the legal proscription against sacking the city. If the Emperor resists—well," he concluded heavily.

Mihrimah pushed on. "How can their Emperor do anything but fight to the end?"

Ahmet was taken aback by her aggressiveness. "Of course, you're right. The customary three days of pillage will be the stuff of nightmares for those who survive."

"And you will participate in these atrocities, Ahmet?" Mihrimah asked, her face tightly balled up in the rigid judgment of an ingenue.

Ahmet considered Mihrimah's reproachful gaze. "I will answer that question if I'm lucky enough to reach that day."

The warmth that had radiated throughout the cottage moments earlier was replaced with ashen desperation. All Mihrimah could do was look at the lamb on Ahmet's plate. "I'm sure you'll do what is right."

İbrahim arched his eyebrows, surprised by Mihrimah's maternal tone. "Perhaps you should spend the week with me, Ahmet. You can help me purchase a flock of sheep."

"You're planning to move?"

İbrahim nodded. "Even this village has become too busy for me. I need the solitude of the hills."

"I wish I could. Unfortunately, Şemsi has secured for me yet another duty—a high honor, or so he claims. He and I are to join a party charged with guaranteeing the security of the Sultan's latest toy. Mehmed has built a massive cannon, the likes of which the world has never seen. It is supposed to be able to hurl a half-ton ball a mile."

"So Mehmed plans to raze Constantinople's walls with his cannon and then push through the breaches into the city," İbrahim concluded. "It won't be easy. Even a defeated people will fight to the death, knowing what fate awaits them."

"No doubt Mehmed agrees. He's left nothing to chance. Constantinople's walls will be hit with the Sultan's machines and a horde unmatched since the time of Tamerlane. Hundreds of thousands of soldiers have been recruited. Fortune seekers are flocking to our banners. Ironically, many of them are Christians. No one seems to have much love for the Greeks."

İbrahim studied his friend. "Ahmet, you're truly a mystery to me. How can this assignment be anything but a sign of favor from the Sultan?"

"Because it makes no sense," Ahmet complained. "Şemsi berated me endlessly after I attended to the *sipahi*. He said the Sultan was outraged and that I would never be admitted into his presence again. But now I've been given an honor? If Şemsi wasn't such a frightened mouse, I'd suspect him of betrayal."

"You don't think Mehmed would plot against you?" İbrahim asked incredulously.

"Of course not. I'm too insignificant to draw his direct attention. Still, Hüsrev's rebellion did bring my own loyalty into question. The Sultan may have placed my fate in the hands of another."

"You sound like you have a suspect."

"Indeed I do: a foul kennelman named Hamza."

"Is this the same Hamza whom Şemsi despises?"

"The very one. He's in charge of my party. But worst of all, he's brought into our midst an unbearable garrison commander from the frontier. No one has explained their connection to me, but Hamza defers to him on every subject. Both of them take an unnatural joy in assigning childish tasks to Şemsi and me. So you see, I'm now being humiliated by a lowly, former garrison commander and a kennelman."

"What is the name of this garrison commander?" İbrahim asked uneasily.

"Abaza."

İbrahim took a deep breath. "I know this man. You're right to be concerned. He's petty and vicious."

"Abaza is the same garrison commander from your days on the frontier?"

"Who else could it be?" İbrahim said. "It's fortunate that I've decided to leave this place. Mihrimah and I aren't safe so close to Edirne. I only hope it's not too late." İbrahim paused for a moment and then asked, "Do you think Abaza knows of our connection?"

"It's quite possible," Ahmet acknowledged, "but then, you are a lost man, vanished from the ranks of the Janissaries for over two years now. Amid the confusion of the rebellion, no one ever pressed me for information about your disappearance. In fact, you weren't even condemned as a traitor. Perhaps that's because you were so quickly replaced by new Janissaries."

"It would've been better if you'd told everyone I was dead. Do you think you've ever been followed here on your visits?"

"I never felt the need to watch my back. You shouldn't worry though. Abaza has only been in Edirne for three months. Since then, I don't think I've visited you more than twice. I cannot imagine Abaza has had the time to make the connection, much less arrange to have me followed."

"But what of Hamza?"

"İbrahim," Mihrimah wailed. She had been standing by the hearth listening quietly. Now her anxiety bubbled over. Mihrimah wrapped her arms in a protective knot around her waist, then threw herself into İbrahim's embrace. "That horrible man," she gasped, pounding her fists into İbrahim's chest. "He will hunt us down and kill us. I know it."

İbrahim held her tightly and soothingly promised, "That bungler will never lay his hands on us. I'm sure he's too enamored with his newfound power to entertain petty thoughts of vengeance."

"You don't believe that," she cried. "You were assuming the worst just a moment ago. We must leave now."

"We cannot just leave. It'll take days to pack up our possessions."

"I want to leave today," she insisted. "I lived my life with nothing. We don't need anything now."

"Mihrimah, we have more time than you think," İbrahim said, trying to convince himself. "Simply because we've uncovered Abaza's presence doesn't mean he's about to fall upon us."

"You may not even be in danger," Ahmet tried to add helpfully.

İbrahim and Mihrimah turned to Ahmet, looking surprised to hear his voice. Ahmet suddenly felt like a stranger invading the sanctity of their marriage. Realizing he had only brought them trouble, Ahmet despondently said, "You must excuse me. My return to Edirne is long overdue." He did not wait for the customary long farewell before bolting from the cottage.

"Wait!" İbrahim called after Ahmet from the door of the cottage as he climbed atop his mount. He raced up to his friend. Hardly a trace of the limp remained.

"You'll have to give my apologies to your dear wife. Şemsi is expecting me."

"You don't have to dream up stories for me, Ahmet. In fact, there's never been a time where it was more important for us to speak plainly."

"Good. Why don't you start by telling me why Mihrimah grabbed her belly when Abaza's name was mentioned?"

"We're going to have a child," İbrahim beamed, "but Mihrimah made me promise not to tell anyone."

"Why wouldn't she want you to share such wonderful news with me?" Ahmet asked, obviously hurt.

"Something about a superstition she learned from the old women in the village. She explained it to me but I cannot repeat the reason. Her story was so strange I only pretended to listen after a while."

"So that's why she's in such a panic," Ahmet concluded. "Tread carefully, old friend. You cannot afford to make the wrong decision."

"Don't worry," İbrahim laughed. "I may have left the corps, but I can still control my emotions. We won't be moving so quickly."

"Don't be so sure you're in control of your emotions," Ahmet warned. "It's an emotional reaction to reject Mihrimah's wishes simply because they're inspired by fear."

"You think she's right?"

"I can't help but think that your life with Mihrimah is—"

"Is what?" İbrahim snapped.

Ahmet hesitated and then tactfully answered, "Uncertain."

"What makes you so sure that my life isn't exactly as it should be?"

"Because you were never destined to live this life."

"This life seems to fit me very nicely," İbrahim huffily disagreed. "Much better than my life as a Janissary. What life do you think I was destined to live?"

"Like a river, a man's life follows natural patterns in the landscape. Even when a river overflows its banks to wreak havoc, it always faithfully returns to its predestined course. Unfortunately, the pattern of your life has always been to stand alone and out of place with your circumstances."

"You sound like an ancient *baba*."

"Then I should return to my natural path as well," Ahmet laughed. A slight, familiar smile creased his face. He maneuvered his horse away from the cottage and firmly said, "I'd rather not say goodbye, if you don't mind. You'll do me the favor of accepting my good wishes."

As İbrahim watched Ahmet slowly disappear, Mihrimah reached under his shoulders from behind and slid her arms around his chest. He had assumed she was watching closely and was not surprised by her unheralded embrace. "Did you and Ahmet say what needed to be said?"

"I don't know," İbrahim thoughtfully answered. He too had not wanted to say goodbye.

"You told him about our baby."

İbrahim's shoulders slumped. "He asked me. I couldn't lie to him."

"I know you couldn't." She squeezed him with all her strength. "Ahmet talks as though he might be executed at any time. What do you think will become of him?"

"Ahmet isn't one to be melodramatic. If he feels he's in danger..." İbrahim heaved a heavy sigh. He turned around and gazed into Mihrimah's eyes. As always, he was instantly enraptured. "We'll leave at sunrise."

Mihrimah smiled appreciatively. Her panic was gone. "I'm sorry. Even the thought of that terrible man freezes me. You were right. It isn't necessary that we leave immediately. Go buy your flock of sheep. Then we'll move to our new home."

"You're certain?" he asked, still ready to yield completely even as he gratefully accepted her concession.

The same brave smile instantly reappeared.

Gesturing towards hundreds of pigeons sunning themselves on the dry grass, Ahmet complained, "Why are we stationed here? We must be a mile from the cannon, left to stand guard with those accursed sky rats."

Şemsi looked back over the long, open field where Urban's cannon was being attended by hundreds of soldiers. More than twenty-six feet in length and eight inches in diameter, the cannon dwarfed its faithful servants, who looked like scurrying ants. The monster weapon was so heavy that fifteen pairs of oxen had been required to transport it. "If Urban is right about the range of his cannon, we're going to have a half-ton ball falling on us."

"Not quite the honor you had imagined, is it?" Ahmet deadpanned.

Şemsi frowned. "May Allah curse Hamza for assigning us to

this duty. Laughter," Şemsi snarled, rage building. "You and I will be the butt of every joke in Edirne for weeks to come."

Ahmet had finally lost patience. "So now I am to become an object of ridicule as well because Hamza is your enemy."

Over the years, an uneasy friendship had developed between them as they plotted together. Now their days were filled with disappointments, reawakening the old hard feelings.

Şemsi cast a scornful look at Ahmet. He understood Ahmet's frustration only too well. "I wondered which one of us would cast the first stone," he coolly said. "Have you become such a fool that you can't see that Hamza is as much your enemy as mine?"

Ahmet bit his lips in silence.

Şemsi smirked. "So, tell me about your trips away from the capital."

"Sounds like you already know."

"That depends on whether Abaza told me the truth. Is it true that İbrahim lives?"

Answered again with silence, Şemsi concluded, "So my association with you has made me party to İbrahim's treason."

Şemsi's words struck a sobering nerve. "What did Abaza tell you?" Ahmet asked contritely.

"Abaza told me our old friend is living with a peasant girl he met in a village along the Wallachian frontier. It seems that Hamza shared the story of İbrahim's mysterious disappearance with Abaza. Once he learned about your close friendship with İbrahim, Abaza asked an endless stream of questions about you. No doubt at Abaza's insistence, Hamza has been faithfully watching your movements for months."

"Mihrimah," Ahmet numbly groaned.

"Yes, that's her name. She must be one of the world's great wonders for İbrahim to have risked so much. It's a shame I won't meet her. Abaza is set upon making İbrahim's 'death' a reality. No doubt this Mihrimah will share İbrahim's fate. I can only guess the indignities İbrahim set upon this man. It's a unique testament to İbrahim's aloofness and arrogance that Abaza is determined to have his vengeance after so many years."

A titanic concussion rolled across the field, angrily charging the air around them. They flinched like young children, ducking their chins to their chests. The flock of pigeons sprang upwards in a singular motion, adding the harsh flutter of their wings to the thunderous report.

Ahmet and Şemsi cast their eyes skyward as the enormous projectile scattered the dense company of pigeons over their heads. Their mouths fell agape in silent response to the accusatory whine of the cannonball. For an exaggerated moment, Urban's creation dominated all earthly elements. After traveling nearly a mile, the cannonball seemed to hang motionless in the air and then fall rapidly towards the earth.

A resounding thud awoke them from their wonder. They sprinted towards the plume of dust spiraling upwards from the gaping hole. "Impossible," Ahmet gushed. "The cannonball must be buried six feet deep."

"I never thought Urban's project would succeed. I was sure the cannon would explode," Şemsi marveled. "With more cannons such as this one, or even cannons half its size, Constantinople will surely be ours."

"Breaching Constantinople's ancient walls will become reality, but not for you."

Ahmet and Şemsi spun around to face a familiar voice. Sitting proudly atop a roan was Hamza, grinning with delight. Behind him rode Abaza and six Janissaries from the First Orta. All were new men.

Ahmet and Şemsi considered Hamza's ominous riddle while subconsciously stepping back from the advancing group. A mile away from their nearest ally, they weighed their odds in a fight against eight men on horseback.

Şemsi cleared his throat and with his customary bravado scolded, "Don't play your games with me, Hamza. Stand in my way and you'll see what a true Janissary can do."

Şemsi's bold offensive did not pale Hamza's spirit. Continuing to enjoy his advantage, Hamza blandly stared back while giving his men time to surround Ahmet and Şemsi. "Şemsi, you always had a way of disturbing my blood. At least that was the case until today. Now your words are no more aggravating to me than cleaning fresh mud from my boots."

"What are your orders?" Şemsi demanded.

"To mount your heads on pikes for the entire corps to see," Hamza said, taking pleasure in slowly pronouncing each word.

"You will show me this order," Şemsi snapped.

Hamza contemptuously sniffed before reaching into his uniform to produce a small piece of paper bearing the Sultan's seal. "'By decree of the state, the men whose names appear herein shall be executed for high crimes against the House of Osman.' You see," Hamza pointed to the paper, "your names and that of your coward friend, İbrahim, appear, at the bottom of the order."

"İbrahim? He died years ago," Ahmet said, feigning disbelief.

Abaza's shrill laugh pierced the exchange. His hatred for İbrahim was palpable. "Your friend does not deserve the respect that comes from a formal execution. I will make him suffer so that he yearns for the rough kiss of death to prick his lips. That's why İbrahim and his woman will be sold to the Mamluks in Egypt. I'm told the Mamluks know how to get the most out of their slaves, particularly the women. I will make sure İbrahim knows about the life of sweet accommodation awaiting her."

While the conversation was focused between Ahmet and Abaza, Şemsi deftly unsheathed his scimitar and withdrew a short dagger concealed in the sash of his uniform. He wanted to strike Hamza first, but Hamza had drifted out of the circle to inspect the cannonball.

"Slavery," Ahmet growled. "Then it's you who is guilty of treason."

"I'm guilty of treason?" Abaza scornfully laughed. "I'm loyal to my Sultan."

"Apparently not," Ahmet shot back. "Where in that order does it say anything about enslavement? You intend to contradict the written command of the Sultan."

Ahmet turned towards the closest Janissary. Like his comrades, he was quietly absorbed in the debate. "What about you?"

Ahmet shouted. "Are you too a traitor to your Sultan?"

The Janissary's eyes opened wide in shock. He then turned to his comrades, whose faces wore the same uncomfortable expression.

"You're being used to settle a personal vendetta," Ahmet confidently continued, sensing he was making headway. "In the end, you'll earn yourself the executioner's knife."

"Don't try to confuse those with innocent spirits," Abaza said, as he cast a worrisome glance towards Hamza. "Enslavement to the Mamluks is a punishment equal to execution. But even if your fanciful claims might be believed, who is going to learn of İbrahim's fate?"

"Who indeed?" Ahmet slyly replied, fixing each man with his charismatic smile. "Dark deeds require absolute secrecy. Where treason is involved, witnesses can be very inconvenient. So tell me, Abaza, what false promises of fortune and advancement have you and Hamza made to these men? Better yet, when will you murder your helpers?"

All eyes fell on Abaza, who was twisting uneasily in his saddle. "You're a wasted talent whose time has ended. Now enough of your serpent tongue. You'll both throw down your weapons and submit or I'll have you cut down where you stand."

Ahmet ignored the command. He turned to the Janissaries and appealed, "You know these men. They have no loyalty to anyone but themselves. Help me arrest them. They have confessed their treason. They are the true enemies of the Sultan. We will prove their treason together and you will receive an award beyond anything they've promised."

Ahmet had succeeded in sowing the seeds of doubt. The Janissaries searched each others' eyes for consensus. All shared the same dire expression.

"Kill them now," Hamza barked as he rode back into the circle with his scimitar raised high over his head.

The Janissaries remained frozen in their saddles. Ahmet's victory was short-lived. In his haste to assist Abaza, Hamza had inadvertently entered the circle near Şemsi. Şemsi could not resist the urge to attack. He ripped into Hamza's leg with his dagger, using it like a meat hook to drag Hamza from his saddle. As Hamza hit the ground, Şemsi brought his scimitar down.

Two piercing screams punctuated the chaos. Hamza had managed to drive his scimitar upward into Şemsi's shoulder just as Şemsi's scimitar grazed his leg. They rolled away from each other in agony. Şemsi struggled to his feet. Three arrows pierced his chest. The force of the arrows propelled him to the ground, severing his spinal cord.

The three Janissaries who fired on Şemsi had answered their doubts through a reflexive call to arms. The other three had also raised their bows and now fired at Şemsi's attackers. Guided by remorse, the arrows missed their mark. The two sides then fell on each other.

Ahmet felt like he was trapped in a nightmare and watching himself slowly drown. As he withdrew his scimitar, Hamza's roan wandered past him. Ahmet turned back to the battle. Hamza was holding Şemsi's severed head in his hand while shouting instructions to Abaza. The men who had rallied to Ahmet's aid were being pushed back. Ahmet could read the equivocation in their faces. At any moment, they might plead for forgiveness.

Ahmet climbed onto Hamza's mount and dug his heels into the horse's sides. Just as the horse started to catch its stride, an arrow caught Ahmet's right shoulder, severing an artery. He yanked the arrow from his shoulder and turned back to see Abaza preparing to fire again. Ahmet pushed his head down and kicked harder. Two more arrows flew over his head before he found the protective cover of the forest at the end of the field. He continued to ride hard for the next hour, his hand futilely clamped over the gushing wound. Ahmet dearly wanted to reach İbrahim, but exhaustion finally overcame his will, forcing him to stop by a small stream.

Ahmet slid off Hamza's roan and fell to his knees. He cut the sleeve off his wounded shoulder. Blood was surging from the gaping hole to the beat of his heart. He tightly wrapped the sleeve around his shoulder and then crawled to the stream to satisfy his thirst. The stench from the brackish, stagnant water forced him to turn away. His energy wrung from his body, he rolled onto his back and stared through the tree branches at the setting sun. As the blood poured past the saturated bandage, Ahmet knew his efforts to stanch the wound were doomed. An oddly enjoyable sense of desperation descended on him as he struggled to keep his eyes open. He began to whisper, "There is no god but Allah...."

İbrahim had quickly negotiated the purchase of a modest track of land and one hundred sheep. Before the owner could thank İbrahim for such a handsome windfall, İbrahim was pushing south again. Using a lantern to travel at night, İbrahim had made the hundred-mile journey in a week. Like an eager young suitor, a light song buzzed about his lips as the vision of Mihrimah's sweet, tantalizing smile hung in front of him.

He had picked an isolated corner of the Bulgarian countryside to make their new home. The nearest village was ten miles away. After Ahmet's dark warning, İbrahim was more comfortable with the prospect of defending his family from marauders than risking detection by Abaza.

İbrahim had assumed that a life of quiet solitude was the final answer to his dreams of contentment. Instead, he found the isolation of the barren countryside uninviting. It never occurred to him that years in the corps had transformed him into a social creature.

As İbrahim neared the cottage, a short gust of wind carried a heavy charcoal odor past him. He instinctively charged ahead. Nothing was spared. The cottage was so thoroughly consumed that even the hearth was completely incinerated. The holocaust had swept beyond the bounds of the cottage, consuming Mihrimah's prized garden and singeing distant trees. The lush, green grass leading up to the cottage was pale ash. The boot and hoof prints pressed into the scorched mat recorded five men.

"Mihrimah," İbrahim grieved. He slowly marched across the cinders that had once formed his home. His despair deepened when he could not find any trace of her among the destruction.

He tried to curse Abaza but the words eluded him. As if he were infused with a forbidden intoxicant, a numbing acceptance of Mihrimah's absence began to distort his anger and pain.

İbrahim turned towards where the barn had been. It too was burned to the ground. Out of the corner of his eye, İbrahim saw two women from the village watching him from the far side of the meadow. They whispered to each other as though they were hatching some base conspiracy. The wind carried their conversation across the open ground to İbrahim. He concentrated on their words, hoping for a clue that might reveal Mihrimah's fate, but he was unable to hold a sentence in his mind.

A subtle change in the wind then drew his attention towards the well. It was a familiar odor. İbrahim clamped his hand over his mouth and nose as he leaned over the edge. The horrid stench of rotting flesh assaulted him from the darkness. He hastily lit the lantern and dropped it down the hole. A pale, yellow glow glistened off the slippery stone walls. İbrahim took a deep breath and peered down. The bloated bodies of the livestock, some mutilated to pass through the opening of the well, met his gaze. With the carcasses piled high on top of one another, it was impossible to tell whether Mihrimah's body was also entombed below.

İbrahim walked towards the women in a mechanical, broken gait, mouth opened wide to speak. İbrahim thought he heard himself asking them what had happened, but his tongue did not manufacture his thoughts. Eyes fixed on İbrahim's gaping mouth, the women stared back at him in stony, fearful silence. Only the rapid flutter of their eyes betrayed any exchange between the two parties.

"The beast has his spirit," one of the women finally lamented. Her words passed through him without impact. She and her friend then ran back towards the safety of their homes, periodically looking over their shoulders to see if İbrahim was following them. He remained cemented in place like a statue.

The sun arched across the sky, casting increasingly long shadows from İbrahim's still-frozen body. Neither the loss of light nor the falling temperature caught his notice. His thoughts drew him back to days at the *tekke*.

The disciple of a great *baba* in Baghdad overheard the Angel of Death talking to a companion at an inn. The Angel explained that he was making calls in Baghdad for the next few weeks. Not wanting to risk meeting the Angel, the disciple fled to Samarkand. The Angel later met the disciple's *baba* and asked for him. The *baba* suggested that the disciple should be found somewhere in Baghdad deep in study. The Angel expressed surprise, saying, "I am to collect him in four weeks' time, but in Samarkand of all places."

As the parable replayed in his mind, the disciple's voice became more feminine, more familiar, except that the voice seemed to echo from a dark, malodorous cavern. It was a deepening nightmare he could not see to the end. He reached out for the last rays of the setting sun and threw open his eyes.

A flickering reflection beamed back at him from across the field, drawing him forward like an irresistible beacon. It was his scimitar, buried butt-first in the soil. The cold steel was pointed skyward. İbrahim grabbed the blade with his bare hand, producing a thick stream of blood. Unmoved, he tore the weapon from the soil.

The Red Apple • May 23, 1453

The twelve-member crew of the Venetian brigantine was exhausted. Since stealing past the naval blockade of Constantinople disguised as Ottomans three weeks earlier, they had desperately searched the Aegean for the long-awaited Venetian relief fleet. No sign of their countrymen had sparked their waning spirits.

With Urban's cannon securely in tow, Mehmed had slowly rumbled through Thrace with an army of eighty thousand, arriving before the walls of the terrified city in early April. All that prevented Mehmed from securing his dearest dream were five thousand Greeks and two thousand Venetians and Genoese manning Constantinople's fourteen miles of land and seawalls. Desperate for food and fresh defenders, the beleaguered city's lone salvation lay in the promised help from its fitful ally and sometime nemesis.

The Venetian Senate underestimated the importance of their participation in the struggle, conveniently assuming that Constantinople's formidable land walls would save the city. Weeks passed as these cautious men struggled over how best to position their trading empire. Finally, the fleet was released from Venice's lagoon, only days after the brigantine had escaped from the Ottoman stranglehold. Realizing that it was only a matter of time before they would have to reckon with Mehmed, the Senate sent an ambassador to push the warring parties towards a peaceful resolution. In no event was the Captain General of the fleet to engage the Ottomans without first reporting back.

The sailors had suffered through the grinding desperation of the siege for a month. They knew the fight to save the city was doomed without aid from the relief fleet. The fresh, unfettered sea air was a tempting contrast to the enervating squalor of the besieged city. Still, thoughts of liberty were brushed aside. Not knowing if Constantine Palaeologus still ruled his capital, they nevertheless renewed their vow to return to his city.

The crew tacked their way through the north wind rushing down the Sea of Marmara, periodically casting a curious eye at the odd man standing at rigid attention on the brigantine's bow. When they had docked at Negropont for supplies, he greeted them as though their arrival had been announced long in advance. Before the captain could take his second step along the quay, the stranger curtly claimed the right to accompany them back to Constantinople. When asked why he would seek out certain destruction, he cryptically answered, "Denial," with no small hint of arrogance.

The captain and crew had inspected the tall stranger, who displayed no interest in currying their approval. His hair was an oily mat of tightly woven curls that brushed lightly against his square shoulders. Set against the tightly drawn skin of his weathered, clean-shaven face, the man's eyes were concentrated into a hard, brooding gaze. The sailors quickly turned their eyes downward as the stranger coldly confronted their curious stares. His soiled, tattered tunic and pants clung tightly to his lean, muscular frame. But for his sturdy pair of boots and finely crafted scimitar neatly secured within the sash around his waist, the crew would have concluded that he had long endured an ascetic existence.

It was easier to yield to the man's demand than resist. The captain granted passage, justifying his acquiescence by assuming that the stranger was a hardened religious fanatic who would prove useful during the hard fighting along the walls. No thanks were offered. Except for later identifying himself as Manuel, the man had not spoken since climbing aboard.

The spray from the light chop of the sea showered İbrahim. He subconsciously stroked the unfamiliar feel of his freshly shaven chin. After Mihrimah's disappearance, he had taken a razor to his finely groomed beard. With his turban cast aside, his childhood curls returned. Deleting the tenets and symbols of Islam from his mind and body were the necessary byproducts of his flight from the past. Even Mahmut's Koran had not been spared.

İbrahim craned his head forward. He tried to catch a glimpse of Constantinople through the fine mist, which was brightly illuminated by the rays of sunshine. He was ready to die in peace if he could deny the Sultan that which had been denied him. "You will know my desolation," İbrahim hissed under his breath. "You will know what it is like to have the world torn from your grasp."

"Raise the Ottoman flag," the captain ordered.

One of the sailors scaled the rigging. The flag of St. Mark was soon safely concealed below.

"Get your axes ready," the captain barked. "If I see a Turkish hand or head on the deck, it better be severed."

"Take it," a sailor said as he warily handed an axe to İbrahim. "Our deck is higher than their ships. Their boarding parties have to climb up," he smiled. "It's easy work if you have the stomach for it."

"Are we near the city?" İbrahim broke his silence.

"Must be," the sailor replied. "Why else would those galleys be making for us?"

İbrahim wheeled to his right. Four vessels flying the Ottoman flag were bearing down on the brigantine. "The flag," İbrahim nodded upwards, "doesn't seem to have fooled them."

The sailor confidently grinned and said, "Don't worry about wasting too much energy on them. I doubt they'll come too close. Their seamanship is worse than their ships. Certainly no match for our skills."

One of the vessels managed to come within striking distance. "Greek fire," the captain sneered. Two sailors loaded a catapult with a large barrel and lit it; then they launched the barrel at the advancing vessel.

The ignited barrel hit the deck of the Ottoman vessel and burst apart. The fiery ooze quickly slid across the ship's deck. The Ottomans madly poured water on the blaze, but the fire was soon licking the rigging. Glued to his position on the bow, İbrahim stoically watched the Ottomans jump into the sea.

The remaining Ottoman vessels continued their pursuit with far less zeal. Soon, their swaying masts receded from view.

With the drama of the battle still pulsing in their veins, the Venetians came upon Constantinople's southern seawalls, which brilliantly reflected the glimmering waves of the Marmara. The awesome sight of the city provoked an unexpected gasp of appreciation from İbrahim. Although less than a shadow of what it had once been, the city remained a hauntingly rich testament to its Roman forebears.

Constantinople's ramparts and towers dwarfed the tiny brigantine. The carefully maintained walls wrapped around the matchless urban expanse of the triangularly shaped city. The stout land walls safeguarded the western boundary. Gently buttressed by the sweet blue waters of the Marmara, the city's southern seawalls ran eastward until they curled upwards into the Bosphorus like a rhinoceros horn. The brimming harbor of the Golden Horn protected Constantinople's northern flank. Across from the Golden Horn lay the walled Genoese colony of Galata, where the Emperor's mercantile neighbors were trying to placate the Sultan through a dubious policy of neutrality.

Hugging the heavens, Hagia Sophia loomed behind the walls, casting its wondrous shadow over the dozens of palaces and proud churches dotting the capital. In a city filled with architectural wonders unimagined in the great cities of Christendom and Islam alike, the breathtaking beauty and majesty of the grand church represented the pinnacle of Byzantium's rich past as well as the central point upon which the people's cherished orthodoxy tightly revolved. No truer symbol of Constantinople's fabled aura existed, making it a beacon to Byzantium's faithful and enemies.

Truly a prize worth denying, İbrahim reassured himself, reflecting upon the Sultan's appetites.

The brigantine speedily made its way towards the security of the Golden Horn. The winged lion flag of the Venetian Republic had been restored to the highest mast. Hopeful cheers greeted the crew from the defenders manning the towers.

At the Emperor's order, the Genoese engineer Bartolomeo Soligo had overseen the construction of a boom that spanned the five-hundred-yard opening of the harbor. The boom consisted of a chain supported by wooden floats. On one end it was fixed to the Tower of Eugenius, which stood below the ancient city's acropolis. The opposite end was attached to a tower on Galata's seawalls.

In combination with a multinational Christian flotilla of merely twenty-six vessels, the boom had prevented the massive, albeit inferior, Ottoman navy from overwhelming the harbor. But Mehmed insisted upon putting pressure on the harbor's seawalls. It was through those very seawalls that the adventurers of the Fourth Crusade had burst into the city two hundred and fifty years earlier.

Following Saladin's reconquest of Jerusalem, Pope Innocent III had called the Christian faithful to the Fourth Crusade in 1198. Led by the blind, octogenarian Doge, Enrico Dandolo, nearly five hundred Venetian galleys carried the Crusaders down the Adriatic. Seduced by the lure of great riches and guided by Dandolo's hatred of Byzantium, the Crusaders soon abandoned their quest and set their sights on taking Constantinople. The ensuing siege ended with the Doge ordering his galleys beached against the seawalls of the Golden Horn. Leaping onto the towers from the masts of their ships, the Venetians had overwhelmed the defenders.

The Crusaders had showed no restraint in plundering their schismatic brethren. Silver and precious jewels were hacked from the altars of Hagia Sophia. Inside the Holy Chapel of Blachernae Palace, they claimed pieces of the True Cross, nails that were driven through Christ's hands and feet, the tip of the Holy Lance, a large phial containing Christ's blood, the Crown of Thorns, and the head of John the Baptist.

A Crusader kingdom ruled the city until it was retaken by the Palaeologus dynasty in 1261. By that time, Byzantium was no longer an effective bulwark against Islam. Forever bankrupt and dominated by the Venetians and Genoese, its eventual conquest became the fantasy of its neighbors, Christian and Muslim alike.

Unable to gain the harbor through an assault on the boom, Mehmed put his considerable manpower to work. The Ottomans built a road that started at the Bosphorus, climbed the two-hundred-foot ridge behind Galata, and then descended into the Golden Horn. The citizens of Galata and Constantinople gazed on in frightened awe as teams of oxen hauled seventy Ottoman vessels over the ridge and into the harbor.

Although the high-decked Christian fleet held the advantage over the smaller Ottoman vessels, the harbor was no longer secure. His forces already stretched to the limit, the Emperor was forced to transfer hundreds of defenders from their much-needed perch along the land walls.

The boom was lowered to allow the brigantine into the harbor. The small ship hugged the seawalls before finding an open quay on which to dock. The captain steeled himself with a heavy sigh and then disembarked. İbrahim and the crew dutifully followed him onto the quay.

The Emperor was waiting for them. Bred more to the life of a common soldier than the life of an emperor, Constantine Palaeologus was wearing a functional suit of armor. His shoulders sagged limply under his heavy breastplate and dark rings framed the gloomy emptiness in his once purposeful eyes, overshadowing his strong, regular features. Still, a dogged determination pulsed from his exhausted, lean body. His serenity in the face of unsalvageable odds had earned him the admiration of his most ardent foreign detractors. Considered by his subjects to be the visible manifestation of God, Constantine Palaeologus dutifully bore the heavy weight of his authority with grace.

Lucas Notaras, the Emperor's valued Megadux and commander of the seawalls along the Golden Horn, stood at his master's side, a respectful half step back. Giovanni Giustiniani Longo, the Genoese adventurer from Chios whose famed expertise in defending walled cities earned him the command of the land walls, and Girolamo Minotto, the Venetian Bailo, competed for position behind them.

In a grand manner that masked his nervousness, the Emperor smiled warmly and said, "Greetings, Captain. What news do you bring us of the fleet?"

The captain's face turned red. "My crew and I searched everywhere." He shook his head side to side. "I fear it may never come."

Giustiniani shook his head in disgust and flashed an accusatory glance at Minotto. "We are six weeks into the siege and the Venetians are no different now than when seven hundred of them disappeared into the night three months ago. Another betrayal is sure to come, Your Highness. I beg you to turn over control of the fleet to one of my countrymen."

"I will not suffer such an outrage," Minotto railed. "I demand—"

The Emperor flinched as though a knife had been dug into his chest. The strain of maintaining peace between the Genoese and Venetians was a constant drain on his energy. "Silence," he snapped in an unusual display of short temper. He then turned to the captain and asked, "Tell me why you've returned, if our plight is so hopeless? Surely you must have thought the city might already be in the hands of the Sultan."

"Our duty was clear, Your Highness," the captain answered. "When we left, we took an oath to report back to you even if it meant sacrificing our own lives."

The Emperor smiled forlornly. In a voice choked with emotion, he personally thanked each member of the crew. When the Emperor finished, he noticed İbrahim, who had deliberately set himself apart from the sailors. "This man," the Emperor pointed to İbrahim, "was not a member of your original crew, was he?"

"No, Your Highness. He joined us when we stopped at Negropont. He wants to fight for you."

The Emperor fixed a hard stare upon İbrahim as though he expected to find an answer to some ancient riddle. He then laughed and said, "Giustiniani."

"Yes, Your Highness."

"Assign this man to the land walls."

"If I may," Giustiniani boldly responded, "we don't know him. We need the utmost loyalty along those fortifications."

"More than anything, we need numbers," the Emperor answered practically. "Thousands of Christian mercenaries are besieging us as we speak, hoping to loot my palace. They may yet succeed. No one seeking my wealth would've joined us at this late date." The Emperor waved for Lucas Notaras to follow him.

Giustiniani sighed and looked at Minotto.

Minotto haughtily sneered, "For once I agree with you. I don't want him either. The man is filthy. Lord knows he may be carrying the plague." Before Giustiniani could respond, Minotto disappeared back into the city.

"Alviso," Giustiniani barked.

A young officer wearing a finely crafted metal breastplate and meticulously fitted armor leggings stepped forward.

"Take this man to your post on the Rhegium Gate. I don't want him near our main defenses along the Mesoteichion section of the walls."

As the young officer watched his commander depart, he contemptuously asked in Greek, "I don't suppose you speak Italian."

"No," İbrahim curtly answered in Greek. Retaining the use of his native Greek tongue had proved useful during his campaigns, but infrequent usage had slowly made it an alien vestige. He now labored to find the right words, certain that each awkwardly accented comment he made marked him as a stranger.

"Save your anger for the pagans," the officer replied. "You mercenaries are all alike. You think you know something about warfare because you carry a sword and have fought a few battles. I won't tolerate any heroics under my command. You'll do what I say when I say it. If you disobey me once, I'll dress you like a Turk and execute you on the highest tower for the Sultan's entire camp to see."

The officer studied İbrahim's face to see if his words were having an effect. İbrahim answered with an amused expression.

The officer shook his head in disgust and asked, "Your name?"

İbrahim heard himself start to say İbrahim. "Manuel," he artificially answered.

"Part of me wants to ask you why you're here, but there really wouldn't be much point, would there?"

İbrahim replied with a stony stare.

"The Rhegium Gate is this way."

İbrahim bit down on his lip and limped after his new commander. He quickly discovered that the seawalls also hid Constantinople's decrepitude. Though the city had once been home to hundreds of thousands of souls, fewer than one hundred thousand citizens remained. The city was fragmented into thirteen distinct towns, many of which were jealously separated by their own well-guarded palisades. The depopulation of the city had caused whole districts to melt away. But instead of meticulously manicured parks and gardens separating the districts as in the city's glory days, fields and orchards filled with wild roses and hedgerows dominated the untamed countryside.

Constantinople's imposing infrastructure was equally impoverished. As İbrahim made his way through the more populated districts along the Golden Horn and then on to the city's central ridge, he saw uninhabited, crumbling buildings interspersed with worn shops and houses. Trees and shrubbery were growing through some of the ruins, reclaiming the city from its weary citizens, who looked past the shells with blind indifference. Except for the state-subsidized Church of Hagia Sophia, many of the city's famed churches had lapsed into disrepair. The Patriarch had even abandoned his residence in the Patriarchal Palace for more comfortable surroundings. Once the city's vital center, the Hippodrome had crumbled into little more than a polo ground for young noblemen. Decay and melancholy cast a gray shadow over all that met İbrahim's eye.

They wound their way through the narrow streets towards the land walls, which periodically peeked over a roof line. An eerie silence had begun to bear down on him. "Where are the people?" İbrahim asked, his curiosity getting the better of him.

The officer had been stealing glances at İbrahim, trying to take his measure. He now took advantage of the opening to study İbrahim more carefully. As much as he wanted to dismiss İbrahim as a base adventurer, İbrahim's upright bearing and stolid mien expressed an undeniable confidence born from the harsh trials of perpetual warfare.

After a long pause, the officer cynically snickered, "I assume you mean the people who didn't sneak away before the siege began." He gestured towards the land walls. "There you'll find the able-bodied men. The rest of the Greeks are either in church or bringing what little food and water is left to the soldiers."

"Are the Greeks good soldiers?" İbrahim asked, trying to envisage his father bravely facing death along the same walls.

"Hardly," the Genoese disdainfully answered, "but they fight as hard as anyone when the call to arms is made. Now tell me, why are you here?"

"I'm a mercenary looking to fill my purse," İbrahim lied, in his usual unconvincing manner. "I expect a generous reward when the Turks retreat."

The officer laughed. "Wait until you look out from the walls. None of us is likely to leave this place. So you're either telling me the foolish truth or an equally foolish lie."

The two men walked in silence for another hour. Upon nearing the walls, they were met by a growing hum. A steady stream of the young and old made their way to the walls, laboring under the weight of heavy stones, planks, barrels and sacks of dirt meant to fill the breaches torn open by Mehmed's cannons. Children carried baskets of bread while their mothers teamed together in pairs to move heavy kettles of water. Stones were delivered to the walls by feeble old men, some of whom carried but one at a time, to feed the catapults and mangonels.

The singular act of community was performed with disquieting urgency. Nervous smiles with tired eyes directed downwards replaced words. No one looked at the walls for too long, fearing that the Turks might burst through them at any moment.

"Your post," the officer announced.

İbrahim looked up at a forty-foot-high wall. He then gazed right to left at the long line of square and octagonal towers that ran from the Golden Horn down to the Sea of Marmara. He followed the officer through a gate and saw a second, twenty-five-foot-high, wall fifty yards in front of him.

As he reached the gate of the nearest tower, İbrahim gingerly reached out to touch the cold, weathered stone, wondering whether this fabled protector of Constantinople's liberty contained its own unique life force. A faint tremor suddenly ran through his hand, accompanied by a deafening blast. Small rocks broke free from the wall and rained down on him.

"The Turks' cannon," the Genoese explained, entertained by İbrahim's startled reaction.

İbrahim followed the Genoese into the dark, musty tower and climbed the steps to the top of the ramparts. A sweet sea breeze washed over him as his eyes adjusted to the sunlight. Some fifty feet past his position was a low crenellated breastwork from which archers could safely pick off the enemy. Immediately past this last defensive line was a deep foss that the Turks were laboring to fill.

"The Theodosian Walls," the officer gestured with a broad sweep of his hands. "They were built over a thousand years ago by the Prefect Anthemius during the reign of Emperor Theodosius II. Of course, they've been rebuilt many times, but never breached. I'm told Attila the Hun brought his army to these walls, took one look and then marched west."

"Attila the Hun didn't have cannons," İbrahim cracked disdainfully, deflating the young officer.

A less powerful blast roared into the sky. İbrahim looked northward. His eyes followed the outer wall over a gradual rise and then down to the Lycus River valley below. A few thousand defenders were scrambling around a makeshift wooden stockade framed by the fallen rubble of the outer wall. The stockade was draped with sheets of leather and bales of wool in the false hope of muting the blows from the cannonballs.

İbrahim looked across the foss where a black cloud of smoke

was slowly dissipating. A crew of Janissaries was struggling to reposition Urban's cannon on its platform. Numerous other cannons focused on the Mesoteichion section of the walls were lined up along the outer edge of the foss. In order to enclose the Greeks, the Ottomans had dug a trench that ran the length of the walls. The trench was backed up by an earthen rampart topped with a low wooden palisade. The Sultan's red and gold tent was safely located behind this line, surrounded by twelve thousand Janissaries and other trusted regiments. The Anatolian divisions were positioned to the south of the Sultan's tent while the European divisions faced the northern defenses. The *başıbozuk*s, the army's mass of shock troops, were settled in behind the lines, ready to move to the next attack at a moment?s notice.

After probing the walls for six weeks, Mehmed had directed most of the cannons to the section of the walls under which the Lycus River flowed into the city. The damage to the fortifications was immense, but every night the Byzantines doggedly rebuilt the walls. As each new cannonball brought portions of the ancient walls tumbling down, the defenders' desperation grew, matched only by the attackers' frustration.

Although rumors about the massive size of the Sultan's army had spread like wildfire as far as Portugal, İbrahim could hardly believe his eyes. Seeing such a mass of humanity drawn to a common purpose awakened a sense of awe and fear that bore into his gut. The mere idea that Mehmed could coordinate such an unwieldy endeavor inspired grudging admiration. İbrahim wondered if so few defenders could ultimately repel them. His goal of denying Constantinople to Mehmed seemed like a faint chimera tossed about in the contrary spring winds. He looked across from his position. The Anatolians were dormant.

"Should we be expecting an assault?" İbrahim asked, eager to shake off his anxiety.

"Oh, they'll be picking up their scaling ladders and grappling hooks soon enough," the officer blithely answered. "They attack at least once a day. You won't be impressed. The Turks haven't mounted a strong attack here for over a week. I think we've only lost ten men since the siege began. They're applying just enough pressure to keep us pinned down so we can't help the defense along the Mesoteichion.

"It's the same everywhere. Their ships pressure us in the Marmara and the Golden Horn. The Emperor refuses to take chances. We've been forced to move men to defend the seawalls. With the way our forces are thinly balanced throughout the city, our doom is assured if the Turks find a penetration point.

"The Turks' energy is astounding. Not only did they haul their ships overland into the Golden Horn, they also built a pontoon bridge linking their forces on both sides of the harbor. The clever bastards built the bridge right where the walls of Blachernae Palace face the harbor. They placed a line of cannons on the bridge that are ripping apart the Emperor's palace. Of course, that's the Venetians' problem. They're defending Blachernae."

İbrahim observed the weaponry assembled along the ramparts. "Do we not have cannons as well?"

The Genoese grimaced. "We had to give up using them. The walls trembled every time we fired."

"What about the inner wall?" İbrahim asked, gesturing to the wall behind him. "Why haven't men been placed on those ramparts?"

"A quick and attentive eye," the officer observed, renewing his interest in İbrahim's background. "Giustiniani decided we only had enough men to defend the outer wall. The Sultan would've turned back by now if he had to breach the inner wall too. Several thousand more men would make all the difference. If the city falls, it will be because of the cowardice and indifference of those who will soon enough face this Sultan."

As İbrahim stoically listened to the Genoese rail against the abandonment of Constantinople, he concluded that the young man gloried in the heroism of his vain sacrifice. İbrahim doubted that the officer would fight to the bitter end should the Ottomans find their small penetration point. After all, who then would tell his story?

The officer's rhetoric boosted his confidence. "Now where did you say you came from?" he clumsily asked.

"Negropont," İbrahim coldly ignored the true intent behind the question, his steady eyes cautioning the Genoese against further inquiry.

The Genoese scowled and harshly reminded him, "Remember what I said about following orders." Leaving İbrahim to introduce himself to his new comrades, the officer angrily marched down the ramparts, barking orders at the fifty-odd men lazily sunning themselves under the fading sky. The Genoese soldiers dutifully stirred, but the Greeks did not flinch.

"Someone should show the little rich boy his eye," a thick, uneven voice hissed at İbrahim from behind.

İbrahim spun around. A hulking man with a large, meaty face and a long, curly black beard stared down at him with hateful eyes. The stranger flashed a black-toothed smile and spit, "My name is Demetrius." Bits of the man's evening meal were sprayed on İbrahim's face.

"Manuel," İbrahim answered, becoming more accustomed to using the name he had been christened.

"Alviso and his countrymen aren't our friends. They certainly aren't our masters," Demetrius seethed. "Just the way they once took Chios from us, the Genoese would be the ones coming through our walls if they could manage it. I wish he and his five hundred brothers would return to Chios tomorrow." Demetrius paused for a moment and concluded with childish simplicity, "I think I should kill the conceited pup the next time he gives an order to one of my Greek brothers.

"Of course, you shouldn't have angered Alviso so quickly," he cackled, one eye drifting up into his head. "You didn't give him a chance to warn you about me." Demetrius playfully knocked his open hand against İbrahim's shoulder, turning him sideways. "I kill," he said, the tone of his voice twisting into an accusation.

The man is mad, İbrahim concluded. He started to walk away, but Demetrius latched onto his shoulder, effortlessly pinching deep into İbrahim's thick muscles and applying pressure to the joint. İbrahim had a dagger at Demetrius's throat before the giant could utter a word.

"Fast," Demetrius snorted with delight through his swollen, bulbous nose. He pressed his neck forward until a trickle of blood stained the edge of the blade.

"Dead is what you'll be if you don't let go of me now," İbrahim slowly chewed his words.

Demetrius's eyes lit up. "A choice?" he laughed, obviously not concerned. "You are a friend."

İbrahim shook himself free. "A cell is where you belong."

Grinning broadly, Demetrius vigorously nodded his head in agreement. "The Tower of Anemas is where I belong. Except I died two days ago," he howled.

"Two days ago?" İbrahim sputtered, withdrawing his dagger.

"I was to be taken from the Tower of Anemas for execution on Monday," Demetrius explained as though he was discussing a trip to the market.

"You seem to be faring just fine."

Demetrius's eyes stopped their mad dance. He sadly tilted his head toward the heavens and said, "Life, death, the most miserable dungeon; it doesn't matter. My pain is relentless."

İbrahim found himself being drawn into Demetrius's world. "What is your crime?"

"Crime?" Demetrius puzzled. "I did nothing wrong. My conscience is pure."

"But you were to be executed," İbrahim gently reminded him, not wanting to incite Demetrius, whose face now hung with depression.

"Oh, I killed three priests," Demetrius admitted, "but that was justice." He thought for a moment and said, "Curse this union with the Latins and their Church. I've not met a single man who wants it. Still, I never paid it too much mind—at least not until several months ago." Demetrius's eyes bore into İbrahim. Finding no sign of interest, Demetrius insisted in an uneven voice, "They told me I was just a lowly baker. That's what they said before casting me out as though the plague were feasting on my organs."

Demetrius caught his breath and mournfully said, "You see, Isaac was all I had left when Anna died. Eleven years old. My sweet boy," he sobbed, digging his fingers into his face.

"I'm sorry." Ibrahim steeled himself for Demetrius's next mood swing. "Hopefully your boy has found peace," he stiffly consoled him, keenly aware that he knew nothing of a father's love for his child.

"I stopped thinking clearly the day Anna's headaches began. How she suffered. The moans were terrible. I think she tried to swallow her cries. But it was the lightly whispered moans that tortured me most. They rubbed their way under my skin like poison, making me want to clamp my hand over her mouth. I prayed for her moaning to end so I would have peace.

"The headaches lasted longer with each new day. The moaning grew worse. A wretched odor fouled our home. I soon realized I had cursed myself with that horrible prayer. Anna raved that I was sent by the devil to tie her in a sack and cast her into the Bosphorus. My anger grew like the madness in her head. I cared for her, but I couldn't bring myself to love her. I never said goodbye. Now, at night, I hear Anna's wails.

"But it was worse for Isaac. He was still of that tender age when a boy worships his mother without fear of what his friends might say. The boy who had once shared everything with me no longer said a word, but I didn't notice. Isaac took to drifting through the streets, sometimes not coming home for days. The day after Anna died, Isaac announced he had found peace in the Roman heresy. They had noticed his pain, he said, and asked him to join their house. I should have begged him to stay. He was all I had left. Too much pain, too much guilt; who knows. He waited for me to protest, but I couldn't. Isaac bared his teeth and then left my home.

"A neighbor told me where Isaac was living. So I went to the compound where the Latin heretics spread their lies. They answered each of my questions about Isaac by spouting their creed. I demanded that they show me Isaac. That's when they mocked me. After a long string of insults, one of them said Isaac had been sent to Rome for formal training as a priest and that he now belonged to them. The rest of my story I cannot recall. It was told to me by others." Demetrius smiled wryly, a steady wave of tears bathing his cheeks. "I can never remember what they say I did. All I know is that three priests died from crushed windpipes."

İbrahim could not resist the disquieting fellowship he felt with Demetrius. The similarities marking their respective misfortunes made him wonder whether madness awaited him as well.

"Of course, I could tell you all about the two guards I killed in the tower." The manic light had returned to Demetrius's eyes. "And yet I've been promised a reprieve if I fight well. Of course, it's all lies. If the Turks don't kill me, they will. I suppose I would feel betrayed if death weren't such a blessing."

"Why do you give up so easily?" İbrahim asked.

"What's left for me to give up?" Demetrius groaned.

"You were told your son is in Rome. Isn't that enough to inspire you? Go to Rome and reclaim your life."

"Go to Rome?" Demetrius was stunned. "You might just as well have told me to find Prester John's fabled kingdom."

"Sometimes the search is all that sustains a man."

Demetrius tilted a curious eye towards his companion. "You're a wanderer?"

İbrahim nodded.

"Tell your story and spare nothing," he said, eyes brightening with interest.

İbrahim's face contorted inwards.

"You needn't be concerned about unburdening yourself on me. I'm a madman. No one listens to anything I say," Demetrius reassured him. No hint of his previous agitation remained.

İbrahim absorbed the request. Then, inhaling deeply, he shared his story for the first time in a low, distant voice. He did not desire absolution, only a kind ear and a chance to testify to what had been.

"And now you search for your woman," Demetrius surmised when İbrahim had finished.

"Everywhere. Over the last year, I've sailed past the Pillars of

Hercules into the Sea of Darkness, trekked through the Sahara's sands and scoured dozens of cities. My Mihrimah eludes me. I'm tortured by the world's emptiness and breadth. It's strange how the world never seemed larger than our cottage when we were together. I'm enslaved by the memory of that paradise and the thought of reclaiming it."

"I've heard that the men who live past the sands walk on one leg and have three faces, with heads of lions," Demetrius said in wonder.

"And the Sea of Darkness boils up into poisonous vapors and sheets of flame rain down from the black clouds above," İbrahim snickered. "Just stories."

Demetrius looked disappointed. "But surely you don't expect to find her here."

"No," he sullenly agreed. "Except for Mihrimah, no thought has occupied me more than the vision of the Sultan's face on the day he's forced to turn back from his prize. I could not resist coming here. Giustiniani may have assigned me away from the fight, but I assure you that I will be in the thick of it when the final charge is sounded."

The maniacal glow abruptly returned to Demetrius's face. "You will destroy the destroyer," he cheered. "Yes, yes," he excitedly swallowed his words. "Then you will rescue your Mihrimah from the land where giant birds scoop up elephants with their talons and take her to a place where the world is her embrace."

"I'll feed your tongue to the dogs if you don't shut that hole of yours," one of the Genoese soldiers yelled, irritated by Demetrius's outburst. "Save yourself from this madman's senseless chatter," the soldier directed his next comment to İbrahim, "or you too will go mad."

Eyes now blazing in full fury, Demetrius's head swiveled side to side until he finally shrieked, mouth oozing saliva, "You obviously don't know a madman when you see one." He mischievously winked at İbrahim, whose heart shuddered. "Here is a true madman," Demetrius cackled, pointing at İbrahim. "He's fool enough to think a Genoese scoundrel like you is worth the piss in this bucket." Demetrius scooped up the bucket and hurled a wave of urine on the dumbfounded soldier.

The doused Genoese jumped to his feet, sword drawn. He took a long, lethal step towards Demetrius and then froze as three successive cannon blasts rocketed the Mesoteichion. The intertwined roar from the Turkish camp and disheartened groan from the defenders followed the echoing concussion into the darkening sky.

Demetrius took advantage of the distraction and launched himself into the Genoese, knocking him to the ground. The Genoese madly tried to free his sword from under Demetrius's hefty bulk. Demetrius sunk his teeth into the soldier's cheek. The officer and several other Genoese responded to their comrade's high-pitched wail. A tangled pile of arms and legs soon lay sprawled on top of one another.

"Order your friend to stop or we'll cut him to pieces," Alviso yelled at İbrahim.

"Friend." İbrahim pondered whether he agreed with the officer's conclusion. He looked at the gathering crowd of Genoese around the pile. Their swords were drawn, eagerly awaiting Alviso's order.

"Demetrius," İbrahim barked. "It's Manuel. Stop."

Demetrius continued to struggle under the pile.

"You need to spare your strength for the journey ahead," İbrahim said. "Alviso has promised to let you free if you give up now. You won't be harmed."

Alviso's mouth opened in protest, which İbrahim blunted with a withering gaze. The officer sighed in exasperation and grudgingly agreed, "It's true. You will not be harmed."

The Genoese released a collective groan. Delighting in their disappointment, Demetrius ended the struggle. He was roughly pulled to his feet to face Alviso. The right side of his face was speckled with blood and both eyes were already swollen.

"What do you have to say for yourself?" Alviso vented.

Demetrius smiled provocatively. "You could all use a good piss bath. Greek piss is perfume next to your stench."

Two Genoese stormed forward.

"Ah!" Demetrius waved a reproachful finger. "Remember what little Alviso promised."

The Genoese looked at Alviso, who motioned them away from Demetrius.

Laughing madly, Demetrius blindly brushed past İbrahim and wove his way down the ramparts like an inveterate drunkard.

Alviso shook his head in disgust. "I'm ordering you to keep that man under control. We don't have time for his distractions. If your friend causes trouble again, I'll hold you responsible."

It is only fitting, İbrahim mused. My lone friend is a madman.

Seventy Thousand Sons of Isaac

A light buzz circulated through the ramparts as the defenders
finished their ablutions and gnawed on stale biscuits seeded with
dirt. A row of men lined up along the edge of the wall were competing to see whose stream of urine would go the farthest. The
sharp angle of the early morning sun cast long shadows from their
bodies over the Ottoman camp, which was also steadily gaining
its usual ominous momentum. The drone of activity was building particularly fast along the Mesoteichion, where the Ottomans
continued to reinforce their positions.

The defenders ignored the Ottoman camp with casual indifference. The initial awe and fear of the Ottomans' vast numbers
and superb cannons was a distant memory. Their fired emotions
had dimmed as the gradual passage of time reduced the extraordinary to the commonplace and the conflict became incidental
to their narrow, predictable routine. As hunger mixed with resig-
nation to weave a stifling grip over the city, the Greek defenders
found themselves torn between loyalty to the Emperor and their
families. Many would steal home at night to bring food or enjoy
what might be their last moments of intimacy.

News that the Venetian relief fleet was nowhere to be found
spread despair. Any hopes of rescue now rested in the unreliable
rumor that Hunyadi had somehow mustered yet another Hungarian army to break the siege. As the incidental passenger on the
Venetian brigantine that had borne the bad news, İbrahim was
treated to bitter frowns from the Genoese.

Anxious to grasp any reason for hope, their spirits rose along with the morning sun when news of a small victory arrived. The Ottomans had conscripted professional silver miners from Novo Brdo to mine under the Blachernae section of the walls in the hope of collapsing the fortifications. But the Greeks had captured the miners, including their commander, who was tortured until he revealed the locations of all the mines.

Another story was unfolding at the Mesoteichion. Hundreds of Ottoman soldiers were rushing across the partially filled foss. Many fell over obstructions and were then trampled by the onward-moving mass. Behind them played the Janissary band. Church bells from within the city answered. As the attackers came within range of the stockade, the defenders launched a hail of arrows, javelins and stones. The Ottomans responded by firing several smaller cannons at the stockade. The splintering wood sprayed deadly shrapnel back upon their own men, who continued on un-deterred. İbrahim noticed a long phalanx of Janissaries standing guard behind the attackers, scimitars drawn, ready to cut down any man who turned back before the signal was given. Finally, the cold clash of steel and chilling cries of the wounded joined together along the stockade.

İbrahim knew that few gains were expected from the assault. The Sultan was simply using his superior numbers to wear down the defenders. Still, İbrahim jealously watched the action. He walked over to Alviso and respectfully advised, "We should be shifting more men down to the Mesoteichion."

"I suppose you think you know something about these pagans that Giustiniani doesn't," the officer snickered. "If you want to be near the Turks so badly, I'll reassign you to Prince Orhan and his fellow Turks." The officer imperiously cocked his head and marched down the ramparts.

"Prince Orhan is in the city," İbrahim muttered under his breath, surprised that the pretender had not fled.

İbrahim had not noticed Demetrius sidle up to him. "He's down by where the Lycus River runs into the Marmara," Demetrius calmly explained. "It's probably the least contested spot along the defenses. You'd never see action there."

Ibrahim noticed that Demetrius's madness was mostly reserved for the Genoese. Upon finishing one of his periodic tirades, he returned to Ibrahim for sanctuary. "Prince Orhan would do well to stay as far away from the Sultan as possible. The Sultan would gladly sever Prince Orhan's head himself."

"Do you think Prince Orhan will flee to Rome?" Demetrius asked.

Ibrahim shrugged.

"I've considered your offer," Demetrius announced. "I will sail with you after the siege as long as we try Rome."

Ibrahim was stunned. Not only had no such offer been made, but he had no interest in turning Demetrius into a traveling companion. Yet Ibrahim could not bring himself to deny him. Instead, he tried to dampen Demetrius's interest.

"Our searches are different," he said in a deliberately smooth, even voice. "I'm glad to hear that you will search for your son, but I think we should pursue separate paths."

Ibrahim's shoulders tightened as he waited for Demetrius to explode. Instead, the giant smiled pleasantly and said, "I don't think you want to find your Mihrimah."

"Of course I want to find her," Ibrahim stuttered in protest.

"It's easier to search for her, though, isn't it?"

"Why do you say that?"

"I won't be pleased with what I find. As long as I'm searching, Isaac is still my boy. He's the way I want him to be." Demetrius's eyes welled up with the tears.

"What do you think you'll find?"

"The world keeps changing," Demetrius agonized. "The Emperor's ancestors thought their city would last forever, but here we are witnessing its final days."

"Don't be so certain," Ibrahim protested. "A long siege can be just as demoralizing for those camped outside the walls."

"Perhaps we will experience a miracle. Still, the city, like my boy, will have forever been changed by what has occurred. I don't think for the better."

"Then why do you want to come with me?"

"Because I'm no different from any other man," Demetrius answered simply. "I cannot resist hope or finding answers."

"It still may not be a good idea for you to come with me. Rome is not in my plans."

"We'll see."

Two more fruitless attacks were launched against the Mesoteichion. Unlike his fellow defenders, who were enjoying another quiet day along their line, İbrahim carefully studied the drama. The Ottomans concentrated on the breaches in the stockade made by the cannon. Each time, the Ottomans' vast numbers were negated by the close quarters fighting, in which the defenders' fierce discipline meant more than their few numbers. Even more impressive was the speed with which the Greeks rebuilt the stockade and repaired the damage to the masonry. No sooner had a portion of the fortifications been smashed than the Greeks were placing the finishing touches on the repairs.

"You'll grow bored soon enough," Demetrius laughed. "Lunch." He handed a rock-hard biscuit to İbrahim, whose eyes drifted over to the Janissary encampment.

As the early afternoon sun vanished behind a murky, grayish yellow sky, İbrahim concluded that the Sultan would have to risk the total commitment of his forces on this critical point. He would have one chance. If the defenders could repel the assault, the Sultan would have to release his prize. No army, not even with Janissaries lethally swinging their scimitars behind them, could be compelled to hurl all their fury again at such daunting defenses once turned back.

"Sometimes I think the earth will open up and swallow the heathens," Demetrius said, leaning over the wall to look at the battered Mesoteichion. "But then I wonder whether the hole will keep growing until it swallows all the evil around us. Why should any of us be spared? I've heard some priests declare that we will soon witness God's judgment."

"Seventy thousand sons of Isaac," İbrahim announced to Demetrius before taking a lusty bite out of the biscuit, which cracked apart in his hand.

A quizzical smile broadened Demetrius's face as his mind raced to unlock the riddle.

"You reminded me of an ancient *hadith* I once heard from our enemies. The prophet Mohammed told his followers, 'Have you heard of a city of which one side is land and the two others sea? The Hour of Judgment shall not sound until seventy thousand sons of Isaac shall capture it.'"

Demetrius shuddered. "The moon is at its fullest. After tonight, it will leave the city. When I was a boy, my father told me about a prophecy that our city was invincible as long as the moon brightened the night sky."

"The moon?" Ibrahim wondered whether Demetrius was starting a new stream of incoherent babble.

"The moon is the oldest symbol of our city," Demetrius proudly declared through his pessimism. "We will surely suffer when it shrinks back to a thin crescent. What could be more fitting?" he observed. "Is not the crescent moon the symbol of your one-time friends?"

"But there was no moon last night. The sky was pitch black." Ibrahim's voice softly drifted off as he recalled the brigantine's swift progress under the nearly full moon the previous night.

"You didn't see the moon?" Demetrius swallowed hard.

"I saw it towards dawn," Ibrahim started to correct himself, "but it was gone earlier in the evening."

"An eclipse?"

"There must have been heavy cloud cover," Ibrahim awkwardly tried to counter Demetrius's growing panic.

"The Divine Presence is leaving," Demetrius trembled.

"Uncle Demetrius," a small, playful voice cautiously whispered, breaking the tension.

The two men spun around to find a four-year-old boy with brilliant yellow locks of hair smiling mirthfully at them. His face was smudged with dirt but his pink cheeks and bright blue eyes cast a warm glow through the colorless gloom along the ramparts.

"Theophilus," Demetrius trumpeted as though the discussion about the moon had never occurred. "My little nephew," he elbowed İbrahim.

A reproachful frown preceded Theophilus's indignant reply. "I'm a big boy, Uncle, just like my daddy."

Demetrius slapped his hands against his knees and said, "A thousand apologies, Theophilus. You're well on your way to being taller than your father."

The boy's face lit up. "Yes, yes. I will serve in the Emperor's bodyguard when I'm all grown up."

Demetrius leaned over to İbrahim. "His father is an officer in the Emperor's Varangian Guard. Comes from a place called Britannia, I think. You should see the man, half a head taller than I, skin as white as snow and hair as golden as the sun on a bright summer day. It's because of his father that this 'big' boy is so fair." His face briefly hardened. "Theophilus looks nothing like my wife's younger sister."

"Uncle Demetrius," the boy impatiently whined. "When are we going to go?"

"Go where?" Demetrius slyly chuckled.

Theophilus stomped his foot. "Why do you always have to tease me? I'm not a baby anymore," he said, planting his hands on his hips and sullenly swallowing his lower lip. "The 'cession is starting soon."

"Cession." Demetrius's face glowed. "You mean procession." Theophilus was not amused by the correction. Ignoring the boy's disapproval, Demetrius grabbed his nephew by the arms and playfully tossed him in the air, high above the swirling conflict below. Theophilus unleashed a delighted, high-pitched squeal. He landed in his Uncle's arms and set to work squeezing Demetrius's cheeks together between his chubby hands. When Demetrius's lips had been forced to pucker, Theophilus darted forward to plant a wet kiss, giggling with ticklish delight. Once Demetrius's face resumed its normal aspect, the boy set to work again.

"You can't simply leave your post whenever you feel like it,"

İbrahim warned. "You'll be giving your friend Alviso just the excuse he wants to open your back with the lash."

Demetrius's maniacal smile returned. This time İbrahim was sure the smile was manufactured. "Now, Theophilus," Demetrius boomed. "Here is where your bread has gone." He pointed a beefy finger at three Genoese soldiers nibbling on biscuits.

"What is that boy doing here?" Alviso demanded from farther down the ramparts. "Children are forbidden."

Demetrius carefully deposited Theophilus on the ground. "Nephew, have you ever seen anything sadder than a grown man afraid of a dog?" Demetrius took a deep breath and then unleashed a horrific howl, followed by a rapid succession of guttural barks. "I need a bone, Alviso," he growled, snapping his teeth at the officer's face.

Theophilus giggled and said, "Uncle, you're silly."

Alviso jumped back and ordered, "Manuel, I want this animal off my wall. And that little rat goes back to his mother's filthy breast. Now!"

Demetrius's barking grew louder, but now he was howling at the clouds and jumping up and down on all fours, drool running down his chin. İbrahim suppressed a smile. He obediently nodded his head to Alviso and then grabbed Demetrius by the neck with one hand while hoisting Theophilus onto his shoulders with the other. He quickly descended the tower while Demetrius continued to howl like a mad dog.

"Who's your friend, Uncle?" Theophilus asked as they made their way back into the city. The boy had wrapped his arms around İbrahim's neck.

"A friend of the family," Demetrius playfully answered.

"Uncle Demetrius," the boy laughed, unconvinced. "We don't know him."

"Can't fool this one," Demetrius said, mostly for Theophilus's benefit. "Theophilus, meet Manuel, my last friend."

"I'm your friend, too, Uncle," Theophilus pouted.

"But of course you are," Demetrius corrected himself. "Please forgive me for being such a silly old man."

"I love you, Uncle Demetrius," the boy said, sorry he had made Demetrius apologize.

Theophilus weighed next to nothing in İbrahim's arms, but the boy, bursting with more heartfelt joy and innocence than İbrahim dreamed might exist, seemed to have the world neatly contained within him. İbrahim protectively wrapped his arms around Theophilus and searched for long-forgotten memories. When did I stop saying sweet things, he asked himself.

"Da, dee, doo, dee, dee, doo," Theophilus melodically experimented with his voice.

"The world shouldn't be allowed to tamper with something so wonderful," Demetrius said, voice heavy with regret.

İbrahim gave the boy a rough, playful hug and said, "Tell me about the games you play."

Theophilus's mouth fell open. "You really want to know?"

"Don't leave out a thing," İbrahim reassured him.

"Open the gates now," a haranguing voice bellowed at passersby, interrupting Theophilus's reply. "The Emperor will abandon us to the pagans' wrath soon enough. He'll leave like the rest of his well-fed noblemen. Do you think the Venetians and Genoese will continue the fight then? Of course not. The time has come to end our sacrifice. Let us beg for the Sultan's mercy before our defiance costs us all."

The passersby pretended not to listen, but İbrahim noticed a number of them deftly turn an attentive ear towards the speaker. "This man must be twice as mad as you, Demetrius. Surely one cannot say such things about the Emperor and expect to live?"

"He's finished if a soldier hears him. If that is his fate, it will be the empty ache in his stomach that betrayed him," Demetrius answered sympathetically. He looked at Theophilus and asked İbrahim, "What will happen to us if the Turks succeed?"

İbrahim had watched hundreds of villages razed to the ground, the inhabitants pitilessly put to the sword. Mercy was only reserved for those who humbly submitted. He knew the only difference between the villages that resisted and Constantinople would be the breadth of the holocaust. Theophilus's endearing smile and innocence would be senselessly swept away. "I think we've found the procession," he said with relief, pointing to the crowd several blocks away.

Theophilus sprang from Ibrahim's arms and sprinted ahead. For a brief moment, the boy's warmth clung to Ibrahim's robe before being carried away by a cool, wet breeze that was sweeping through the streets with growing force. The wind curled its way through the tatters in his robe and came to rest where the boy's body had rested. Ibrahim contracted in a protective shudder.

Theophilus jumped up and down trying to see the procession. He was blocked by a somber wall of humanity. An equally withdrawn huddled mass on the opposite side of the wide avenue stared blankly back. Between them marched a long parade of priests, dressed in their finest robes, solemnly chanting prayers for the city's deliverance. The crowd was oblivious to the priests. All necks were craned towards the great icon making its way up the avenue.

"Uncle Demetrius," Theophilus complained. "I can't see."

Demetrius hoisted his nephew on his shoulders. Theophilus gasped and excitedly tugged on Demetrius's thick mop of hair. The boy could have torn handfuls of hair loose without provoking a single complaint from his doting uncle.

"I can see the holy icon." Theophilus took a long look. "She's not as pretty as Mother," he whispered with more pride than guilt.

Demetrius laughed. "A boy your age is allowed to think his mother is the prettiest woman alive."

"But she is," Theophilus insisted.

"An angel's hair away from being the mirror image of your aunt."

"Mother says I can't talk about Aunt Anna with you. She says thinking about Aunt Anna makes you sad."

"She did, did she?"

Theophilus blushed. "She really said thinking about Aunt Anna makes you mad. I think she really meant to say sad. I don't want you to be angry with me, Uncle."

Demetrius reached up and gently stroked the boy's soft, rosy cheek. "I love you, Nephew."

İbrahim jealously watched the tears well up in Demetrius's puffy, bloodshot eyes.

A loud murmur redirected the threesome's attention back to the procession. Hundreds of onlookers were now kneeling down in prayer, pleading for God's favor. Hundreds of Greek soldiers were mixed among the worshipers. The defense of the walls had temporarily assumed secondary importance. For a people whose religious fervor dominated their world, raising the full might of their collective voices to the Lord in this final appeal was far more important.

The icon of the Mother of God was secured to a platform supported on the shoulders of a dozen men. İbrahim was drawn to the Virgin Mary's face, which was crowned by a lustrous, golden halo. A deep mystery peered out from the unusually large blue eyes painted flatly on the tall wooden panel. As he locked on the advancing icon, her watchful, protective eyes and tightly withdrawn mouth alternated between poised potency and perilous concern. It seemed that the Byzantines were relying on the Mother of God's fierce maternal instinct to guarantee their safety, just as the Christ child had once done.

Although it was impossible to mistake the concern on the faces of the Byzantines, they remained ignorant of the fate that faced them. İbrahim felt a vague kinship with these people who were facing envelopment by the same irresistible wave that had carried him off into servitude.

A powerful wind suddenly erupted down the avenue. The crowd turned their backs against the blast and shielded their eyes from the swirling debris. "The Virgin!" an old woman cried out. All eyes turned towards the empty platform. The icon had been torn loose from its moorings and was lying face up on the street.

Its bearers immediately dropped the platform and knelt down to lift the icon. For a long moment, the men gripped the icon, their faces contorting as they tugged at it. Several of them then lost their grip and stumbled back, looking at their empty hands with obvious surprise, while the others continued to pull at the icon.

A group of soldiers rushed from the crowd to help the bearers, who were quizzically looking at the icon as though it was a giant foundation block. Uttering groans that penetrated the angry howl of the wind, they managed to restore the icon to its platform. The shaken bearers braced themselves against the wind and slowly moved ahead.

"Is it bad that the icon fell?" Theophilus quietly asked amid the hushed assembly. The wind carried his voice across the avenue. Fearful faces turned towards Demetrius, who simply stared after the icon in numb silence.

"It was only the wind," İbrahim soothingly counseled.

"But why was the icon so heavy?" Theophilus pressed.

"It wasn't. Sometimes people can't do simple things when they're surprised," İbrahim replied.

"It's not God then?" Theophilus skeptically considered the explanation.

"I don't think so." İbrahim resisted the urge to laugh at the boy's comical innocence.

"But the sky's so angry," Theophilus objected.

A swirling green witch's brew, accompanied by a pungent, gangrenous odor, poisoned the afternoon sky. As though he were eating a spoonful of steaming stew, İbrahim's tongue was set afire by a light raindrop that found his open mouth. His face felt like a pincushion as several more sharp raindrops pricked his cheeks. He snapped his head down and said, "We need to find shelter."

The sky fell on them like a wave rolling over a ship. A series of thunderous claps seemed to ring out heaven's judgment. Surrounded by a blinding wall of water, the worshipers collided with each other as they scurried for safety. Hailstones, some the size of a man's fist, splashed in the flooded streets.

Demetrius pulled Theophilus from his shoulders and surrounded him with his robe. Then they rushed over to a nearby house and pounded on the door.

"Go away," a frightened voice called back.

Demetrius tried to answer, but the rain filled his mouth. He spit the water out and then threw his shoulder into the door, which splintered from its frayed hinges. For a moment, the door hovered precariously in front of them and then toppled forward. Like a fire searching for oxygen, the rain followed them for the first several feet into the house.

"Good afternoon," Demetrius smiled with maniacal glee at a middle-aged woman staring back at him in disbelief. "Thank you for allowing us to enjoy the pleasure of your home until the storm passes."

The woman's face was puckered into an angry scowl. Her eyes darted from İbrahim to Demetrius as she decided whether to protest. Finally, she heaved a helpless sigh and retreated into the dark interior.

Demetrius beamed at İbrahim. "You see, my people have earned God's love," he said sarcastically. "It's a wonder the lightning hasn't found this home already."

They silently stood in the doorway for the next hour watching the street transform into a river. The deadly torrent swept away everything in its path, including carts loaded with sorely needed food.

"What do you think happened to the icon?" Theophilus finally broke the silence.

"I'm sure it's fine," Demetrius answered. "I'm more interested in getting you home to your mother. She must be worried about you."

Theophilus was unimpressed with his uncle's concern. "Do you have to go back to the walls?"

Demetrius nodded.

"I don't want you and your friend to get hurt, Uncle."

Demetrius patted Theophilus's wet hair. "Don't worry, Nephew. Not even the Turks fight in this kind of weather. I'll be safe enough."

Theophilus frowned and then hugged Demetrius's thick leg.

"I've lived here all my life. I've never seen a storm like this one in May. It's unnatural," Demetrius whispered to İbrahim. "Surely we're witnessing a bad omen."

İbrahim nodded his head contentedly and said, "I'm sure the Sultan is thinking the same thing right now as his cannons slide off their moorings and the foss bubbles with mud. We should celebrate God's blessing."

Demetrius squeezed some of the water out of his robe. He watched it trickle into the street, where it was carried off by the rushing river. "You won't find many people on our side of the walls who share your opinion."

When the storm finally slowed to a steady rain, İbrahim and Demetrius brought Theophilus home. His mother unleashed an hysterical greeting and explained that the boy had disappeared without a word early in the morning. She treated Theophilus to a harsh lecture and a snap of her hand on his bottom before banishing him to a small room.

Eager to return to her good graces, he took two swift, obedient steps before being halted by his mother's shouting, "Theophilus!" She nodded towards Demetrius. The boy's face lit up and he launched himself into his uncle's waiting arms. "Thank you for taking care of me, Uncle Demetrius," he slyly said, hoping to spare his uncle from a similar lecture. "I'll pray for you tonight," he sweetly promised. Theophilus planted a big kiss on Demetrius's cheek and jumped to the floor.

"And say goodbye to Uncle Demetrius's friend," she reminded him, her voice softening.

Theophilus's eyes narrowed as he decided how he should bid farewell. He pressed his cheek into İbrahim's leg and gave a mighty hug.

İbrahim patted Theophilus on the back and said, "You have a rare gift, Theophilus. You know how to make people happy."

Theophilus turned expectantly to his mother, who was glad to reward him with a proud smile.

Theophilus's mother waited for him to disappear into the room and then reignited her wrath against Demetrius. Rather than protesting his role in the boy's misadventure, Demetrius happily absorbed the harangue while basking in her resemblance to his wife. When she finally dismissed him, he kissed her on the cheek as though she had sung his praises. İbrahim expected her to explode, but her eyes melted. She ran her hand along Demetrius's beard and said, "We've missed you at the dinner table."

No one had missed İbrahim and Demetrius on the walls. Demetrius surveyed the Genoese, trying to decide whether to antagonize them. They looked too exhausted to raise their heads. Demetrius shrugged and said to İbrahim, "Perhaps I will spare them this one night."

The rain periodically regained strength before finally being replaced by a soupy fog that enveloped the city. Constantinople echoed with the panicked voices of people crying out to children and companions who had taken one step too many into the fog and were now lost from sight.

Demetrius was right. The arrival of the storm on the heels of the eclipse the night before had awakened every dark superstition held close by the population. It was roundly believed that only a blind man might miss such obvious bad omens. The people held their breath waiting for the next portent.

They did not have to wait long. As the fog lifted, it clung to the Church of Hagia Sophia's dome. The setting sun lit the fog, turning the cross at the apex of the dome into a brilliant beacon towards heaven. And then the light passed, leaving the cross lifeless and cold.

İbrahim and his companions along the Rhegium Gate had been watching the spectacle with fascination. "God has abandoned us," one soldier lamented. "His presence has left the city. He will not return."

Heads vigorously nodded in agreement.

"That may be so," a watchman announced, "but perhaps we may still be saved. Look to the west," he shouted. "I see lights. It must be Hunyadi's army."

"Campfires," one soldier exalted.

"The lights are too large," another man sneered. "They've built bonfires to sow terror in the Turks."

"We will crush the Sultan between us."

Like a siren's song, the lights mesmerized the defenders for the next several hours until they inexplicably vanished just as quickly as they had first appeared. The most hopeful watchman never saw the lights again.

"The City is Ours"

"Soon my friends will be as mad as I," Demetrius complained, his voice hollow from exhaustion, as another cannonball slammed into the walls. He pulled at his ears, trying to relieve the hurtful ring.

The Greeks and Genoese had worked side by side to repair the crumbling walls for the last two days. The Ottomans had been pounding the defenses with a relentless barrage that sent tremors throughout the city. The churches overflowed with worshipers praying for the bombardment to end even as they sensed that a greater danger awaited them when the last cannonball was fired.

"Do you think the Sultan really offered a peace treaty to the Emperor?" Demetrius asked, longing for a reprieve.

The Ottoman camp included many Christians, some of whom shot arrows over the walls with messages attached informing their besieged brethren about the Sultan's plans. The Sultan had been as unnerved as the Byzantines by the numerous omens. Rumors of Hunyadi crossing the Danube and the Venetian relief fleet reaching Chios were badly damaging the morale of his forces.

Halil Pasha had never approved of the siege and now pleaded with the momentarily unsure Sultan to negotiate an honorable peace before disaster befell the empire. Yielding ever so slightly to the rapidly aging minister, the Sultan toyed with the Byzantines. He blandly offered them two choices: pay an impossibly large annual tribute or abandon the city with their lives and possessions intact. Some claimed that the Emperor offered to surrender everything he owned but the city itself.

Wherever the truth lay, the negotiations lasted no longer than a day, all the while complemented by the thunderous claps of cannon fire. To the Sultan's delight, the dialogue petered out when his more aggressive younger leaders conveniently produced a mandate from the troops demanding an immediate attack.

Not receiving an answer, Demetrius changed the subject. "You repeatedly muttered Theophilus's name in your sleep last night."

İbrahim was not surprised. Theophilus had been on his mind since they parted company. Watching the boy smear food all over his face or just miss finding the proper words to express his thoughts had left İbrahim spellbound. He thought of the unborn child in Mihrimah's womb and felt a hard ache fill his throat.

"Have you considered that your search is only prolonging your pain?"

"Where has your mad bark gone?"

Demetrius smiled. "It's served me well enough."

The deep thud of a cannonball exploding several yards away nearly knocked them off their feet. The walls groaned and they could hear pieces of stone tumbling away. "Of course," Demetrius said, "none of us might leave this place."

A fiery glow stretched its way up into the dark sky hours after sunset. Excited shouts and the driving rhythm of trumpets and pipes echoed deep into the city. Drawn by the possibility of a miracle, the Byzantines gravitated to the Theodosian Walls. They were hoping to see the Ottoman camp engulfed in flames. Instead, they foresaw their own demise and dropped to their knees in prayer.

The staging for the final attack was under way. By the light of countless flares and torches, thousands of workers were busily filling in the foss like a colony of ants. The work continued at a furious pace until midnight. Then, the lights went out, leaving the faint crescent moon as the lone illumination. A malevolent silence reigned in the Ottoman camp.

Arrows were shot over the walls informing the defenders that the Sultan had ordered Monday to be a day of rest. On Tuesday, every point along the walls would be attacked in order to keep the defenders pinned to their positions while the Mesoteichion suffered the main thrust.

Although the Sultan had granted his army a day of rest, he was busy the next day inspecting his forces and giving orders in preparation for the coming assault. A lifetime's worth of treasure was promised to the first man who breached the stockade. The Sultan then gathered his commanders and reminded them that it had been the sacred duty of the Faithful to capture Constantinople since Mohammed's heirs had first assaulted the city eight hundred years earlier. He enticed them with images of the riches that awaited them within the walls. He intended to send an endless swell of soldiers until those riches were his to bestow.

The momentary reprieve from the cannon fire gave the defenders little to cheer. Like a merchant calculating his losses, they methodically counted down their last hours, preferring the arrival of the final assault to the nerve-wracking wait. For once, the odd coupling of allies set aside their mutual distrust of each other and joined together in mournful prayer before the badly damaged fortifications.

Constantine Palaeologus reminded his Greek subjects of their glorious past and their duty to die for their faith, country, family and sovereign. He then thanked his Italian allies and assured all that God would inspire them to victory. Always a man before an emperor, he humbly asked their forgiveness if he had ever offended them.

Back on the ramparts, İbrahim stonily eyed the Janissaries' camp. The First Orta's flag was waving lazily in the soft breeze. He subconsciously ran his hand along the tattoo of the camel branded into his shoulder. He was certain that Abaza would come into view if he gazed long enough.

"Counting friends or enemies?" Demetrius smartly asked.

"It's an awesome sight, isn't it?" İbrahim slowly answered through his distant haze.

Demetrius sniffed quizzically. He looked at the Janissary encampment and said, "All I see is darkness."

"They are the soul of the army, the heart of the empire, a force equal to nature's angriest storm," İbrahim explained, voice trembling with pride. "The fire breathed by the Sultan is borne from their molten fury. Tomorrow, they will rise above fear and self-doubt. They will wash away their personal weaknesses and seamlessly merge into a single relentless wave, immune to the wounds and suffering of their brethren as they heartlessly perform their master's bidding. You will witness the Janissaries' charge and know that it's possible for majesty and darkness to fit neatly together."

Demetrius huffed, "They are only men. Even the greatest warrior can be killed." He deliberately held his gaze on İbrahim's ruined leg.

İbrahim's eyes turned raw.

"Uncle Demetrius," Theophilus melted the tension. The little boy burst into his uncle's arms.

"Does your mother know you're here?" Demetrius asked, understandably suspicious.

"Demetrius, it's Helena," the boy's mother called over to him. "I need to speak to you," she nearly sobbed.

A grave look crept across Demetrius's face as he deposited Theophilus at İbrahim's feet. "Why don't you amuse my nephew?" he tried to say cheerfully.

İbrahim dutifully took Theophilus's little hand and joined the crowd of Greek families who had flocked to the ramparts. They strolled past Alviso, who was pretending not to notice the break in military discipline. Theophilus squeezed hard on İbrahim's hand, all the while tilting his head away from the Ottoman positions. The phosphorescent glow of his face was extinguished.

İbrahim wondered why Theophilus was now so uncomfortable standing safely above the Ottoman army. He stole a glance at Demetrius and Helena. She was holding Demetrius's hands at arm's length. Her smooth, oval face shimmered like a still lake being lightly doused with a sun shower. Her eyes squeezed tight and her mouth spread wide with pain. Demetrius moved forward to engulf her in his massive chest.

Theophilus looked at his mother, then at the other families huddled together. His lip quivered as he asked, "Why does everybody else get to say goodbye?"

Ibrahim imagined his own father. He patted Theophilus's curly hair and tried to think of something to say. The moments slipped by in silence. Nothing mattered more than finding a way to ease the boy's pain. Ibrahim's body stiffened with frustration. Only the thought of striking out against their mutual enemy presented itself as an answer.

"Theophilus," Demetrius called out on Helena's behalf.

Theophilus smiled at Ibrahim, gratitude etched on his rosy cheeks. He hugged Ibrahim's legs and then ran over to his mother, who embraced him with a hauntingly familiar desperation.

Demetrius stumbled over to Ibrahim as though he had sunk his head in a barrel of wine. Demetrius turned to watch Helena and Theophilus leave the ramparts. Theophilus was doing his best to appear brave. "His father was at the stockade. Four feet of timber tore through his waist."

"Did he die quickly?"

"Of course not," Demetrius bitterly answered. "We live in a city draped with a curse. He was still screaming madly in his native tongue when poor Helena arrived. He was too blind with pain to even notice her. It took two awful hours for him to die. Helena said she was ready to drive a sword through his heart just to end the agony for both of them."

"And the boy?"

"My nephew only knows that his father died a hero."

Ibrahim kicked a cluster of stones. "Not much consolation for a boy who's lost his father."

"I had held out hope that Helena and Theophilus might somehow be saved even if the Turks forced their way into the city. Now Helena's husband is gone and his family is as vulnerable as every other family in Constantinople. They are my responsibility now. They have no one else. When the sun sets, I will join them."

"To do what?" Ibrahim snapped. Saving Helena and Theophilus had suddenly ripened into a virtuous cause. "Do you think standing in the doorway of their home will stop the Turks from doing as they please? You'll be one man surrounded by many. The only thing you'll succeed in doing is forcing poor Theophilus and his mother to see you butchered. If you want to save them, stay on the walls where every man makes a difference. Stop the Turks from entering the city. Then you'll have fulfilled your duty."

Demetrius shook his head like a trapped animal. "You're right. Of course, you're right. I wanted to say the same things to Helena but I couldn't find the words. She begged me to come to the house. She looks so much like my Anna. I couldn't say no. What choice do I have now?"

"You can choose to live by your honest convictions rather than by a few poorly chosen words said in a moment of weakness."

Demetrius heaved an unhappy sigh. "A man must live by what he says."

"I know your heart right now," İbrahim said sympathetically. "I've sworn oaths to a master I now stand foursquare against. But I'm not an impious man. When I took those oaths, I made a contract. A good contract speaks to morals and true balance. I did more than swear fealty to a man, his successors and their empire. I also swore to uphold my own inner beliefs. You must do what's right. You know what you must do to save your family."

Demetrius gazed at the rapidly descending sun, which looked like it would plunge into the earth and never reemerge. "They will throw everything at the Mesoteichion."

İbrahim nodded.

"And you will be there when the fighting grows thick."

Again İbrahim nodded.

"I will be at your side."

As the last rays of sunshine departed, crowds descended on the Church of Hagia Sophia to make their peace with God. Greek priests who had exhausted themselves opposing the union with Rome served at the altar with the Latin clergy. Confession and communion finally occurred in true unity.

The Ottomans had also been busy after sunset. An anxious hum buzzed through their camp as they prepared for battle. Under a heavy rain shower, workmen completed filling in the foss and brought the cannons closer to the walls.

The defenders watched in silent impotence. Giustiniani ordered the gates of the inner walls locked behind them. The only path for retreat would be through death.

At 1:30 in the morning, the eerie pallor was abruptly shattered by the distinctive blast of Urban's cannon. After a respectful hesitation, the rest of the Ottoman guns fired in rapid succession, setting the night sky ablaze. The deafening sound of drums, fifes and trumpets mixed with bloodcurdling war cries. A supernatural potency pulsed through the Ottoman camp, infusing each man with a sense of invulnerability.

Like a doomed man fighting for his soul, Constantinople responded with its own fury. The church bells near the walls sprang to life. The signal quickly spread through the city until every belfry was alive, warning the terrorized population that the feared moment had arrived.

The Ottomans wasted little time sending in the first human wave. The *başıbozuk*s, armed with an odd collection of scimitars, slings, harquebuses and, of course, scaling ladders, hurled themselves at the walls with undisciplined abandon. The Sultan held little hope that this multinational throng of Christian and Muslim treasure seekers would win the day. He simply planned to wear down the undermanned defenders. In order to make sure the attack was pressed until the formal retreat was sounded, military police stood behind them with weapons in hand. Never leaving anything to chance, the Sultan ordered his Janissaries to stand behind the police. Cowardice was not an option.

The Ottomans attacked by land and sea at every point along the walls, looking for that single penetration point. Although menacing, these attacks were designed as feints to keep the defenders narrowly pinned down to their positions. It was in the Lycus Valley, at the Mesoteichion, that the Sultan intended to win the Red Apple.

Like the rest of the defenders, İbrahim made quick work of the *başıbozuk*s, who clumsily tried to scale the walls against a hail of arrows and stones. Those who made it to the top of the walls were dispatched with well-aimed, downward sword strokes, leaving the outside of the walls bathed in blood.

İbrahim had kept a careful, northward eye on the Lycus Valley, where the *başıbozuk*s' attack was far more ferocious. Their concentrated mass interfered with their own movements and made them easy targets. Still, they were serving their master well. The defenders were expending a tremendous amount of energy to earn their victory.

Demetrius had been stealing glances at İbrahim. He had expected İbrahim to unleash hell's fury. Instead, İbrahim approached his task with all the passion of a palace maid washing the laundry. Rather than calming his anxiety, this sight made Demetrius tremble at the thought of an entire corps of soldiers pressing the attack with such calculating precision.

"When do we go to the Lycus Valley?" Demetrius asked.

"Don't be in such a hurry," İbrahim answered. "We'll need all our energy for later."

"But the battle is now."

"This?" İbrahim sneered. "It's just the beginning. The Sultan hasn't even sent in his Anatolian *yaya*s. We're being exhausted with their blood."

"These men have been sent only to die?" Demetrius was aghast. He suddenly felt guilty about the slaughter.

"The Sultan is not concerned about a momentary boost to our morale. He wants a tenderized foe for his Janissaries."

More than two and half hours after Urban's cannon had first sounded, the *başıbozuk*s were finally recalled. Breathing hard, the defenders hurled well-won insults at the vanquished. Then they set about repairing the damage to the fortifications.

As İbrahim had predicted, it was a fleeting moment. Urban's cannon soon signaled the second act. The Anatolian *yaya*s were sent forward. The battle between the Ottoman bands and Constantinople's church bells sounded again. Unlike the *başıbozuk*s, the *yaya*s were well-trained and devout soldiers. They yearned to claim the holy prize. The combination of their zeal and discipline placed a formidable strain on the weakening defenders, who now faced men who jumped on each other's shoulders to scale the defenses. All the while, the cannons tore into the walls with increasing effect.

"I'm leaving for the stockade," İbrahim announced.

Demetrius dutifully followed.

"Deserters," Alviso swore. "My sword has plenty of work left to do tonight and by God, I'll put it to work on you if you don't return to your positions."

Demetrius's eyes rolled madly and he brayed like a mule.

"It's the cannons," İbrahim awkwardly explained. "They've driven him mad. He was spitting at the Turks as they climbed their ladders."

"Why should you spare me an honest word now?" A cannon blast shook the walls, knocking Alviso backwards. When he righted himself, they were gone. "Give my regards to the Devil," he shouted after them.

İbrahim stoically dragged his leg, steeling himself against the pain. He had planned to save his energy for the Janissaries, but the *yaya*s looked like they might force their way past Giustiniani's weakening forces at any moment.

Just as İbrahim and Demetrius reached the stockade, a ball from Urban's cannon found its mark. The stockade emitted a terrible groan and a thick cloud of dust and debris blew through the defenders. A lengthy section of the stockade was obliterated, leaving a yawning gap. Lungs burning, the defenders dragged their swords on the ground like lead balls. Now, only their swords and shoulders stood between the Ottomans and the city.

"*Allahu akbar!*" İbrahim heard hundreds of *yaya*s cheer through the murky mist. Encouraged by their own guttural roar, a few hundred *yaya*s overcame their fatigue and rushed the gap.

"Follow me," a Greek voice bravely rallied the defenders.

It was Constantine Palaeologus. Like a common foot soldier,

the Emperor, sword drawn high over his head, led his subjects into battle. The defenders' spirits revived as they scrambled to meet the *yaya*s.

"Come," İbrahim ordered Demetrius. He raced into the fray as fast as his ruined leg could carry him. It was his first chance to unleash his full fury since he had lost Mihrimah. Now that İbrahim was unable to maintain his disciplined conservation of energy, his scimitar furiously hummed with quick, lethal blows. Before long, he was breathing heavily by the Emperor's side at the front of the attack.

The *yaya*s' losses mounted quickly and soon the survivors were racing back to the foss. Like a wounded bull, İbrahim chased after the stragglers, hacking down those he could reach from behind. If his leg had been whole, he would have found his way into the foss, himself soon surrounded.

"You are the madman," Demetrius gasped for air, his massive stomach heaving up and down. He was taken aback by İbrahim's lack of discipline. "I hope you don't expect me to run after you again. I've seen starving beggars attack a stray loaf of bread with less fire than the way you hacked at the Turks. I thought your arm would fly off."

İbrahim's already flushed face turned a brighter shade of red. He had thought the reckless habits of his youth were nothing more than distant memories. "It won't happen again," İbrahim promised, remembering his hand in İshak's death.

Reports were now coming in from the rest of the city. "The defenses are holding," a runner from the Blachernae section of the walls announced. He was answered with a hearty cheer.

"We're winning," Demetrius rejoiced.

"No," İbrahim corrected him. "Look at these men." Most of the defenders had their hands planted on their knees as they gasped for breath. "The stockade is more splinters than planks."

"And your friends haven't entered the battle yet," Demetrius soberly finished the equation.

"We don't have much time. The Sultan will not allow us to catch our breath. When the Janissaries come, swing your sword thinking of your son and hold your shield thinking of Theophilus. And if you wish to see another day, don't stray from the line."

"You will do the same?" Demetrius asked skeptically.

İbrahim reflexively looked skyward. A hail of arrows and stones rained down, sending the defenders scrambling for cover on their leaden legs. The pounding beat of the Janissary band rose above the cannon blasts and echoed in their ears. The church bells angrily answered back.

"They're coming again." A watchman grimly called the defenders back to arms.

İbrahim raced to the stockade and peered across the foss. Positioned at the front of the Ottoman line was the Sultan's standard, horsetails pointing towards the city.

Mehmed had led his favorites to the foss and was shouting encouragement. All of his carefully laid plans hung in the balance of this charge. He dared not contemplate the fate of his empire should the Janissaries be turned back.

A proud chill rippled down İbrahim's spine. Trying to awaken the dead with their primeval war cries, the Janissaries crossed the foss in a solid phalanx. The defenders had regrouped and were now hurling their own missiles at the Janissaries, who absorbed the punishment without flinching. The Janissaries fell by the dozens, but their disciplined rows marched forward with the relentless intensity of the incoming tide, all the while contemptuously staring down death as though it were some petty nuisance.

Giustiniani had moved to the head of the defense at the stockade. "Hold this ground with your lives," he boldly shouted in an insistent voice that denied challenge. "We will not yield a single step until the accursed scum are running back to the bosom of their devil master."

Greeks and Italians alike took heart seeing their commander confidently standing before the onrush. Giustiniani beamed with a victorious aura, which the defenders clung to like a stray plank in a churning sea. Shoulders defiantly pinned back, they found courage in unleashing their own hellish roar at the charging Janissaries.

The clash of steel calmed İbrahim's racing heart. İbrahim wielded his scimitar like a great portrait master applying the first bold brushstrokes to a new work. Within minutes of his delivering the first blow, three Janissaries lay dead before him. As the bodies piled up near him, İbrahim felt like he could walk over the heads of the Janissaries to the Sultan. He fought back the urge to wade into the grinding advance, reminding himself that he was engaged in an endurance test.

Demetrius stood in tight formation to İbrahim's left. Confident that İbrahim would protect his right, Demetrius concentrated on protecting his own left while slashing at the Janissaries with short, deliberate blows. It was an effective combination. The Janissaries began to drift away from them, probing for softer spots in the line.

Success had made the time pass quickly for the defenders. The same was not the case for the Janissaries, who were frustrated by their inability to take advantage of their superior numbers and skills in the compressed battle zone. After an hour, the Janissaries were no closer to breaking through than when they had started their assault.

İbrahim's dream of denying the Red Apple to the Sultan was taking shape as he had planned. Still, he found no satisfaction. Slaking his thirst for vengeance had exposed him to an even greater void. "What will be left for me should the Greeks hold their city?" he asked himself.

"Abaza," İbrahim spat, suddenly redrawn to the conflict.

"What does 'Abaza' mean?" Demetrius asked almost jovially, sensing victory now like the rest of the defenders.

İbrahim tracked Abaza, whom he had spotted trying to reach the stockade with elements of the First Orta. Abaza and his men were pressed several rows deep against the backs of their fellow stymied Janissaries, safe from İbrahim's venom.

İbrahim's face glowed red with rage. His discipline collapsed into instinctive fury. "Mihrimah," he bellowed. İbrahim drew back his scimitar and leveled an overhead blow that split open the skull of an onrushing Janissary. Then he stepped over a pile of fallen Janissaries and onto the foss.

Like a blast from Urban's cannon, İbrahim hacked his way forward. His eyes were locked on Abaza, who was being carried northward amid the flow of men to a point on the stockade that had just been broken open by a fresh cannon shot.

"Would fate toy with me so," he asked himself as Abaza drifted farther away. "Abaza," İbrahim madly yelled, expecting Abaza to meet him once alerted to his presence.

A sense of danger prevailed on İbrahim to spin around. He dodged sharply to the left, narrowly avoiding the rushing blade. His left leg collapsed under him just as he felt a new blow coming. Sprawled on the muddy foss, İbrahim drove his scimitar through the man's ankle. The Janissary's chest landed on his own severed foot. İbrahim then buried his scimitar into the fallen man's throat.

İbrahim shuddered as he thought of King Ladislas at Varna surrounded by the Janissaries. As he began to push himself up, İbrahim's eye was drawn to his right. His heart sank. Lying lifeless on the ground was Sinan. The top of his head was cracked open.

A powerful hand grabbed his shoulder and yanked him to his feet. İbrahim turned to see his executioner. He sighed heavily.

"You'll kill yourself yet," Demetrius berated him.

İbrahim pushed himself up on his toes, looking for Abaza. He was gone, swallowed up in the swarming mass. "How can this be?" İbrahim muttered.

"We cannot stay here," Demetrius shouted.

An irresistible swell of men began to draw them southward. The two friends struggled to hold their ground against the flow of Janissaries, whose singular focus on the walls blinded them to the intruders.

İbrahim started to nod in agreement but then snapped his head sharply to the left. "Abaza," he snarled, mixing venom with triumph.

Abaza had broken free from the driving mass. Although he

was winded by the struggle, his still neatly pressed uniform and shimmering scimitar reflected his freshness to the battle. Wearing a puzzled expression, he quickly turned his head in a wide circle, searching for the vaguely familiar voice.

"You might have survived this day had you remained with your friends," İbrahim seethed as he made his way towards Abaza.

Abaza coolly examined İbrahim's tattered robe and exhausted body before settling on his ruined leg. As if he had been always prepared for this moment, Abaza said, "What part of her do you miss the most? Perhaps we finally share something in common."

İbrahim struggled to control his rage. In a low, trembling voice, he growled, "We will share something. You will tell me what you've done with her."

Abaza's eyes sparkled. "Surely it is Allah's will that we found each other on this battlefield. How then can I deprive you? She now lives in a harem. With beauty such as hers, I have no doubt she daily serves the most corrupted appetites."

"Where?" İbrahim slashed the air in front of him with his scimitar.

Abaza took two giant steps and drove his sword downward. İbrahim parried the blow, but the force of Abaza's assault was too much for his leg. He crumpled to one knee. İbrahim narrowly avoided the next blow by using his good leg to launch himself backward. He grimaced as the small of his back landed sharply on the head of a fallen Janissary. The dead man's scimitar lay impotently on the ground beside him. Abaza confidently pursued İbrahim, who raised his scimitar in defense. In one broad swipe, Abaza ripped the scimitar away.

Towering triumphantly over İbrahim, Abaza gloated, "Until now, your woman's sweet flesh had been my most prized memory." He winked lewdly. "Although I'll chew this morsel more quickly, I'm sure its taste will be even more savory."

As Abaza raised his scimitar to strike the deathblow, İbrahim produced a small dagger from his sash. Abaza scoffed, "a trinket." As he kicked the dagger away, Abaza's midsection was set ablaze. He looked down in disbelief to find İbrahim, bathed in fresh blood, digging the fallen Janissary's scimitar up into his torso. Abaza grabbed the scimitar with both hands, stopping İbrahim's progress. For a long moment, they stared into each other's eyes with blackened hatred. A stricken gasp then squeezed past Abaza's bloodstained lips. He collapsed to his knees, inches away from İbrahim, looking at the blood oozing from his body in disbelief.

İbrahim grabbed Abaza's rapidly graying face. "Where is Mihrimah?"

Abaza drooled a thick torrent of blood. "With me."

"No," İbrahim shouted. "You said she was in a harem. Now tell me where."

"The woman you knew is dead," Abaza wheezed, pleased with his revenge. "Live with her suffering." His eyes rolled skyward and then fell empty.

İbrahim felt the gnawing frustration of an uncollected debt as he watched Abaza's secret elude him. He looked back at Demetrius, who frowned disapprovingly.

"Now that your vengeance is satisfied, we must go," Demetrius said.

"Vengeance is not what I wanted," İbrahim protested. "I wanted answers."

"Vengeance is yours just the same." Demetrius pulled İbrahim to his feet and pushed him towards the stockade.

On reentering the stockade, İbrahim detected a difference along the defenses. "Something's happened," he told Demetrius gravely.

Demetrius sensed it as well. Their eyes were drawn towards a small gate in the inner wall. The Emperor was kneeling beside Giustiniani, who was twisting spasmodically on the ground in obvious pain. Blood was pouring from a small hole in his breastplate. Giustiniani's staff was demanding the key to the gate. Against the Emperor's protests, Giustiniani's bodyguards carried their leader from the battle towards a waiting ship in the harbor.

Giustiniani's countrymen lost their nerve and followed him from the field through the same small gate before the Greeks could lock it shut again. Now vastly outnumbered, the Greeks were left alone to defend their city.

Further north near the Blachernae section of the walls, the Ottomans had penetrated through an unlocked postern gate controlled by the Venetians. Fifty Ottomans unfurled their flag atop a tower. Rather than marking themselves for quick slaughter, their bold move had sown panic among the Venetians. The Venetians failed to seal the gate, allowing a growing stream of Ottomans to pour into the city.

The Sultan noticed the retreating Genoese and jubilantly declared, "The city is ours!"

"Let every blow count," İbrahim cried, racing back to the front line to face the rallying Janissaries.

As they neared the stockade, the Janissaries cheered, "Hasan!"

A giant man leading thirty Janissaries was standing atop the broken timbers of the stockade. The Greeks were trying to throw the Janissaries off the beachhead, but they were being knocked back by Hasan's thunderous blows. More Janissaries were flowing towards their comrades. If Hasan and his men could hold their position, the corps would soon be poised to burst past the defenders.

Realizing that each moment Hasan stood firm spelled the demise of the defense, İbrahim picked up a large rock and threw it at Hasan's head. The stone found its mark. The giant swayed for a moment and then dropped to his knees, now easy prey. Still, Hasan's comrades managed to hold on without their leader. A sudden surge from behind then drove the Janissaries forward. The Greeks fell back, exposing the first leak in the dam.

Demetrius shook his head and said, "It's time to get Theophilus."

İbrahim craned his head to watch the Janissaries streaming through the widening breach.

Demetrius tugged on İbrahim's sleeve. "Let's go."

İbrahim wrenched his arm free and continued to look towards the stockade.

"You never said you came here to die," Demetrius thrust his

chin in İbrahim's face. "So your Sultan will have his prize. It was never yours to deny him. Be my friend. Help me save my nephew."

The Greeks were being pushed back to the inner wall. During the siege, they had dug deep ditches by the base of the wall, using the dirt to fortify the outer wall. Now they stumbled into their graves, falling under a hail of arrows.

Demetrius anxiously watched the Janissaries unleash their pent-up frustration on the reeling defenders. The Greeks were broken into clusters struggling to make their way through the gates of the inner wall. Demetrius grabbed İbrahim's forearm and yanked him towards the same small gate the Genoese had used.

Suddenly exhausted from hours of fighting, İbrahim dutifully followed Demetrius like a lost boy. A heavy, dull sensation throbbed inside his head, reducing the harsh battle cries to a faraway buzz.

Dodging errant projectiles as he knocked aside his fellow countrymen, Demetrius ground to a stop just short of the open gate, where the Emperor and his staff were having a heated discussion.

Astonished, Demetrius proudly said, "I thought for sure the Emperor would've escaped already."

The Emperor's aides were begging him to retreat to the harbor. Constantine Palaeologus's eyes glowed with feverish intensity. He had demanded that his people give up their lives for his empire. He could do no less himself. The signs of his rank were cast to the ground. Now dressed like a simple soldier, he raised his sword to heaven and charged.

The Emperor caused a momentary tremor as he dove into the sea of Janissaries. İbrahim thought he saw a scimitar strike the Emperor's jaw. A moment later, Byzantium's last ruler was gone forever, an undigested morsel left for carrion.

"Let us act with purpose," Demetrius shouted, concerned that İbrahim might follow the Emperor's example. Any second, the Janissaries threatened to consume them as well. Demetrius plowed into a mass of Greeks who had turned their backs to the onrush. Terrified cries chastised them as they bulled their way through the small gate.

"We're out," Demetrius triumphantly declared.

"But hardly safe," İbrahim answered, starting to regain his footing. "The real slaughter will begin soon."

"We will get Helena and my nephew, board a ship in the harbor and then sail to freedom." Demetrius made his plan sound too simple not to succeed. A nervous smile betrayed him as he hurried down Constantinople's twisting streets.

Vanquished

Under the relentless glow of the rising sun, word rapidly spread that the Ottomans had breached the walls. On the verge of being silenced forever, the church bells rang with furious defiance. The alarmed population fell into chaos. People blindly crashed into each other as they raced towards their home, church or the harbor. Some of the walled communities locked their gates, hoping the Ottomans might bypass them in favor of easier bounty. Each person's heart fluttered in fear of that first moment when the Ottomans would come into view. The disarray was all the Sultan could have desired.

"You must go faster, Manuel," Demetrius nervously bellowed.

Ibrahim was falling behind again. The painful struggle to keep going had overwhelmed his senses, temporarily blocking any contemplation of the lost battle. He bit down and pushed harder on his good leg. His stricken grimace seamlessly matched the faces of the Byzantines.

After several more minutes of hard labor, they reached the small, wooden house. "Helena, open the door. It's Demetrius." He waited a moment and then burst through the door into the darkened house. They hesitantly held out their hands, trying not to trip over the furniture. "Helena?" Demetrius softly appealed. An uncomfortable silence greeted them.

"You don't think it's possible that the Turks could be here?" Demetrius asked, unnerved by such total silence after being barraged with the thunderous reports of war for hours.

"Impossible. They couldn't—"

"Wait. What's that?" Demetrius's heart jumped. He pointed at a small shadow creeping along the wall.

İbrahim's eyes snapped shut and he inverted his back in pain before toppling to the floor. Moments later, a heavy foot trampled his battered leg. The two sources of trauma gained momentum, setting ablaze every nerve in his body. As İbrahim writhed on the cold floor, distant voices dully echoed in his head until the pain was washed clean by unconsciousness.

İbrahim was unsure how long he had been lying on the floor, bathed in sweat, when his eyes fluttered open. His hands slowly searched outward until they pushed against the pieces of a broken chair strewn by his side. He held one of the legs above him and stared blankly at it, waiting to regain his focus.

"I told you it was me," Demetrius bitterly complained. Thin steaks of blood were running down his left cheek.

"Theophilus and I have been waiting hours for you," she sobbed.

"Does that mean your ears no longer—"

"He's awake," Theophilus shouted, thankful he could interrupt the argument.

Head swimming with pain, İbrahim dropped the chair leg and rolled over onto his knees. With a heavy groan, he tried to stand up, but his left leg gave way underneath his weight. Demetrius's meaty hands grabbed hold of İbrahim and held him steady. "I'm going to carry Theophilus. You'll help Manuel."

"I don't need you to carry me," Theophilus protested. "I'm a big boy. You said so yourself."

Demetrius kneeled down and hugged his nephew's shoulders with trembling hands. "You're also a very good boy. The streets are different today. They're no place even for a big boy like you. People are in a hurry. They're scared. We might see and hear some bad things. You must trust me and do as I say. Promise me you'll do that."

Theophilus nodded. His lip curled down and his eyes filled with tears. Demetrius kissed Theophilus on the forehead and then scooped the boy up in his arms.

İbrahim struggled to keep up with Demetrius, who was using his bulk to plow a path through the swirling throng of desperate souls. The briny smell of the harbor revitalized İbrahim. He shrugged off Helena and tried to walk on his own, but immediately stumbled to his left. Before he could fall, she was back by his side, fixing him with a stern glare. İbrahim answered by clutching her close to his side.

As the Ottomans deepened their penetration into the city, the sound of church bells was replaced by screams. İbrahim wondered whether the Ottoman navy had taken the quays. He trudged on, knowing their only chance for survival lay in boarding an outgoing vessel. Even those taking refuge in the churches were destined for no less than the sword as the Ottomans exhausted weeks of pent-up fury on their new subjects.

They reached a dock teeming with refugees besieging a vessel flying the winged lion standard of St. Mark. A skeleton crew of thickly muscled Venetian sailors blocked the gangplank, beating back their erstwhile allies with thongs.

İbrahim examined the harbor. The Ottoman ships were abandoning their positions. The sailors had no intention of leaving the spoils to the army.

At the same time, Constantinople's defensive perimeter was rapidly collapsing. Some defenders, such as Prince Orhan and his followers, fought to the last man, knowing clemency would not be offered. But more often the defenders recognized their lost cause and opened the gates in exchange for their lives. In either case, the city was being absorbed from all points. Before noon, Byzantium was to be no more.

"They'll never let us board," Demetrius groaned.

"Why are they waiting, Uncle?"

"Because Minotto hasn't returned," İbrahim answered, sizing up the situation. "It can be no other reason. They'll wait for the Bailo as long as they can."

"Let me pass," an elderly man imperiously commanded in flawless Greek.

Out of habit, the Byzantines respectfully cleared a path for the nobleman and his family. After a brief conversation, the Venetians ushered them aboard.

"I didn't see him fighting on the walls," Demetrius bitterly complained.

İbrahim stared at Theophilus. A sly grin thickened on his face. "Thankfully, we are blessed to be in the presence of royalty."

"What do you mean?" Demetrius looked at İbrahim as though he was mad.

"Get us to the ships and I will take care of the rest."

Screams wafted down the streets onto the quay. Several men lost their nerve. They abandoned their families, dove off the quay and made for several Venetian ships waiting for their countrymen in the middle of the harbor. İbrahim wondered if the men would choose to sink beneath the gentle waves when the Venetians rebuffed them.

Demetrius's heart beat furiously as he watched the spectacle. Theophilus felt his uncle's anxiety. He squeezed his arms around Demetrius's thick neck until the giant man's face turned bright red. Demetrius gently rubbed his nephew's back. He then threw back his shoulders and waded into the crowd.

Demetrius's bulk was an irresistible force. İbrahim supported the charge by waving his blood-soaked scimitar with sufficient menace to stifle challenge. He pulled Helena close in order for it to appear that he was supporting her rather than she him.

When Demetrius finally pushed his way to the front of the swarming mass, İbrahim discreetly sheathed his scimitar. A smooth-skinned, young man with wavy auburn hair was at the front of the gangplank, barking orders at his fellow sailors. İbrahim studied the man's hazel eyes, which brimmed with shallow, youthful bravado. A quick blow to this sailor's confidence will collapse his resolve, İbrahim concluded.

İbrahim offered a short prayer for strength and released Helena. He slowly maneuvered around Demetrius, trying to affect the imperious dignity he had witnessed in the Sultan. "Let us pass," İbrahim condescendingly ordered the sailor.

Demetrius flinched.

The sailor lifted his thong in reply.

"You'll answer to his Excellency himself if you lay a single finger on any of us," Ibrahim said smugly, appearing indifferent to the prospect of being struck by the thong.

The sailor held the thong steady over his head. His eyes squinted with a mixture of aggravation and surprise. "And just which Excellency do you mean," he snarled, trying to return the contempt.

"Why Girolamo Minotto, of course," Ibrahim smiled as though he had caught the sailor committing an unpardonable gaffe.

"You know his Excellency?" the sailor asked, voice weakened by uncertainty.

"I know many people," Ibrahim sneered. "And what is your name?"

"Paolo."

"Time is short, Paolo," Ibrahim said curtly. "I certainly wouldn't bandy about his Excellency's name for no reason. Now hurry up and move aside before the heathens are upon us."

Paolo stood his ground. "How do you know the Bailo?"

Ibrahim pointed to Theophilus. "The boy's name is Jacobo. Look at him. Surely I need not say more."

Paolo leaned forward to take a long look at Theophilus. "You mean to say this boy is the Bailo's—"

"I mean to say nothing unseemly," Ibrahim testily rebuked him. "How can I be more clear than I've been already?"

"And who are these people?" Paolo pointed to Demetrius and Helena, squinting to get a better look at the streaks of blood drying on Demetrius's cheek.

"He is the boy's uncle," Ibrahim graciously smiled, now trying to break the sailor with a well-timed, unexpected kindness.

Paolo relaxed but managed to retain a small measure of his skepticism. "And the woman?"

Helena turned a dark shade of red and dropped her eyes to the ground.

Ibrahim shook his head in amazement. "Is it really so confusing?"

Paolo swallowed hard, afraid that any further questions might expose his naiveté. It was time to make a decision.

"Paolo," another sailor yelled as he pushed his way through the crowd. "We must sail at once."

"But what of his Excellency?"

"Who's to say?" The sailor elbowed his way onto the gangplank, violently knocking an old woman to ground. "But I just came from Blachernae Palace. It is surrounded and the flag of St. Mark no longer flies. The Bailo will have to be ransomed if he lives."

"Is there no possibility of a rescue?" Paolo asked, afraid not to exhaust every avenue before giving up on the Bailo. For a long moment, Paolo quietly listened to the terrified screams echoing across the city. "You," he snapped at İbrahim with as much dignity as he could muster, "board."

Demetrius looked at İbrahim as though he had stopped the sun from advancing in the sky. İbrahim answered by pushing Demetrius up the gangplank.

The heavy groans of the ship pushing away from the quay were drowned out by the piercing lament from the stranded refugees. Several men leaped off the quay and grabbed hold of the gunwales. Showing a thin measure of compassion, the sailors only used the butt ends of their axes to knock them loose.

The ship's deck was jammed with refugees, who were standing on their toes to catch the last glimpses of their city. They listened to the morose valediction of their brethren trapped on the docks in stony silence.

"What will happen to them?" Theophilus asked from his perch on Demetrius's shoulders.

Demetrius struggled to find the right thing to say before settling on, "We will remember them."

Several refugees nodded their heads, tears rolling down their cheeks.

"Don't count yourself among the mourners just yet. It'll be a short trip if the boom is still locked in place," İbrahim soberly reminded Demetrius.

All eyes turned east. The ship was picking up speed as a strong north wind opened its sails. The captain appeared intent on ramming the boom if it were still in place. Already beaten victims, the passengers expected to feel the rough tug of the boom cutting through the bow of the ship. They tilted their heads skyward and prayed that the peaceful blue waters would kindly accept them.

"Our ships are waiting for us in the Marmara," a sailor called down from atop the rigging. "The boom has been cut loose. It's drifting out to sea."

No one cheered. No amount of good news could spark celebration on such a dark day.

The captain steered the ship close to Galata's walls. The passengers stole a quick glance at the Genoese colony, whose gates were tightly locked. The only question that remained for the inhabitants of Galata was whether they would freely hand over their sovereignty. For the moment, the Sultan was content to let the horrified screams of his victims waft across the Golden Horn as a grim warning to those who might resist him.

The ship sailed out of the harbor in a wide arc around the ancient acropolis and joined the mixed fleet of Venetian, Genoese and Imperial galleys. Two more Christian vessels, sped along by the increasingly powerful north wind, made their way out of the harbor. Like the rest of the flotilla, the ships dropped their sails and waited in the Bosphorus for more ships to join the venture.

İbrahim turned his gaze towards Constantinople. Pillars of smoke rose up from various points in the stricken city. Even the Sultan would have to wait before he could savor his prize. Still, the Red Apple was firmly within his grasp.

A medium-sized Genoese galley, listing dangerously with refugees, plodded out of the harbor. The ship continued to sail by the flotilla, daring not to stop should she lose her momentum and flounder.

A mass of Ottoman ships had set sail from farther up the Bosphorus and was now bearing down on the stationary Christian flotilla. With a heavy heart, the order was given to set sail for the

Aegean. Using the north wind to its advantage, the flotilla safely made its way down the Marmara.

The refugees solemnly watched their city fade beneath the horizon. The most stout man's eyes were swollen with tears, prayers for heaven's mercy parting his lips. When the last rays of sunlight flickered off Hagia Sophia's golden dome, each family searched for their own space on the deck.

İbrahim stood at the ship's bow and looked at the refugees huddled closely together, arms wrapped around each other in a comforting embrace. Their soft moans reminded him of the sheep he had tended as a child.

İbrahim absentmindedly ran his fingers along the butt of his scimitar. It felt raw and uninviting, an alien presence. He slowly withdrew the scimitar from his sash and held it out to catch the sun's light. The sharp reflection caught the attention of the sailors, whose muscles coiled in preparation to strike. İbrahim ignored their nervous stares and concentrated on the cold metal burning in his eyes.

İbrahim pulled the scimitar back behind his shoulder and held it steady for a long moment, allowing the last of his fury to pour into his arm before launching it into the air. The scimitar spun end over end, quickly at first, flashing brilliantly above the untroubled, azure sea. Then it sliced harmlessly into the water with hardly a splash.

İbrahim tried to staunch the hint of sadness he felt as the scimitar disappeared forever into the deep, another lost attachment. He slumped down on the deck and faced his shipmates. They too were cast adrift, stripped bare by the same nemesis. None of the refugees had asked about the ship's destination. Wherever they landed would not be home. Gone was the neighbor who shared the news of the day in the evening, the familiar alley they strolled down to buy a loaf of bread, and the church where they had pledged their spirits to the Almighty. A life of carefully drawn connections had been irretrievably washed away.

Their emptiness struck an intimate chord in İbrahim. It gave him no joy to see others reduced to his own unhappy state. Still, he felt welcomed on their passage.

Demetrius was deep in sleep, leaning heavily against Helena and Theophilus. Helena clung to Theophilus, alternately caressing and kissing the boy's hair. After several minutes, she felt İbrahim's stare and looked into his unflinching eyes. She evenly returned his gaze with an enigmatic combination of gratitude and compassion.

İbrahim tried to smile, but his muscles would not release his lips from their brooding frown.

Helena whispered in Theophilus's ear. He lifted his head from her breast to look at İbrahim and then threw his head back down. She hugged him tightly and continued to whisper. Theophilus stubbornly burrowed his head deeper into her bosom, but Helena refused to relent. Finally, Theophilus climbed to his feet and faced İbrahim. He was sent on his way with an adoring pat on the behind.

"My mother says I should talk to you." Theophilus paused for a long moment, fists planted defiantly on his hips. "But she didn't tell me what to say."

İbrahim laughed.

Theophilus responded with a hurt scowl.

İbrahim instantly drew a serious mask over his face. In a gentle, dignified voice, he said, "I'd like to know what you think of this ship."

Theophilus knitted his eyebrows in protest but then turned in a clockwise rotation, carefully taking in his surroundings. "It's a very sad ship," he said with an expression that demanded approval.

İbrahim was surprised by his response. "What is sad about this ship? Do you mean the creaking sounds it makes?"

"They're not creaking," Theophilus scornfully corrected him.

"I see. You mean the passengers."

"No, I mean the people," he threw his arms wide as though he might gather up all the passengers in his arms.

"They are sad," İbrahim agreed.

"Are you sad too?"

İbrahim recalled his days as a young boy in the Thracian hills. He forced a smile and said, "You and I should be good friends."

"But you're my uncle's friend."

"Sit, Theophilus. I want to tell you a story that no one has ever heard."

"No one?" he gasped.

İbrahim had expected the boy to sit beside him. Instead, Theophilus settled comfortably into his lap. Helena beamed contentedly with pride.

"Is your story about a mean monster?"

"It's a story about a boy," İbrahim said hesitantly, afraid to disappoint Theophilus.

"Does this boy look like me?"

İbrahim thought for a moment and then nodded.

"And is he my age?"

İbrahim nodded again, heartened by Theophilus's growing excitement. "Many years ago," he started, "a young boy was tending to his flock of sheep in the high hills. It was a bitter, windy day and one of the sheep, his favorite, had strayed from the flock while the boy was daydreaming. So he went to look for his sheep."

"Did he find the sheep?" Theophilus asked with great concern.

"His dearest sheep was being feasted on by a large, gray-backed wild dog. Several other wild dogs were pacing around the kill, waiting for their leader to release the remains to them. Well, the boy was very sad. He wanted to cry but he also wanted to have his revenge against the dog."

"Was the boy sad because he let the sheep wander away?"

"Do you think it was his fault that the dog ate the sheep?"

"It was his fault," Theophilus answered with all the imperious certainty of his four years.

"Then that is why the boy was so sad," İbrahim conceded. "Should he have also been mad at the dog?"

"Of course he—" Theophilus stopped and rubbed his fingers along his chin, squinting with an intense, inward stare. "Well, the dog might've been hungry."

"Do you think a hungry dog can afford to pass on an easy meal?"

"He has to eat," Theophilus unhappily decided.

"Agreed," İbrahim said, "but the boy was still very angry at the dog. He wanted to kill the dog more than anything else in the world. But he was just a young shepherd boy, alone. He didn't have a single weapon and the dogs were hungry for more." İbrahim leaned his head forward and gazed thoughtfully at the boy. "What would you have done?"

"I would've been afraid that those dogs would've eaten me."

"But imagine the boy's anger for a moment. Wouldn't you have attacked the dog anyway?"

Theophilus struggled with the question, wanting to please İbrahim with the best answer he could muster. He sighed heavily and gave up. "I think I would've asked my mommy what to do."

"But the dog would've been gone by then."

Theophilus chewed on his lip in frustration. "What did the boy do?"

İbrahim looked deeply into Theophilus's searching eyes. Then he let his eyes wander over to Demetrius and then Helena, whose hazel eyes were ripening into a richer, more beguiling melancholy. The faces of the other refugees answered his gaze with an arresting calm.

"What did the boy do?" Theophilus asked again.

İbrahim's eyes filled with tears. Drawn together in his tired mind were a bursting flood of memories: too many miles marched in bad weather, piercing wails from butchered mothers, and faces of lost friends. But most painful of all was the memory of Mihrimah. Her loss was the suffocating ache that had chilled his heart and left him without purpose. He wanted to be free from all of it, even Mihrimah.

"Manuel, what did the boy do?" Theophilus urgently demanded.

"The boy followed his heart. He picked up a rock, the biggest, sharpest one he could find, and pulled it back behind his shoulder. His arm was just starting to move forward when he heard something behind him. He wheeled around to find the flock, faintly bleating for him to return with them to safety."

"Did he throw the rock?" Theophilus anxiously asked.

"How could he? The dogs would have turned on the entire flock. No, he put down the rock and silently followed the flock back to safety." İbrahim nodded his chin forward sharply to indicate that the story was over.

Theophilus eyed İbrahim suspiciously. "Is this a true story?"

"It's part of one," İbrahim answered, voice cracking. His lungs quickly gasped for air as he gently squeezed Theophilus in a tender embrace.

Theophilus pulled himself free and beamed at İbrahim with a sweet expression that defied İbrahim's understanding even as it blunted the sob on the edge of his lips. The boy took İbrahim's hand and led him back to his mother and slumbering uncle. Theophilus stood still for a moment and then directed İbrahim to Helena's side.

İbrahim dutifully sat beside Helena, who collected Theophilus into her lap. She gazed far ahead at the soft waves shimmering in the bright sunshine. After several minutes, she said, "My husband never liked the sea. He always wanted to feel the ground pushing up against his feet. So I disliked the sea too." She brushed a tear from her eye. "It's really quite beautiful, though."

İbrahim nodded. He squeezed her accepting hand and let the peaceful roll of the ship carry him off to sleep.